JUSTICE UNHATCHED

JUSTICE UNHATCHED

EXCEPTIONAL S. BEAUFONT™ BOOK 5

SARAH NOFFKE

MICHAEL ANDERLE

DISRUPTIVE IMAGINATION

Copyright © 2020 Sarah Noffke & Michael Anderle
Cover by Mihaela Voicu http://www.mihaelavoicu.com/
Cover copyright © LMBPN Publishing
A Michael Anderle Production

LMBPN Publishing
PMB 196, 2540 South Maryland Pkwy
Las Vegas, NV 89109

First US Edition, April 2020
Version 1.04 June 2021
eBook ISBN: 978-1-64202-873-7
Print ISBN: 978-1-64202-874-4

THE JUSTICE UNHATCHED TEAM

Thanks to the JIT Readers

Angel LaVey
Dave Hicks
Deb Mader
Debi Sateren
Diane L. Smith
Dorothy Lloyd
Jackey Hankard-Brodie
Jeff Eaton
Jeff Goode
Larry Omans
Micky Cocker
Nicole Emens
Paul Westman
Peter Manis
Veronica Stephan-Miller

If we've missed anyone, please let us know!

Editor
The Skyhunter Editing Team

For Crystal, for being my constant comic relief.

— Sarah

To Family, Friends and
Those Who Love
to Read.
May We All Enjoy Grace
to Live the Life We Are
Called.

— Michael

CHAPTER ONE

"Are you ready for it?" the scientist asked Trin Currante, as her men worked around them in the makeshift laboratory at the back of the airplane hangar.

She bit down on the mouthpiece and nodded, willing the specs cascading across her visual cortex to stop. The green words that usually streaked over her vision and told her everything from distance to destinations, temperature, wind, or a dozen other things about her environment disappeared.

Alexander Drake turned the knob on the control panel, a tentative look in his cold eyes. Electricity coursed through the cables attached to Trin's chest, making her instantly convulse. Her brown eyes rolled back and she trembled continuously, her head knocking back into the padded chair.

The others in the warehouse looked up from their jobs, no concern on their faces for the woman being electrocuted.

After a full minute, Drake turned the knob back and stopped the electric voltage. Trin shook less, and her head lolled to the side as the electricity subsided. Unconcerned, Drake watched the woman strapped into the padded chair.

"Well?" he asked in an impatient voice, tapping a button to release her restraints. The locks around her arms and legs opened simultaneously.

Slowly, she lifted her chin and blinked, trying to clear the tears from her eyes. She assessed her internal program, pulling up the diagnostics on her main screen. The green words began scrolling on her visual cortex.

Cyborg functionality...seventy-nine percent.

Human functionality...twenty-one percent.

She spat out the mouthpiece and shook her head of mostly wire hair. "It didn't work."

Drake typed on the computer next to the voltage box and concluded with a nod. "Yes, no changes in your functionality. Guess you are glad you have those dragon eggs as an option."

Trin Currante unhooked the wires connected to the open panel in her chest. She threw a nasty look at the scientist she was forcing to help her become human once more and wondered if she might kill him if he didn't improve his bedside manner.

She shook off the anger. Trin needed Drake. He was on the team of scientists at Saverus Corporation who had made her and the other men what they were presently, which was less than human. He had done it against his will he'd declared when she held the gun to his head months ago, after she'd taken over the facility and released all the prisoners and killed most of the staff.

Trin wasn't sure she believed the old German man, but she knew she needed him to reverse what had been done to her. Once she, like all the men in the warehouse, had been a normal magician with all human parts. Then one man with a corrupt vision and too much money took out most of what made her real and replaced it with metal, wires, and magitech.

Thad Reinhart was dead now, thanks to Hiker Wallace.

His corporation, Saverus, was destroyed, thanks to Trin and her men.

What had been done to her and the men would live on forever, unless she found a way to reverse things. Everything she'd tried so far didn't work. According to Drake, she couldn't remove the magitech inside of her and survive.

That was where the dragon eggs might help. It was a gamble. According to Trin's research, the blood of a newborn dragon could be used to fix her. One dragon egg was hard enough to come by. She'd nearly lost it all trying to get into the Gullington the first time. When she learned she needed at least two dragon eggs, she'd gone on a rampage and nearly destroyed the place she called home, Ash Research.

She looked around the airplane hangar, realizing her men were pretending to work. They were not. They were studying her, and wondering if she'd flip again, knocking over shelves, and damaging the planes and equipment.

She wouldn't.

The company was all Trin had left. She just had to learn to control her temper, not easy to do when her emotional control center was mostly wires, much like her hair.

Slapping the metal door shut on her chest, Trin buttoned up her blouse and began retying the corset around her midsection. Some might think she was dressed for a strange renaissance fair. The truth was that much like her men, she was covered in a corset and had leather straps around her legs, chest, and arms to hold in hardware that never should have been there in the first place.

"Any changes to the eggs?" Trin asked the scientist. Drake had worked with Thad Reinhart, so she figured he might also be a resource on the dragons, although he was proving to volunteer very little information.

"No dragons have hatched yet if that's what you mean," he told her, looking around the hangar and watching the cyborg men as they loaded a plane for a contract job.

Trin sighed. "How can we speed up the process?"

He shook his head. "I don't think you can. And even if you could, there's no way to tell if the thirteen eggs you got are going to be right. They might all be angels."

Angels versus demons.

According to what she'd learned, dragons were born two specific ways, always. Some were born "angels" like the ones who formed the Dragon Elite. The others were born "demons."

Good and bad. That's how the world was made up. It was no different for dragons.

It was still strange a dragon was predisposed to a certain affiliation. It wasn't a nature versus nurture situation, but there had been a reason. When Michael the archangel's blood infiltrated the Earth, soaking into the dragon eggs, according to the legend, other blood was spilled at the same time by the demon Nergal. Half the eggs absorbed the angel's blood and the other half, the blood of the demon.

Those who had read the *Incomplete History of Dragonriders* knew about the angel blood. It wasn't until Trin had gotten access to a different text she learned the full history. Everything in the world was about balance. While the Dragon Elite was created to protect the Earth and rule over the affairs of mortals, they couldn't exist without an evil counterpart.

It was only after Trin had stolen the single dragon egg that she'd learned she'd need at least two, the blood of an angel and a demon. She now had thirteen eggs. One of them had to be an angel and the other a demon, she reasoned. She wouldn't know for certain until they hatched, and that apparently took an indeterminable amount of time.

"There's something I've heard of that you can try to speed up the hatching time," Drake offered, combing his hands through his long white beard. "I don't know if it will work."

Trin narrowed her eyes at him. "What is it?"

"You aren't going to like it," he said, a bit of amusement in his voice.

She nodded. "That's the status quo at this point."

Drake pointed to one of the planes getting ready for a mission. "The good news is you've got what you need to make it happen."

She made a silent promise to herself. Drake would die. By her hands.

But not until she didn't need him anymore.

She opened her hand, the metal joints making a mechanical sound as she combed her fingers forward at the man. "Tell me what I have to do."

CHAPTER TWO

Sophia Beaufont knew it was still dark before she opened her eyes. She pressed her lids together more firmly and tried to will herself back to sleep.

It was no use, and from recent experience, she knew it.

She cracked open her eyes in the large bedroom in the Castle to find she was in fact correct. It was still dark outside the Gullington.

She knew what time it was.

A cold laugh fell out of her mouth when she looked at the clock.

3:33 a.m.

Every single morning recently, Sophia had awoken at the same time.

She had no idea what the significance was, but Sophia thought it had to be of importance somehow.

Swinging her covers off, she rolled out of bed and stretched to an upright position. The flames of the candles in the torches and fireplace sprang to life.

"Thanks, Quiet," Sophia said, stumbling around to find her clothes.

It was still incredible to her that the Castle, Expanse, and Gullington were managed by the tiny unassuming gnome. She wasn't sure how it worked, but it was the most impressive source of magic she'd ever witnessed. It made sense it had come from Mother Nature.

Sophia pulled on her boots and her eyes drifted to the note beside her bed she found the other morning upon waking up at the ungodly hour.

It read:

"The morning breeze has secrets to tell you. Don't go back to sleep. – Rumi."

Sophia knew the note with the great poet's wisdom was from Quiet, or rather the Castle. They were one and the same. Quiet was telling her she needed to get out of bed when she awoke so early in the morning at the same time. She quit tossing and turning and getting frustrated about not getting enough rest.

Sophia slipped out of her room silently and strode through the Castle. Each morning she'd gotten up, she found it impossible to stay confined inside her room. Something always seemed to be calling her to the Expanse, although she hadn't found what it was yet.

She knew Quiet had a way of orchestrating things around her, like when he'd been preparing the Nest for the new dragon eggs. She trusted him and was willing to be led to a certain point. It was also frustrating. Sophia didn't know why the sage sources in her life like Quiet, Mama Jamba, Papa Creola, Subner, and Mae Ling didn't just tell her what they were up to.

"They may be surprised to find I follow direction quite easily if they are straightforward with me," Sophia joked to herself as she exited the Castle to find the morning air crisp.

You know straightforward is too easy for them, Lunis offered in her head.

A moment later, the blue dragon landed quietly beside Sophia on the damp grass. She smiled affectionately at her dragon, lifting a hand and resting it on his thick neck in greeting.

"Morning," she said in a hush. "Have trouble sleeping too?"

He nodded. *That which affects you is also my affliction.*

"Why do you think we are having trouble staying asleep?" Sophia asked, starting forward, headed for the Nest.

7

Maybe Mercury is in retrograde, the dragon joked.

Sophia shook her head at the ancient creature. "Or the moon is full, or the change in seasons or some other dumb cosmic reason."

Or maybe it's because you had a last cup of tea with dinner or ate the food Ainsley served or had a nap, Lunis offered.

"I didn't nap," Sophia snapped, a rude expression on her face.

Oh, really? he argued. *You and Wilder didn't fall asleep on the beach next to the Pond?*

She scratched her head. "I can't really recall. That doesn't sound like something I'd do."

It really isn't, but it's one of the reasons I support it, he said discreetly.

There was never any keeping things from Lunis for Sophia which was how it should be. It was never an invasion of her privacy. That would be like getting mad at herself for spying on her own thoughts.

Of course, Lunis continued. *I know of others who wouldn't love the idea you are napping with Wilder so much...*

He was referring to Hiker. There was a good reason the two drag-onriders spent their lunch breaks on the beach of the Pond, which couldn't be seen from the Castle, and it wasn't because they both had an affinity for water.

"Well, I'll simply tell Hiker if he asks, that my early wake-ups are requiring an afternoon siesta," Sophia declared.

Lunis gave her an annoyed expression as they continued toward the Nest, their steps in time. *I don't think the napping is what would make him red-faced angry.*

"I'm certain naps or rest in general would actually put his kilt in a wad," Sophia said with a laugh.

Yes, and of all people in the world who I wouldn't want to piss off, Hiker Wallace is at the top of the list, Lunis told her as they approached the fog that always clung around the Pond and Nest these days. *I mean, that Viking scares me and I'm a fire breathing dragon who is friends with his bestie.*

Sophia laughed, knowing Lunis was closest to Bell, Hiker's dragon. It was strange her dragon, the youngest of all at the Dragon Elite had aligned with the oldest.

"It's like she's taken you under her wing," Sophia joked.

Stop, Lunis said with a bite as they cut through the fog. It cloaked them as they approached the Nest, making each step a mystery.

He knew she got nervous as they approached the Nest each time, worried about her thousand dragon eggs. They weren't hers, Sophia knew, but they felt like it since she'd spawned them. Another reason she felt guilty was that there was roughly a dozen missing. They were going to get them back. As soon as they knew where to look and who to kill.

So, are we again simply sitting there and watching the eggs until the sun rises? Lunis asked.

That had been the routine for the last few days, since the strange wake-up schedule. Sophia didn't know why, but there wasn't anything else she cared to do with her time, just be near "her" eggs and her dragon and wait for the sun to rise before she joined the others.

"Yeah, does that work?" she asked.

As well as you and me, Lunis answered.

So it was. Their routine was as good as them, and there wasn't anything better than Lunis and Sophia.

CHAPTER THREE

The rain was pounding against the Castle windows when Sophia sat down at the dining table for breakfast. Usually there was a large assortment of pastries or fruit sitting on the surface of the grand table that stretched the length of the dining hall. It was empty, save for dirty dishes that looked to be left over from last night's dinner. Sophia definitely recognized the shepherd's pie sitting in front of her—or what was left of it.

She sat straight, her hands in her lap and her eyes tentatively skirting back and forth, and wondered what Ainsley the housekeeper was up to this time. As if cued by her thoughts, the shapeshifter staggered into the dining hall, not at all looking like her usual self. She hadn't changed into a different form or anything, but she also hadn't brushed her hair or buttoned her brown burlap dress properly.

"Ains?" Sophia questioned. "Are you okay?"

The elf turned her head side to side like she was having to search for the source of the voice. Finally, she squinted in Sophia's direction.

"What are you doing down here so early, S. Beaufont?" Ainsley asked, her words slurring.

Sophia's eyes darted to the grandfather clock on the far wall. "It's ten minutes past breakfast time."

Ainsley narrowed her gaze. "What? That's impossible! Where are the others? Evan's hardly ever late for a meal, nor Mama Jamba."

Sophia shrugged. She didn't really know the answer. Evan usually preferred to rush down to breakfast so he could nick all the best pastries.

"And why are you here on time?" Ainsley continued to grill her, hands now pinned on her narrow hips.

"I don't know," Sophia answered honestly. She awoke early, strolled the grounds with Lunis, checked on the dragon eggs, and had been planning on watching the sunrise, but the rain had started, sending her straight to the Castle for shelter and Lunis to the Cave.

She glanced out the window and noticed the storm seemed to only be inside the Expanse. In the distance, the hills appeared clear, with rays of sunshine cascading down and illuminating the morning dew on the green grass. Sophia shook her head, sure Quiet was behind this somehow.

Ainsley combed her hand over her head, her fingers catching in her red hair. She pulled it away in confusion. "What do I look like right now?"

Sophia scrunched up her nose, not wanting to say it. "Sort of like you just rolled out of bed."

Proudly, Ainsley nodded. "I did. I always do, but the Castle puts me together. Gets me ready, fixes my hair, and takes care of my clothes."

She looked down at her dress, her eyes suddenly bulging. "Oh, dear. I look like a right mess. What the hell?"

"The Castle...I mean, Quiet gets you ready every day?" Sophia questioned.

"Well, of course," Ainsley answered, trying to fix her buttons. "I mean, I have got things to take care of and don't really have the energy to fix myself. I haven't brushed my hair in eons. Or dressed me, for that matter."

"Then, if that's the case, why isn't Quiet doing it now?" Sophia asked.

Ainsley held a finger in front of her face and pressed her eyelids together like she was about to get painfully pinched. Her red hair instantly smoothed back into a low ponytail, more polished than usual. The wrinkled brown burlap dress was replaced with a clean, pressed one. She opened her eyes, relief filling her gaze.

"That's better, but what an effort it takes to get oneself presentable," she said, shaking her head. "You do that every single day?"

Sophia shrugged. "I'm sort of used to it."

"Well, no wonder the guys hardly do more than the bare minimum," Ainsley stated. "Again, I applaud your hygienic efforts, S. Beaufont. I knew you were a real class act, but I had no idea how much energy it cost you."

"It really isn't that big a deal," Sophia protested. "I like being clean."

"That you do," Ainsley answered with a smile. "You are such a modern city girl, ain't ya?"

Sophia didn't answer since she didn't think washing behind her ears or brushing her hair should associate her with modern city life. It should be a human thing. It reminded her of the flu season in Los Angeles when everyone was constantly reminded to wash their hands. Liv often remarked, "What the hell have you all been doing before?" Hygiene was a full—time job, not a seasonal one.

"To answer your question," Ainsley went on, "I suspect that insufferable gnome is mad at me, and that's why he's not been doing my hair and getting me ready or waking me up on time."

"Mad at you?" Sophia scratched her head, wishing she had a cup of tea since she'd been up so long.

"It's just a guess," Ainsley answered. "He's been super sensitive. I realize now that I know he was the Castle all along. I didn't like learning about it the way I did. At first, I was okay, but the more I started thinking, the more it burned me up." She shook her head, her face flushing red. "You'd have thought my best friend of the last five hundred years would have indulged me with the information. But oh no. He made me think the Castle was this grumpy, eccentric building that demanded my constant attention. Now I know it was him. So I gave him a piece of my mind last night."

"It's understandable you'd be upset," Sophia consoled. "He kept something important from you, but he did have a good reason. No one knew but Mama Jamba. I'm sure you didn't say anything he won't get over."

Ainsley's laugh was shrill and loud. "Oh, you don't know that petty little jerk. He's quite stubborn and manipulative."

"He has a very difficult job to do, Ains," Sophia argued. "I realize the Castle can be…" She paused and lowered her voice, deciding she should choose her words carefully. The Castle was always listening, meaning Quiet was. "It can be particular and all-powerful, but he has his reasons, I'm certain."

"Particular?" Ainsley laughed again. "Do you know how many times I have cleaned the floors and turned around to find them a mess again? That's just spiteful. Before, I thought this place was possessed by some ornery spirit who did as it liked. Now I know, the gnome I thought I could sympathize with because he had his own challenges managing the Expanse, was behind it all."

The housekeeper folded her arms across her chest, a hurt expression in her green eyes.

"I'm sure there's a reasonable explanation," Sophia reassured her. However, she didn't know what it would be. The knowledge Quiet was the Gullington had changed everything and brought many things to light. It definitely highlighted why the gnome didn't want his secret out, but she didn't think Quiet was a spiteful person. The Castle was often very playful. Maybe that was just how Quiet's personality manifested inside the walls, or maybe Quiet had a good reason for why he had it behave in certain ways. He was privy to much more than anyone else, being omnipresent and all.

"And the Castle let me oversleep," Ainsley complained, gauging the time on the old grandfather clock. "Now I hardly have any time to prepare breakfast. Hiker will be livid. Mama Jamba will be starving, and Evan will complain bitterly."

Sophia glanced around at the empty table. "I don't think you have to worry about it since none of them are here yet."

A low growl fell out of Ainsley's mouth. "Which makes me wonder what that gnome is up to." She glanced up toward the rafters of the ceiling and waved her closed fist. "Whatever you are orchestrating, you better be careful. I'll quit on you and get a job in the village. Then who will care for your stupid Castle?"

She strode for the kitchen, continuing to shake her fist.

Sophia knew there were no second career opportunities for Ainsley in the neighboring village. She was stuck at the Gullington for the foreseeable future. At least until Sophia had a chance to investigate and see if there was a cure to fix Ainsley after the attack by Thad Reinhart. Quiet might be mad at her. He was definitely a trickster who liked his pranks, but it was because of him Ainsley was still alive when she should have died long ago.

Sophia rose to clear the table of the dirty dishes from the night before when racing footsteps stole her attention. She looked up just as Evan materialized in the entryway, his face pinched with embarrassment. She didn't have to wonder why though because the dragonrider was nearly completely naked. The only thing covering his privates was a much too small painting he held in front of himself.

CHAPTER FOUR

Sophia slapped her hand over her eyes, shielding them the best she could. The portrait was of an old dragonrider, Bruce Campbell, a man with a boxy jaw and a patchy beard. The painting used to hang outside of Evan's room and must have been the only thing he could locate to cover himself.

"Um...are you going for a new look?" Sophia asked, her eyes still covered.

"I wasn't planning on it, but imagine my surprise when I woke up to find all my clothes gone," Evan retorted. Sophia made out the telltale sounds of his bare feet slapping the floor and him drawing closer.

"I would encourage you to keep your distance," Sophia told him, pressing her hand more firmly to her face.

Evan snapped. "Give me your cloak."

She shook her head. "No, then it would touch your bare skin."

"Is that worse than seeing my bare ass —"

"Yeah, yeah. Fine," Sophia interrupted. She pressed her eyes shut tightly as she pulled off her long traveling cloak. "Why didn't you pull your sheets off your bed or use a towel to cover yourself?"

Sophia remembered when the Castle had taken all of Hiker's clothes and replaced them with retro suits. The Viking had fashioned his bedsheets into togas to cover his body since he wasn't about to put on Napoleon Dynamite suits.

"Believe me, I would have," Evan answered. "The Castle, which we all know who that is now, took every piece of material in my room, including the throw pillows on my sofa. The armor outside my room was even gone. I only managed to snag Bruce here before I'm sure the conniving gnome realized his oversight."

"Poor Bruce," Sophia grumbled.

"Poor Bruce?" Evan questioned. "Try poor me. It's freezing out here."

"I can see that," Mama Jamba sang, her southern accent strong.

Sophia heard the rustling of fabric as Evan sighed.

"I won't take offense since you have obviously seen me in my birthday suit, Mama Jamba," Evan said with a laugh.

"Seen you in it." The old woman laughed. "I made it. But still, it appears you are extra chilly this morning." Sophia heard a snap of fingers and then flames rose in the fireplace.

"Okay, you can look," Evan told her. "I'm all covered."

"I'm not sure I can," Sophia joked. "I think my vision was burned by what I saw already."

He sighed dramatically. "Don't be a pain. I need your help figuring out what that short guy's problem is."

With great hesitation, Sophia opened her eyes to find an even more comical sight than before. Standing beside her was Evan, barely covered in her tiny cloak, straining at the seams to cover him. "You can keep that for good."

He chuckled, turning sideways to admire himself in a mirror. "I think it looks all right on me."

"You look like Tommy Boy," Sophia joked.

"Tommy who?" he questioned.

"It's a pop reference to a Chris Farley movie, dear," Mama Jamba explained, taking her usual seat.

Sophia smiled at her and winked. "Fat man in a little coat."

Evan clapped his hands to his chest. "How dare you call me fat?"

"It's a movie reference," Sophia explained, afraid he'd rip off the cloak and expose himself.

"You are obviously not fat, dragonrider," Mama Jamba said, looking back at the kitchen expectantly. "I wonder where my pancakes are."

"Ainsley had a late start," Sophia explained.

"Did the Castle take all her clothes too?" Evan asked.

Sophia shook her head. "It apparently let her oversleep and didn't get her ready."

A speculative glint passed across Mama Jamba's eyes, but she didn't say a word as her mouth twitched.

"What I don't get is, I have been extra nice to Quiet," Evan wondered, his gaze on the floor.

"You might want to stay still," Sophia advised, worried her cloak wouldn't hold up.

He shook his head. "No, moving helps me to think."

"Is that what the problem is when you are sitting at the dinner table then, dear?" Mama Jamba asked, her eyes still expectantly on the kitchen door.

"Mama Jamba, I expect that from the others, but not from you," Evan complained.

Sophia pointed a finger at the other dragonrider, trying to put an expanding spell on her cloak. To her surprise and utter disappointment, it didn't work. She grimaced at her finger.

Evan halted, lowered his chin and regarded her with contempt. "Don't you think I tried that already? I tried to magic some clothes. Tried everything I could think of. I really hope you know I wouldn't have ventured down the freezing cold corridors of this place with a portrait of Bruce covering my manhood if I had any other option."

Sophia's eyes darted to the abandoned painting on the table. "It really is such a small painting, isn't it?"

"Haha," Evan said, not at all appearing amused. "I'm serious, though. Last night, I lavished the Castle with compliments. I was nice to Quiet. I even offered him the larger slice of pie."

Sophia thought for a moment about Ainsley and her predicament with Quiet. "Maybe he doesn't want you to be nice to him."

"What?" Evan questioned, throwing his arms in the air, making the cloak rise dramatically.

Sophia jerked her head to the side to avoid seeing something that would be burned into her memory. "Keep your hands down."

"Fine," Evan said, tugging the cloak back down to cover himself. "But you have to start making sense. Why wouldn't the little guy want me to be nice to him? When I wasn't, he, like the Castle, used to throw all my belongings on the Expanse or throw me out of bed. He did all sorts of other things to torment me."

Sophia deliberated on the idea formulating in her head. "Maybe he liked that because it was your dynamic and he enjoyed it."

Evan gave her an astonished expression. "What a weird masochist that gnome has turned out to be."

Sophia glanced at Mama Jamba, but she wasn't giving anything away it appeared from the tight-lipped expression on her face. "I think there's a lot more going on behind the scenes for Quiet than we realize. He didn't want us to know he was the Gullington. Now we do, it changes everything. It changes how you treat him, and we know he doesn't want that."

Ainsley hustled through the swinging kitchen door, carrying a platter of pastries and fruit. "Apparently, he doesn't like to be called a sneaky little toad who has ruined the last five-hundred years of my life."

She laid the tray on the surface of the table, sticking her hands on her hips and running a curious gaze over Evan.

"You don't say?" he joked. "I'm astonished he wouldn't like to hear such sweet things. I think you'd get punished either way. I told him he was a brave soldier who had my undying respect and look what he did to me." He threw his hands in the direction of his chest.

Ainsley blinked at him. "What? I don't get it. What is different about you?"

Evan rolled his eyes. "My clothes."

The housekeeper shrugged. "Black isn't your color. I have always told you that. Nor is green, blue, white, red, orange, yellow, indigo—"

"I think Evan is referring to the fact he's been forced to wear my cloak since Quiet stole his clothes," Sophia interrupted.

Ainsley tilted her head to the side. "Oh, well, whatever. It isn't like anyone even looks at him." She swung around and strode back in the direction of the kitchen.

"Pancakes, dear," Mama Jamba called to the shapeshifter.

"Yes, I'm working on it," Ainsley replied. "Little behind this morning since the Castle doesn't appear to want to help me at all."

"Oh, for the love of the angels," Hiker said, coming to a swift halt in the entryway. Behind him, Mahkah and Wilder peered around his large frame, trying to see what the cause of the stress in his voice was from.

Mama Jamba nodded, looking around the table. "I know. It's half past the hour, and I don't have any sweet, buttery pancakes in my mouth."

Hiker shook his head, continuing into the dining hall. "No, I was referring to Evan wearing a cloak a size too small for him."

Sophia gawked at the leader of the Dragon Elite. "Excuse me. You think I'm simply a size smaller than that massive guy? Thanks a lot!"

He narrowed his light-colored eyes at her. "Why is Evan wearing your cloak?"

Wilder slid into the chair next to Mama Jamba, giving Sophia a pirate's smile across the table. "Oh, this is going to be good."

Mahkah appeared equally amused as he took the seat next to Wilder.

"Because I didn't want to have my retinas burned out," Sophia answered.

Hiker sighed loudly and took his normal seat at the head of the table as Ainsley rushed from the kitchen carrying the tray of tea and cups.

"Pancakes?" Mama Jamba asked expectantly as Ainsley bustled back to the kitchen.

The housekeeper swung around, her face pinched. "What? You like pancakes? I had no idea. I'm not in here trying to make ten different dishes in half the time I normally do with none of the help I always have."

"Okay, then," Mama Jamba sang good-naturedly, a napkin appearing in her hands that she set into her lap. "Then I'll expect the pancakes next."

Ainsley threw her hands in the air as she burst back through into the kitchen with an annoyed sigh.

"Will someone," Hiker began, looking at Sophia, Evan, and Mama Jamba, "tell me what is going on?"

Evan continued to pace. Mama Jamba hummed to herself and swayed slightly. Sophia realized the burden of explanation was going to fall on her.

"Well, Quiet appears to be upset about the status of things around here," she began. "Ainsley told him off for keeping the secret he was the Gullington, so he didn't get her ready and let her oversleep—"

"Me too," Wilder cut in, stretching his arms into the air and yawning. "Best sleep I have had in ages."

Mahkah nodded, apparently having slept like a baby too.

"Must be nice," Sophia remarked, shaking her head.

"You aren't sleeping?" Hiker asked with concern.

She shook her head. "No, not really. Been up since three this morning."

"Interesting," Hiker said, combing his hands over his beard.

"Not to me. Just annoying," Sophia disagreed. "Anyway, Evan, who is really trying to test the strength of my cloak, had all of his clothes taken by the Castle for being nice to Quiet."

Evan paused his pacing. "You really think he doesn't like me being nice to him?"

Wilder pointed over his shoulder toward the entrance of the dining hall. "You could always try the novel approach of asking him yourself."

Standing squarely in the archway was Gullington Quiet McAfee, the groundskeeper for the Expanse, but more importantly, the all-encompassing and powerful source of the Dragon Elite's home.

The gnome was who kept the Barrier in place over the Gullington. He was the Cave where the dragons lived. He was Expanse all around them, and The Pond to the North and the Castle where the dragonriders rested. He was their home, and based on the expression on his face, he was pissed.

CHAPTER FIVE

"Q uiet, what is the meaning of all this?" Hiker began, throwing his meaty arms wide. "You didn't wake Ainsley up, took all Evans clothes, won't let Sophia sleep, and I swear the three of us had a bloody awful time trying to rouse." Hiker shook his head. "It took everything I had to get out of bed this morning when I realized the time."

"If you hadn't thrown that bucket of water on me, I'd still be asleep, sir," Wilder said, throwing his fingers through his chaotic dark hair, which Sophia realized was wet.

"On the bright side, you've now had your weekly bath, so there you go," Evan joked.

Quiet didn't appear obligated to offer an answer to the leader of the Dragon Elite as he strode into the dining hall and took a seat next to Sophia.

Evan peeled back like he was afraid the tiny gnome would assault him. "Not that I'm complaining, great and noble Gullington. I was just wondering if you might know where all of my clothes are?"

"Oh, keep your pants on, would you?" Wilder joked with a laugh. "Let our groundskeeper eat without being bothered with your constant nagging."

Quiet's eyes skirted to the pile of pastries in front of them and sighed as if disappointed to find no one had touched them and left him with only scraps.

"Haha," Evan said without amusement. "I'd ask to borrow a pair of your pants, Wilder, but we all know yours would be much too small for me."

"I have got a sock you can shove in your—"

"Enough," Hiker boomed, interrupting Wilder. He leaned forward, rapping on the table in front of Quiet. "What is going on? Why are you acting in this peculiar way?"

"I don't think he's acted in a peculiar way," Sophia observed. "It's only that we know it's him now, whereas before we subscribed the behavior of the Castle to some unknown entity."

Hiker sat back. "Will no one else at this table speak unless your name is Quiet?"

Ainsley hurried from the kitchen, a platter of pancakes in one hand and a plate of bacon and hash browns in the other. She narrowed her eyes once she spied Quiet. "There he is, the reason I'm working double-time this morning. I had to actually fry the breakfast foods myself, and S. Beaufont saw me with my hair an atrocious mess."

Hiker threw a contemptuous glare at the elf.

"What?" Ainsley spat. "You said for no one at the table to speak, and I'm clearly not at the table."

Sophia was highly amused that Ainsley hadn't even been in the room when Hiker had made his declaration, but that was always the way with the housekeeper. She always chimed in on conversations she wasn't even present for.

Sliding the tall stack of pancakes in front of Mama Jamba, Ainsley stared daggers at Quiet, who had his stumpy hands in his lap and his cap pulled down low over his eyes, making his expression unreadable. "You didn't get me ready this morning, Quiet."

"You stole all my clothes," Evan declared angrily.

"You nearly put me in a coma," Hiker fired.

All eyes at the table landed on Sophia, but she merely shook her head, unwilling to join in against the groundskeeper. Instead, she reached over and grabbed the biggest pastry on the top of the stack.

"I don't know about you all, but I'm starving," she said, taking a large bite.

The gnome's eyes flickered up to meet hers, a strange expression in his gaze. He muttered something she couldn't make out before reaching over and grabbing his own pastry from the stack.

Ainsley threw her hands in the air as she backed for the kitchen. "Oh, that's bloody great! We confront you for being a calloused jerk, and you lavish her with compliments for treating you like there's nothing different about you. Very bloody well. Just see if I dust the cobwebs this century. I might not even scrub the floors properly anymore."

Hiker shook his head. "When have you ever scrubbed the floors properly?"

Mama Jamba, who didn't seem to have heard a word, licked her fingertips and smiled across the table at Hiker. "You should eat, son. You were asleep for nearly twelve hours."

"Yeah," Hiker growled, piling hash browns onto his plate. "That's what I was trying to get to the bottom of. I can't go to sleep at night, not knowing when or if I'll awake."

"Sir," Evan said, still standing, "Since you are built like a real man, could I borrow a pair of trousers from you?"

"No," Hiker spat, picking up his fork and knife and going to work on his food, although his gaze was still on Quiet. The gnome had polished off his pastry and seemed to be studying the platter in front of him, deciding which one to go after next.

"But sir," Evan complained.

Quiet reached for a large croissant, but Sophia cut him off, getting to it first and stealing it from him. Everyone at the table but Mama Jamba gasped at the risky move. Sophia had punished Evan for bullying Quiet like this when she'd first come to the Castle. He'd done it to Quiet to be mean. Sophia was doing it to test a theory.

Right on cue, as she took a bite of the croissant, the gnome as old as the Dragon Elite and just as powerful, smiled up at her. She grinned back and winked at him.

"I don't know why you're waking me up early or what secrets you want me to hear, but I'll keep doing it," she said in a whisper to him. She knew the others could hear her, their dragonrider senses making them privy to the quietest sounds. Sophia looked at them. "The rest of you, well, if you don't want to oversleep or lose your panties..." She glanced back at Evan, "then stop tiptoeing around Quiet. He doesn't like it, obviously."

Ainsley threw open the kitchen door and stomped over to the table, another tray of breakfast food in her hands. "I gave him a right piece of my mind, I did. I'm not sucking up or tiptoeing. Even so, that repugnant jerk is making my life hell, more so than usual."

"I wouldn't say I have ever tiptoed a day in my life," Hiker complained.

Sophia nodded. "Then figure out what he's been trying to tell you. Both of you."

Hiker seemed to consider this before he cut into his food, but his strength was too much for the ceramic plate and it broke, sending bits all over the table.

"Damn, Hercules," Evan said, shaking his head. "Maybe you need to lay off the Wheaties."

"And maybe you need to stop watching modern television with this one," Hiker suggested, throwing his chin in Sophia's direction.

"She is right, though," Mama Jamba agreed. "You all have to redefine your relationship with Quiet. He is in charge of the Gullington."

"He *is* the Gullington," Mahkah corrected.

Mama Jamba shrugged. "It's semantics at this point, love. My point is, he has an important role to do. I gave it to him long ago. He is the perfect person for the job, and you might not always like how he carries it out. I dare say, most of the time, you'll not even understand his methods, but I trust him implicitly. Figure out how to live under his roof, or you'll suffer."

Evan pressed down Sophia's cloak, suddenly uncomfortable. "Tell me about it. It's quite drafty in here."

Hiker stood and glared at his broken plate and ruined food. "I'm going to be in my office. You all will join me there when you are done eating." He narrowed his eyes at the gnome, who was polishing off a third pastry, seeming to ignore the conversation at the table. "Quiet, you might want to be treated the same, but that's a mighty big hope for someone who has us all by the reins. It's too lofty of a wish to ever consider we will treat you differently, knowing you are so powerful."

Mama Jamba giggled like she'd just remembered a joke.

"What is so funny?" Hiker questioned.

"Oh, nothing, son," she said, wiping her mouth. "Just ironic the most powerful magician in the world would somehow think he wasn't going to be treated differently now that rumors are circulating about his incredible strength."

Hiker's mouth twitched with annoyance. "You are talking about me, aren't you?"

Mama Jamba elbowed Wilder. "He's pretty obtuse, isn't he?"

Wilder shook his head. "I'd prefer not to weigh in on this, actually."

"I don't see how anyone will know about my powers," Hiker argued.

"Yes, because there weren't representatives from the House of Fourteen who witnessed your incredible display of power," Mama Jamba told him.

"Liv Beaufont?" Hiker questioned. "She won't talk."

"No, she won't want to make the Dragon Elite, the organization she's been lobbying for, that her little sister is a part of and who has constantly met restrictions from, seem like it shouldn't be threatened anymore," Mama Jamba said, rising from the table.

Hiker considered her for a moment. "Okay, well, fine. I need time to absorb all this. As I said, the rest of you are to come straight to my office after you finish breakfast. I have assignments to make." He turned to face Sophia, his eyes briefly flicking to Quiet, who was gnawing on a piece of bacon. "I want a private word with you when you are done."

Sophia rose immediately, her eyes meeting Wilder's. His usually playful expression dropped as worry sprang to his gaze. "Yes, sir," Sophia answered. "I'll follow you up now. I'm all done anyway."

Hiker nodded and marched from the dining hall. Sophia gave Wilder a tentative expression before following the most powerful magician in the world to his office, worried he knew her secret and was going to punish her for it.

CHAPTER SIX

It wasn't that Sophia was afraid of Hiker Wallace as much as she was...no if she was honest with herself, really honest, she was absolutely terrified of the Viking. He'd absorbed his twin brother's powers when he killed him.

It wasn't like when Sophia absorbed her twin Jamison's powers when he died at birth. That had made her more powerful as a magician for all of her life. Hiker had absorbed the powers of a five-hundred-year-old dragonrider.

Thad Reinhart's powers had always been legendary, and now Hiker possessed all of it, along with his own. It had been very difficult for Wilder to get Hiker to embrace his new strength. Now that he had, there seemed to be other issues unrelated to the initial concerns surrounding guilt and frustration.

Controlling the power was incredibly difficult for Hiker, as Sophia had witnessed at the breakfast table. She knew all too well, large amounts of power could corrupt people or make them irrational, especially when they discovered news they didn't like so much. Like two of his dragonriders were romantically involved, spending hours together regularly, not doing one of the three main activities Hiker encouraged, namely training, resting, and studying.

Hiker was quiet as they strode through the Castle to his office. He didn't say a word once they were inside the warm study, the fire making the only noise in the room as it crackled.

Every one of the Vikings' movements seemed deliberate as he strode over to the Elite Globe and ran his hands over it, making it rotate in the large, intricately decorated stand.

"This globe can tell me a lot about my dragonriders," Hiker began, his words carefully chosen. "For centuries, I have relied on it to tell me their locations and status or confirm their deaths. It's never, ever wrong."

Sophia tensed and held in a breath as she considered her exit strategies.

She could probably run faster than Hiker for a little bit. Maybe Quiet would take pity on her and help with her escape, throwing down things in Hiker's path, slowing his progress and giving Sophia a chance to survive his deadly wrath.

Sophia saw the different red dots on the Elite Globe when Hiker's fingers paused over Scotland, where the whole of the dragonriders were located. Five riders and their dragons were all that remained in the world.

He lifted his gaze, a sober expression in his eyes. "What I can't understand is why it's suddenly changed."

"It has?" Sophia asked, rising on her toes to get a better look at the Dragon Elite Globe.

"Yes, but only for two dots," he stated, a speculative glare in his blue eyes that seemed to cut through her.

Sophia remembered something she read in her father's journal before giving it over to Liv and Clark. The pages were full of Theodore Beaufont's wisdom. Some of his thoughts were complex and profound, blowing Sophia's mind, but most of his ideas were simple and peaceful. Like when her father had written simple words on one page that came to her now:

Always accept responsibility for your actions.

"Sir, I can explain," Sophia started, finding her voice strong.

He turned, facing her directly. "How can you explain? I haven't even told you what is going on yet."

She combed her hands through her long blonde hair, trying to cover her nervousness. "Well, I just figured it out."

He shook his head at her. "Okay, then tell me why."

Sophia knitted her hands together as Mama Jamba entered the office, a nail file in one hand as she stroked it against the lavender nails that matched her tracksuit. "Don't let me interrupt. I just figured I'd get here early to enjoy the show."

Hiker scowled at her. "What show?"

She plopped herself down on the leather sofa, her attention staying on her nails. "The one going on now."

His eyelids fluttered with annoyance. "There's no show, Mama." Returning his gaze to Sophia, Hiker cleared his throat. "Now, go on. Explain yourself."

"O-O-Okay," she began.

"Don't stutter dear," Mama Jamba cut in. "It makes you seem unconfident."

Which is exactly what Sophia was. She was about to have to tell the most powerful magician in the world, a man always prone to anger, that she and Wilder were romantically involved, something they both knew he wouldn't be happy about. He'd be livid. He wouldn't allow it, and it was because of these worries Sophia hadn't allowed herself to really think much about the relationship. She spent most of her energy avoiding it, darting her gaze from Wilder's, making excuses and avoiding getting closer.

"Right," Sophia agreed, giving Mama Jamba a pleading look, hoping she could rescue her. Mother Nature didn't look up from her nails to see the begging. "It just sort of happened..."

"I know that," Hiker said with a sigh. "I watched it happen."

Sophia gasped. "You did?"

"Of course, I did," he declared, looking offended.

Worried thoughts began racing through her head. She didn't understand. Sophia thought they had been so careful. "When? How? Where?"

"Oh, what does it matter?" Hiker questioned, glancing back at the

Dragon Elite Globe. "I was standing right there, and then all of a sudden, well, it's unexplainable."

He pointed to the spot next to the window that looked out at the Pond. It was a spot where Wilder and Sophia had spent most of their time together when she allowed for such luxuries. She'd thought on the beach, they couldn't be seen. Apparently, she was wrong. Maybe Hiker's new powers allowed him to see through the rocks and cliffs that shielded the beach from the Expanse. Or maybe they had just been sloppy.

Sophia sucked in a breath. She couldn't run from this. "Sir, it isn't really unexplainable. It's feelings and although I realize you don't always understand those—"

"Feelings!" Hiker roared abruptly.

Sophia peeled back. As she suspected, his temper was heightened by these new powers.

He sprang into his normal pacing, and his boots thundered louder across the floor than usual.

Mama Jamba pulled her gaze away from her nails. "Now, it's getting good."

"How can you find this entertaining?" Sophia asked her, offense heavy in her voice. "This is my life. It isn't some joke for you to laugh at."

Mama Jamba simply smiled. "Oh, I flipped ahead and saw a spoiler. Can't tell you, though."

Sophia sighed, shaking her head. "Anyway, sir, we have feelings for each other. I know it doesn't make sense to you, but—"

"Feelings?" Hiker repeated, his face growing redder. "Of course, you'd make this about emotions."

"It's about emotions," Sophia argued. "I know you haven't really allowed dragonriders to have them in the past, but you can't control me."

This wasn't how Sophia pictured dying. As she stared at the angry eyes of the man towering over her, she waited for her life to start flashing before her eyes. Instead, the strangest, most unexpected thing happened.

Hiker Wallace started laughing.

Mama Jamba also appeared quite amused.

"What is so funny?" Sophia asked, the offense in her voice growing.

"Control you?" Hiker questioned, continuing to laugh. "Yeah, I think I know better by now. I wouldn't even waste my time with such a lofty goal at this point."

Sophia's chest was buzzing with adrenaline. Maybe this wasn't going to be so bad. She opened her mouth to say something, but Hiker beat her to it.

"I do expect if I put down my foot, you'll listen to me, Sophia." Hiker resumed his pacing. "I'm reserving that for other situations I suspect will arise, like you running an adjudication mission your own way or going over my head to Mama or when one of the other riders falls for you or when—"

"Wait, what?" Sophia interrupted, her insides freezing. Heart-stopping. Breath hitching.

"Oh, don't think I don't know you are just waiting until you disagree with something I say and supersede my rule by going to Mama," Hiker said, throwing an arm at the old woman curled up on the sofa, who was watching the exchange with a curious smile.

"No, not that," Sophia disagreed. "That part about the other riders…"

She couldn't believe she actually came out with the sentence without throwing up. Her breakfast was definitely not sitting right in her stomach.

"Well," Hiker began, throwing his hand through his short blond hair. "I'm not a fool. You are the only girl in his Castle and—"

"I believe Ainsley would take serious offense to that," Mama Jamba interrupted.

Hiker rolled his eyes. "I meant eligible bachelorette."

"Again, do you want to have your mustache shaved off in the middle of the night?" Mama Jamba asked seriously. "Keep that up and I'm certain our lovely housekeeper will do it for you. The last time I checked, there was no ring on Ainsley's hand."

Hiker protectively touched his mustache, as if checking it was still there. "I simply mean, that of all the options in the Castle, Sophia is the only one I suspect one of the other riders would be interested in. Ainsley has been here with them all the while, and they don't think of her that way."

"No, *they* don't," Mama Jamba sang, an emphasis on the middle word.

He shook his head. "Anyway, my point is that's something I'd put my foot down on, but for the most part—"

"Wait, what are we talking about?" Sophia asked, completely confused now. Hiker was speaking about a romantic relationship with Wilder like it wasn't happening but could become a possibility.

He threw his arm at the Dragon Elite Globe. "You and me. I realize you say this is about feelings, but all due respect, this is a logistical issue, Sophia. I know women like to think of things in terms of emotions, but I really need you to focus on the concrete."

Mama Jamba sat up straighter. "Oh, it's getting good now."

Hiker threw a contemptuous glare at the old woman. "Would you mind?"

She shook her head of short silver hair, which moved together like a helmet. "I don't mind at all."

"Sir, what do you mean, this is about you and me?" Sophia asked her eyes on the Dragon Elite Globe. "And the globe? I don't understand."

"I thought you did." Confusion covered his face. "You said you could explain. If you know why our dots on the globe are different than all the rest, I need you to tell me."

Sophia's eyes widened with understanding. "Our dots are different than all the rest... That's what this is about."

Mama Jamba smiled at her and winked. "There's the spoiler. I told you this would be fun."

"Oh," Sophia said, putting it all together. She'd thought Hiker knew about her and Wilder. He was referring to the Dragon Elite Globe. That was curious, but what she'd just learned was of even more interest to her. What had he said? A relationship with a dragonrider would be something Hiker would put his foot down for. So, the good news was he didn't suspect anything. The bad news was he wasn't an idiot and knew it was a possibility. The worst news was he'd put his foot down, and probably not in the figurative sense. It would probably come down straight on Wilder's head.

Sophia had been trying to tell herself when she allowed herself to think about the complexity of her new predicament that Hiker needed them. He only had four riders, but that was exactly why this wasn't going to be tolerated. She also had to remind herself there were just under a thousand dragon eggs sitting in the Nest, which meant there would be many more dragonriders in the future. Ones who could easily replace Sophia and Wilder when Hiker killed them.

The confusion was heavy on the Viking's face as he looked between Sophia and Mama Jamba. "What is going on here?"

"Oh, nothing," Mama Jamba sang. "Now, Sophia, the Dragon Elite Globe. I bet you have some questions about that, dear, don't you?"

Sophia allowed herself to finally breathe properly. She nodded. "So our dots are different?"

Hiker pressed his eyes shut and vigorously shook his head. "You said you already knew about it and you knew why."

"Right," Sophia said, drawing out the word. "I thought you were talking about something else."

"What did you think I was talking about?" Hiker questioned with authority in his voice.

"So the dots?" Sophia asked, trying her best to change the subject. "You said you watched it change from right there." She indicated the spot next to the Dragon Elite Globe. Now things were starting to make sense from earlier. Hiker hadn't spied her and Wilder at the Pond. They had been careful.

He gave her a discriminating expression. For a moment, she thought he was going to question her again. Instead, he seemed to think better of it and shook his head. "Yes, so I was studying the Globe this morning when I noticed your and my dots changed."

Sophia strode over and studied the Globe from a closer distance. There were three red dots. Even though they were all huddled on top of each other at the Gullington, she could still read the labels: Evan, Mahkah, and Wilder.

Next to them, and distinctively different were two other dots that were red, outlined with blue. They were labeled: Hiker and Sophia.

CHAPTER SEVEN

Sophia studied the dots on the Dragon Elite Globe for a long minute, thinking something would occur to her to explain why theirs were different. When nothing did, she glanced up at Hiker. "Why are we different?"

He threw his hands up, obviously irritated by the question. "I thought you could explain it. That's what I'm wondering."

Sophia glanced at Mama Jamba, a question in her expression. "You know, don't you?"

"She won't tell us anything helpful," Hiker said with a growl.

"My helpful and yours are different," Mama Jamba argued. "I think I offer you a lot of helpful information, but you just don't value it the same way as me."

He huffed. "This morning you told me I had pillow marks on my face from sleeping when I asked you about the Dragon Elite Globe."

"And that was helpful," she stated. "Imagine if you'd have shown up to breakfast with those. It would have been rather embarrassing."

"What is embarrassing is Sophia and my dots have changed, and you know and won't tell us," Hiker protested, his voice rising.

"Maybe it's because we are twins," Sophia muttered.

Both Hiker and Mama Jamba looked at her. He had a skeptical expression on his face. Mama Jamba had a proud smile.

"You'd think the old man would have figured that out already, but he's getting slow in his old age," she commented, clasping her hands together in front of her chest.

"That's it?" Hiker asked, looking between the two women. "But why?"

"Because..." Mama Jamba answered, a hint of mischief in her voice.

"Mama..." Hiker said, disapproval in his tone.

"Hiker," she fired back, matching his tone.

"What is the deal with the twin factor?" Sophia asked.

Mother Nature pursed her lips, indicating to Sophia. "She knows how to ask the right questions. You should take notes from her."

The annoyance was evident on Hiker's face. "Are you going to answer the question?"

"Do you think I'm going to?" Mama Jamba asked in reply.

He shook his head as Wilder, Mahkah, and Evan strode into the office, none of them seeming to notice they were interrupting.

"I can do some research," Sophia offered.

"You mean you are going to read through my book," Hiker argued unpleasantly.

"You can have it back if you like," Sophia offered.

"No, because every time you try to give me the *Complete History of Dragonriders*, it just ends up back in your room," Hiker said. "One of these days, I'm going to lay into Quiet for reducing my office to nearly a closet for several weeks."

"Yeah, because that won't backfire on you." Evan threw himself down next to Mama Jamba and put an arm around her shoulder.

She smiled at him, running her eyes over the clothes he was wearing, which didn't appear to fit well at all. They must have belonged to Wilder or Mahkah, who were smaller in stature.

"Fine, Sophia," Hiker relented. "Do the research and let me know what you find out."

"Research about what?" Evan asked.

"That's none of your concern," Hiker told him. "I have missions for you all."

"Although I'd like to help," Wilder began, "I'm afraid Subner has something that demands my attention."

Hiker sighed. "Fine, Sophia you'll have to take on another mission because—"

"Actually, Subner wants her on this particular mission as well," Wilder boldly declared.

Sophia was careful to keep her eyes away from Wilder's gaze. He was being bold, but he didn't know that Hiker already suspected something broadly. He was going to kill them, and she already had enough to do. She'd promised to help with the Cupid mission and couldn't let them down now. It was just with the Trin Currante situation and lost dragon eggs, she felt torn.

"Remember when I mentioned putting down my foot earlier?" Hiker asked Sophia.

"You don't have any leads yet, son," Mama Jamba cut in.

He swung around to face the old woman. "What are you going on about?"

"Well, sometimes, when you are looking for something," Mama Jamba started, "it's a good idea to go looking for something else to find it."

He sighed heavily. "That makes zero sense, Mama."

"No, I get what she means," Evan stated.

"Of course you do," Hiker agreed, rolling his eyes.

"Seriously, sir," Evan went on. "When I was looking for clothes earlier because someone took all of mine, I found the yoyo I lost last summer and also an entire package of chocolate." He pulled a candy bar from his pocket and offered it to Mama Jamba.

She shook her head. "No, I'm watching my girly figure."

Evan winked at her. "I'm watching it too."

"Will you not hit on Mother Nature," Hiker said with irritation.

"I'll try, but no promises." Evan sent a flirtatious glance to Mama Jamba. "Anyway, I get what she means about finding something else

38

when you are looking for another thing. I think there's merit in the idea."

"Then we are probably doomed," Hiker grumbled.

"Hey now," Evan complained. "I'm one of the dragonriders who will actually take on your adjudicator missions, unlike some people." He gave Sophia and Wilder very pointed expressions.

Wilder snapped his fingers. "Guess you don't need to borrow that shirt after all, do you?"

The flannel long sleeve Evan was wearing disappeared, leaving him sitting topless on the sofa next to Mama Jamba. He didn't budge but just shook his head. "That's fine. I don't need a top." Then he grabbed on to his pants, his eyes wide, giving Mahkah a pleading expression. "Please mate, don't take my clothes. Don't be like this guy." He indicated Wilder on the other side of the room.

"Don't worry," Mahkah replied calmly, his hands pinned behind his back. "I think we all want you to keep your pants on."

"Amen to that," Sophia sang.

"Well, they are tight enough they aren't coming off unless someone really pries," Evan said, batting his eyelashes at Sophia.

She caught the paranoid expression on Hiker's face. He was worried about something happening between her and one of the men, and she understood. Something had transpired between her and Wilder. It wasn't because she was the only new girl in the Castle in centuries, or she at least hoped so. That thought was enough to ruin it for her. There were so many doubts revolving around her and Wilder. She'd told herself they had a spark, and there was chemistry, but maybe it was just because she was a woman who lived in the Gullington.

"Fine," Hiker finally agreed. "Sophia and Wilder go on this mission for Subner, but I do want you keeping an eye out for information on Trin Currante. We need to find out where she is. We need to find those eggs. We also need to find out how she got the advantage over us in the first place. Otherwise, we might fall victim to another attack."

Sophia nodded. That had been her concern too. "I'll add it to my research."

"Very well." Hiker turned his attention to Evan and Mahkah. "You two will have to take on the adjudicator missions and pick up the slack."

Evan sprang to his feet, his eyes wide with excitement. "You can rely on me, sir. I won't let you down like Sophia and Wilder."

Sophia was about to defend herself and make an antagonizing statement to Evan, but she didn't have to, because the sound of the seam of his jeans bursting filled the room, making everyone but the young dragonrider laugh.

CHAPTER EIGHT

Something wasn't adding up. Sophia knew it. Hiker Wallace knew it. The dragonriders all suspected it. But no one knew what they were missing. There were more questions when it came to Trin Currante than there were answers.

The cyborg knew more than anyone believed possible. She'd managed to poison Quiet. Sophia reasoned it was a blanket attempt to poison all the Dragon Elite. The herbs that had been sold to Ainsley at the village market were gone and so studying them wasn't an option. The vendor hadn't returned to the market, which wasn't a surprise to anyone.

She'd returned a second time, having taken only one dragon egg the first time. Her next trip, she took a dozen eggs. Trin Currante got what she wanted. There was no reason to return.

"What am I missing?" Sophia asked herself as she opened the *Complete History of Dragonriders*. The book was so large that finding something related to the topics she was researching would take time.

On top of trying to learn more about Trin Currante and the Saverus, Sophia now needed to figure out why she and Hiker's dots were different on the Dragon Elite Globe. It had to do with the twin factor, but that wasn't something new. They had been twins since the beginning.

"So why was the Dragon Elite Globe just now noting us as different? We have always been twins." Sophia continued to talk to herself, wondering if maybe Quiet would answer. He probably knew the answer to all these questions, but similar to Mama Jamba, he wasn't talking—and if he were, no one would be able to understand him. Not since he told his name to Sophia and thanked her for saving him, had he spoken in an audible voice. He was back to whispering and acting in his usual mysterious ways.

Sophia flipped through the enormous volume, overwhelmed by the information. Similar to Bermuda Lauren's book, *Mysterious Creatures*, the physical size of it didn't really tell one how large it actually was. It was glamoured to appear smaller for easy transport. *The Complete History of Dragonriders* was even larger than Bermuda's hand-held book, which worried Sophia.

She needed to rest up for her mission the next day with Wilder, something she'd committed to and wanted to run as far from as possible after the strange conversation with Hiker. She'd dodged a bullet there. It made her cringe. She'd been moments away from confessing to something she thought he already knew and revealing something he didn't know. All the while, sneaky Mama Jamba was sitting by watching and completely entertained.

Sophia shook her head, and flipped through the book, wishing it had a table of contents or an index. She could look up the twin factor and be done with it since she didn't know what to look for to find out how Trin Currante learned so much about the Gullington. Maybe it had been a good guess on Trin's part, poisoning Quiet and taking down the Barrier. Or maybe there was something in the large volume that stated this explicitly. It was hard to know, and with time ticking down to bedtime, she feared she wasn't going to find any answers that night.

Hiker'd had the book for centuries, and even he hadn't read the whole thing. Those who had answers like Mama Jamba and Quiet literally weren't talking. Sophia was about to give up when her head snapped up with an idea.

She jumped to her feet. "Trinity!"

The librarian for the Great Library had read the *Complete History of Dragonriders*. The skeleton would know the answers to her questions. At least he might be able to point her in the right direction for reference.

She grabbed the large book and hurried from her room. The torches on the long corridor of the Castle lit as Sophia progressed. She didn't know how Quiet did it, how he was everywhere and also a person. It was a strange bit of magic, more powerful than anything she'd ever witnessed before.

When she got to the portal door that led to the Great Library, Sophia paused and made a silent prayer. Before, Trinity had locked the other side, saying the energy between the Castle and the Great Library was connected through the portals. He further explained that if something happened to the Castle or the Gullington, then since it was the major organ connected by the portals, it could affect the Great Library and the House of Fourteen.

Sophia stiffened her fingers on the handle to the closet door. "He knew," she said in a whisper. Just after Trinity had put the lock on the portal, Quiet had fallen ill, and the Gullington had begun withering away. The grounds had started to die, and the Castle fell into ruin. Everything connected to the Gullington began to degrade.

The House of Fourteen had been okay because of the presence of the giants who stabilized chaotic energy. But the Great Library would have been affected if Trinity hadn't put a lock on it. He'd said it was simply a precaution based on what he learned in the *Complete History of Dragonriders*. Now, the timing seemed odd.

He'd have more than just a few questions to answer. Sophia pushed down on the handle and to her frustration, found it locked.

She searched around, wondering how she could get into the Great Library. Before she had to make an appointment with the librarian, but he'd sent the meeting request. She had no clue how to get a hold of him. The only other way into the Great Library involved going to

Zanzibar, finding the Fierce, and following its path. That wasn't a quick task and involved enlisting her friend King Rudolf who always made everything more complicated.

No, she didn't have time for such an excursion. She was curious how Trinity had known to put the lock on the portal between the Castle and the Great Library when he had. Something was needling at her brain, telling her something wasn't right, but what, she didn't know. It would have to wait. For right then, she was going to tuck in so she wasn't exhausted for what she had to do the next day.

CHAPTER NINE

The rain was unrelenting when Sophia exited the Castle the next morning. She could make out a figure in the distance, his chin in the air unconcerned about being splattered by the large droplets of water.

Wilder Thomson was made for the unforgiving weather of Scotland. He'd never shrunk away from the chilly winds since Sophia had known him. He never threw his hood up when they were out together and the rain started. Instead, he seemed at ease with whatever Mother Nature threw at him, or the Gullington in this case.

The sun hadn't risen over the hills in the distance. The two dragonriders had agreed to set off for their mission as early as possible. Sophia could have left much earlier since she'd been up at 3:33 that morning. Like before, she got up as Quiet had encouraged. The morning breeze wasn't talking to her. As she sat in front of the fire, reading the *Complete History of Dragonriders*, she expected to get some epiphany, but the hours went by with no revelations. When it was time to meet Wilder, she got ready and exited the Castle to find him standing squarely in the middle of the Expanse, rain rolling off his cheeks.

In the distance, where the glow of the sun was starting to edge around the hills, it appeared it wasn't raining outside of the Gullington. Sophia didn't know why Quiet was insisting on making it rain pretty much full time on the Expanse. She trusted his reasons, though, whatever they were.

Sophia pulled up her hood and marched across the Expanse, making quick progress in Wilder's direction. He smiled at her when she approached.

"You awake?" he asked when she was closer.

She wanted to return his grin, which made both his dimples surface, but she couldn't. Sophia had never been good at pretending. She couldn't pretend to be happy when Clark was sad, or fake confidence when Liv was worried. At the end of the day, the emotions the others saw on Sophia's face were real, never an act.

"I have been awake since the wee hours," she answered, noticing his dark hair was drenched, but he didn't seem to care.

"Did you say 'wee'? I do believe our Scottish vernacular is rubbing off on you," he said with a wink.

"How could it not?" she replied, pointing to the Barrier. "Shall we get to drier land?"

He nodded. "Yeah, I was just wondering why the little guy is making it rain so much more here."

"Maybe it's a part of his recovery after the whole ordeal," she suggested.

He didn't answer but rather studied her with a sideways expression as they strode toward the Barrier. "What is it? Something bothering you?"

And there it was. There was no hiding things from this one, she realized. Wilder always seemed to see right through her, even from the beginning.

"Hiker…" she started and let the word trail away.

"Yes, I have met the grumpy goose," Wilder answered with a laugh. "He can really be delightful after a bit of whiskey, though."

"He suspects us," she explained, not laughing.

Wilder's light expression fell away. He swallowed and pulled his gaze forward.

"He said it was one thing he wouldn't tolerate," Sophia continued.

"We figured as much." Wilder's voice was suddenly cold. His eyes narrowed.

"He doesn't know it's you, but he is not an idiot," Sophia stated. "I'm the first eligible bachelorette to enter the Castle in centuries and—"

"Is that what you think this is about?" Wilder interrupted. "You think I like you because you are the only option?"

Sophia shrugged. "It goes to reason."

He shook his head. "You are ridiculous. I don't need to be with someone just because. I don't need you. I want you." The frustration was immediately palpable between them, but there was no avoiding it, and Sophia had known that. Wilder let out a breath and continued. "I'm not alone. I have Simi. You should know a dragonrider doesn't need companionship the way others do. Our dragons provide us with so much. But I chose you because, well, I want to be with you. There could be a hundred girls here at the Gullington, and I'd choose you. Over and over. I don't know how to convince you of that."

Sophia sucked in a breath, her chest suddenly feeling extra tight like she'd caught a novel virus that was about to take hold and destroy her life. She shook off the dramatic notion and met Wilder's gaze. "I wasn't wrong to have such a thought based on what I knew."

Wilder smiled at her, one that was so full of warmth and understanding it made her chest ache even more. "No, and I hadn't said what I just did until presently. But now I have, and now you know. I hope you have no further doubts."

"It isn't that easy, Wild," she argued. "Hiker, if he finds out then he'll be angry. It's not like we have the luxury of time or anything else to explore this. There's so much demanding our attention."

"Don't do this," Wilder warned, all lightness leaving his face at once as the realization of what was happening set in.

She swallowed. "I have to. We don't make any sense together. How long can we really keep this up?"

"As long as we choose," he declared, his voice suddenly louder as the rain began to dissipate. They were almost to the Barrier at the edge of the Gullington.

"Inevitably, there's an expiration date on us," she explained. "Hiker won't accept us. He said as much. It's one of the few things he'll put his foot down for. You've got Subner and adjudication missions. I need to find the dragon eggs. That leaves little time for anything else. This was a pipe dream all along. You know that."

Wilder halted just beside the Barrier, the rain continuing to splatter down his face and drenching him. Sophia paused, looking up at him. On the other side of the Barrier, she could spy clear skies as the sun rose over the hills, making it appear like a fresh day full of possibilities was dawning. Outside the Gullington, things didn't appear dreary and beyond their control.

"We could make it work," Wilder argued.

"For a little while," she agreed. "But at the end of the day, we are just postponing the inevitable. Break our hearts now or later. Regardless, this always ends the same way."

"Please, Soph," he pleaded. "I want you in my future."

She struggled to swallow. "And I'll be there. As your friend."

Before she could change her mind, Sophia stepped through the Barrier into the crisp morning air, devoid of rain and the problems she wished she could leave behind in the Gullington. Just as Wilder stepped through after her, she knew her problems would always follow her. It might not be raining on them anymore, but that didn't mean she didn't feel a storm cloud overhead.

CHAPTER TEN

Wilder and Sophia didn't exchange any more words after they crossed the Barrier and stepped through the portal to Roya Lane. Things were going to be awkward now, especially since they were required to go on this next mission together.

There was no avoiding it. Sophia could have tried to pretend everything was okay, but as she'd already seen, Wilder would always see through things with her.

No, she'd decided to end things right away before it got any more difficult. Things had just gotten away from them, but she was redefining their relationship, and they would both be better off for it. They could do this, she reasoned. They could be friends. That was what they were before.

Roya Lane was as crowded as ever, and their drenched appearances earned them more than a few curious glances, or maybe it was because most recognized them as the Dragon Elite. It had been many centuries since a dragonrider freely stomped around Roya Lane, and they were still considered quite the novelty. Sophia looked forward to when they marked hope and gave others encouragement. They still had some work to do, taking on their roles as adjudicators. It wasn't an overnight change in perception.

They had to resolve one worldly affair after another in order for nations and people to stake their fate in them once more. That's why Mahkah and Evan were off on adjudicator missions presently. Each one helped to earn the favor of mortals and bolster the reputation of the Dragon Elite. That was the hope, but Sophia reminded herself Evan was one of the dragonriders on these missions, so there might be some cleanup needed.

"Closed?" Sophia asked, reading the sign in the window of Subner's shop, Fantastical Armory. "How is it closed? Didn't he tell us to come here and meet him at this time?"

Wilder eyed the pocket watch he retrieved from his cloak. "Yeah, and he even stressed not to be late, which is why we got up at the crack of dawn."

"Well, I was already up," Sophia teased, wishing her comment would bring a smile to the other dragonrider's face. It didn't.

He sighed. "You'd think Father Time's assistant would be punctual."

"I wouldn't actually," Sophia said. She tested the door handle and found it locked. Peering through the windows, she searched for a sign of the hippie elf. The shop was dark and empty.

Sophia shook her head. "If I know Subner, he wanted us to get here early and be locked out."

"Because?" Wilder asked.

"I don't know, but that's how he and all the other irritatingly powerful entities in our lives work," Sophia explained, thinking of the pocketknife Subner had given her, knowing she'd drop it for Wilder to find. Or how Mama Jamba was always orchestrating something in her life, and how Quiet was setting her up for something with the early morning wake up calls.

"So, what should we do?" Wilder asked.

Sophia's stomach rumbled, and she remembered she hadn't had breakfast yet. Wilder must have heard the complaint from her stomach with his enhanced hearing. His eyes darted to her midsection, and to her relief, a sideways smile whisked to his face. "Hungry?"

"According to my stomach, I'm apparently starving," she answered, hopeful things could be normal between them once more.

"Well, we all know how you Los Angeles girls never eat anything unless it's a cucumber or ice chips infused with mint leaves."

Sophia scowled at him. "As if I'd break my diet with something as indulgent as mint leaves."

"As if," he fired back, pretending to flip his hair over one shoulder.

"Come on, I could use a cookie the size of my face," she said, striding down the stairs of the Fantastical Armory and setting off for the bakery they had found the last time they were on Roya Lane.

"A cookie for breakfast?" Wilder questioned. "That sounds mighty indulgent."

Sophia, like all magicians, fueled much of her magic with food. The higher the fat and sugar content, the better it was for replacing reserves. It was one of many perks of being a magician. They were rarely ever fat since they burned calories so quickly. This was in contrast to gnomes who could bank their magic for long periods of time but then also had weight gain as a result.

"Well, I won't tell Hiker we didn't have a protein-rich breakfast if you don't," Sophia bartered, remembering all too well the leader of the Dragon Elite always pushing them to eat more meat and eggs instead of carbs at the morning meal.

"Funny," he muttered, the light expression dropping from his face. "So, there are certain secrets you are okay with keeping from Hiker."

Sophia rolled her eyes, realizing Wilder had to get his jabs in. She didn't expect this to be the last one.

"When I was little—"

"Last week, you mean," he interrupted.

Another eye roll. "Like a child little," Sophia explained. "Anyway, my brother once allowed me to have cookies for breakfast because I was sad."

"Because the training wheels on your pink bike got tangled in the ribbon for your balloon?" he asked with real curiosity.

"Because my sister and brother had been murdered," she fired back immediately. The events hadn't happened very long ago and the wound was still fresh, although Sophia suspected it always would be.

Wilder sighed with defeat. "That isn't fair. I thought we were joking around."

"Did you?" Sophia asked. "Then why aren't you laughing? People usually laugh when they joke."

"Touché, Soph," he said, shaking his head at her. "You are really going to have a cookie for breakfast? Is it because you are upset about something?" It was a leading question, and she wasn't taking the bait.

"The way I figure it, we only have one life to live," Sophia explained, walking backward through the streets and flashing him a grin.

He worked his jaw, a hooded expression in his eyes as he strode after her. The crowds parted for them, although Sophia paid little attention to the passersby.

"Yes, one very long life," Wilder stated matter of factly. "As dragonriders, you can pretty much bet on being on this planet for a millennium. Might as well be happy during that time, or really careful and appease the grumpiest person on Earth."

Sophia spun around as they came to the alleyway where the Crying Cat Bakery was located. "I know what you are talking about, Wild. Maybe you should write about this in your diary."

"I will, once I have scrapbooked the occasion in my rose-scented journal," he grumbled.

Sophia opened the bakery door, enjoying the chime of the bells signaling their arrival.

The smell of baked goods was enchanting. So were the fairies flying overhead, doing various chores. What wasn't so inviting was the masked murderer leaning against the display case, cleaning blood from her machete.

CHAPTER ELEVEN

"Um, what is going on here?" Sophia asked the masked person she was fairly certain was Lee, one of the owners of the eccentric bakery.

She shrugged. "Caught us right before rush hour."

Lee must have realized she was wearing the mask because she ripped it off and threw it dramatically behind the counter. "Oh, sorry. You didn't see that."

"See what?" Wilder asked, sidling up next to Sophia, his hands pressed casually into his pockets.

"I don't know," Lee started. "The lighting in here makes people see weird stuff sometimes." She lifted the machete and licked the blade, the red substance getting on the edge of her lips before she wiped it off with the back of her sleeve.

"Like you cleaning a sharp blade with your tongue?" Sophia asked, her hand flexing by her sword. She didn't trust this one, although she found Lee amusing.

Lee didn't pay her any attention as she called over her shoulder, "Cat, the raspberry compote is too sweet."

"It's supposed to be like that to counteract the rhubarb, which is naturally bitter," Cat yelled from the back, her face popping into view through the delivery window in the back.

"Naturally bitter," Lee said with a laugh. "Just like you, my love."

"What was that?" Cat asked, striding in carrying a tray of pastries.

"Nothing, dear," Lee stated. "Do we have something for a broken heart?" She pointed at Wilder with her machete. "This one needs it."

He shot her an annoyed glare. "I don't either. I'm simply hungry." He thumbed in the direction of Sophia. "This one never lets me eat. It's always go, go, go."

"And also, no, no, no," Lee protested, pushing off the display case and walking around to the other side. She dropped the blade of the machete into a bucket of flour, where it fell with a satisfying grace.

"Something for heartbreak," Cat muttered, her words slurring as she glanced over the pastry case. "Let's see…" She tapped her fingers on her chin, thinking. "Was it a man or a woman who broke your heart, dear?"

Seemingly bored, Lee pointed at Sophia with a small knife, which Sophia hadn't noticed her pick up. "It was that one there."

Sophia blushed, looking over her shoulder like Lee might be referring to someone behind her.

"Yes, you, blondie," Lee said, taking the knife and picking her teeth with it.

"Okay, so a woman broke your heart," Cat remarked, continuing to browse the pastries.

"Actually, if I could just get a couple of cookies," Wilder cut in.

Cat waved him off. "No, we are going to fix you."

"Or we are totally going to screw you up," Lee stated matter of factly. "It's like a fifty-fifty thing."

"So, I can't have a cookie?" Wilder asked, sounding amused.

"You can have a pastry I choose, a pat on the head and a gold star," Cat said, swaying slightly.

"Are you drunk?" Lee asked her wife. "The sun has hardly risen."

"If it makes any difference, I'm not freshly drunk," Cat answered proudly, waving her hand in front of her face. "This is residual drunkenness from last night."

Lee wiped her hand over her forehead, feigning relief. "Oh, well, that makes a difference." She glanced around as if looking at a crowd of people there to bear witness. "No, ladies and gentlemen, you can't have her. She is all mine."

"Can I get a cookie?" Sophia asked, daring to cut into the conversation.

"No, Heartbreaker," Lee admonished, pointing to the corner. "You are on time out until you realize hearts aren't made of paper and can't simply be glued back together."

"But—"

"You are telling me," Cat said, seemingly stumped. "I mean, there really isn't a way to repair a broken heart. Just bandage it."

"Is there any more whiskey left?" Lee asked.

Cat laughed. "Yeah, right, dear."

"And here I have been poisoning your mashed potatoes," Lee joked.

Cat continued to laugh. "No, always spike my drinks. That's the only way to ensure you don't waste the poison."

"Wait, you want to be poisoned?" Sophia asked.

"Didn't I tell you to get in the corner, Succubus?" Lee scolded, making Sophia take a step back out of concern for her safety.

"And yes," Cat declared proudly, studying Sophia. "I mean, a good buzz takes me a whole bottle, but mix it with some of the chemicals Lee keeps testing and I'm sleeping like a baby."

Sophia cut her eyes to meet Wilder's, but he didn't seem to want to commiserate with her.

"Okay, so your heart was broken by a pretty blonde," Cat commented, searching over the pastries again.

"Actually, if we couldn't do this, that would be ideal," Wilder said, embarrassment edging into his tone.

Lee waved him off dismissively. "No, we are doing this. You came in here damn well knowing the craziness you were going to encounter. We aren't doing our job if we don't fix your problems, fill your bellies and give you a rash that will ensure you come back for the antidote."

Wilder, who had been scratching his arm, suddenly stopped. "Wait, what?"

"Nothing, dear. Now I want you to eat this in one bite," Cat told him, picking up a cupcake that said, "Treat Yo Self."

She handed it over to Wilder, and to Sophia's surprise, he actually took it and crammed it into his mouth. After what looked like some really uncomfortable chewing and a dry swallow, he turned his attention to Sophia before shaking his head, a sober expression in his bright blue eyes. Through still a full mouth, he said, "It didn't work."

"Of course, it didn't," Cat agreed, putting a couple of chocolate chips in a bag. "We told you there was no cure for a broken heart." She handed the sweets over the counter to Sophia, then leaned forward and whispered loudly in her ear, booze heavy on her breath. "How about you make some racist statements?"

Sophia shrunk back. "No, why would I do that?"

Lee nodded, joining the group, brandishing the knife she'd been using to pick her teeth. "Great idea. I could probably ugly her up, too. What do you think of a facial scar?"

"I-I don't like that idea," Sophia stammered.

Cat shrugged. "Do you want this young man to suffer? We are trying to repair the damage you've done."

"First off," Sophia began, unable to meet Wilder's gaze, "he is not young. And secondly, other people's emotions aren't my fault."

Lee elbowed Cat. "She reminds me of you when you were younger and spritely."

The other woman nodded. "Yeah, and she hasn't allowed herself to fall, which is why it doesn't hurt yet."

"It's only a matter of time," Lee said to her wife, talking in front of Sophia like she couldn't hear every word they were saying.

"Then it's going to hurt like hell," Cat added.

"We should go into the liquor business," Lee suggested.

"We both know that wouldn't be a wise investment," Cat explained and hiccupped.

"Right," Lee chirped.

"Speaking of failed businesses, are you going to be here all day?" Cat asked her, seeming to forget they had two patrons.

"Maybe," Lee answered and then strode over to Wilder and leaned in his direction but kept her gaze on Sophia. "Hey, I know how to fix your problems. I take out Shorty over there, and I bet you feel a lot better. Maybe not at first, but after a few years, you'll forget about her."

"She is a dragonrider for the Elite," Wilder said. Sophia was grateful to see the amused expression back on his face.

"So, what are you saying?" Lee asked loudly, like she wasn't being overheard by the "target."

"I'm saying it might be hard to kill her," Wilder answered with a laugh.

Lee nodded, like this made perfect sense. She tapped her wife on the arm. "He's tried to kill her already. Apparently, they are much more in love than I thought."

Cat batted her eyelashes at Lee. "Reminds me of us."

"Right," Lee agreed before shrugging at Wilder. "Well, maybe you'll have better luck killing your other half than I have. All my best efforts don't work on this one. I swear she's got as many lives as a cat. The other day, I pushed her down the stairs, and wouldn't you know, that was the day they had delivered all the paper goods."

Cat giggled. "It was a great landing, after a fun ride."

"You rode your ass down the stairs," Lee corrected.

"And landed like a baby on a pile of clouds," Cat sang.

Lee gave Wilder a serious look. "Kill your girlfriend now. That's my only advice."

He shook his head. "She isn't my girlfriend."

Lee peeled away, nodding like she had a sudden realization. "Gotcha."

Cat gave her a confused expression. "What is it?"

Lee whispered loudly into her ear. "Another man. Really powerful one. Blue eyes over here would probably lose a limb, and Shorty over here is simply trying to keep him from getting killed."

Cat's eyes widened with astonishment before glancing at Sophia.

"Good on you, dear. That must have been very tough to do. To end something to save the other person. Now that's true love."

Sophia wanted to cover her face and run from the bakery. Instead, she managed a meek smile. "What do I owe you for the cookies and the cupcake that didn't work?"

Lee shook her head. "Don't worry about it. I'd feel bad taking your money when you've already lost so much. But do have a great day."

"Thanks. I'll try," Sophia said, turning for the door.

"You probably won't," Cat insisted before Sophia could tune her out. "If I had to work with the guy I couldn't be with, well, that would make for a torturous experience."

"They have to live together too," Lee added.

Cat whistled, shaking her head. "Talk about an awful existence. If you want to end this, contact Assassin Lee. We could work out a two for one thing."

Lee laughed. "Great idea. Sort of a Romeo and Juliet. But why did you have to use my first name?" she asked Cat. "I told you I was going by an alias."

Cat shook her head. "Don't worry. They don't know I'm referring to you." She glanced at the two dragonriders with a serious expression on her red face. "Not this Lee. I was referring to another one. Let me know if you want to put a hit out on yourself."

Sophia nodded, encouraging Wilder to follow her from the bakery. "For sure. Thanks."

CHAPTER TWELVE

"Well, that went...strangely," Sophia commented as they strode back down Roya Lane toward the Fantastical Armory.

"You are telling me," Wilder complained, rubbing his stomach. "I wonder what was in that cupcake."

She offered him one of the cookies in the paper sack. Unsurprisingly, she'd lost her appetite and didn't much feel like eating anything after leaving the bakery. Sophia tried to not let the guilt the bakers had unintentionally placed on her overwhelm her. She knew she had to remain focused, but it was difficult with her partner being the source of her current problems.

"I'm good," Wilder said, holding up his hand to decline the cookies. "I think I'm off sweets for a while."

"Yeah, I don't think we should go back to that bakery," Sophia agreed. "Although stopping an assassin would fall under our jurisdiction."

"I don't know," Wilder related. "Lee is a magician and probably needs to be regulated by the House of Fourteen."

"Oh good," Sophia said with relief. "I'll have Liv take care of her. They'll probably become best friends, and my sister will subcontract her to do side jobs."

Wilder flashed her a grin. "That does seem like the Beaufont way of handling things."

"Look who has decided to open up." Sophia pointed to the Fantastical Armory. The front door was propped open and the sign on the front read, Open.

Wilder placed a hand on Sophia's elbow, pausing her. "You think Subner didn't open on purpose so we'd go to the Crying Cat Bakery?"

She studied him, trying to force herself not to look at where his hand was resting on her arm. "I'm not sure, but we are about to find out."

The pair didn't say a word, simply looked at each other, so much transpiring in the expressions in their eyes. Sophia knew whatever was being communicated between them, had to be silenced. Tortured looks and quiet wanting wasn't going to do them any good, so she pulled her arm from his grasp and strode through the entrance to the shop only to find one thing she was waiting for and one she wasn't expecting.

Subner was looking like his usual self, leaning casually against a case of knives, his long stringy hair partially obscuring one eye. He was dressed in his usual denim cut off shorts and a t-shirt that read, "Leave nothing but footprints. Kill nothing but time."

Behind him, appearing to be involved in a very heated conversation with Papa Creola, was the person Sophia had just been talking about—Liv Beaufont. She had a flustered expression on her face, but it receded at the sight of her sister. Father Time didn't appear stressed as he braided together pieces of twine, making a rope bracelet.

Similar to Subner, his assistant, his elfish form was very hippie, with loose-fitting clothing and his long hair tied back into a low ponytail. Over his tie-dye pants, he was wearing a shirt that read, May I live like the lotus flower, at ease in muddy water.

"Hey, love bug," Liv said, her face brightening. "What are you doing here?"

Sophia lowered her chin and spoke from the corner of her mouth. "Maybe don't call me that at work, sis."

Liv gave her an annoyed expression and pointed to Wilder at her back. "You need to check yourself. I was talking to him, S. Beaufont."

Wilder batted his long eyelashes in Liv's direction. "I hadn't realized we had picked out pet names for each other yet. How about I call you by your given name, Olivia?"

Sophia gave him a quick nod. "I wouldn't do that if you want to live long."

Liv laughed and pushed her long blonde hair out of her face. Similar to the hippies she worked with, her unmanageable locks were always in her face, unlike Sophia, who tried to at least corral hers back in an orderly fashion. The sisters were dressed similarly in dark armor, long black cloaks, and knee-high boots.

Papa Creola snapped at Liv. "Let me see your wrist to see if this fits."

"I'm not wearing your Bohemian hemp bracelet. I thought I made that clear."

"And I thought I made it clear that if you want to withstand the charms of the Tooth Fairy, you are going to need a protective element." Father Time grabbed her wrist and began measuring the length of the bracelet.

"Why couldn't you have fashioned the protective element into a badass weapon?" Liv threw her arm wide at the assortment of knives, swords, and other items on the walls and in the display cases. "It isn't like you have a shortage here."

He shook his head. "You have to leave your weapons here. Tooth fairies will flee at the first sign of violence."

"You are going after a tooth fairy?" Wilder asked, amused. "That does seem dangerous."

Liv sighed and gave the bracelet Papa Creola had fashioned onto her a wrist a repugnant glance. "Apparently, something has happened to the tooth fairies and they aren't collecting teeth, which is stalling the development of children and causing them not to grow older. So someone, me, has to find out what is happening and get them to do their job again."

Wilder laughed. "I have so many questions after hearing those few short statements."

"Tooth fairies collecting teeth cause children to age?" Sophia asked.

"Naturally," Papa Creola answered like this was common knowledge. "It's actually tooth fairies requesting the discharge of teeth from children that triggers them to grow up. They simply collect them to complete the process. It's an archaic part of the progression they didn't want to relinquish, afraid of losing job security when I flattened the org charts centuries ago."

Liv gave Sophia a wicked grin. "Yes, our fearless leader, Father Time, has the worst processes to control the aging of mortals, passing of time and essentially keeping this planet in balance. One tooth fairy falls out of line, and everything goes to hell."

"Seems about right," Sophia said.

"Isn't there a regulatory board for tooth fairies that can intervene?" Wilder asked. He and Sophia had laughed when they strode down Roya Lane, reading the signs for all the strange magical regulatory headquarters like the Pegasus Corrections Facility and the Unclassified Magical Creatures Office.

Father Time nodded. "I normally would, but the same agency which controls the tooth fairies is in charge of the fairy godmothers, and they are overwhelmed with quite a few issues there. Since Mama Jamba is in charge of that one, she trumps me."

Liv shook her head at Sophia. "Isn't it cute? He is being serious. This isn't a strange dream, and our day jobs aren't jokes."

"Yeah, which reminds me," Sophia said to her sister. "There's a woman who works at Crying Cat Bakery here on Roya Lane I think you need to look into. She is an assassin of sorts."

Liv nodded. "Oh, Lee. Yeah, I have been over there for a few domestic disputes. They make a great cup of coffee. Just don't eat the cupcakes."

"Too late for that advice," Subner remarked, finally joining the conversation. He held out a hand to Sophia. "I'll take the peanut butter cookie."

Sophia narrowed her eyes at the all-knowing hippie. "How do you know I got peanut butter?"

"Because I wanted it," he answered. "You can have the chocolate chip. Throw the oatmeal raisin in the trash since Wilder won't be eating anything for a while."

"Also because it has raisins in it," Papa Creola added. "I thought Mama Jamba was trying to get rid of those."

"She's having issues with health nuts who insist on keeping the dried fruits around even though they ruin everything they are in," Sophia said, having had an entirely too long conversation with Mother Nature on this particular subject.

"You intended for us to go to the Crying Cat Bakery, didn't you?" Wilder asked, conviction in his tone. "That's why you told us to get here early and then had the shop closed."

"I can't leave here to get cookies." Subner took the cookie Sophia offered him.

"No, why do that when he has minions like us to do his errands," she complained.

Liv nodded, pointing at Father Time. "This one makes me pick up his dry cleaning."

"You dry clean your T-shirts?" Sophia asked the elf.

"Only my bamboo pants and linen jackets," he explained and then shivered. "Being a hippie still doesn't feel right."

Subner agreed with a nod, pointing at his own shirt. "I think it should be illegal for me to wear this, and yet, it's what I woke up in this morning."

"Yeah, the protector of weapons, being against killing seems ironic," Sophia said.

"And the assistant to Papa Creola, killing time, makes it even better," Liv added.

"Well, now that we have fetched your breakfast, as you intended," Wilder began, "do you want to tell us about this mission?"

Subner lifted a bushy eyebrow at him. "That wasn't the only reason the shop was closed and I wanted you to go to the Crying Cat Bakery."

Sophia couldn't help but roll her eyes. "Told you, Wild. It was all orchestrated for some devilish agenda."

"But what, I wonder," he questioned, eyeing the protector of weapons. "It seemed like a waste."

Subner pressed his hands together as if in prayer. "The time you wasted is not wasted time." He shook his head. "Sorry, what I meant to say was, make a wish, take a chance, and make a change."

Sophia and Wilder exchanged confused expressions. "Say what?"

Subner sighed. "See, that's why I need your help. I can't stop talking in hippie phrases. Maybe it's because I want to be wild, beautiful, and free, just like the sea." He shook his head. "That isn't what I meant to say." He bit down on his knuckle, seeming to try and restrain himself.

"What is going on?" Sophia asked.

"It's Cupid," Subner said through gritted teeth. "There's a problem with his bow and arrow, which is causing resonating effects worldwide."

"Resonating effects?" Sophia questioned.

"Yes, the calibration is off," Subner explained.

"And people like us," Father Time indicated Subner and him, "are particularly attuned to it."

"You mean hippies?" Liv questioned.

He nodded. "Yes, but that isn't the biggest concern. Cupid's arrows are having unintended consequences, causing mortals to become lustful. Those who shouldn't fall in love are. And vice versa."

"Oh," Sophia said, drawing out the word.

"You aren't affected by this," Subner explained, reading her thoughts. "Magicians are notorious for their cold hearts. The resonating effects of Cupid's bow don't affect your type unless you are struck directly. Which is why I want you to go together. If Wilder went alone, I don't think he'd have much luck getting the bow from Cupid. He won't want to part with it easily, afraid I'm decommissioning him, as I tried to all those years ago."

"You want me to go and help distract him, is that right?" Sophia asked.

Subner nodded, taking a bite of the cookie. "Yes, and then Wilder can get the bow and arrow, recalibrate it and give it back to the little runt."

"You are starting to sound like your old self again," Sophia observed.

The elf nodded. "The cookie helps. It's why fairy godmothers live on a diet entirely made up of sweets. It balances them out so they can be objective when it comes to love."

"Great," Wilder said, not sounding amused. "Where do we find this Cupid?"

Subner shrugged, taking another bite. "I haven't got a clue."

"That seems about right," Sophia muttered.

"But your partner here has an inside resource who will know where to find him since they are in the same business of matchmaking," Subner explained, finishing the cookie.

"Do you mean…" Sophia trailed away, knowing Subner was referring to Mae Ling at Happily Ever After College, the place where fairy godmothers were trained.

He nodded. "Your resource is in class for another hour, so you'll have to find a way to kill time until then."

Papa Creola put his hands to his ears. "Please, Sub, can you rephrase that?"

"Yeah, sorry, Papa," he amended, glancing back at Wilder and Sophia. "May every sunrise hold more promise and every sunset hold more peace." He shook his head.

"You are getting worse again," Liv observed.

"Yes, the cookie didn't help as much as I would have liked," Subner stated, rubbing his belly as if it was suddenly bothering him.

"Actually, Liv," Sophia started, looking at her sister. "Maybe you can help me track down a lead? I need to find some information on Trin Currante, the pirate who stole our dragon eggs."

Liv nodded. "I might have someone who can help." She gave Papa Creola a tentative expression.

The hippie gave her a reassuring look. "It's fine. You can't track down any tooth fairies until nightfall. That's the only time they are visible. During the day, I can't even find them."

"Sunshine is my favorite accessory," Subner said, all dreamy-eyed.

"Okay, we have got to fix this one," Sophia told Wilder, pointing in Subner's direction.

"Whatever makes your soul happy, do that," Subner related.

Wilder agreed with a nod. "First, let's go check up on this lead for Trin. Then we'll find out where Cupid is hiding."

Liv strode over and put her arm around her sister's shoulder. "Who would have thought you'd make me feel like I had a normal job?"

Sophia smiled back. "If I make you feel normal, you have a lot of problems."

"Let your smile change the world," Subner called to the three of them as they left the shop. "Not the world change your smile."

CHAPTER THIRTEEN

"So, where are we headed?" Wilder asked when the three of them were outside the Fantastical Armory.

Liv spun around, halting him. "We aren't going anywhere. Sorry, but my inside source can't be risked."

"But I'm a Dragon Elite," Wilder argued. "You can trust me."

The warrior for the House of Fourteen huffed. "Sorry, Blue Eyes. I don't trust anyone except my sister and brother. Oh, and Rory Laurens. On occasion, King Rudolf. Oh, and my boyfriend, Stefan Ludwig. Most of the other Warriors for the House, and some of the Councilors. Other than that, I don't trust anyone."

Wilder offered her a friendly smile. "Well, maybe one day I'll earn your trust."

Liv pursed her lips and gave Sophia and then Wilder scrutinizing expressions. "Maybe. Answer me this question. You can only have three toppings on your nachos. What are they?"

Wilder grimaced. "I actually don't like cheese."

Liv threw up her hands, striding off. "You are dead to me, Blue Eyes. Simply dead to me."

Sophia spun to face him, walking backward after her sister. "Wrong answer. She probably won't ever talk to you again."

"Is it really that serious?" he asked. "It's only nachos."

"For the love of all that's magical!" Liv roared. "Where did you find this one? Next he's going to say he's vegan."

"Nah," Wilder retorted. "If I was vegan, you'd have already heard about it."

"Ha!" Liv fired back. "My heart really goes out for those who are vegan and do CrossFit. I bet they struggle with what to tell people first."

Wilder followed after the two sisters, a hopeful smile on his face. "What do you say? Can I come on this fact-finding mission? Soph will attest I can be trusted."

Liv didn't even give Sophia a chance to say anything. "It isn't her call. I don't trust anyone with this source."

Wilder's hopeful expression dropped. "Okay, well, then I'll meet up with you, Soph, when you are done."

She halted, making the other two pause. "Sorry, but you can't go with me when I meet with my source either."

"But it's to find information on Cupid, which is our case," Wilder argued.

Sophia shrugged. "Sorry, but my source has strictly forbidden me from bringing others with me." Sophia wasn't sure if men could even enter Happily Ever After College where Mae Ling was. She was fairly certain the school for fairy godmothers was full of only women.

"Then I'll be at the Castle," Wilder said, disappointment on his face.

Sophia nodded, wishing she could say something to make him feel better. It appeared all she could do was let him down with everything she did.

CHAPTER FOURTEEN

"Are we talking about how you are ruining his life?" Liv asked Sophia as they started down Roya Lane.

Sophia was used to getting looks when she went down the magical street in London, but not like this. As she walked beside her sister, Warrior for the House, Sophia noticed the people gave them a wide berth. Gnomes headed their direction suddenly turned and ran off in the opposite direction as fast as their short legs would take them at the sight of Liv Beaufont.

"I think I'd rather talk about how you have ruined all these magical creature's lives," Sophia joked, deflecting.

Liv reached out and grabbed what Sophia thought was a mop. Not until the warrior shook it did Sophia realize it was an old magician with long hair that looked like a mop head. He was so boney she'd have mistaken his arm for the handle. He apparently had been glamoured to look just like the cleaning instrument. As Liv shook him continuously, his actual appearance came into view, although it really wasn't much different than that of a beat-up old mop.

"Hey, Gary," Liv said, looking the magician straight in his beady eyes. "What are you doing here?"

"H-Hey, Warrior Beaufont," the man stuttered. "Just volunteering my time to help disadvantaged pixies."

"You mean, take advantage of naïve fairies," Liv corrected, holding the man's arm tight, her expression fierce.

"You say potatoes and I say—"

"All lies," Liv interrupted. She reached into the man's coat pocket and felt around.

"Hey, there, Missy," Gary complained with a sneer. "Although I'm flattered, I'm not attracted to you like that and would kindly ask you to stop with your advances."

"I just can't help myself," Liv said, continuing to feel around in the man's pocket, although it appeared much deeper than a usual garment.

"It appears I might have to make a harassment complaint to the House of Fourteen regarding you," Gary threatened and then added, "Yet again."

"Oh, no. Please don't," Liv protested, feigning fear, then grabbing his arm and twisting it behind his back, making his face pinch with pain. "Please don't tell them I used unnecessary force on you." She threw him back into the brick wall, making his head hit hard. "And please don't tell them I assaulted you. I'll do whatever it takes."

Gary laughed through the pain. "This time you are leaving bruises. How can I not tell your bosses you aren't following protocol?"

Liv pinned Gary to the wall with her elbow as she continued to feel around in his pockets. "First of all, I don't have a boss. Second of all, if I find any more pixies on you." Liv pulled a restrained and gagged fairy from the man's pocket and held it up in front of his face. "Then you are going to be turning yourself in and hoping the House of Fourteen locks you up before I can get my hands on you. I swear their punishment will be far more kind than mine."

"Oh, how did she get in my pocket?" Gary asked with a nervous giggle.

Liv handed the pixie back to Sophia, who went straight to work untying its bindings. The warrior continued to check Gary over.

When she'd determined he didn't have any more pixies on him, she shoved him harder into the wall.

"Let's get one thing straight," Liv said, her mouth inches from his dirty face. "I have my eye on you. If I so much as imagine you are trafficking pixies again, I'm going to take you down to Merlin's on all you can eat Tuesdays."

"You wouldn't," he gasped, his voice suddenly a hoarse whisper.

"Try me, Gary," Liv threatened, shoving him into the wall again as she stood back.

He shook out his arms, visibly shaking now. "Fine, Liv. I'll be good. You'll not catch me with any more pixies."

"Just remember that if you slip up, I'll catch you," Liv warned as the wooden looking man hurried off through the crowd, nearly tripping on his feet to get away from her.

"You think it was safe to let that jerk go?" Sophia asked, looking the blue-haired pixie over before determining she was uninjured. She bowed as she rose into the air, her wings working double-time to make her fly.

Sophia smiled and waved her off before turning her attention to her sister.

"Gary won't slip up again," Liv stated with confidence. "But if he does, I'll know about it since I just implanted a tracking device on him. If he goes near a pixie, I'm going to get a notification of his whereabouts."

"And this Merlin place?" Sophia asked. "He appeared legitimately scared about an all you can eat buffet."

Liv laughed. "As he should. Merlin is a man-eating serpent, and on Tuesdays, he fills up on the low-lifes I decide aren't worthy of clogging up our dungeons in the House of Fourteen."

"Wow, I never took you to be one for corporal punishment," Sophia said, surprised by her sister.

Liv winked and leaned forward. "I'm not. But what I'm good at is spreading rumors about man-eating serpents that don't really exist."

"Oh…" Sophia was thoroughly impressed.

Liv wrapped her arm around her sister's shoulders, steering her in the opposite direction. "The key to justice is giving people the right motivators not to break the law. Oh, and technology. It's our friend and keeps tabs on the offenders."

The area of the street where they were walking was mostly empty now. Many had taken the altercation with Gary as their chance to get away before Liv could rough them up. She gave a few gnomes dirty looks before turning her attention back to Sophia. "What were we talking about? Oh, you broke that boy's heart. Want to tell me about it?"

"He's not a boy," Sophia corrected. "Wilder is two-hundred years old."

Liv whistled. "Oh, breed with that one. He's got great genes."

"Hold up, there," Sophia said, pulling away from her sister. "As you so appropriately noticed, I have broken his heart, and there's nothing going on between us anymore."

"Right," Liv agreed, pausing in the Lane. "But you were able to break his heart because he cares, which is telling in itself."

"There's nothing to tell," Sophia insisted. "We can't be together. Hiker would kill us."

"I'm certain he wouldn't," Liv argued.

"No, he had," Sophia explained. "He has an awful temper and would rather kill off half his riders than have two of them going against his rule."

"Remember, when I started dating Stefan, warriors and councilors for the House of Fourteen were forbidden from being together," Liv explained.

Sophia nodded. She remembered this recent history. "Yeah, but you changed the law because you are Liv."

Her sister smiled. "I changed the law because it was dumb, and I do what I want when I think it's good and true and within reason."

"Yeah, well, I can't change Hiker's mind on this, and also, there are a lot of other reasons Wilder and I don't make sense together," Sophia told her sister. "Remember when I said he was over two hundred years old?"

Liv nodded. "Yeah, it's sounding a bit like a Bella and Edward scenario."

Sophia shuddered. "Did you just make a *Twilight* reference?"

"Hey, don't knock it until you've tried it," Liv argued. "It's no Great Gatsby, but to each their own. I get what you are trying to say, but you aren't any normal girl, Soph. You are wise beyond your years. I dare say someone a hundred years older than you'd probably be too immature."

She laughed, thinking of Evan. "That's accurate."

"Just don't close your mind off to possibilities," her sister encouraged. "You never know how this part of your story will go. Maybe an angry Viking will dictate your personal future, but I sort of hope I raised you better than that. Maybe you'll run from love because it doesn't make practical sense in your already complicated world. I, for one, have been there, done that, and would fault you none. Just don't tell yourself the story has already been written before the ink has dried because in this day and age, there are so many ways to erase and tell things differently. Just be open to a different ending, is all I'm saying."

Sophia managed a tender smile, grateful she had a sister who was so thoughtful and could also kick serious butt. "Thanks, Liv. Now, where is this secret contact you think can help me find information on Trin Currante?"

Liv pointed at a solid brick wall and smiled victoriously. "Right here."

CHAPTER FIFTEEN

The solid brick wall didn't appear to have any doors Sophia could discern, but she'd spent enough of her life in the strange magical world to know appearances were often deceiving.

"Glamoured?" she asked her sister.

Liv nodded proudly, stepping forward and rapping on the brick wall. "Warrior Beaufont from the House of Fourteen with special guest Sophia Beaufont, rider for the Dragon Elite."

A moment later, a small door materialized in the seemingly solid wall. Liv held out her hand in a welcoming fashion.

"We are supposed to go through there?" Sophia questioned, wondering how she'd fit through the narrow opening.

"Well, if you want a shove, I'll give you one," Liv offered.

"I think I'm good." Sophia knelt and opened the small door to try and determine if her hips would fit through.

"If I can fit, then you can," Liv told her, reading her thoughts.

Sophia nodded. "And where are we going?"

"You'll find out," Liv said, a hint of mischief in her voice.

"Fine," Sophia stated, trusting her sister but pretending to be skeptical.

Getting onto her hands and knees, Sophia poked her head through the small door to find a waiting room with a receptionist desk waiting on the other side. A long hallway ran the length of the space and at the back was a single door. All the furniture was small, as though designed for magical creatures bigger than fairies but smaller than gnomes.

Sophia glanced back at Liv, blinking in confusion. "Is this a shrink's office?"

Liv shook her head and gave her sister a mischievous expression. "No, do you really think I'd take you to a therapist for help?"

"Do I have to answer that?" Sophia joked, thinking she could probably use a session or two on a psychologist's couch.

Turning her attention back to the empty office, Sophia crawled through, rising to stand when she was all the way into the space. Her head brushed the ceiling, but what caught her attention was the little creature that jumped out of the corner and attached itself to her leg.

Sophia nearly screamed until she realized the creature was an adorable brownie with wide eyes, large ears, and a brown body.

"Biv Leaufont!" the little guy squeaked.

"Ticker," Liv grunted, coming through the narrow door. "That isn't me."

The Brownie glanced over his shoulder as Liv stood and then back up at Sophia.

Ticker was fairly cute, with a round face and elfin ears. On his head, he wore a hat with a long pointy end, like Santa Claus.

"Lwo Tivs?" Ticker asked, continuing to look between the two magicians.

Liv bent over and pulled the Brownie from Sophia's leg. "No, not two Livs. Thankfully for the rest of the world, there's only one of me." She held her hand out to her sister. "This is Sophia Beaufont, my younger sister."

"Nice to meet you, Ticker," Sophia said, bowing slightly to the little guy.

"Tou yoo," Ticker answered, smiling wide.

"That means—"

"You too." Sophia interrupted Liv, having figured out the brownie switched the first letters of two-word phrases. If at all possible, it made him even cuter.

"Oh, there are you, Ticker," a not much larger, female brownie said, striding in from the other side of the hallway, having come through the door at the back. She was carrying a small, wiggling bundle wrapped in blankets.

"Hiv lere!" Ticker exclaimed, pointing at Liv.

"I see that." The woman smiled politely at Liv before turning her attention to Sophia. "And you must be Liv's sister. The resemblance is uncanny."

Sophia nodded, curtseying slightly. "Yes, I'm Sophia."

"Hi Pricilla," Liv stated. "Is Mortimer busy? Could we pop back to see him?"

"For you, he is never busy," the Brownie declared, holding out her arm to her son, who jumped from Liv's grasp to his mother.

"Oh, thanks," Liv said, grabbing Sophia's arm and dragging her down the hallway.

"This is your secret contact?" Sophia asked, realizing they must be in Official Brownie Headquarters. "This is genius. You get all your inside tips from the Brownies."

"Well, they do have eyes everywhere, and they are incredibly nice to work with," Liv exclaimed proudly.

"However did you strike up such a partnership?" Sophia asked.

Her sister rolled her eyes at her. "Oh, don't pretend you don't have your own insider sources. You know what I'd do to get a fairy godmother?"

Sophia blushed. "Well, I could see if they've got an opening."

Liv shook her head. "No, I think to become a Cinderella, you have to be chosen. You can't request it."

"A Cinderella…" Sophia said, playing with the term. "That's what I'm considered?"

Liv smiled at her. "You really should read more of Bermuda Lauren's book, *Magical Creatures*. Then you'd know this."

"Sure thing," Sophia agreed. "Right after I finish the *Complete*

History of Dragonriders, which will only take me another century or two."

Liv pushed through the door at the back, knocking as she entered.

"Warrior Liv Beaufont for the House of Fourteen," a man's voice chimed when they entered.

The office, unlike the waiting area and reception desk, was completely unorganized with stacks of papers everywhere. There was a false window at the back behind Mortimer's desk, and in the Brownie's hand, he had a foam stress ball.

"How is my favorite brownie?" Liv asked him, continuing to duck to avoid hitting her head on the low ceiling.

Mortimer, who was dressed in a smart three-piece suit, beamed from across the desk. "Business is good. I can't complain. Although, Pricilla and I are behind on filing, as you can see."

"A new baby will do that to you," Liv said good-naturedly, looking around at the many stacks of paper precariously stationed around the office. "I thought you were going paperless."

He sighed, his large lips making a drumming sound. "We tried. I'm just not as technical as you and fear I don't have it in me."

Liv offered him a kind smile. "I might be able to offer you some magitech to speed up the process and take the burden off you and Pricilla."

Mortimer squeezed the stress ball and smiled. "You really are too good to me, Warrior Liv Beaufont. Now, will you please introduce me to the stunning dragonrider by your side?"

Liv beamed in her sister's direction. "Well, of course. This is Sophia Beaufont."

Mortimer stood, but his height didn't change. He bowed dramatically, his nose nearly hitting his desk. "Oh, yes. Sophia Beaufont wears size seven shoes and wipes the soap film off the bathroom mirror while brushing her teeth in the morning. Doesn't separate her whites from her colors when doing laundry, but always washes her hands thoroughly."

Sophia gave Liv a curious expression. "That's quite a lot of information you know about me, Mortimer. I'm sorry all I know about you is that you have a beautiful family."

He giggled. "Thanks to your sister, who encouraged me to lose weight, take better care of myself, and start dating."

Liv shook her head, giving Sophia a sideways look. "None of that happened. He did it all on his own."

Mortimer dismissed her with a wave. "Anyway, it's a brownie's job to know the habits and traits of the good around the world. Although we don't directly serve magicians, because you are a Beaufont, I have had my brownies look after you from time to time."

Liv's eyes widened. "Um...Mort..."

Sophia pieced it all together and gave her sister a mock look of offense. "Have you had them spy on me?"

"In the past," Liv admitted. "But not since you've been at the Gullington. Brownies can't get in there."

Sophia laughed. "And yet, Plato can."

"He does what he wants," Liv admitted. "But yes, when you were living at the House of Fourteen or staying with me and I was gone on extended missions, I had Mortimer's brownies pop in to ensure you were doing well. It gave me peace of mind, but your privacy was always respected."

Sophia couldn't help but smile. Only Liv would enlist brownies, who went unseen by most and took care of mortal's homes while they slept, to watch after her. She was full of creative solutions.

"So, what brings you here away from your dragon?" Mortimer asked Sophia, coming around the desk to stand opposite her.

"Well, I was hoping you could help me track down a person who stole over a dozen dragon eggs from us," she explained, then proceeded to tell him about Trin Currante and the band of pirates she'd enlisted to storm the Gullington.

He listened thoughtfully, stroking his pointy chin and "oohing" and "aahing" as she spoke. When Sophia was done, he nodded before striding around his desk and taking a seat once more.

"Can you help?" Liv asked, her tone anxious.

"One-hundred percent I can," he said victoriously.

Sophia found herself clapping with excitement. "Thank you! This is great news."

He held up a single finger to pause her. "The timeline is the worrisome part. I can't guarantee it will be a short process to find this mysterious person. For one, my Brownies look after mortals, so having them track down magicians isn't always straightforward."

"But this magician is unique," Liv countered.

"True," Mortimer agreed. "I'm certain a person like this, with associations like you've described, has left behind a trail we can pick up. I simply want to set expectations. I could find her whereabouts fairly fast, within a week or two, or much slower, within a decade or two."

Sophia couldn't help but sigh with defeat. "That's quite the gap."

He shrugged, regret on his face. "Rest assured, I'll put my best on the case. A friend of Warrior Liv Beaufont for the House of Fourteen is a friend of mine."

Sophia bowed to the small fairy and smiled at her sister. She really had the best family and the best friends. Hopefully, that meant the best chance of winning against Trin Currante.

CHAPTER SIXTEEN

After demolishing the chocolate chip cookie Sophia got at the Crying Cat Bakery, she wasn't in the mood to eat a macaroon, but that was the only way she was aware of to get to Happily Ever After, the college for fairy godmothers.

She pulled one of the blue cookies from the bag after finding a less crowded place on Roya Lane. Liv had left her, grumbling something about having to go deal with diva tooth fairies. It was ironic that one Beaufont sister was off to meet with a fairy godmother and the other was taking care of tooth fairy business. They were two industries with a huge rivalry.

Sophia took a bite of the crispy macaroon and waited for the portal to form in front of her. When she stepped through to the campus for Happily Ever After College, she was grateful for the peace and quiet of the grounds. They were a welcomed sight after the craziness of Roya Lane. Sophia was always better when surrounded by trees and green grass, which was another reason she did so well at the Gullington and considered it her home. There were other reasons unconnected to her dragon she wasn't going to think about right then.

She set off for the pink doors at the front of the brick building and noticed a strange woman approaching at the same time as her. What made her strange was she wasn't dressed in the usual fairy godmother uniform of a rainbow pleated skirt and pink blouse. Nor was she dressed in clothes like the professors. Like Sophia, the woman was wearing a long traveling cloak and had a worried expression on her face.

"Are you a Cinderella?" Sophia asked the woman, who appeared confused.

She glanced up, slightly spooked as if she hadn't seen Sophia right beside her. The woman looked at a piece of paper in her hand and shook her head. "No, I'm not a godchild. I'm a professor. At least that's what the note I received said, but I'm not sure I'm in the right place."

"Oh, maybe I can help," Sophia offered. "Who are you looking for?"

"Professor Mae Ling," the woman explained. "She is apparently my new supervisor."

Sophia's face brightened. "That's who I'm going to see. I'll show you to her office."

"Thanks. I'm Amy," the woman said, offering her hand to shake.

"Nice to meet you, Amy. What will you be teaching here? Creative writing? Pottery? Music?" Sophia opened the door to the school. The long rainbow floor of the hallway was empty, all of the students in class.

"No, nothing like that, actually," Amy answered. "It's actually strange. I'm not a fairy godmother."

"You are not?" Sophia asked, confused.

"No, I didn't even know about them until I got this note." She held up the piece of paper she was holding onto fiercely, a buzzing excitement in her eyes.

"So, what are you going to be teaching?" Sophia questioned.

"That's just the thing," Amy began, waving the note in the air. "The course is brand new, and I have no idea why they are suddenly going to be offering it. Or why they picked me to do it."

Sophia laughed, leading the way to Mae Ling's office. "Well, if you wanted to get my attention, then you have it."

Amy gave her a nervous expression. "Yeah, this whole request to teach at Happily Ever After College has gotten my attention as it seems to have taken over my life."

"Are you going to tell me what art you'll be teaching?" Sophia questioned.

Amy shook her head. "That's just the thing. I'm not into the creative arts. I'm a quantum equations professor. I teach math."

CHAPTER SEVENTEEN

Math?

The last time Sophia was at Happily Ever After College, she learned math was used as a punishment for struggling students. It drained their creativity and made it harder for them to excel in their studies. So why in the magical world was the college about to start offering classes on the subject?

Sophia had so many questions, but before she could bombard Amy with them, Headmistress Willow came out of a classroom and caught sight of them.

"Oh, good you made it," Willow said, her long brown hair cascading down her back and her reserved smile, making her appear elegantly beautiful.

Amy looked at Sophia as though Willow was talking to her.

"Willow," Sophia began. "Amy says she's been brought here to teach—"

The Head Mistress held up her hand, pausing the question. "Yes, there are a lot of changes going on here. The world is changing. The ways we used to fix problems aren't working. That means we must adapt. Mae Ling will explain this all to you, I'm sure. I appreciate you leading Amy to me. I'll take things from here."

Sophia hadn't intended to lead Amy to Willow, but she probably had unintentionally. Such was the way of the fairy godmothers. She was dismissed with a wave as Willow led the new professor back through the door she'd just exited.

Sophia stood in the empty hallway, questions streaming through her head rapidly. The world was changing. The solutions of yesterday were no longer good enough to fix tomorrow's problems. That was what she'd been trying to tell Hiker since she arrived at the Gullington. And if the fairy godmothers were shifting their practices, it meant everyone would have to adapt—the Dragon Elite included.

"Very good," Mae Ling exclaimed to Sophia when she entered her office. "You haven't been filling up on vegetables and instead have opted for sweets. Your color is much better than the last time I saw you."

"Um...thanks," Sophia said, always so confused by the strange world at Happily Ever After College where up seemed like down and right seemed wrong. "Didn't you tell me last time math was a punishment here?"

Mae Ling pushed her short black hair off her forehead. "That's right, but timeouts are also punishments for small children, and I know more than a few adults who would beg for such a reprimand."

Sophia laughed, taking a seat across from her fairy godmother. The office was just as colorful as the first time she was there. The large pink chair had a long back and a sort of a roof and made her feel comforted at once.

"You aren't using it as punishment anymore?" she questioned, still unclear on why things were changing at the college.

"It's true certain types of math will drain mental faculties," Mae Ling explained. "But that's true of any taxing difficulty. Willow has expanded her thinking to consider creative math could be potentially beneficial for our students. You see, we are facing some real challenges at the college right now. The current student body...well, they aren't cutting it. Not in the real world or their magical endeavors."

"I thought you said magic could be used to replace math for when the students went out into the real world to open businesses?" Sophia questioned.

"That's true," Mae Ling confirmed. "However, the lopsided nature of our curriculum might be contributing to other problems. We have always done things the same way here at Happily Ever After. And that has worked, but it doesn't anymore. So we are going to try something new. Now, if I start eating salad for lunch, well then, we might have a problem, but for now, I think these changes will be worth trying out."

"What do you usually eat for lunch?" Sophia asked, curious.

"Chocolate chip cookie dough," Mae Ling answered, smiling wide, her white teeth sparkling.

Sophia's stomach still felt uneasy from the cookie she had for breakfast. She couldn't imagine eating something so rich as cookie dough every day.

"You need answers, don't you," Mae Ling asked. "Go on. You know how it works. Ask your questions."

The fairy godmother placed her hands calmly on the desk in front of her, a placid expression on her face.

Sophia knew why she was there. It was to find information on Cupid's whereabouts. She could also ask about Trin Currante, so she was surprised at the question that actually tumbled out of her mouth.

"You're a love expert, right?"

Mae Ling smiled. "Yes. That's the chief job of any fairy godmother. You and I have more of a unique setup since you were assigned to me directly by Mother Nature. You have a bit more responsibility than most, and Mama Jamba felt you could benefit from having a fairy godmother's assistance in your life."

"Oh, so like with Cinderella, your job is to what? Make matches?" Sophia asked.

"That's right," Mae Ling confirmed. "Love is what makes the world go round."

"Yeah, that makes sense." Sophia chewed on her lip, considering her next question. She sometimes felt like Mae Ling was a genie, and instead of wishes, she got questions. Their sessions were always short, and her fairy godmother kicked her out when she was done. It was usually before Sophia had asked everything she wanted.

"Well, since you are a love expert, I'm hoping you can help me find the whereabouts of the notorious Cupid," Sophia asked.

Mae Ling studied Sophia for a long moment, a discerning expression in her wise gaze. "That's your question?"

Sophia tilted her head to the side, wondering if she hadn't asked it right. "Well, yeah, although I also would welcome information on Trin Currante."

Mae Ling shook her head. "I can't help you track down the cyborg, but I suspect the Brownies will be able to, eventually."

Of course, her fairy godmother knew she was relying on the Brownies for information. She seemed to know everything, which was why the look she was giving Sophia made her uncomfortable.

"Isn't it funny that as soon as we get what we want, we don't want it anymore?" Mae Ling asked, a musing quality to her voice.

"I'm not sure how that helps me to find Cupid," Sophia stammered, trying to wrap her brain around what the older woman was saying.

"It isn't meant to," Mae Ling imparted. "He is in the hottest desert in the world."

"The Sahara?" Sophia questioned. "Where? That's also one of the largest deserts."

She knew even knowing the location wouldn't help her to find Cupid unless she narrowed it down.

"Go there with someone you care for and you'll find Cupid," Mae Ling told her. "Or rather, I should say he'll find you."

"What did you mean about getting what we want and then not wanting it?" Sophia dared to ask, not sure if she wanted her fairy godmother to answer.

"I think that was pretty straightforward."

Sophia argued by shaking her head. "But I never wanted anything more than to be one of the Dragon Elite. I didn't ask for anything else."

"No, and when the time came, you ran, dropping the glass slipper, didn't you?" Mae Ling challenged.

Sophia continued to chew on her lip. "It's not about want and desire. It's about doing the right thing. People in our positions don't get options for love."

Mae Ling sat back in her oversized chair, appearing impressed. "Well put, S. Beaufont. There are certain people who fall into those categories of having to be exempt from love. Unfortunately for you and your need for excuses, you aren't one of them. Whether you are prepared for it or not, your story will be one for the pages of the greatest fairytales. I daresay, all my contemporaries are keeping a close eye on how this one will unfold."

"Why?" Sophia asked, feeling the pressure.

"Because it will change everything," Mae Ling answered simply.

"How?" Sophia continued with the one-word questions.

"I can't really say, but you already knew that didn't you," she teased coyly.

Sophia did. She should have expected that answer.

"I can offer you something, but you'll only think it's more riddles, and maybe it is. On the way to finding love, we often find ourselves," Mae Ling began. "Isn't it ironic we become that which we love when we start searching for the person we hope will complete us?"

Sophia sighed. This was a riddle, and it only made her more confused. She worked to keep the look of frustration off her face as she thanked her fairy godmother for the help.

"You have one more question," Mae Ling said, catching her before she left the office.

Sophia halted, thinking. She wanted to ask about Cupid, Trin Currante and...she couldn't remember another question plaguing her, but there were so many mysteries that she could be forgetting something. Then it occurred to her, making her mouth pop open.

"Ainsley?" she asked.

Mae Ling nodded proudly. "There it is."

"You know how I can save her and recover her memories?" Sophia asked, hope filling her chest.

"I don't actually," Mae Ling stated at once. "But the next time I see you, I will."

"And that will be?" Sophia asked, hoping for a specific.

"At our next meeting, when you need me once more."

Feeling slightly defeated, Sophia nodded, realizing she should have expected this visit to bring up more questions than answers. Such was the way of the most helpful people in her life.

CHAPTER EIGHTEEN

All the way back to the Castle, Sophia turned Mae Ling's words over in her brain.

"On the way to finding love, we often find ourselves," Mae Ling had said. "Isn't it ironic we become that which we love when we start searching for the person we hope will complete us?"

Sophia couldn't make sense of it. Maybe at her early morning wake up it would be clearer. She'd been trying to find herself in one way or another since becoming a dragonrider and coming to the Gullington.

Right then, more important than her and Wilder were the missions that demanded their attention. Sophia had to find Cupid or the repercussions would be far worse than Subner spouting hippie phrases. And she had to figure out where the dragon eggs were that had been stolen. Almost as important was her need to rescue Ainsley. Of course, there was the need to strengthen the reputation of the Dragon Elite. That was how Sophia needed to find herself, but she had no idea what it had to do with Mae Ling's advice.

The Castle was bustling with noise when Sophia entered, the smell of garlic and other savory herbs strong in the air. "Wow, something smells good," Sophia declared, talking to herself and strangely grateful

Ainsley had made real food. She couldn't have another meal of sugar and baked goods that day.

"I have gone all out," Ainsley said proudly, buzzing by Sophia carrying a large vase of flowers as she made for the dining room.

"What is the occasion?" Sophia asked, following behind her.

"Well, since Quiet is mad at me and refuses to help me with meals, I have decided to show him I don't need his help," Ainsley explained, putting the arrangement on the table and eyeing it before moving it a few inches. "You know that squatty fellow has been helping me as the Castle for the last five hundred years, sometimes making my life more difficult, but also helping me with meals and whatnot. Now that we have had this falling out, I'm doing everything myself. I'd say I'm winning at it."

The housekeeper pushed her shoulders back and held her chin high. "He probably thought I'd fail without his help. Probably hoped I would, but I won't. I'm going to show him."

Sophia was proud of Ainsley. This just proved to her she was a fighter, and worth saving. Ainsley and Quiet would make up. It just was a matter of time. Ainsley had been hurt about being kept in the dark, but this was a good thing for now. It was empowering the shapeshifter, and maybe that was what she needed.

"What did you make that smells so good?" Sophia asked.

"Beef roast with neeps and tatties, fresh rolls, and a flourless chocolate cake for dessert," Ainsley stated.

"Oh, why flourless?" Sophia asked.

"Because I'm working on ways to be a pain in Hiker's ass, so I have decided everyone is going gluten-free," she told her proudly.

Sophia laughed. "That will definitely infuriate him."

Ainsley joined in, slapping Sophia's arm as she giggled. "I have got recipes for scones made out of things he will loathe. He's going to complain bitterly about all the bread made out of tapioca and milled nuts."

"I can't wait to see this," Sophia said. She was about to say something else when a familiar voice chimed in her head.

Soph, Lunis called, an urgency to his voice.

"What is it, S. Beaufont?" Ainsley asked, the light expression dropping from her face. She must have seen the change in Sophia's face.

She held up a finger, pausing the housekeeper so she could hear Lunis. *What is it?*

It's the dragon eggs, he answered. *The first of them are starting to hatch.*

CHAPTER NINETEEN

Sophia ran all the way to the Nest, Ainsley on her heels. She'd have gone up and gotten Hiker, but Ainsley had said he was out. Lunis followed up with something about how fewer people were for the best.

Once they were at the Nest, Lunis met the pair and told them Ainsley shouldn't enter the cave area.

I'm sorry, he said remorse in his voice. *It's really better if they aren't overwhelmed when they first enter this world again.*

"Again…" Ainsley clasped her hands to her chest, looking all starry-eyed and not seeming disappointed by the news. "Dragons are so romantic in that they really never die since they hold the collective consciousness of their ancestors."

"Thanks for coming to the Nest with me," Sophia said to the elf. "I'll give you a report when I return to the Castle."

"You'll give me a report when you exit that cave," Ainsley corrected. "A new dragon has not hatched…" She pointed at Lunis. "Well, since that one, but still, we didn't think there would ever be another dragon on this planet. Now there are a thousand, all thanks to you, S. Beaufont. You are going to march in there, watch history happen and come out here and tell me all about it."

Sophia didn't know how she could argue with that, so she nodded and followed Lunis into the Nest, unsure what to expect, but her nerves buzzing with excitement for what she'd witness.

The hundreds of colorful eggs spread over the grounds of the Nest glittered in the flame lit cave. Sophia at first thought Lunis had been mistaken and maybe the dragon eggs weren't hatching. The entire area was silent save for the crackling of the flames.

Then her ears heard an unmistakable sound. It was also a cracking sound, but distinctively different than that of embers and fire. It was the sound of birth. Of awakening.

Sophia remembered hearing it once before. The night Lunis was born.

A few yards away, surrounded by unmoving eggs, was a single one with a crack running down the side. It was black with white spots.

Sophia sucked in a breath and squatted to get a closer look. She glanced at her dragon, feeling a unique fondness to witness such an event with him. He mirrored her emotions in his eyes.

"What happens when the first one is here?" Sophia asked in a whisper.

We will move it to the Cave and take care of it, showing it the way, Lunis answered and then shrugged. *Or we might eat it if the little one gets on our nerves.*

She scowled at him. "You are ruining the sentimentality of the moment."

Am I? Lunis argued. *That black dragon is taking his sweet time getting out of his shell.*

He was right, Sophia realized. Lunis had broken through his shell pretty quickly when hatching, but his egg was much larger. This one was about the size of a bowling ball, the same size as all the rest of the eggs in the Nest. They were growing at roughly the same rate. Some dragon eggs would hatch when their eggs were smaller and some would hatch when much larger. Eggs would stop growing at this point until they were ready to hatch or magnetize to a rider. There were no hard and fast rules when it came to dragons, she'd learned. She and Lunis had set new standards, and Sophia suspected the dragons in the Nest would set their own, along with the new generation of riders.

A black dragon's head poked out of the top of the shell, finally breaking free. He popped his head up, blinking shining eyes around the Nest before landing his gaze on Lunis and then Sophia. He regarded them with a strange expression that filled Sophia with both sentimentality and also a foreboding fear.

The new dragon was unmistakably beautiful with its shiny black scales and horned head. She recognized the ancient wisdom of the dragon in his eyes, the same as Lunis when he first hatched. Unlike human babies, dragons were born with inborn intelligence. They had the gift of seeing the history of their ancestors, but that also could be counted as a burden. It was impossible to be an individual as a dragon who shared the memories of all.

The black dragon crushed his shell with its front leg, knocking the rest of the way through its binds. It shook its tail and spike-covered back, turning the shell to bits, and sending pieces flying.

Sophia ducked to avoid being hit with flying bits of shell. When she returned her gaze to the black dragon, she was astonished by its beauty.

This wasn't her dragon, but she was unmistakably drawn to it—as all humans were tethered to dragons on some mysterious level.

Respectfully, she bowed her head to the dragon, the first of many, and offered a single word she hoped imprinted her on its soul.

"Welcome."

CHAPTER TWENTY

Sophia left Lunis in the Nest to look after Blackey. That was what they were calling him between the two of them. His name wouldn't be revealed until he did it or magnetized to a dragonrider.

She'd nearly forgotten about Ainsley waiting for her until she ran into the shapeshifter, who was in the form of a barn owl. She landed on Sophia's shoulder and flapped her wings excitedly. Sophia couldn't help but laugh at the strangeness of the elf, who was always doing silly things, especially during heightened moments.

"He is beautiful," Sophia said, knowing what Ainsley wanted to hear. "It's a him, although I only know because Lunis told me since I don't know how to sex a dragon."

Ainsley hooted in reply, encouraging Sophia to keep talking.

"Well, he is all black and has these old soul eyes, the same as all the other dragons, but it's very striking when you see it right after they are hatched," Sophia went on, trying to remember all the pertinent details Ainsley would want to know.

The housekeeper hooted again as they descended the hill in the direction of the Castle. The sun was beginning to set on another day in the Gullington, which was fitting since they had just had the first dragon egg hatch there in...well, forever. Sophia would have to ask

Hiker and maybe consult the *Complete History of Dragonriders*, but she was almost certain no dragons had actually hatched there.

The Gullington was the home of the Dragon Elite and the place dragons and their riders were brought to once they magnetized to each other. However, Sophia didn't think eggs had ever hatched there, even back in the day when the first thousand were in existence. She considered that Ainsley might know the answer to the question, but she seemed so excited in owl form and being the first one to hear about the new dragon she didn't want to make her shift to answer the question.

The barn owl hooted again on Sophia's shoulder, to encourage her to keep talking.

"Right," Sophia chirped, trying to think what else to tell her. "Well, the dragon is very small by our standards. Much smaller than Lunis when he came to the Gullington." Sophia laughed, the fond memory washing over her. "Remember he was small enough to enter the Castle and sleep in my room. He was like a Great Dane."

The owl hooted with delight.

"This one is the size of a poodle, but no doubt will grow fast, just like Lunis did," Sophia continued. "Although Mahkah will undoubtedly be able to tell us much more about its growth potential. I seem to remember dragons grow faster when paired with a rider, right?"

The owl hooted as they approached the Castle steps.

Sophia paused just before the door. The owl froze on her shoulder, sensing her trepidation. "There was something else about the black dragon…" Sophia thought for a moment, replaying the memory of the newly hatched dragon in her mind. "A spark in his eyes."

Ainsley flapped her wings excitedly.

"Yeah," Sophia said, sensing what she meant in the movement. "But I don't know. The spark wasn't like the one I witnessed in Lunis' eyes or Bell's or the others. It was something else. Like a sinister spark. I remember having the urge to draw my sword, but I'm certain it was just my nerves."

Sophia shook her head, wondering if she was reasoning away her instinct, or her excitement was coloring the experience. What she didn't say to Ainsley and nearly didn't want to admit to herself was the spark reminded her of something she'd seen only two times before. Once in the eyes of Sulphur, the dragon who belonged to Gordon Burgess, a lone rider and his dragon.

The last time Sophia had seen that strange spark was unmistakable. It was in Thad Reinhart's dragon—Ember.

CHAPTER TWENTY-ONE

Sophia shook off the trepidation and forced a smile. "Well, it looks like we have something to celebrate," she said to the barn owl.

Ainsley squawked, springing off Sophia's shoulder and taking her usual appearance, nearly knocking into Sophia as she took up more space.

Sophia was about to ask what the matter was when Ainsley burst through the Castle doors, her red hair flying behind her. "My dinner! The roast! The rolls!"

Sophia wanted to tell Ainsley everything was going to be okay, but as soon as she stepped over the threshold, she knew dinner wasn't going to be all right. The smell of burned food was strong in the air.

Sticking her arm up to her nose, Sophia caught sight of Quiet on the stairs, a guilty expression on his face. She shook her head at the groundskeeper. "You can't give her a break, can you?"

He muttered as he toddled past her and through the doors of the Castle.

Sophia hurried for the kitchen, her phone already out. "Don't worry, Ainsley. I'll call for food."

The smoke in the kitchen was strong, making Sophia's eyes

instantly water. The housekeeper was already fast at work, trying to put out a fire and throwing towels over a smoking mound of meat.

"Oh, I can't believe this," Ainsley cried, working fast to lessen the damage. "The first meal I have made entirely by myself in centuries, and it all went to hell because you dragged me out of the Castle."

Sophia lowered her phone and regarded Ainsley with a mildly annoyed expression. "I totally take the blame for all of this."

Ainsley nodded, swiping her hand through the air to try and dispel some of the smoke. It only partially worked. "As you should, S. Beaufont. Now go ahead and order Chinese, but ensure it's all gluten-free. You know how my allergies spring up if I have breaded chicken."

Sophia paused, scrolling through her phone for the Uber Eats app, but decided now wasn't the time to argue with the housekeeper. She wasn't sure if after this there would be a good time. She'd really been looking forward to the dinner that night, but no one would enjoy it more than Ainsley.

"Hey, you can always try again tomorrow," Sophia offered. "Same meal, but this time, without the distractions."

Ainsley shook her head, continuing to clean up. There was literally nothing from the dinner that could be salvaged. "Oh, what is the point. Quiet probably made that black dragon hatch just to get me distracted and mess up. He's always got the upper hand."

"Well, then maybe you two have to find a way to make up," Sophia suggested.

Ainsley considered this, pausing from her cleaning to look up at her. "Do you think I like being his best friend for the last five-hundred years and also kept in the dark?"

"No, of course not."

"He is always playing pranks on me," Ainsley went on. "And being elusive, but now I know it was him whereas before I thought it was just a possessed Castle."

"I get you are upset—"

"Upset," Ainsley replied. "I have half a mind to leave this place for good. Hiker treats me like I'm a second-class citizen. Quiet is a jerk, and the rest of you have your own lives to live. Where does that leave me?"

Sophia could tell the housekeeper was close to tears, but Ainsley didn't realize how much sadder her story could get, because there was no escape for her.

After tapping her screen several times, Sophia offered her friend a sympathetic smile. "I've ordered some food. I'll just go out past the Barrier to get it. We will put it in dishes and tell the gang you made it."

Ainsley sighed. "Thanks, S. Beaufont."

"Also," Sophia said, a hint of mischief in her voice, "I ordered mostly tofu and all gluten-free options."

That seemed to make Ainsley feel slightly better. She pulled a set of small plates off the shelf using magic. "Do you think these will do? I'm hoping they are just small enough they anger Hiker when his kung pao tofu keeps tumbling off the plate."

"I think they are perfect, but you are missing something," Sophia teased, winking and flicking her hand in the air. Beside the plates appeared a set of chopsticks. "That will surely irritate him to no end, trying to use those."

The smile that broke across Ainsley's face made Sophia feel immeasurably better. "Thanks, S. You are the best."

CHAPTER TWENTY-TWO

"Forks," Hiker grumbled, irritation heavy in his voice as he eyed the wooden chopsticks sitting beside his undersized plate. "Would you fetch them?"

Ainsley slid into a chair next to Sophia and smiled discreetly at her. "No, for several reasons."

The Viking rolled his eyes. "Reasons you'll no doubt tell me instead of giving me a fork."

"First off," Ainsley began. "My name is Ainsley, not Would Ya."

"That joke got old several centuries ago," Hiker said, taking one of the dishes of Chinese food being passed around the table.

"Good, then it's working as intended," Ainsley fired back, feistier than ever. "Secondly, we are eating with chopsticks tonight to keep festive."

"I don't know how to use chopsticks," Hiker remarked, spooning rice onto his plate.

"You don't know how to use a fork either, just like most of the rest of you," Ainsley said, pointing around at the other men.

"Haha," Hiker grumbled, obviously about to lose this battle and realizing it. Thankfully the hatching of the first dragon's egg had put him in a better mood to deal with Ainsley's rebellious behavior.

SARAH NOFFKE & MICHAEL ANDERLE

"And lastly, I'm not a dog, and therefore, I don't fetch," Ainsley declared, looking at Hiker and then Quiet, a serious expression in her green eyes. "I don't clean up fake messes only to turn around and find them there again. I don't appreciate finding my things missing on a regular basis. I'm thoroughly sick and tired of you all being ungrateful. Yes, I take care of this Castle. I take care of you all. I value my job and take it quite seriously, but things are going to change unless you all buck up and start showing me some respect and gratitude."

Everyone at the table froze, having never seen the housekeeper act like this. It was overdue, really, but still, to see her face grow two shades darker as her voice rose was quite chilling.

Finally, Hiker broke the silence as he picked up the chopsticks. "Are you quite done?"

Ainsley, undeterred, narrowed her eyes at him. "I can be. Are you going to stop being so grumpy and demanding and show a bit of courtesy?"

"Where is this coming from?" Hiker asked in response to her request.

To Sophia's horror, her new bestie, Ainsley, indicated her. "S. Beaufont has encouraged me to stand up for myself."

Evan let out a low hiss like he'd been burned.

Wilder slid down in his seat, covering his face.

Mahkah gave Sophia a commiserate expression.

Mama Jamba and Quiet didn't appear to be listening to any of it, continuing to dig into their Chinese food and using the chopsticks.

Hiker rotated to face Sophia directly. "I should have guessed."

"The food is great," Sophia said, paying extra attention to her tofu and broccoli.

"I'm having a hard time finding the meat," Hiker complained.

"If you find any, then it means a rat crawled into one of the dishes because I didn't put any in this meal," Ainsley said with a delighted cackle.

"You what?" Hiker asked her. "And we don't have rats."

Ainsley shrugged. "It wouldn't surprise me if we did. The Castle is a real hell hole."

Quiet's chin jerked up. Apparently he was listening. His eyes turned into narrow slits as he muttered something inaudible.

"What is that, Gullington?" Ainsley asked, having way too much fun with torturing the two men who had spent centuries torturing her. "There's an infestation of roaches. That does not surprise me. This place is falling apart."

"Maybe the problem is the housekeeper doesn't do her job," Hiker seethed, not eating any of the food on his tiny plate.

"Probably," Ainsley chimed. "You should fire her."

"I'm very much considering it," he grumbled back, pushing his plate away.

"This food is delicious, Ains," Mama Jamba sang, having finished and digging into the rice for seconds.

"Thanks," the shapeshifter announced proudly. "I made it myself."

Quiet shook his head, muttering again.

"What is that, Gullington?" Ainsley asked. "You have another bad bout of gas? Maybe you should excuse yourself from the table."

Evan, who was sitting closest to the gnome, scooted closer to Mama Jamba.

She smiled at him, pointing to a dish. "Be a dear and please pass the dumplings."

"Why is there no meat in this meal?" Hiker questioned. "And what is with the small plates?"

"It was S. Beaufont's idea," Ainsley said because she obviously wanted to make enemies out of everyone at the table.

Hiker leveled his gaze at the young dragonrider. "You must really tell me why you want to ruin this meal. I'm quite curious."

Sophia cleared her throat. "Lo mein? For sure, I'll pass that over, sir."

She indicated the dish beside Wilder. When their eyes met, there was an obvious hesitation in his gaze. "Will you please?" Sophia asked, pointing to the noodle dish.

"I don't want vegetarian lo mein," Hiker complained.

"Well, I do," Sophia said, her gaze still connected to Wilder's. He was unmoving and just stared at her with so many messages in his eyes.

Quiet glanced between the pair and muttered something.

Ainsley leaned forward, forgetting she was mad at the gnome. "I know. I didn't realize it until now, but Quiet, you are completely right."

"Right about what?" Hiker asked, slamming his palm down on the table and making the dishes hiccup slightly.

"Nothing, son," Mama Jamba remarked, pushing her food around on her plate as she eyed the table, trying to decide what platter to empty next.

"Not nothing," Hiker said, his gaze drifting between Sophia and Wilder, who still had their eyes locked on each other.

It was almost a point of pride for Sophia now, a staring contest she wasn't going to lose. He was mad at her—that much was obvious. But he didn't have to do it right there at the table, making things exponentially more tense with so many other things going on.

"What is going on between you two?" Hiker asked, still studying the pair.

"Nothing," Sophia stated. "I think Wilder is just excited about our upcoming mission for Subner tomorrow."

"So excited," he commented, sticking a bite of noodles in his mouth and chewing without taking his eyes off her.

"Where are your adventures taking you?" Ainsley asked.

"The Sahara," Sophia answered.

"Lucky," Ainsley drawled, doing a Napoleon Dynamite impression.

"Yeah, you two get to go trudge around the hottest place on Earth," Evan whined, taking a bite of an egg roll. "I bet you can't contain your excitement."

"It's taking all my restraint," Wilder said with no inflection in his voice.

"Mine as well," Sophia fired back.

"Well, I vote we make a toast to the newest dragon being born," Mama Jamba declared, holding up her goblet.

Reluctantly everyone at the table joined in, holding their own glasses. Wilder was the first to pull his gaze from Sophia's, making her feel silently victorious.

"Cheers," Mama Jamba began. "To the beginning of a new generation. To the new crop of dragons."

"Cheers," everyone said collectively, clinking glasses.

The laugh that fell out of Hiker's mouth made everyone tense as they regarded their fearless leader. He froze, realizing he'd gotten everyone's attention without meaning to.

He offered them an embarrassed smile. "I was just thinking how weird it's to have all those dragon eggs. This is just the beginning. Soon we will have more dragons and then riders. It would be good if we all take a moment to remember how far we have come." He glanced down the long thirty-person table. "One day, all those seats will be filled. One day, the Castle will be full, and it all rests with us. Men...Riders," he caught himself, correcting his usual way of calling on his own. "Don't ever allow yourself to forget the dark times, for they make the journey to the light that much richer."

Mama Jamba smiled wide at Hiker. The rest all wore dumbfounded expressions.

It was Ainsley, though, who broke the silence. "Are you running a fever, sir?"

He shook his head, not even angry at her comment. "No, I'm well. I could use some meat at the next meal. But even your antics tonight can't get me down." He dropped the chopsticks and picked up a dumpling and put it in his mouth, chewing with a smile in his eyes.

"Who knew it just took a dragon hatching at the Gullington for you to not be such a grump." Ainsley shook soy sauce onto her fried rice.

"Yeah, it doesn't take much to put a smile on this man's face," Evan teased.

Hiker stood suddenly, pushing his chair out with his legs. "You two," he indicated Sophia and Wilder. "Finish up this Subner mission fast. I need you both using your efforts to find the missing dragon eggs."

"Oh, isn't it nice you two get to go on another mission together after this one." Ainsley patted Sophia's hand resting on the table.

"That's fantastic," Sophia said dryly, this time refusing to look across the table at Wilder, sure they would stay locked in another staring contest.

Quiet mumbled as he finished off another serving of fried eggplant.

"Even though you are a repugnant and conniving runt, I agree. They do make a smart match," Ainsley agreed, nodding at the gnome.

He muttered in reply.

"Awe isn't that sweet," Evan gushed. "Ainsley and Quiet are making up."

"Not yet, we aren't," Ainsley declared, pushing up from the table and standing beside Hiker. "Now, I'm going to go clean up the kitchen, which will take me much longer than usual since I have no help."

"I'll help," Evan offered with a wink, not moving.

"You'll rest up for your adjudication missions tomorrow," Hiker ordered before glaring at Sophia and Wilder. There was a heated suspicion in his gaze, but he shook it off as he strode for the exit. "Don't stay up late partying, you all. No whiskey, Wilder. Mahkah, ensure Evan does not eat too much. And Sophia?"

She jerked her chin up. "Yes, sir."

"Try not to fill my housekeeper's head with ideas that ruin my meal again," he ordered.

"I'll try, sir," she retorted, realizing no matter what she did, she'd probably be in trouble with Hiker Wallace.

CHAPTER TWENTY-THREE

"Oh, morning breeze," Sophia muttered, curling up on her sofa in front of the fire. "What is it you want to tell me so desperately you'll not let me sleep?"

She pulled *The Complete History of Dragonriders* closer to her. She couldn't sleep since her usual wake up at 3:33 in the morning, and yet her thoughts were too unfocused to allow her to read. She was being forced to stay awake, with nothing to do with the time. It seemed like a waste.

Finally, she abandoned the impossible task of reading and got ready. By five in the morning, she was ready and out the door of her room. She and Wilder had planned to meet at the front of the Castle, but she decided since she couldn't sleep, he wouldn't either.

A moment after exiting her room, she knocked on Wilder's door. There was quite a bit of rustling noise followed by the sound of something falling.

"Ouch," she heard him grumble as he stomped in the direction of the door.

When he pulled it back, she laughed at the sight of him wrapped in a sheet.

"What are you doing?" he asked her, his eyes squinting from the firelight.

"Waking you up in case Quiet had you oversleep again," she answered.

He glanced over his shoulder at a clock on the wall. "We're not supposed to go for another two hours."

"Why wait?" she argued.

He grunted in protest. "Okay, fine. You win. I'll get ready."

Wilder turned, dragging his sheet behind him.

Sophia used the time it took for Wilder to get ready to send Lunis a message, knowing he'd communicate to Simi, although her rider probably had too.

A short while later, Wilder pulled the door back again to reveal himself fully dressed in armor, his brown hair more presentable than before and his blue eyes bright and awake. "You just couldn't wait to go on this mission, could you?"

"Something like that," Sophia answered, kicking off the wall where she'd been waiting.

"The Sahara, huh?" Wilder asked. "Sounds romantic."

"Cupid must be up to something there," Sophia related, having thought about the reason why the God of love and desire would pick a place that wasn't inhabited by many to hang out, especially if he was on a streak with a faulty bow and arrow.

"I've heard a rumor the Sahara is quite large," Wilder mentioned as they strode through the quiet Castle.

Sophia gave a mock huff. "I guess. If you consider three and a half million square miles large."

He tilted his hand back and forth. "Sort of. Please tell me you packed the snacks."

Right on cue, Sophia held up the rucksack she put together the night before when she was helping Ainsley do dishes. The housekeeper kept giving her sideways looks, filled with curious expressions. Sophia assumed she knew something about her and Wilder but was thankfully being polite enough not to say anything.

"See, you are my perfect partner in crime," Wilder said, flashing her a grin.

"We are world adjudicators," she corrected. "We do the opposite of crime."

"It's an expression, Soph." He rolled his eyes at her. "Are you going to be this difficult for the whole mission?"

"Yes, and also for the rest of my life," she stated.

"Challenge accepted," he told her, pulling the front door to the Castle back and waving her through.

She shook her head at him, wondering if he was going to keep saying things like that all through this mission that made things even harder between them. Probably, Sophia reasoned, spying their dragons waiting for them on the Expanse.

"So the Sahara," Wilder began, catching up with her after pulling the heavy Castle door shut. "Do we comb over all three and half million miles, or do you have a more specific location for Mr. Bare Butt?"

Sophia shuddered. "Do you really think he's still naked? I know what the mythology says, but it's the twenty-first century."

He chuckled. "You are such a millennial."

"You take that back," she fired at him.

"I won't."

"I don't take constant selfies and say hashtag awkward, and I'm not obsessed with indie folk music while sipping on an energy drink," Sophia said in a long sentence, rushing through each word while hardly taking a breath.

"But you do love to invest in startups and play frisbee all the time, right?" he asked.

"Obvi," Sophia answered, trying not to laugh. "And when did you learn about startups and frisbees, old man?"

Wilder winked at her. "I get around."

Sophia did laugh now. "That's what she said."

He shook his head. "Hashtag awkward."

"Anyway, my source—"

"Your top-secret source you can't share with me," he interrupted.

"Yes, that one," Sophia continued. "They simply said to go to the Sahara, and I'll find Cupid or he'd find me."

Wilder gave her a skeptical expression. "That seems weird. Are you sure that's what they said? Just drop yourself into the middle of the desert and what you are looking for will find you?"

Sophia felt the urge to grab her sword. She talked herself down. Don't cut him...not yet.

"My contact told me to go with someone I care about, and Cupid would find us," Sophia reluctantly explained.

"Oh," Wilder drawled, sounding pleased.

Sophia nodded, sidling up next to her dragon and combing her hand down his long blue neck. "So naturally, I'm going with Lunis. That should be enough to draw Cupid out."

"Well played, Soph. Well played."

CHAPTER TWENTY-FOUR

That was hashtag awkward, Lunis said in Sophia's head when she slid into the saddle on his back.

"Seriously, you aren't allowed to use any hashtag phrases," she replied.

But I'm totally a millennial, he argued. *So are you two going to be okay on this mission?*

With her single intention, Lunis began to run and launched into the clear skies of Scotland as the sun started to peek over the horizon.

"Yeah, I'm going to figure out how to make him despise me," she declared. "By the end of this mission, he will beg Hiker to move me out of the Castle."

Well, then it might be a blessing you two are going on this mission together, Lunis said, his blue wings gliding effortlessly through the Scotland skies, headed for the Barrier.

The pair had taken off before Simi but also, Lunis was faster than the white dragon on most days. Simi had the advantage of wind, employing it to her advantage in multiple ways. Lunis having grown up with his rider gave him advantages over the other dragons.

He was already bigger than Bell, the largest of the current dragons, and he was still growing by Mahkah's assessment. Not only did his size, speed, and skills increase on a full moon, but any time the moon was out, no matter what phase it was. The crescent moon at their backs was giving him increased speed, but he'd slow down as the sun rose, taking over the skies.

It's pretty interesting the particular case you two are going on, Lunis observed, headed for the Barrier, the terrain below growing smaller as they rose higher.

"I don't think it's that interesting," Sophia disagreed. "Subner needs me to help with distracting."

You conveniently left out who you are distracting, Lunis snickered.

"I don't see that it matters that it's Cupid," Sophia insisted. "The god matters very little. I have a job, and I'm going to do it. Just like when I helped Wilder to recover Devon's bow from the Pond."

But how do you plan to distract Cupid, Lunis asked.

"With my devilishly good sense of humor and a fancy dragon," she answered.

And when that doesn't work, he continued.

"Then I'm going to have you eat him."

Lunis glanced over his shoulder at her, his blue eyes sparkling in the morning light. *I could use a snack.*

"I think if we take out the God of Love then we will have some explaining to do," Sophia said with a laugh.

Okay, I won't eat him, Lunis grumped. *But sooner or later, you need to find someone I can eat. Nothing tastes as good as a human.*

"You really shouldn't say that." Sophia pretended to tense on the back of her dragon.

Don't worry, I won't eat you, he offered. *I'm not a cat. Those jerks turn on their owners faster than any animal. Sleep for more than twelve hours and they start nibbling.*

"We should probably pass this along to Liv," Sophia suggested. "I always knew Plato couldn't be trusted."

That cat is the only reason she is alive, Lunis stated. *But he does cheat at poker.*

"How do you know that?"

We play, Lunis explained.

"When?"

When you are sleeping, he answered. *You sleep a lot, human.*

"Just don't eat me," Sophia begged as they exited the Barrier. Soon she'd need to create the portal, but they slowed down to allow Simi a chance to catch up. With a thought, her dragon slowed, gliding on the chilly wind.

So how are you going to get Wilder to despise you, Lunis asked as the white dragon and his rider pulled up next to them. His dark hair flew back from his face making him appear more rugged than usual.

Sophia sighed, pulling her gaze away from him. "I don't know. I'll figure something out. Maybe I'll make a few racist statements."

There you go, Lunis laughed. *You don't mess around when you want someone to not like you.*

"Operation Loathe Sophia is important," she insisted. "I can't fail."

What if you make sexist statements? he offered.

"Or told knock-knock jokes," she teased.

Hey, I happen to like...Oh, I see what you did there, he grumbled. *Why don't you keep using all those puns? That's pretty annoying.*

"Totally, right after I offload the large supply of bad jokes I've stolen from you," Sophia joked.

Have you heard the one about the deaf magician, Lunis asked.

She opened a portal, shaking her head, but deciding to play along anyway. "No, I haven't."

Neither has he, Lunis said, roaring with laughter as they flew through the portal.

CHAPTER TWENTY-FIVE

The heat in the Sahara was real. Really sticky, hot and instantly overwhelming.

Well, I figured out how you can turn Wilder off you, Lunis commented, circling over the red desert below. It looked like waves of the ocean with ripples created by the wind and sand dunes. In the distance, there were palm trees and more blue sky than Sophia had ever seen.

"How is that," Sophia asked, grateful for any tips on how to make Wilder not like her. Even more useful would be tips on how to make her not have feelings for him.

Just hang around in this desert for a few minutes, he stated, preparing to land. *You are already starting to smell ripe. No offense.*

"None taken," Sophia answered with a laugh. "I think I'll stick with my bad puns and your jokes."

And racial slurs, Lunis added, landing on the sandy desert.

"You know why I love bad puns so much?" Sophia asked.

Why?

"Because that's how eye roll." Sophia was laughing out loud as Wilder and Simi landed next to them.

"What is so funny?" Wilder asked her, appearing amused.

It isn't funny, and that's the point, Lunis explained dryly.

Sophia slid off her dragon, pulling off her cloak immediately and wishing she wasn't wearing heavy, hot armor. "I was going to wear camouflage pants," she offered as Wilder joined her.

Don't, Lunis warned, shaking his head.

"Yeah," she continued. "But I couldn't find them."

Wilder rolled his eyes. "That one was cute."

You'll have to try harder, Sophia, Lunis said in her mind.

She nodded in reply. "Don't worry. They will get old. Just wait until I start making jokes about blondes."

"But you are a blonde," Wilder argued.

"Yeah, and I'm a total airhead," she told him.

"Is that why you landed us here instead of..." He turned in a complete circle. "I don't know, anywhere else."

She shrugged. "It was here or over there where there's sand. Or over there where there's also sand. Did you have a specific place you wanted to land?"

He fanned himself. "In the air-conditioned place."

"I think there's a Starbucks that way." Sophia pointed toward the palm trees in the distance.

Maybe we should scout, Simi offered.

"That's a good idea," Wilder said. "Soph and I can go on foot."

Lunis gave her a sneaky expression. *Tell him the deaf magician joke.*

She shook her head. "I don't remember how it goes."

The dragons took to the air, Lunis blending into the blue and Simi looking like a dragon-shaped cloud.

"What was that about?" Wilder asked, amused.

"My dragon tells the worst jokes and thought you'd enjoy them."

He laughed. "The fact your dragon tells jokes at all is pretty impressive. Simi laughs at mine only about half the time."

"That's a lot," Sophia jabbed. "I've heard your jokes. They aren't funny half the time."

He pretended to be hurt, holding his hand to his chest as his mouth popped open. "You scare me, Sophia."

"Then Operation Loathe Sophia is off to a fantastic start."

"Oh, is that a thing?" he asked.

"It's now," she answered, holding out her arm. "Well, shall we go and find Cupid?"

"That way?" he questioned, arching an eyebrow at her.

"Which way do you want to go?"

He rolled his eyes, pointing in the opposite direction. "He is obviously this way."

"Then maybe you should go one way and I'll go the other."

He shook his head. "No, that isn't how it works. Your source said you had to be with someone you care about, and since Lunis is gone, you are going to have to settle for me."

It was Sophia's turn to roll her eyes. "Fine."

They started walking in the random direction Wilder had chosen in silence. After a bit, he started, "So maybe this is as good as time as any to talk about us."

"A sheep, a drum, and a snake fell off a cliff," Sophia said in a rush.

He gave her a sideways expression, encouraging her to continue.

"Baa-dum-tsss," she finished, laughing at her own joke.

"Wow, that was horrible," he said, not amused.

"As intended," Sophia assured him.

"As I was saying," Wilder continued, a serious expression on his face.

"What religion are you?" Sophia asked, hoping she could use that as kindling to make the Operation Loathe Sophia fire hotter.

He gave her a curious expression. "I'm agnostic."

"Yeah, I figured you'd safely ride the fence like that," she jabbed. "How about your nationality?"

Wilder did laugh now. "You know I'm Scottish and can't use forks and apparently chopsticks. Also, you can't understand a word I say, and I drink way too much."

"This isn't going to work if you make the offensive statements for me," she muttered, kicking up sand.

"Then it isn't going to work, and you should abandon this mission of yours."

Sophia shook her head. "How about greatest dreams and aspirations? I'm sure I can poke some holes in those."

"You already have," he said, giving her a tender expression that made her want to punch him in the face. It might actually work. If they sparred, then she could take all her frustrations out, maybe out strategize him and then kick his ass. He couldn't like her then.

"You can't best me in a fight," he told her, grinning.

Sophia's mouth popped open. "How did you know I was thinking about that?"

"Because when you spar or are about to, with me, you get this look on your face. Currently, you are wearing it."

"Oh, yeah, well, when you are thinking, you twist your tongue in your mouth."

"It's cute you noticed that about me." He batted his eyelashes at her.

"It rarely happens," she fired.

Undeterred, he laughed. "Because I never think. What can I say, you make me lose my wits."

Sophia halted and swung around to face him as she pulled out Inexorabilis. "Come on, then. Let's do this."

"Are you serious?" he asked. "It's hotter than hell out here. We are walking through a giant desert, looking for Cupid, and you want to throw down right now?"

"Why not?" Sophia fired. "Unless you're scared and think I can kick your ass."

His chin tilted back as laughter spilled from his mouth.

"What are you laughing at?" Sophia tapped the side of her sword against his shoulder, trying to encourage him to pull his own weapon.

"You," he responded. "You are ridiculous."

"I'm so ridiculous," she said, continuing to knock the side of her sword into his shoulder. "Why don't you teach me a lesson."

Easily he deflected her blade, spinning her around in a swift move and grabbing her from behind, pinning her hands down. Over her shoulder, he spoke into her ear. "Would you stop this?"

"Stop what?" she challenged, struggling to free herself from his tight grip. "If I'm insufferable, you simply have to say so."

"No, this whole thing you are doing to make me not like you, only makes me like you more."

Sophia grunted, dropping her weight, but Wilder had anticipated this and fell with her, flipping her over and straddling her. The sand was scorching hot on the back of her hands he'd pinned to the ground. "You are pretty corrupt if my attempts to make you loathe me only make you like me more. Maybe you need therapy."

He laughed. "It makes me like you because it's so Sophia-like. You always employ strategy. And your bad jokes are very endearing."

"Don't worry," she said, struggling to free herself from his grip but to no effect. "I'm going to start spouting prejudiced statements soon. There's no way you can find that endearing."

"Maybe I will," he countered.

"Wild," she started, her resolve waning as she looked into his eyes. "We—"

"Shh." He looked up suddenly.

Sophia narrowed her eyes at him. Just when she was about to cave, he pissed her off. "Don't shush me."

"Soph," he whispered. "You hear that?"

She clapped her mouth shut, listening. Actually, she didn't hear anything, but now she was paying attention, she did feel a rumbling underneath them.

In an instant, Wilder jumped off her and yanked her up to her feet. "Just when I had you where I wanted you, something had to ruin it."

"What is it?" Sophia asked, now hearing what he was talking about. It was a rattling sound, and it was growing louder, and the ground under their feet was visibly trembling.

"Trouble," Wilder said, pulling out his sword.

CHAPTER TWENTY-SIX

From the sand of the Sahara Desert, a thing that could only be described as a giant worm shot out of the Earth. The scream that spilled from its mouth nearly made Sophia drop her sword to cover her ears. She recalibrated her hearing so her senses weren't so acute.

"What the hell is that?" Wilder yelled, putting his back to Sophia's and holding his sword the same as her. He scanned the area, looking for other potential monsters to spring up from the desert floor.

"Angels above," she said in a hush. "It appears the movie *Tremors* is about to get real."

"Please explain," he urged as the thing writhed in the air before flopping down in front of them, throwing up a cloud of sand and covering them instantly.

"It's a movie from the nineties," she said, watching as the ground began to ripple behind the giant worm thing. Sophia grabbed his arm and pulled him away. "Run!"

"Nineties?" Wilder asked, taking her lead. "You weren't even born then."

"And yet," she continued, sprinting as the ground behind them exploded from the monster surging after them. "I've seen the movie and know how to get away from this thing."

"How?" he asked, almost passing her.

"Call our freaking dragons!"

CHAPTER TWENTY-SEVEN

The dragons weren't responding. Sophia had only had that happen once, the nightmarish time Gordon Burgess used magical tech to sever their connection.

She continued to try and communicate with her dragon as they sprinted across the desert, running as fast as her feet could take her. That wasn't nearly fast enough. The giant worm was tunneling behind them at an alarming rate. There wasn't anything in the distance but sand and more sand. They needed something that got them off the ground. The palm trees in the distance weren't really a great option.

A dragon. That would be nice, Sophia thought.

She was just about to call out to him again when Wilder grabbed her and halted suddenly. Sophia twisted around, wondering what suicidal idea he was playing with.

"It's stopped," Wilder said between ragged breaths.

Sophia shook her head. "No, it's just changing its strategy."

"What is that thing? And what is this movie it's from?" Wilder asked.

Sophia sucked in a breath, her chest aching from the heat and running. "First, can you communicate with Simi?"

He shook his head. "No, for some reason, I'm blocked. It's most likely to do with the magnetic field of the Sahara. We have had this issue before."

Sophia rolled her eyes. "Of course the reception is spotty in the freaking Sahara. How did I not guess that?"

"We just have to keep trying," Wilder offered, searching the area.

The path they had taken was well mapped by the darker sand that ran the length of where the giant worm had sprung up from the ground.

"So that thing," Wilder started, running his hand over his face, which was completely covered in red sand. It made him look like he had a bad sunburn.

Sophia could taste the sand in her mouth, making it gritty when she spoke. "It's a worm-like monster that eats flesh."

"I sort of figured out it wasn't friendly when it thundered after us." Wilder narrowed his eyes. "I think it's coming back."

Sophia knew what he meant by the way the ground moved under her feet. Growing up in Los Angeles, she was used to minor earthquakes, which is what this felt like, but she didn't think it was caused by seismic plates shifting.

"So we portal out of here," Sophia suggested.

Wilder shook his head again. "I already tried that. The magnetic field or whatever it is…"

Sophia rolled her eyes. "How convenient. No dragons. No portals. It seems like we are going to have to slay this beast to survive."

"Looks like it," Wilder agreed, watching the ground around them as it started to swell in places, like waves in the ocean. "Running isn't a long-term option, I'm thinking."

"What we need is Kevin Bacon," Sophia mused, considering their options.

"Please explain," Wilder encouraged, tensing as the swelling sand got closer to them. The thing was trying to figure them out or trap them. Maybe make another grand entrance.

"Actually, we need bombs," Sophia decided, recalling the movie Liv made her watch, stating it was a classic and her education wasn't complete without it. How strange it might be exactly what saved her in this situation.

"I'm a weapons expert, but bombs aren't really my forte," Wilder explained.

She nodded. "But you can use spells. Fire magic will be extremely helpful."

"On it," Wilder said, holding out his hand, drawing energy to him for a spell.

"Now what we need is a structure," Sophia explained, realizing summoning something so large was going to significantly drain her powers. Staying on the ground was a really bad idea since it was the giant worms home turf.

"It can tunnel through sand..." Sophia said, thinking through her options. "But rock would slow it down."

"Rocks!" Wilder exclaimed. "That's brilliant." He pointed in the distance, maybe a mile off. It was hard to tell in the desert where the sandy terrain went on for miles.

Sophia gave him a tentative expression. "Do you think we can make it?"

He flashed her a grin. "I have no doubt."

As if the monster had been eavesdropping on their conversation, it burst through the sand roughly fifty yards away. Its mouth opened, and weird hooked fangs unfolded from its jaw as another snake-like thing exploded from its mouth, licking the air as it screamed.

CHAPTER TWENTY-EIGHT

Wormy, as Sophia decided to call him, towered high above them, over the height of a two-story house. Sophia desperately hoped that was as long as it was, but she also hoped not to find out.

"That's our cue to run!" Wilder exclaimed, throwing a fireball straight at the monster and hitting it in the side.

It was a very effective attack and knocked the monster, which was about five feet wide, to the ground. When it fell, the ground trembled violently under their feet, nearly throwing Sophia off balance.

Even though the attack had been well placed, Sophia knew it wasn't enough to stop the beast, but it would slow it down. She was about to launch her own attack, but before she could, the monster began to slip back down into the hole it had come from, quickly slipping out of view.

The ground rocked so hard and began to split in places that for a moment, Sophia thought they might get sucked under the sand. She used the momentum to push herself in the opposite direction, running again so fast her feet hardly felt as though they touched the ground, Wilder on her heels.

The attack had hopefully injured Wormy, but to kill it was going to take much more than magic, she suspected. Sophia slid her sword into its sheath as they sprinted, the rock structures in the distance growing closer.

She chanced a glance over her shoulder. As Sophia expected, Wormy was in hot pursuit, although it didn't appear to be moving quite as fast.

The red sand exploded up from the ground as it progressed, following them with an angry force. Even moving slower from the injury, it was still gaining on them because the heat of the desert and trudging through sand, even with superhuman powers, was taxing on the two dragonriders. At this pace, the creature would catch them and eat them.

Sophia had to do something unexpected to save them.

CHAPTER TWENTY-NINE

Sophia halted, spinning to the side.

Wilder caught sight of her, and his face was the first part to register his shock. "What are you doing?"

"I'm buying us some time," she shouted, pointing in the distance. It wouldn't work for long, but if Sophia's assumption was correct, then this would at least give them enough time to get to the rock structure. Or it wouldn't work, and she'd have lost valuable time. It was a risk she was willing to take. She had to rely on her greatest asset—strategy.

"Stay absolutely still," Sophia urged, hardly parting her mouth to talk.

To her surprise, Wormy froze under the ground.

"What is happening?" Wilder asked in a whisper.

"As I suspected," Sophia began in a hush, talking so low only another dragonrider could hear her. "It tracks us by sensing motion."

"Was that in the movie?" he questioned.

"Think about it," Sophia started. "It doesn't have eyes or probably smell. Its ability to follow us is based on vibrations."

"If we remain still, then it won't be able to find us?"

The timing was a beautiful and ironic thing. On the heels of Wilder's statement, Wormy exploded up from the ground, flopping onto the sand, and its giant, disgusting head landed only feet from Sophia.

She didn't move.

From her peripheral vision, she noticed Wilder tense, like he was about to push her out of danger. However, he followed her lead and remained frozen.

"It can't find me unless I move," Sophia stated, watching as the creature writhed, making sweeping motions in the sand.

"Yeah, but it knows we are here, and it's feeling around in the dark, so to speak," Wilder agreed.

She nodded. Sweat dripped profusely from her forehead, falling into her eyes and dripping down her chin, then splattering on the sand in front of her.

Wormy froze too.

Had it sensed the movement? The dripping of sweat was ever so slight, but Sophia knew it carried a vibration.

The hideous monster opened its mouth, and a putrid smell spilled out. Wormy's hooked fangs popped out to the side as the mini-me inside of it sprung out, flying in the air like a gross kite. It flew only inches from her face, but she didn't budge. It was only a matter of time before the thing haphazardly knocked into her.

She knew it. Wilder knew it. And she suspected the monster knew it.

"Soph..." Wilder said more stress in this voice than she'd ever heard before. "You have a plan?"

Answering him would have been a death sentence. So instead, she lifted her hand and pointed in the distance. Because she learned magic from giants as well as other magical races, she could do complicated Earthquake spells most magicians couldn't master easily.

Squeezing her eyes shut, she focused all her energy on the spell. This had to work, or at any second, the monster was going to find her, and it would all be over.

CHAPTER THIRTY

In the distance, there was an explosion, followed by a great rumbling. Sophia's eyes popped open to find the spell had worked. There appeared to be a disturbance about a hundred yards away. The ground there was shaking, splitting, and sand sprang into the air, making a huge dust cloud.

Wormy froze. Although he didn't have eyes or other features to communicate his facial expression, it seemed to say, "What was that?"

It turned its ugly head toward the upheaval in the distance. The ground continued to shake, the tremors spreading all the way to Sophia and Wilder.

She didn't even dare take a sip of breath as she waited to see what the giant worm would do. It seemed to be weighing its options as well, indecision tunneling in its tiny brain.

Sophia considered her next options if this didn't work. She'd have to resort to attacking the monster up close, which she had her doubts about based on its size. The only way they were going to defeat this thing was to have an advantage. Right now, standing on soft sand, with few defenses, wasn't going to cut it.

Thankfully, she'd bought them some time.

Wormy dived, plummeting into the sand like a serpent in ocean waters. Its body arched up high as its head made progress, swimming through the sand in the direction of the earthquake Sophia had caused.

"Don't move yet," she urged Wilder.

"Copy that," he answered. "And that was genius."

"Thanks. Let's hope it buys us enough time," Sophia said, watching the monster moving farther away, tearing up the sand as it progressed.

"Well, we might want to consider making a run for it now," Wilder stated. "That thing is about to figure out it's been tricked."

"You really think Wormy is that smart?"

A chuckle fell from his mouth, earning a warning glare from Sophia.

Wormy froze. The laugh had been enough to signal to it there was something back in the direction it came from.

"Damn it," Sophia spun around and began sprinting at once for the rock structure.

Wilder took off after her, easily keeping pace. "Sorry, but it caught me off guard you'd name the monster trying to eat us."

"I always name the monsters I have to slay," she explained. "I already know what the next one will be called."

"Wilder, huh?"

"Bingo," she answered, running fast, trying to force herself not to look over her shoulder, although the sounds of Wormy in hot pursuit were unmistakable.

Again, she tried to reach out to Lunis but got no answer. Whatever was up with the Sahara was especially annoying. No portal magic. No telepathic communication. Maybe that was exactly why Cupid was here. It couldn't be to create romance among ugly worm monsters. At least, Sophia hoped not. Those things needed to go extinct, not breed more.

The first of the rock structures wasn't far. It was a smaller one that included an archway made of what appeared to be sandstone shaped by the harsh Sahara Desert winds. Beside it were two towers that unfortunately were just under the height of Wormy.

Farther away were larger rock structures, but getting there would be a risk, and Sophia thought her luck was about to run out.

She felt the sand pushing up under her feet, almost seeming to launch her forward. However, she didn't for a moment delude herself into thinking Wormy was trying to give her a boost up to the top of the rock formation. He was going to get right underneath her and suck her down with him, swallowing her whole.

Wilder made it to the rocks first and was already climbing up. He was safe, at least for now.

Sophia could feel the monster under her, making her progress slower. In an act of faith, she used her magic to propel herself, combining it with a leaping spell.

She flew forward as two things happened simultaneously.

The beast rose out of the sand springing after her, a familiar scream echoing out of its mouth as it opened wide.

And Wilder threw another fireball straight at the beast, hitting it hard in the body.

CHAPTER THIRTY-ONE

The blast of heat flew right by Sophia. She couldn't imagine feeling hotter, and yet, she thought she'd catch on fire as the flaming ball soared by.

The monster screamed as the fireball hit it, again knocking it in the opposite direction, and sending a great cloud of red sand into the air that rained back down on them. Sophia was momentarily blinded as she landed on the rock structure, her chin knocking hard into it.

She didn't allow the blunt hit to slow her. Instead, she continued to move, her hands and feet working hard to find holds. Wilder, who was nearly to the top, spun around and held out a hand for her. She took it, allowing him to yank her up to where he stood.

Sophia was impressed by his strength. Never in sparring had he shown that kind of power against her, but he never really pushed himself against her, not wanting to actually hurt her.

She rocked back from the momentum, catching herself before tumbling back in the other direction. One thing was clear to Sophia from her vantage point on the top of the rock structure—Wormy was pissed.

It jerked in the sand below, a weird green substance oozing from its body. Wilder had really wounded the thing with the fireball, but he hadn't killed it, and now the monster was madder than hell.

Sophia was surprised by how well she was able to discern the emotional state of the sightless creature. It was as if in such a short period of time, they had come to know each other. Hopefully, it knew how much she despised him. She pulled Inexorabilis from its sheath and brandished the sword her mother had used until the day she died. Sophia hoped Wormy knew these were its final moments on Earth.

CHAPTER THIRTY-TWO

"What is the strategy?" Wilder asked, holding a protective hand to steady Sophia as Wormy thrashed around and made the rock structure shake.

Several times, the creature tried to lift itself up, but the injury seemed to be preventing it.

"Well, how about we reverse roles from the Cupid mission," Sophia suggested. "You've got that fireball attack down."

"But I don't think that's going to kill it," Wilder observed as Wormy rose up slowly, teetering dangerously and close to crashing down on them from its instability.

"I don't think so either," Sophia agreed, having studied enough of Bermuda Lauren's book *Mysterious Creatures* to know how a beast of this sort had to be killed. "We have got to sever its head, I believe."

"You want me to distract it while you do that?" Wilder asked.

Sophia could hear the reluctance and uncertainty in his voice. "I get you are stronger and have the larger sword but—"

"But you are the better choice for it," he interrupted, dodging an attack from Wormy as it swung and nearly knocked Wilder off the rock structure.

"Really?" Sophia was surprised to hear him say that.

"One hundred percent," he insisted, kneeling and grabbing a handful of rocks at their feet and throwing them. Like a dog, Wormy swung around, sensing the distraction at its back. "Your magic reserves have to be low after pulling off that earthquake. More importantly, I think you are nimbler than me, and your size will make it easier for you to get into position."

Sophia had been prepared to argue with him, but Wilder was surprising her at every turn.

The distraction was short-lived. Wormy swung back around, facing them straight on. It was go time. They had one chance to get this right and end things before the giant beast ended them.

CHAPTER THIRTY-THREE

The beast opened its mouth, revealing darkness worse than any nightmare. The second head shot out, reaching for them.

Sophia was about to swing her sword and sever the little head, but something told her that it was a bad idea. It was like when she faced Hydra and learned severing one of the heads only made another one grow back. She pictured three heads replacing the single one and making the monster somehow stronger from the inside.

No, she needed to cut off the main artery, but getting a clear shot would be a challenge. Currently, Wormy was too far away, making it impossible for her to reach him. Even Wilder, with his longer sword and arm span, couldn't reach the monster that swiveled, trying to find them.

"Another fireball?" Wilder asked, backing away from Sophia, sensing she was preparing for her attack.

"No, you need to bring it closer, not farther away."

He nodded, reluctance heavy in his eyes, although it was soon replaced with determination. "You got it, Soph."

Wilder held his hands in front of his face, cupping his mouth. "Hey, you ugly deformed maggot!"

Wormy, who had been rotating back and forth trying to find them, halted. Robotically it swiveled until it was facing them directly.

It had found them. Wormy knew it.

The monster seemed to be overwhelmed with excitement, salivating for the meal it was so hungry for.

"Yeah, that's right, you horrendous smelly worm!" Wilder yelled.

Sophia shook her head. "We really need to work on your name-calling skills."

The monster struck, making Wilder dive to avoid being dinner. "Later," he roared, rolling forward and nearly falling off the rock structure.

The beast crashed into the archway, nearly breaking it in two. It threw Sophia off balance, making her fall on her back. Thankfully she kept her sword in her hand. Unlucky for her, the worm sensed her only a few feet away. It opened its mouth and the other head slithered out.

Wilder was trying to climb back up into place on the other side of the monster, but the formation he was on continued to break apart, making him slip back down with each attempt to secure his footing.

Sophia rolled to the side and jumped to her feet.

The second head rose into the air. She could feel its delight about what it believed was an inevitable win. It might be. Behind her was a stone wall. She could jump down, but that would involve running, which she knew wasn't the way to survive. Wormy would be on her in seconds and it would all be over. It rose up higher, now towering above her. If she was going to strike, now was the time, but getting around the smaller head to sever the larger one was impossible.

Then, from behind Wormy, Wilder rose, having recovered from his fall. "All right, you, son of a dirt-eating mother of all that's despicable! It's time you met your match!"

Wormy screamed and swung around to face Wilder. The name-calling must have finally hit a nerve because the beast was furious based on the long piercing sound that came from its mouth. It vibrated with hostility. Sophia spied the muscles on its back telegraphing the striking move it was about to do next to take Wilder down, who had nowhere to go to escape.

At that moment, faced with so much stress and the potential loss of Wilder, she knew something with certainty. Something that surprised even her. She was utterly in love with the man on the other side of this beast. No matter what divided them, monsters, Vikings, or age.

She didn't hesitate and swung Inexorabilis around with a furious force, combining the effort with a combat spell. Her sword sliced through the veiny monster, cutting off its head in one quick movement.

Blood and guts, covered in a slimy green shot up from the body of the beast like a volcano erupting. They covered Sophia and Wilder at once, drenching them in a hot liquid that smelled like sewage. The head of the monster flew backward, landing and creating a cloud of red sand that rained down, also covering them, sticking to the glue-like substance of Wormy. The creature's body swayed slightly before it crumbled to the ground in a heap.

Looking horrible and gross, Sophia offered Wilder a relieved smile when it was only them standing on the rock archway, nothing dividing them anymore.

CHAPTER THIRTY-FOUR

"What? No bad puns about how we have been tarred and feathered?" Wilder asked as they got down, careful not to land in the swamp of dead Wormy pooling underneath them.

"I think the joke would go something like, looks like we have been slimed and sanded," Sophia teased, finding her skin tightening up from the guts and sand covering her.

"I hope this stuff isn't poisonous," Wilder remarked, seeming to read her thoughts on their current predicament.

She nodded. "Yeah, because I doubt there's an Airbnb we can go rinse off at anywhere nearby."

"What is an Airbnb?" he questioned.

"Or a pond," she remarked, too exhausted to explain her modern reference right then.

"Yeah, there usually aren't many bodies of water in the desert, hence making it the desert." He surveyed the area they had come from.

Sophia was still having no luck calling her dragon or creating a portal, which was frustrating. On a positive note, they were alive and not being hunted by a giant man-eating worm anymore.

She'd learned to count her blessings at this stage of the game. Right now, she could use a drink of water and steak dinner but guessed there was no Outback Steak Houses in these parts either.

Pulling the canteen from the snack bag, she took a sip and then offered some to Wilder.

He gave her a grateful smile. "Thanks. So what do we do now to find Cupid? Do you think Wormy was part of leading us in the right direction based on your inside source?"

"I think he was a bonus to this whole mission," Sophia joked, searching through the bag of snacks but not interested in any of it. "I'm certain later I'll find out we just slaughtered the last remaining tiggly wig worm in existence and Bermuda Laurens is going to chew me out for it."

"Why does this sound like something you've encountered before?" Wilder asked with a laugh.

"Because I did in the Australian Outback," Sophia explained. "Leave it to me to find the last remaining Spindle spider during my walkabout. Lunis and I killed it and all her babies."

"That's so you," he said with a laugh and held out his hand. "Shall we walk and find out what is on the other side of these rock structures? If nothing else, they should provide some shade so we can enjoy the snacks you brought."

Sophia nodded, thinking it was impossible for her to enjoy the taste of anything with her mouth coated in sand and the smell of dead Wormy covering her body.

"You almost gave me a heart attack when you stopped running when that monster was after us," Wilder remarked, his eyes continually scanning the terrain.

"It was a risk," Sophia agreed.

"It's funny the way you wager on certain things," he stated, giving her an impressed look. "Your brain doesn't work like anyone else's I've ever known."

"I'm just glad my wager paid off. I can thank movies from the nineties for it all."

They strode around a large set of rocks to find a mirage. It had to be. There was no other explanation.

Sophia clapped her hand to her forehead, her mouth popping open. "Oh, good. I have lost my damn mind."

Wilder's expression mimicked hers. "Then they can cart us away to the looney bin together because I have too."

CHAPTER THIRTY-FIVE

Sophia reasoned she must be losing her mind and the heat of the desert was getting to her. She'd heard about mirages in the desert. They were brought on by dehydration, heat exhaustion, and apparently near-death experiences. That pretty much summed up her life right then.

"If this is a dream, don't wake me up," Sophia said in a whisper.

Wilder reached over and pinched her arm.

"Ouch," she yelled, yanking away.

"It isn't a dream, Soph."

"But that can't be real." She pointed.

Her version of an oasis would include a regal mansion on a vast estate flanked by her and Wilder's dragons and is what stood in the distance, completely out of place with the Sahara framing it.

Oh good, you two found us, Lunis said, striding over like a golden retriever who had been lost from his owner.

Conversely, Simi appeared much more elegant as she walked over to Wilder's side and lowered her head down close to his, an unmistakable expression of affection in their gaze. "Simi, are you real?"

He reached out and stroked the side of her face, and she nuzzled into him.

Of course I am, she declared.

"Lunis, where have you two been, and why couldn't we communicate with you?" Sophia asked, thrilled to see her dragon and also a bit miffed to find them casually hanging out next to a mirage.

He lowered his head and nudged her, looking for the same attention Simi was getting. She giggled, nudging him back with the side of her head.

We were stuck here until you found us, Lunis explained.

"I don't understand." Sophia looked between the two dragons.

We don't either, Simi explained. *We could only determine we couldn't leave from this spot or communicate with you.*

We guessed you had to complete a challenge in order to find us, and that would lead you to Cupid, Lunis added on.

"Those are a lot of assumptions, but I'll go with it." Sophia pointed at the mansion. It was right out of a movie, rising up from the grassy lawn surrounding it.

A circular drive ran the length of the space in front, and pulling up in old fancy cars were elegant guests dressed in their finest clothing. They were greeted by men in jackets with long tails and white gloves, who dutifully took their keys and drove the cars away.

The whole picture was very confusing, and not just because a mansion flanked by large columns on an elegant lawn was something she didn't expect to find in the middle of the Sahara Desert. The cars appeared from nowhere and then disappeared as though there was a mysterious street that brought everyone to the house party and then away again.

"Are we hallucinating, or can you two see that mansion too?" Sophia asked.

Lunis blinked around, a dumbfounded expression on his face. *Mansion? What are you talking about?*

Yes, we see it, Simi said at once.

Lunis rolled his eyes. *It's a joke. They are these devices we employ to interject a bit of humor into things. You should try them sometime.*

That's quite all right, Simi pointed out, turning her attention to

Wilder. *It isn't a mirage from what I can tell. I believe it to be the place where Cupid is inhabiting presently.*

Lunis coughed snottily, and looked at Sophia. *Yes, we have deduced through constant observation if we hold our noses high in the air and think only serious thoughts we can talk like we are stuffy old dragons.*

"I see your time together has only brought you closer to one another," Sophia joked. "Good team building."

Simi didn't appear amused, but thankfully Wilder was for the both of them. "Are we just supposed to waltz onto this fancy property and attend whatever soiree?"

"What is going on? Why is everyone speaking so strangely?" Sophia asked.

Wilder grinned at her. "Oh, all of a sudden, I'm not allowed to talk like I've got a bit of sophistication?"

Sophia glanced down at her outfit, covered in slime and sand. "I feel like we are a bit underdressed for the party."

We aren't going to see Cupid for social reasons, Simi stated dryly.

Lunis shoved his face in close to Wilder's. *Make her stop. Please.*

Wilder laughed. "I get Simi isn't as colorful as you, but she also didn't grow up watching modern television or with an eccentric rider like you."

"I'm not eccentric," Sophia argued.

Need I remind you all we are here for a mission, Simi interjected.

Need I remind you all that...what the hell happened to you two when you left us? Lunis asked.

Sophia nodded. "Yeah, I guess we could use magic to clean ourselves up."

I wouldn't until you've filled your magic reserves, Simi suggested. *Wilder's is quite low.*

Yours are too, Sophia, Lunis pointed out. *But I almost think you should risk it because you are hard to look at and that's almost more important than anything else.*

Sophia laughed. "Thanks, Lun."

"Well, I guess we better pop off to this strange party even if we weren't invited," Wilder teased, giving Sophia a proud expression. "If we pretend we don't look horrid, you think they'll notice?"

"I think they will smell us a mile away," she stated.

He nodded, holding out his arm for her. "Shall we then?"

She took his arm, not even hesitating. Things had changed once more between them after they faced Wormy.

Oh, hey Sophia, Lunis said at her back.

She swung around to face him. "Yeah?"

You've got a little something on your face, he offered.

She rolled her eyes, which were probably the only part of her not covered in slime and sand. "Thanks. You're a doll."

CHAPTER THIRTY-SIX

Just as when Sophia and Wilder had come around the rock structures and found their dragons, it felt like they crossed through a strange barrier, similar to the one that surrounded the Gullington.

Sophia imagined she'd walked through a portal as she stepped from the soft sand of the Sahara Desert and onto a paved driveway surrounded by manicured hedges and a pristine lawn. If any of the party guests were surprised by their appearance, they didn't show it as Sophia and Wilder approached the front entrance.

The cars, many of them driven by chauffeurs, pulled up to the front steps, and let off distinguished individuals wearing the finest clothing from the 1920s. Women in flapper dresses and pearls spilling down their front and men in three-piece suits with bow ties and flasks giggled as they were greeted by a butler standing on the first step. They all had paper invitations they showed to the man with a boxy jaw and a dignified expression.

"We don't have invitations," Sophia said in a hush to Wilder.

He patted his side, where his sword was sheathed. "I've got my invitation right here."

She gripped his arm tighter, smiling. "I like the way you think."

"Same to you, Soph."

She glanced over her shoulder to find both dragons were following them up to the door, although she was certain there wouldn't be much room for them inside. Maybe in the back where she noticed signs of an outdoor area and could hear orchestral music. It was more than strange none of the valet staff seemed to think it was weird that two people covered in worm guts and sand or their dragons were casually strolling up to the party.

The desert was still all around them, although Sophia had expected when they stepped into this strange land, the Sahara Desert would disappear. Something very curious was at work in this place...wherever it was.

"Excuse me," Wilder began when the butler brought his chin up and smiled politely at them. Suddenly the constant flow of cars with guests dissipated, and it was only Sophia and him at the front of the house, their dragons behind them.

"Good evening, Mr. Thomson," the man said kindly. He nodded to Sophia. "And a pleasure making your acquaintance, Ms. Beaufont. I know our host will be happy to have you attending tonight."

"You know who we are, and we are expected?" Wilder asked, arching an eyebrow at the butler.

"Naturally," the man replied.

"We don't have invitations," Wilder explained as if looking for a reason to keep them out of the party.

Sophia understood. This could be a trap. One of their many enemies could have set up a whole ruse to trick them.

"You don't need one," the man told him. "Mr. Cupid is expecting you and hoped you made it through the obstacles to get here."

"He knows we are here?" Sophia asked, wondering if everything was ruined. They needed to get the bow Cupid didn't want to part with, afraid of being decommissioned by Subner and Father Time. If he knew they were coming, getting the bow away might be impossible.

"Of course," the butler answered. "Mae Ling, a wonderful friend of my masters, called ahead and said you'd be coming."

"Mae Ling?" Wilder questioned.

Sophia tugged on his arm, still locked in hers. "My inside source."

He nodded. "Of course. And these obstacles?"

"Well, all guests have to get through them to get here," the butler explained. "Mae Ling asked for yours to be a bit more unorthodox. Usually, they require a lot of self-loathing and doubt. That's what the path to love is paved with, my master always says."

"Oh…" Sophia said, everything dawning on her. She knew Mae Ling's, as well as most other fairy godmothers' missions were to arrange love for couples. She must have used that excuse to get them into this party. Cupid thought they were there to find love.

"Now, would you like us to valet your dragons for you?" the butler asked them like this made perfect sense.

Sophia glanced over her shoulder at Lunis and knew she was going to enjoy this a lot more than she should. She held out her hand and a key fob appeared. "Sure, that would be great."

A man in a short jacket ran over at once, grabbing the key from her hand.

He clicked it, pointing it at the blue dragon.

Right on cue, Lunis beeped like a car being unlocked. The valet strode off, all perfectly natural, Lunis trotting off behind him.

Have fun, he called to her, Simi rolling her eyes and following behind him.

CHAPTER THIRTY-SEVEN

"I can't help but point out we aren't really wearing the same attire as the other party-goers," Sophia told the butler.

He nodded. "Not to worry, Ms. Beaufont. Just cross the threshold to Mr. Cupid's house and all will be taken care of for you."

"Um...do you mean there are clean clothes and a shower waiting for us?" Wilder asked.

The butler shook his head. "No, Ms. Beaufont's fairy godmother has ensured you'll be dressed appropriately. All you must do is cross the threshold."

"Fairy godmother, eh?" Wilder gave Sophia a curious expression.

"I guess my secret is out now," she said, smiling at the butler before making for the house where wonderful smells and sounds were emanating.

"Are you like Cinderella and about to be transformed?" Wilder asked her. "Do you have a curfew?"

"I have no idea," she answered, pausing at the threshold to the mansion. Sophia drew in a breath, catching sight of the elegant entryway and the party going on inside. "I guess we're about to find out."

In unison, Sophia and Wilder stepped across the threshold. She instantly felt clean, all the grit and slime magically washed from the many crevices where it had been stuck. Sophia was no longer wearing her armored clothes and boots. Instead, she was adorned in a tight black dress with a fringe on the end that shook when she walked. Draped around her neck were several strands of pearls and heavy earrings hung from her lobes. Around her sleek blonde hair was a headband filled with feathers and beads. Without looking in a mirror, Sophia knew she appeared exactly like she'd stepped out of the 1920s, ready for a roaring party.

Just as impressive as her was Wilder by her side. He had on a three-piece suit that matched her dress. Hanging from his pocket was his usual watch, and around his neck was a plaid bow tie to match his pocket square. But the best part of his outfit was the wing-tipped shoes, which made him look like he was ready to do the Charleston.

"I do declare, Sophia Beaufont, you look like a sight for sore eyes," Wilder declared, giving her a devilishly handsome smile.

She couldn't help but return it. "Why, you do as well, Mr. Thomson."

Gracefully he reached out and grabbed two champagne flutes as a waiter passed with a tray.

"I think we deserve a cheer to this adventure," he said, handing her one of the glasses.

She took it and held it up. "To defeating Wormy."

"To passing the obstacle that inevitably led us here," he said, clinking his glass to hers.

Sophia took a sip, the bubbles nearly making her hiccup. She remembered she was hungry. Thankfully, looking around the party, they were in the perfect place for dining.

CHAPTER THIRTY-EIGHT

The entryway to Cupid's mansion was as impressive as the outside. The polished white and black checkerboard marble floor made Sophia feel like she was a queen on a chessboard. Framing the oversized foyer were two sets of staircases and a large balcony at the top where she expected to find Cupid, looking down at them. However, there wasn't anything there except for giggling girls all dressed in mink coats and drinking martinis. The area was lit by one of the largest chandeliers Sophia had ever seen.

Gently Wilder led her forward, straight into a ballroom where the party was going even stronger. In this room, waiters buzzed by with white gloves, holding trays high above their heads and offering artfully arranged appetizers to the guests.

Sophia grabbed two puffed pastries, handing one to Wilder and shoving the other into her mouth, hardly chewing before she swallowed. She was famished.

"So, what is the plan?" Wilder asked in a whisper.

"Eat all the food and get tipsy," she offered.

He grabbed some stuffed mushrooms from a tray as it passed. "I'm as delighted by our change of events as you are, but unfortunately, we are here for a reason, remember."

She sighed, inhaling the food. "Yeah, fine. I just don't understand. Why is Cupid throwing a 1920's party that looks like it's hosted by Jay Gatsby?"

"Nice reference," he said proudly. "I can't think of a character who romanticized his love affair more than Gatsby, so it makes sense Cupid would entertain in this fashion."

"This is very weird, though," Sophia admitted. "We had to go through the desert and fight a giant worm so we could get here. But what do other people do to show up at these parties to find love?"

"Remember what Subner said about the bow having a resonating effect that was creating problems." Wilder led Sophia through the dancing guests to the outside area at the back. "Notice everyone here appears to be...what is the word?"

Sophia nearly gasped as they stepped out onto the terrace. The sprawling backyard was lit with beautiful white bulbs scattered throughout, hanging in trees and draped over another dance floor and dining areas where guests chatted up close, many of them looking moments away from doing a lot more than converse.

"They are in lust," Sophia observed, looking around to notice it appeared more like a high school party where everyone was pairing up.

"Yes, a malfunction of the bow," Wilder said. "There's no precision, and then it has a rippling effect, it seems."

Sophia nodded. "Causing the elves to be overly hippie-like."

"And who knows what else," Wilder stated. "If so many are haphazardly falling in lust, how many aren't actually falling in love with the right person? Are they missing their soul mate?"

Sophia considered this, her gaze dancing around the party, the emotion of the festivities starting to sweep her away. "I'm not sure I believe in such things, but I get what you are talking about. Cupid is causing more problems than anything else. People are losing their objectivity."

"We might too if we aren't careful," Wilder warned, his face unusually serious. "It's important we get that bow and fix it."

"And not get struck by it or be in the vicinity when it's fired," Sophia added. "I think that's when this reverberating effect happens."

"What's the plan?" Wilder asked again.

"Well, first, I think we have to divide up," Sophia suggested. "But you should keep an eye on me, so you know where I am and when I've distracted our host. I'll get him to put his bow down somewhere and you can swoop in and fix it."

"How are you going to get this naked cherub to put it down?" Wilder asked, a challenging expression on his face.

She shrugged. "I don't know. I'll tickle his tummy."

Wilder shook his head, taking a step backward. He pointed at his eyes and then her, giving her the universal message for "I'll be watching you."

She nodded, turning around on the terrace and looking out at the most magical party she'd ever seen.

CHAPTER THIRTY-NINE

Enchanting wasn't quite the word for the festivities going on around Sophia. She had to check the party goers around her weren't fae. They had a way of seducing and making those around them feel drunk.

No, they were mortals, she realized. But they were definitely under a spell.

Below the terrace, two stories down, beside the dance floor and dining area was a large pool with Gatorade-colored water. The swimmers splashing around in it were even wearing 1920's bathing suits. Everything about the party was on point. She couldn't even fathom the details paid to make this party so much like she'd expect Jay Gatsby to throw.

Her sister Liv had left the classic book on her dresser one afternoon, hinting it would change her life if she read it. Sophia would never ignore such a subtle hint from the person she respected most. In one afternoon, she became acquainted with a work of art that forever endeared her to thoughtful and romantic prose.

As Sophia stared around the mesmerizing party, she tried to determine how she'd distract Cupid. She was going to wing it at this point. Hopefully something brilliant would occur to her. She had a hard time picturing a little naked child flying around the elegant party, firing off arrows. Then her eyes landed on the fountain in the middle of the large lawn. It had three levels and was the size of a motorhome, but the sparkling, cascading water wasn't what caught her attention.

It was the man standing beside it. He was probably the most handsome man she'd ever laid her eyes on. He was young with firm skin and had a timelessness about him, with a sophisticated expression in his brown eyes. Like many of his guests, he wore a smart tuxedo, and his blond hair was gelled and pushed back from his face, which was composed of perfect features. His nose wasn't too big for his face nor too small. His lips were the right shade of pink and his jaw was strong, making the smile that formed appear like the perfect accessory to his already polished appearance.

Sophia wondered who the man was who had stolen her attention amid the hundreds of guests at this lavish affair, and then she saw it and knew without a doubt.

Cupid had changed and wasn't at all what she expected.

CHAPTER FORTY

Sophia wouldn't have believed the man standing by the fountain was Cupid if it hadn't been for the bow slung over his back. It was a strange thing to wear over a formal tuxedo, but it made him appear more attractive if that was at all possible. He was an elegant gentleman with a warrior's spirit.

His discerning eyes swiveled around the party until they rose and centered directly on Sophia. He lifted a champagne flute at her, a silent cheer in the movement. She reflexively lifted her own, suddenly feeling drunk, although she'd only taken a sip.

Cupid smiled, and the words from when the main character met Jay Gatsby came to her as if she had them memorized, although she hadn't remembered reading the words of F. Scott Fitzgerald more than once or twice. They fit Cupid perfectly right then:

"He smiled understandingly—much more than understandingly. It was one of those rare smiles with a quality of eternal reassurance in it that you may come across four or five times in life. It faced—or seemed to face—the whole eternal world for an instant, and then concentrated on you with an irresistible prejudice in your favor. It understood you just as far as you wanted to be understood, believed in you as you'd like to believe in yourself,

155

and assured you it had precisely the impression of you that, at your best, you hoped to convey."

Sophia found herself descending the long staircase, her eyes pinned on Cupid as her hand glided down the banister. Party guests instantly moved out of her way, as if repelled, clearing her path. Cupid's eyes followed her all the way down, not taking his gaze off her until she was standing in front of him.

She'd made it to him quicker than she'd have thought, and the journey to get there had been a blur, like when commuting home through traffic and one forgets actually driving.

"Ms. Sophia Beaufont," Cupid said, extending a hand to her, his tone refined. "You made it after all."

She gave him her hand and he lifted it to his mouth, kissing the back of it softly. "Thank you for inviting us to your party."

He batted his eyelashes at her. "You can thank your fairy godmother for arranging this. I don't usually allow magicians at my parties. Their practical nature and concrete hearts usually spoil the vibe, but two dragonriders...well, how could I resist?" Cupid brought his gaze up, searching the house area. "Where did your friend, Wilder, go?"

Sophia pretended she didn't know and didn't care. She shrugged.

"Oh, there he is." Cupid pointed toward the house. "Enjoying the company of other party guests, as I intended."

Sophia turned to find Wilder on a balcony, surrounded by women, his arms around the shoulders of two. She had to refrain from throwing her hand in the air and sending a stunning spell at the jerk. He was supposed to be keeping an eye on her and ready to swoop in at any moment. How could he do that if he was entertaining a bunch of bimbos?

"Looks like he's had enough champagne," she said, working to keep the bitterness out of her voice. Just when they had made progress, she felt like they were taking several steps backward. Maybe that was their destiny—never to find their way to each other completely. She hoped not.

That was the key. Hope. What we stake hope on is what is important. Everything else is the options we didn't choose, she thought.

"Now, Sophia Beaufont, dragonrider for the noble Elite," Cupid
began, leading her through the garden around the fountains, "tell me
why you wanted to attend one of my affairs? Does this have to do
with Hiker Wallace?"

Sophia had to stop herself from yanking away in alarm. Hiker, she
wondered. Why would this have to do with him?

She was going to have to play this just right to get the information
she wanted. Not only did she want to have Cupid supply her reason
for being there, but she wanted him to fill her in on what he knew
about Hiker. "It definitely has something to do with the leader of the
Dragon Elite."

"You are much smarter than most magicians and definitely much
more open to strategic ways than the dragonriders I've encountered
in the past," Cupid said, steering her to a less congested area of the
party.

"Thank you," Sophia replied. "I feel we need to evolve our
practices."

"Evoking love in adjudication rather than force is about the
smartest thing any Dragon Elite has thought of in all my time," Cupid
commented. "Which for the record is about as long as they have been
on Mama Jamba's Earth."

"Yes, that's why I wanted to meet with you," Sophia said, latching
onto the excuse he'd given her.

They had come to a grassy knoll with a gazebo that wasn't filled
with lustful party goers.

"What you have to understand about using love to create solutions," Cupid began, taking her hand and spinning her about in time
to the music from the orchestra by the house, "is that it has to be
forced on people. Otherwise, people get inundated by work demands
and daily responsibilities and dreary Mondays."

Sophia took a single finger and drew it down the front of Cupid's
tuxedo jacket. "Tell me more."

He hazarded a smile. "Well, I think the best way to explain how to employ love to solve the world's problems is to explain how the weapons of love work."

Cupid took a step away and pulled the bow off his back.

So far, so good.

Sophia chanced a glance over her shoulder. Where was Wilder, she wondered.

When she looked back at Cupid, his gaze was worried.

"I was just checking that we were alone," Sophia explained, giving her attention back to Cupid, and making his soft expression return once more.

He nodded. "As I was saying, I can't let you have my bow, but I can show you how to use it. Then you can find your own weapon of love and use it for your dragonrider missions. That's what Hiker Wallace needs. He's been in hiding for too long and is paralyzed. After the Ainsley situation, I guess I understand."

Cupid came around behind Sophia, holding the bow at the ready as he braced himself beside her.

She tensed as he grabbed her arms and placed his bow into her hands. "What was the thing with Hiker and Ainsley?"

He directed her with his fingers on hers, indicating she should pull back the bowstring. "That's it. Get used to the way it flexes before we use an arrow. Dare I say, I couldn't actually put one in my bow with you around."

Sophia didn't know what that meant, but she had other competing worries right then anyway. "You were saying? Regarding Hiker and Ainsley?"

He chuckled deeply beside her ears. "I wasn't saying. You were the one trying to get information out of me about Hiker and Ainsley. I do many questionable things, but telling other people's secrets is not one of them."

Sophia gulped, feeling Cupid pressing up against her. She pulled back the string of the bow, trying to focus on whatever he was directing her to.

"Do you see how your aim needs to be on finding matches rather than judging?" Cupid asked, a soft whisper in her ear. "If you are doing your job as a dragonrider, then you no longer need to pick the right or wrong side. You don't need to fix disagreements, but rather make everyone love one another. It's that easy."

It wasn't Sophia argued in her head. That was the opposite of what the Dragon Elite did. They created justice. They created peace, and that wasn't about making others love each other. That was simply forcing solutions that would backfire. Making others love each other would only simmer over and erupt in their face later.

Sophia chanced a glance over her shoulder, her attention stolen by the many arguments erupting from the party close by. She caught sight of couples bickering in the distance. One woman threw champagne on a man. Another couple looked close to pushing one another.

Sophia held her bitter feelings inside, hiding them from the God of Love. This was what Cupid was doing with his corrupt bow, and it was wrong. Not only that, but his approach to justice would only prove detrimental. No wonder he was worried about being decommissioned. It was good Subner had made it so he could only intervene in the affairs of mortals. He was dangerous, spreading his toxic blind love.

Love, real love, wasn't blind. It saw the flaws in the other person and loved them still. It saw problems and decided to conquer them. It saw the debt and wanted to pay it.

"I'm not sure I'm a bow and arrow kind of girl," Sophia commented, pulling the instrument of Cupid's affection out of his grasp. He allowed it, confusion in his gaze.

"Well, that's understandable," he said, his eyes on her as she lowered the bow by her side. "What would work best for you to spread love?"

She pretended to think. "I don't know. What do you think would suit me?"

Sophia had never done it before, but she tried to adorn her best pouty face. To her surprise, it worked on Cupid. He put his fingers under her chin and lifted it up slightly to look deep into her eyes. "I think that you, Sophia, need to employ your gaze."

"Like Medusa?" she dared to ask.

He smiled brilliantly. "Like Medusa, but without the stone and killing part."

Sophia giggled, like the women she'd overheard that night. "I think I could do that. But how would that work for an adjudication mission?"

"Well, eyes, like sounds and like arrows, can be hypnotizing," he explained. "Here, let me show you."

Cupid took the bow from her grasp and set it down on the bench of the gazebo behind her. His gaze never left hers. Nor did his hand.

With a force to make Sophia gasp, he tugged her back, his hand on her hip and the other in hers. "Now, to change others with magic, using love, you simply need to find a part inside of you that's full of lo—"

He paused. His chin tilted to the side, revolving in the direction of the party where the music halted.

"What is it?" Sophia asked, stalling. She wondered if Wilder was still on the balcony with the mortal women or what. She was going to put him in a headlock later.

"The party," he answered, his tone suddenly stressed.

"Oh, is everything okay?" She tried to figure out how to stall as the sounds of crickets took over the music that had been playing.

Cupid pushed her back and turned toward the twinkling lights in the opposite direction. "Something is going on with the party."

Sophia's eyes skirted to the side. The bow was gone from where Cupid had left it. That was something, at least. Wilder had it. She glanced around the dark and didn't see him, but knew he was close fixing Cupid's bow.

She grabbed Cupid's arm. "Actually, I think it means the party is going well. Where were we?"

He tensed under her grasp, but then seemed to think better of it. "I guess you are right. I really will enjoy teaching you the ways of love and how to use it to seduce the other side into agreement."

Sophia couldn't believe what he was saying and that he thought it was okay. She covered the expression on her face and nodded, smiling. "Absolutely. Please teach me."

He leaned in close to her, his lips inches from hers. His breath brushed across her face. His eyes were locked on her. All she was thinking about was Wilder recalibrating the bow and fixing it so mortals and elves and everyone else were no longer affected with lustful feelings. She hoped she was playing the right part. She thought she was.

And then, Cupid quit leaning her back and instead yanked her straight up, his chin jerking to the side. His eyes narrowed.

"My bow!" he boomed.

Sophia tensed.

She prepared to see the bow still missing, but when she looked over her shoulder, Cupid's bow was there again. "What about it?" she asked, using the giggle the mortals had perfected.

"It's been moved," he complained, pushing her from his grasp and stalking over to the instrument on the bench.

"I'm sure you're wrong," she argued. "It was probably the wind."

His glare was anything but warm when he looked at her, a red heat in his eyes. It glowed as she'd seen demons' do. How funny the two weren't that far apart. The God of Love and evil demons, like love and hate. They were divided by such a thin line.

Sophia tensed and stepped back, nearly tripping in her heels, unaccustomed to walking in them. "Maybe we should return to the party. You could tell me more there..." Silently she thought, where there are witnesses.

Never before had she had such a distinct idea that she was in the presence of a psychopathic crazy person. It was crucial she didn't push things with him.

Cupid grabbed his bow, menace in his every movement. "Sophia, what is going on?"

She feigned a smile. "I don't know what you mean. I simply wanted your help."

"My bow," he said, looking between the weapon in his hands and her, the red in his eyes glowing brighter.

"I don't know what you are talking about," she protested. She tried not to look to the side for Wilder but sensed he was there close and ready to defend her.

"You know quite well," Cupid said, stalking forward and throwing his chest up close to her, pressing his nose in against hers.

Sophia didn't back down. She kept up the pretenses of innocence and batted her eyelashes at him. "What is wrong, dear Cupid?"

"What is wrong is that I'll tear your heart out with my teeth and I was just starting to like you—"

A loud explosion echoed on the other side of the gazebo, followed by a bright array of light. Sophia ducked and Cupid, unsurprisingly, dove for cover.

Sophia was just about to pull the sword she didn't have from her hip, forgetting she'd lost it when dressing for the party. A hand wrapped around her wrist and yanked her to the lawn, where her high heels sunk into the grass immediately, pinning her in place.

"Come on!" Wilder urged, pulling her through the grounds.

Sophia took his lead and ran fast after pulling off her shoes and leaving them behind to sprint barefoot.

She looked back and spied Cupid rising from his hiding place to find them fleeing.

A yell that rocked the ground roared from his mouth.

Then he pulled back his bow and fired an arrow that magically appeared in his hand.

She saw the arrow fly.

Saw it whiz past her.

Saw it strike the man holding her arm, pulling her to safety. It tore through the shoulder of his jacket and continued on.

They continued to run, not stopping from the attack or looking back at the crazed God behind them.

An instant later, they were at the edge of the property, their dragons waiting for them and a portal open. Wilder must have created it as they ran. He pulled her with a great force, although Sophia felt safer now with Lunis standing there ready to guard her.

Wilder pulled her through the portal and they tumbled through, falling onto the grounds next to the Gullington. With his arms around her, Wilder rolled several times, clearing the space next to the portal and making room for the dragons. Sophia didn't notice the dragons come through after them. She saw nothing but the guy hovering on top of her. They had stopped rolling and Wilder was covering her with his body, his legs on either side of her. He kissed her like she'd never felt before. He looked deep into her eyes with unmistakable love.

"I love you, Sophia," he said, shaking his head. "I love you more than anything. I'm absolutely obsessed with you."

Sophia could hardly believe what was happening and what he was saying. It made her feel their life could have romance and dinner parties. The cough that sounded behind Wilder cut into the surreal moment. It was the most frightening thing she'd heard in all her adventures.

She and Wilder tensed, and they both looked up to find Hiker Wallace standing at Wilder's back. His arms were crossed, and murder was written on his face.

CHAPTER FORTY-ONE

"Sir, we can explain," Sophia exclaimed, wiggling to get out from under Wilder. He appeared in shock and had stiffened up at the appearance of their leader.

She was finally able to roll him off her and spring to her feet.

Hiker's eyes were dark slits as he regarded them. In the distance, the portal was closing, and the dragons stood watching the exchange.

Pissing off the most powerful magician in the world with the one thing he said he wouldn't stand for, seemed to evoke dread in the ancient dragons, which did little for Sophia's own confidence.

"I'm fairly certain there's no explanation that won't make me kill the both of you," Hiker stated through clenched teeth.

It was just as Sophia had feared. The leader of the Dragon Elite would prefer for them to be dead than together. She understood, having been counseled on the subject by Liv. Her sister had encountered something similar when she started dating Stefan, a fellow warrior for the House of Fourteen.

These magical organizations didn't tolerate relationships within their ranks because it was thought to corrupt individuals and distract from their responsibilities. Lineage was also important, especially for a governing body like the House of Fourteen that relied on royal families to fulfill roles.

But for Hiker, Sophia sensed this was more personal after learning a tiny bit of information about him and Ainsley from Cupid. She'd gathered as much after learning Ainsley's history that there had been something between her and Hiker.

Why else would she risk her life to save his when his brother tried to kill him? It was more than just a close friendship or partnership between the elves and the Dragon Elite. Hiker and Ainsley could once have been in love.

Things had obviously broken apart, and Hiker was the only one left with the memories since Ainsley couldn't remember anything after the incident. Now he had a vehement reaction to the idea of a relationship among those in the Gullington.

Sophia also knew he was struggling to build the Dragon Elite back, and a relationship among riders would complicate everything.

"Sophia, I told you this wouldn't be tolerated—"

"He was shot by Cupid's bow," she interrupted, speaking fast. Pointing over her shoulder, Sophia indicated Wilder, who was lying flat on the ground after having been tossed off her in her attempts to get up. He was staring at the starry sky, a mesmerized expression in his eyes.

"He what?" Hiker asked in disbelief.

"The God of Love," Sophia began to explain.

"I know damn well who Cupid is," Hiker said furiously, his eyes darting between Wilder and Sophia.

"Subner ordered us to go after Cupid because there was something wrong with his bow," Sophia explained.

"He has it, and that's the biggest problem," Hiker grumbled. "Did you destroy the weapon?"

She shook her head. "No, Subner just wanted Wilder to recalibrate it."

Hiker growled. "He should have ordered you to kill the treacherous man."

Sophia actually agreed with this after meeting Cupid. The bow wasn't entirely the problem. It was the man who wielded it. She suspected he'd probably corrupted the bow over time with his flawed thinking on love.

"Wilder fixed the bow," Sophia continued. The man was still lying on the grass and starting to mutter under his breath. The hit from the arrow must have had immediate and strange effects on him.

"But he was hit by an arrow," Hiker guessed.

She nodded, bracing herself for whatever his wrath brought.

To Sophia's surprise, Hiker sighed, resigning slightly. "Of all the reasons you could have given me for what I just witnessed, that's by far the only one I'll understand and not punish you both for."

Sophia's chest rose and fell, overwhelmed with relief. "Thank you, sir."

She couldn't believe she was thanking him for not doing something awful to them. However, he'd warned her.

"We need to get him to the Castle," Hiker insisted, striding over to Wilder. "I don't know if there's any way to combat Cupid's arrow."

Swiftly, the leader of the Dragon Elite bent over and yanked Wilder up to his feet, who appeared drunk. His head lolled to the side before he jerked it up.

"Well, hello sir, aren't you looking lovely tonight," Wilder said, his words slurring.

Hiker rolled his eyes. "Oh, you are going to be a mess now, aren't you?"

He pulled his gaze to Sophia and winked. "For that one, I am."

Hiker shook his head, encouraging Wilder to walk with him, although most of his weight was supported by the Viking. "Hit by Cupid's arrow. You two really know how to get yourselves into trouble."

CHAPTER FORTY-TWO

"Cupid...Hm...Where have I heard that name before?" Ainsley asked, tapping her chin and thinking.

Hiker halted pacing in his office and narrowed his eyes at the housekeeper. "God of Love. Or rather of infatuation, and now he's struck Wilder, and he's in love with Sophia."

Ainsley laughed. "Oh, that's what you think? Wilder has been—"

"Yes, Ains," Sophia interjected. "That's how it happened. Wilder was struck by one of Cupid's arrows when we were fleeing his estate. That's what happened and why he is regrettably in love with me now."

"That's weird because I could have sworn that—"

"Oh, Mama Jamba is here!" Sophia exclaimed, interrupting the nutty housekeeper who was about to reveal their secret.

The small woman with immaculate hair smiled at the greeting as she strode into the office wearing a teal velour tracksuit and bunny slippers. "I just saw you outside of Wilder's bedroom, dear. Did you get struck by one of Cupid's arrows too?"

Sophia shook her head. "No, I'm just so happy to see you and get an update. Can Quiet fix Wilder?"

Mama Jamba gave her a knowing expression as she took her normal place on the leather sofa, curling her feet up underneath her.

"Quiet's powers don't work like that. The Castle, fueled by Quiet's magic, can cure an illness or repair an injury, but when it comes to love, he can't change things." Her eyes flitted to Ainsley and then Hiker. "You know well, don't you, son?"

Hiker grunted, looking out the bank of windows at the Pond lit by the moon. "Yeah, I guess."

"Anyway, Quiet can repair the wound from the arrow, but as far as the magic, well, that's beyond his powers," Mama Jamba stated.

"That won't do," Hiker argued. "I've seen firsthand how Cupid's arrows ruin perfectly reasonable men, making them slack from their responsibilities, pining after flighty women."

"Hey," Sophia complained.

"Oh, not you. I'm just recalling from experience," Hiker said with a tired sigh.

"He is asking for you, dear," Mama Jamba informed her.

"She will stay away from him until he's been fixed," Hiker ordered.

"Fixed?" Mama Jamba questioned with a laugh. "You really are cynical about love, aren't you, son?"

"He isn't in love," Hiker argued. "Sophia being around him will only deepen the spell. We have to find a cure."

Mama Jamba gave Sophia a pointed look. "I can only think of one person who will know how to 'fix' Wilder. The same one who told you how to find Cupid. But she is currently administering exams, so you'll have to wait to get a session with her."

"What are you talking about, Mama?" Hiker asked, his tone heated.

"Oh, it's nothing," she said, waving him off dismissively.

"Nothing," he growled. "This is my rider we are talking about."

"And Sophia is in the prime position to help out," Mama Jamba explained. "She knows that. I know that. And it appears Ainsley knows."

Hiker shook his head. "Whatever you are talking about is making my head hurt. How much longer is Wilder going to be like this?"

Mama Jamba shook her head. "Hard to say. Some believe love is forever."

"He is not in love!" Hiker bellowed.

"Of course, son," Mama Jamba assured him. "But I think this will have to wait because Sophia needs to go to Roya Lane."

"She what?" Hiker questioned. "She just got back from doing a mission that wasn't adjudication."

"Well, she will have to report to Subner in Wilder's absence," Mama Jamba explained. "And then, of course, if you want her to recover the dragon eggs then—"

"Absolutely! I want those dragon eggs recovered," Hiker nearly yelled, his fist by his side.

"Dear," Mama Jamba said, pointing to her pocket. "You have a message I think you'll want to see."

Sophia pulled her phone from her pocket and read the top text. To her surprise, it was from Mortimer. The message read:

Hello S. Beaufont, rider for the Dragon Elite. Be here in one hour. I have information on Trin Currante.

Sophia's head jerked up. "It's about Trin Currante. I might have a lead."

Hiker threw his hands in the air, relief finally overtaking his sullen expression. "Thank the angels. At least we are making progress somewhere."

Sophia rushed for the exit. "I'll be back as soon as I've got the information."

"I don't suppose you are going to tell me where you are getting your information from," Hiker protested, but didn't sound as angry as she would have expected.

She glanced over her shoulder at him. "I wish I could, but this isn't my contact, so I can't risk it."

He nodded. "Most powerful magician in the world and my riders still don't fear me enough to tell me everything they know."

"They fear you all right, son," Mama Jamba said with a laugh. "So much so, you wouldn't believe the things they keep from you." Mother Earth gave Sophia a sneaky grin that made her tense. She and Ainsley were enjoying teasing her too much with this secret regarding Wilder.

"What is that supposed to mean?" Hiker questioned.

"Nothing, son," Mama Jamba answered. "But at some point, you and Sophia really should work together. I think she is the only one who will help you to stop cutting yourself shaving and breaking plates when you eat."

"Sophia?" he questioned.

"Well, there's a reason your two dots are different on the Elite Globe." Mama Jamba pointed to the large object next to the bank of windows.

"Because we are both twins," he supplied.

She nodded. "As such, you two share the same struggles. Rely on each other and you'll get stronger. Do it on your own, and you are sacrificing resources at your fingertips."

Hiker nodded but rolled his eyes at the same time. "Obviously it makes sense the only person who can help me learn how to control the power I wield now is the newest, most inexperienced dragonrider."

"I'll try not to take offense to that," Sophia joked.

"Do what you will," Hiker stated. "But get out of here for now. I want information on Trin Currante. Then you can help me with this power issue. And I want you to figure out how to fix Wilder."

"That's all he is asking of you, S. Beaufont." Ainsley laughed. "Work yourself tirelessly to solve all the problems of the Dragon Elite, and for centuries of servitude doing everything he asks, he will repay you handsomely with rude stares and constant criticism."

Hiker cast an angry glare at the housekeeper. "Would you get out of here and make yourself useful?"

Ainsley curtsied, a sneaky grin on her narrow face. "Thank you, sir. Would-You'll go make dinner." She glanced at Sophia and winked. "See, his affections are so much better than hearty wages, employment benefits, or supportive management."

CHAPTER FORTY-THREE

Sophia knew feeling overwhelmed by all that lay before her was normal. However, feeling lost also seemed appropriate too. How was she supposed to help Hiker to come to terms with his new powers after killing Thad Reinhart? Yes, they were both twins, but they had very different experiences as such. And now she was supposed to fix Wilder of something she didn't think was entirely caused by Cupid. All of that would have to wait, though, because first she was going after Trin Currante and getting her dragon eggs back.

She still had a bit before she was expected at the Brownie head-quarters for her meeting with Mortimer. That would work out great because she also needed to report to Subner.

Stepping through the portal onto Roya Lane, Sophia noticed how deserted the usually crowded street was. It was a late hour, but still, the magical road was a lot like the Las Vegas Strip in that it was never quiet.

Speaking of Las Vegas, the city run by the fae, Sophia recognized the only other person on Roya Lane. It was none other than King Rudolf Sweetwater. He didn't notice her. He appeared completely in his own world as he danced through the street to music she couldn't hear.

As her eyes adjusted to the dark of the lane, she noticed the fae was wearing headphones and jumping around like he was doing hopscotch drunk. Not far from him was a three-baby stroller where she suspected the Captains were sleeping.

Hoping to spook the king, Sophia walked straight up to him as he turned about, throwing his hands in the air and shaking his butt as he rocked his head. She tapped him on the shoulder.

Rudolf tensed. "Captain Morgan, is that you?"

Sophia rolled her eyes, disbelieving anyone could be so dumb, but that was the brilliance that was King Rudolf. He was so dumb it was incredibly perplexing how he'd survived this long on the planet, and yet, there was something indescribably intelligent about the strange fae.

"Nope," Sophia said loud enough she thought he could probably hear her through his headphones and the music they were blaring.

He pulled them off as he turned around and gave Sophia a look of shock. "What are you doing here?"

She shook her head at him. "I'm working. More importantly, what are you doing here, and what have you done with everyone?"

"Isn't it obvious?" Rudolf asked, a serious expression on his face.

She actually smiled. "It's not. Please indulge me."

"I'm doing a silent disco," Rudolf explained.

"What? Why?" Sophia asked. "And what is that?"

"It's a disco, but you have headphones on." He pointed to the devices he'd pulled off his head. "It's this great thing where you dance through the street to music others can't hear. They all think you are looney, but if you do it in a large group, then they think you are having a party they aren't a part of."

"Okay," Sophia said, drawing out the word. "But there aren't any people around."

He nodded proudly. "I sent them all away so they wouldn't laugh at me dancing in the street with the Captains."

Sophia's eyes darted to the strollers. "They aren't listening to music, are they?"

"Of course not," Rudolf replied. "But they are dancing, I can assure you."

Peeking at the strollers, Sophia spied three sleeping babies. "Right. So what is the point in doing this silent disco if there's no one around to watch the craziness? Or why do you not have anyone else dancing with you...besides the Captains." She added the last part quickly, knowing Rudolf would instantly correct her otherwise. "Why not just dance alone in the comfort of your palace?"

"I don't like to dance alone," Rudolf stated. "And Serena kicked me out again, saying something about how she was social distancing from me."

"The woman you brought back from the dead and killed a powerful queen for kicked you out of your kingdom?" Sophia questioned.

"Yeah, she said my constant affections and support of her was really getting on her nerves," Rudolf explained with a handsome smile.

"What a catch that one is," Sophia said, sarcasm overflowing in her tone.

"Hey, don't get any ideas," Rudolf scolded at once. "She is all mine. You can't have her."

Sophia held up her hands as if in surrender. "No worries. I have my own romance issues."

"Yeah, you and the gnome having relationship problems?"

"Quiet?" Sophia questioned. "We aren't together. He is in charge of the Gullington. Well, he is the Gullington after all." Rudolf had been there the night of the battle, where Quiet almost died. He, as well as the Rory, Bermuda, Liv and the rest of the Dragon Elite, knew the truth about the gnome.

Rudolf nodded like that information wasn't the strangest thing in the world. "So, you'll not be with him because he isn't rich enough, huh?"

She shook her head. "I prefer to understand what my men say."

"Oh, you and Serena are complete opposites," Rudolf declared. "If you really want to understand what your boy says, that means none of those Scotsmen you work with are potential love interests. I can't understand a word that guy Rougher says."

Sophia squinted at him. "Do you mean Wilder?"

He shook his head. "I refuse to call him by that amazing name."

Sophia laughed. Rudolf was right about something. Sophia often struggled to understand what Wilder and Hiker said, their accents were so strong. That almost made it better because then she just made up what she thought they said.

Rudolf held up his headphones. "If you promise not to steal my dance moves, I'll allow you to join my silent disco."

"Thanks for the offer, but I've got a couple of meetings and actually have to run right now."

"Okay, next time then." Rudolf waved as Sophia strode for the Fantastical Armory at the end of Roya Lane. "Don't forget to set your clock forward one hour."

"Thanks," Sophia said, pausing with surprise. She'd forgotten in Europe it was daylight savings that night.

"I mean," he continued, something seeming to occur to him, "most of your smart devices will do it on their own. But if you know someone with something like a pocket watch, they will have to manually reset it. Wouldn't want them to lose track of time."

Sophia nodded, wondering how the fae had done it again, saying something so elegantly poignant and related to her. She'd have to reset Wilder's pocket watch for him. With all that was going on and everything that was bound to happen in the future, the last thing she wanted was for him to lose track of time...or for them to lose time together.

CHAPTER FORTY-FOUR

No one appeared to be social distancing in the Fantastical Armory when Sophia entered. She was surprised to find the shop full of patrons, especially since she couldn't remember ever seeing a single customer in the place. She'd assumed the business was a tax write-off for Father Time or they did all of their orders online.

There were gnomes, elves, and magicians all crowding the shop. They were all chatting excitedly, many of them sounded like they were bartering over products.

"Okay, we are going to have to limit items to one per customer if there's going to be hoarding," she heard Subner order from behind his usual counter.

"What is going on?" Sophia asked a figure in the corner sitting on a stool. He had a hood over his head, partially obscuring his face.

However, when he lifted his chin, Sophia recognized Papa Creola. "You started an outbreak of panic. There has been a rush on weapons."

"Me?" Sophia questioned, pointing to her chin. "What did I do?"

He shook his head. "Don't worry. Things will balance out soon. It's just the way the pendulum swings. When you fixed Cupid's bow, it made emotions swing the other way dramatically. Now instead of feeling euphoria and spreading love, elves are all angry about one thing or another. They started disputes with their neighbors, some being gnomes and magicians, and they have all shown up here for weapons."

"Well, you aren't going to sell them any are you?" Sophia asked. "They aren't rational, obviously."

"Obviously," Father Time said. "But of course we will sell them weapons. We are in the business of making money. By the time they get back with the sword they overpaid for, emotions worldwide will have stabilized, so don't worry."

"So you and Subner know Wilder and I were successful with fixing Cupid's bow," Sophia guessed.

"Yes, and thanks to you both, I don't have to hear Subner spouting hippie wisdom," Papa Creola stated. "I also realize you completing the mission came at a cost for you."

Sophia sighed. "Yeah, Wilder was hit with an arrow, but thankfully it was after he fixed the bow."

"Right," Papa Creola said, his eyes darting to the side.

"Do you by chance know how to fix him?" Sophia asked.

"Fix him?" Papa Creola questioned.

"Hiker's words," she answered.

He nodded understandingly. "Yeah, that seems about right. Gods more powerful and knowledgeable than me have been unable to cure the disease of love."

"You are as cynical as Hiker calling it a disease," Sophia observed.

"I reason it's a disease," Papa Creola imparted. "It infects its host, taking over with universal symptoms and usually can only be managed, but never cured. Once you fall in love, I think there's only one cure."

Sophia regarded the elf with an expression that urged him to continue.

"Time, Sophia," Papa Creola explained. "Time is the only cure for love I'm aware of, and it doesn't always work."

CHAPTER FORTY-FIVE

Sophia squeezed through the small door at the Official Brownie headquarters and crawled through to find Ticker playing on the floor close by. She smiled at the baby brownie, hearing his mother humming a lullaby to the youngest child in her arm.

"Si Hophia," Ticker said, bouncing a ball at his feet.

"Hi Sophia," his mother, Priscilla, echoed.

She pushed up from the floor, which was ironically dirty for being the headquarters for a place related to magical creatures who cleaned the world's houses.

"Hi," Sophia said. "I hope my meeting with Mortimer didn't keep Ticker awake."

Priscilla shook her head. "No, as brownies, we are used to being awake at night. And if you are Mortimer, then you are used to being awake all the time."

Sophia nodded. "He works hard, doesn't he?"

"Tirelessly," his wife replied. "I can hardly ever get him to take a break, but he loves his job, so time away from it isn't pleasurable for him. That's the way it should be, am I right? When you love what you do, you don't really need a vacation from it."

Sophia smiled at the notion. She'd rarely thought of her role for the Dragon Elite as a job. Even with the overwhelming stress staring her in the face with all the new responsibility, it didn't feel like work. It was more like she had a series of puzzles begging for her attention and the world was a rainy day, giving her the opportunity to sit down and put puzzle after puzzle together at her leisure.

"Yeah, I think you are right," Sophia answered the brownie, keeping her voice down so as to not wake the baby sleeping in Priscilla's arms. "I think if more people felt the way about their jobs as Mortimer the world would be a different place. People wouldn't be looking for an escape but rather living in the moment."

"I think," Priscilla began, seeming to muse on the words as she spoke, "the key is to feel essential in this world. Mortimer has that with his job. He knows what he does makes a difference. When we feel that, when we feel valued, it's easy to show up to a job even when it's hard."

"Well put," Sophia said, not having any way to improve upon Priscilla's words.

"He is expecting you, so please don't let us keep you."

Sophia nodded, waving to Ticker and making for Mortimer's office.

She found the manager of the brownies concentrating on paperwork when she entered his office.

"S. Beaufont." He cheered at the sight of her. "Thank you for coming on short notice."

"Thanks for your help," she offered.

"I wouldn't have sent a message for you to come so quickly, however, my brownies found something of great interest I thought you'd want to know about as soon as possible."

"This is about Trin Currante?" Sophia questioned, deciding to stand rather than sit in the tiny chair in front of Mortimer's desk.

"Yes, and like I said, it's time-sensitive," Mortimer stated. "I know from my position timing is very important."

There it was again. The mention of time. It was starting to create a theme in her life, and Sophia wasn't sure how she felt about it. First daylight saving and the pocket watch. Then Father Time's statement and now this from Mortimer.

"You see," Mortimer continued, "In my line of work, reconnaissance is of the utmost importance, but when to do it's really the key. I discovered where your villain, Trin Currante, spends most of her time. I also found out she is soon leaving on a mission, which would be a good time to sweep in and do this investigation. Not that I have any enemies, but if I did, learning about them before confrontation would be my strategy for beating them."

"You are as wise as your wife," Sophia told him proudly.

Mortimer beamed. "Why, thank you. She pretty much taught me anything of use that I know."

He thumbed through several papers on his desk, licking his fingers before pulling out a certain page. "Here it is. Yes, Trin Currante runs a company in the Pacific Northwest of the United States that's about to embark on a mission. They leave tomorrow morning, so that seems like the ideal time to find more information on the organization like schedules, routines, security measures, and so forth. Maybe you'll even happen upon what you are looking for, saving you much time and effort."

"Maybe," Sophia agreed hopefully, taking the page he handed across the desk to her.

"There's something else, though," he said a serious expression on his face.

Of course there was, Sophia thought, deflating.

"The organization Trin Currante runs was easy for me to find," he told her.

"Oh?" she asked, intrigued.

Mortimer nodded. "Yes, you see, the Brownies have been cleaning it for quite some time, even though it's mostly run by magicians—who, yes, happen to be cyborgs much like Trin Currante."

"I'm listening." Sophia urged him to continue.

"Well, we usually don't clean the establishments of magicians, since they have magic and can do the work themselves," Mortimer explained. "There are some mortals who work for Trin Currante, though. Anyway, the reason I deemed her organization worthy of our efforts is because of what they do."

Sophia drew in a breath, lowering her chin. "What do they do?"

"S. Beaufont, they make the world a better place," Mortimer answered. "I don't know much about Trin Currante, and I understand she stole something very valuable from you. But her organization, well, it has an altruistic mission."

CHAPTER FORTY-SIX

All Mortimer gave Sophia was an address for Trin Currante's organization and a warning expression that seemed to say, "Proceed with caution."

He couldn't tell her exactly what this altruistic company was or what they did. Mortimer said that wasn't really how the Brownies worked. They didn't always know the specifics of what good deeds the people they took care of did. Brownies worked through feeling, sensing when someone was good or when efforts were noble. He explained it was like a frequency. Apparently, there was a positive frequency that came from Trin Currante's organization. He couldn't speak about the woman herself, though, saying her cyborg equipment made it hard for her to read.

The company, Medford Research, was located in the Pacific Northwest in an airplane hangar in a small, idyllic valley. According to Mortimer, they were leaving the next morning on a mission, which would present the perfect opportunity to scout the area. Sophia didn't really understand what that meant or how they had discovered information if most people were gone from the company, but she trusted Mortimer. If he thought she should act fast, then that's what she'd do.

As she strode through the Castle, she paused beside Wilder's door. It was late in the Castle, and she reasoned he was probably asleep.

She pushed open the door, finding it unlocked.

He was sitting up in his bed, staring at the door like he'd been expecting her.

"Hey," she said, suddenly feeling shy.

"Hey there," he answered with a smile.

"You are awake," she remarked, surprise evident in her voice.

"Were you expecting to find me asleep, and if so, what were you planning to do to me?"

She laughed, shaking her head at him. "I was going to reset your pocket watch. Tonight is daylight saving."

He glanced at the watch on his bedside table. "That was thoughtful of you. I sort of suspected you'd drop by tonight, which is why I'm still awake."

"You did? How?"

Wilder picked up the pocket watch and turned the knobs to reset it. "I just had a feeling. I think that's common when you have a connection with someone."

Sophia tensed, taking a step closer to the door. "I'm sorry Cupid hit you."

Surprise crossed over his face before he seemed to recover. "Is that right?"

She nodded. "I've got to leave first thing in the morning on a mission related to Trin Currante. Then there's a thing with Hiker where he is making me do extracurricular work in my spare time. But once I have a chance, and my source is available—"

"Your fairy godmother," he supplied, interrupting.

"Yes, my fairy godmother, Mae Ling," she affirmed. "Anyway, once I get a chance and some more information, I'm going to find a way to fix...to undo what Cupid's arrow did."

The tender expression of hurt was unmistakable on his face. "Yeah, okay."

She nodded, backing for the door. There was so much she wanted to say, and so much she didn't know how to.

"You know, Soph," he said, pausing her when her fingers were on the door handle. "You might want to consider there's nothing wrong with me." He held up his watch, having reset it. "Maybe it's just timing."

CHAPTER FORTY-SEVEN

Timing, Lunis mused, having heard Sophia's conversation with Wilder the night before.

Sophia thought she'd sleep in to at least the time when she and Mahkah planned to go to Medford Research on their stealth mission. She reasoned she hadn't had a proper night's rest in days, and she was exhausted from the Cupid mission.

Alas, even after going to bed after midnight, she still woke up at exactly 3:33 in the morning.

She and Lunis had then spent the first part of the morning going over the strange conversation with Wilder and the others.

I wonder what the deal is with timing on all this stuff, her dragon continued, talking in her head. *Multiple people have mentioned that now.*

"Yeah, and why do you think he doesn't think getting struck by Cupid's arrow was a problem," Sophia related. "I feel like he isn't being realistic lately about our situation."

I think this runs deeper than the two of you, Lunis suggested.

"That's an interesting statement that by no means makes me want to know more," she joked.

Cool, he said. *I'm not telling you any more.*

"Well, now I don't want to know." She tried using reverse psychology.

Then say no more, Lunis sang. *You should head down here to the Expanse.*

Sophia stretched out in front of the fire, having been lounging for the last few hours. "I'm cozy, though," she explained to her dragon.

Yeah, but you said you wanted a dragon, and now you aren't even taking care of it, he lectured using his best "mom" tone, which was pretty spot on. *You said, and I quote, "If you get me a dragon, I'll take it for walks and brush it and feed it every day." And now your dragon sits alone in its cave with no one to pay attention to him.*

Sophia rolled her eyes and pushed up. "Lun, you are acting out again. Are you feeling ignored?"

No, he answered at once. Then amended by saying, *Maybe. If I'm honest, I can't really get enough attention. The other dragons say I'm needy. I say they are boring and emotionally cold and then the name-calling starts, but they aren't nearly as good as I'm at it.*

"I do hope the new batch of dragons has more colorful personalities," Sophia said sympathetically. She thought it must be tough for Lunis to be the only dragon on Earth with a sense of humor.

Well, so far, Blackey doesn't seem to have much of a personality, but he likes to try and evoke pain on the rest of us in the Cave. He chomps on Bell's tail when she is about to fall asleep and steals Coral's food.

"Wow, he sounds mean," Sophia exclaimed, not used to hearing of dragons acting badly. The others in the Cave were so mild-mannered they bored Lunis to death when he only wanted a bit of banter from them. A dragon who was unthoughtful and ruthless; well, that was a first, as far as Sophia knew.

"Blackey isn't mean to you, is he?" she asked Lunis. "Because if he is, then I'm going to show that bully who is boss."

Lunis laughed in her head. *Thanks, Mom, but don't worry. He doesn't come near me ever since I threatened to toss him out of the Cave. Since he can't fly yet, that would be quite the unforgivable fall.*

Sophia didn't mean to laugh, but it tumbled out of her mouth anyway. "I'm sure that scared him from bullying you like the others."

Yeah, but then Bell said I was taking advantage of my position as the senior dragon, Lunis explained.

Sophia smiled, guessing how this played out between the dragons. "And what did you say to Bell," she asked Lunis.

I told her if she wasn't careful, I was tossing her out of the Cave too and changing the lock so she couldn't get back in.

"I'm sure that went over very well," Sophia remarked.

I've been on the Expanse ever since Lunis admitted. *They kicked me out of the Cave last night until I had, and I quote, an attitude adjustment.*

Sophia shot into a sitting position. "Oh, Lun, why didn't you tell me?"

She'd been so busy she hadn't scried her dragon and seen he was sleeping on the cold grounds of the Gullington.

"I'll get down there right away," she promised, pulling on her boots.

And brush my scales and take me for a walk, Lunis said with a pouty quality to his voice.

She shook her head but laughed regardless. "No, but I'll keep you company until Mahkah and Tala show up."

Soph, even when you aren't talking to me, you still keep me company. That's the thing about the ones we love. They are in our head, regardless of where they are.

CHAPTER FORTY-EIGHT

Sophia felt so close to her old home and still so far away. The Pacific Northwest wasn't anything like Los Angeles, and yet it held many similarities only a local would understand.

As she and Mahkah slipped through the portal in the sky on their dragons, she felt a familiarity wash over her as her eyes took in the terrain below. The way the hills rose and fell into one another in this part of Oregon was very similar to the ones around her childhood home in Los Angeles.

The smell in the air was reminiscent of the pines and crisp mountain breeze. Many thought that Los Angeles smelled of smog and filth, but that wasn't her experience, or not how she chose to remember it.

After surveying the area, Sophia and Mahkah landed a safe distance away from the airplane hangar located on the south end of a small town. She'd asked Mahkah to accompany her because she wanted to maximize her eyes and ears during the reconnaissance mission, and she needed someone even-tempered. There was no one more so than Mahkah.

Sophia was still perplexed by Mortimer's strange warning about this mission. He seemed to want her to be successful while also not taking out Trin Currante or her company. That was a first for Sophia.

There were enemies and those she protected. There wasn't this strange middle gray area.

She needed more information about Medford Research. Then the Dragon Elite could reconvene and figure out how to take Trin Currante down...or not take her down. They were getting the dragon eggs back regardless. Sophia was certain of that.

Sliding off her dragon, Sophia surveyed the warehouse below. It was a large blue building at a small airport. There were several small jets and helicopters parked around the building, but not much else to give them information.

All of her attempts to find anything on Medford Research online had come up dry. The company had a very low profile. That was why they were going to go incognito.

Sophia figured since many of the "employees" were leaving Medford Research that morning for a mission, only a bare-bones crew would be left behind. Those types usually looked forward to lying back, playing games, and eating snacks while the boss was away. That was perfect for their purposes and the disguises they were going to pull off. The only concern for Sophia was Mahkah and his ability to act.

"Okay, remember to let me do the talking," Sophia urged him, watching as a crew by the airport fueled up a plane. They were about to take off on their mission.

They could follow the plane, but Sophia reasoned she needed to know what the company did, and the best way to do that was to get inside.

Mahkah nodded. "I'm the ears and eyes. I can do that and feel most comfortable with that assignment."

"Good," Sophia agreed, looking him over. "Now what we need to do first is make you look official. I'm thinking a starched suit. Something that looks like it's supposed to be expensive but isn't. Like a low-end department store suit."

"I don't have any idea what you're talking about," Mahkah admitted sheepishly.

She nodded. "No need. Just close your eyes and hope I get this right the first time."

Obediently, Mahkah pressed his eyes shut.

Sophia flicked her hand in the air, muttering a disguising spell she'd used a hundred times on her sister.

Just like that, Mahkah was transformed to look like a traveling salesman. He wore an inexpensive suit with a tie done up like he'd watched on a YouTube video about how to fashion them. His long black hair was redone into a long ponytail, making it look like he arrived in a Toyota Corolla instead of on the back of an ancient dragon.

Tentatively, he opened his eyes and peered down at his starched appearance. "This makes me appear credible?"

"It makes you look like someone who would call on a company that needs resources," Sophia explained. "Now, I need to look as equally polished." She pointed at herself, and a moment later, she was wearing a pinstriped skirt and jacket. Her long blonde hair was folded into a loose braid, and to complete the look, she was holding a clipboard. Everyone appeared more official when they had a clipboard.

She spun to face the airport hangar, grateful the glamoured dragons were hiding their location at the top of the hill. Currently, the dragons, who were magnificent at looking like normal terrain when in the mortal world, were disguised as shrubbery and trees.

The roar of the plane taking off was deafening for a moment. It was followed by a couple of helicopters, and then the large door to the blue airport hangar closed.

It was go time.

CHAPTER FORTY-NINE

Sophia found the main entrance, which wasn't as easy as she'd have guessed. This place wasn't like a Target that welcomed customers through the front. Instead, it seemed Medford Research would prefer no guests and didn't advertise their business. Things were getting more curious by the moment.

Sophia felt strange knocking at the door to a business, but it seemed so stuffy she decided that was the best way. She rapped at the "front" door.

A moment later, a squatty woman who smelled of cigarettes and appeared interrupted, answered. "What can I do for you?"

"Hi," Sophia said, swallowing and peering past the woman into a cluttered office with muted colors. There were several workstations and loud rock music blaring. "I'm here with Best Designs, an inventory organization business. We're all about providing solutions for expanding businesses who are losing track of their supplies because they are growing at an alarming rate and can't keep things together. If you have a moment, then—"

"We're good," the woman stated, about to shut the door on Sophia.

"Did I mention you automatically get a two-hundred-dollar Amazon gift card just by allowing us to do a consultation for you?"

Sophia asked, holding her clipboard up more prominently for the gatekeeper to see.

"Me or Medford Research?" the woman asked skeptically.

Sophia shrugged. "Doesn't matter to me. Whoever hears my presentation after making my assessments. Is the boss here?"

The woman shook her head, a smile breaking through on her face. "No, you'd have to pitch to me, which sounds like I'd get that gift card."

Sophia nodded victoriously. "Absolutely, you would."

The woman waved them in. "Then get in here. The draft is bringing in all sorts of dust."

Sophia and Mahkah walked through to the cramped office. There were several workstations, but the computers were off on all but one, which probably belonged to the woman. Sophia's eyes darted to her workstation, and she read a business card sitting behind some papers.

Tammy Swindle, Office Administrator.

This was perfect, Sophia thought.

"Okay, throw your pitch at me," the woman said. "I have about ten minutes until my smoke break."

Sophia nodded. "We'd love to, but first we have to do a quick assessment of your company. It won't take long, but it gives a general scope of your needs. You see, most businesses of this type lose valuable assets because they don't know how to inventory properly and we—"

"Don't care," Tammy stated. "Just go through to the main hangar. That's where you'll see a bulk of the inventory, but don't touch anything. Don't go into the offices on the second story, and when you're done, I'm shaking you down to ensure you didn't steal anything. Then I want a thirty-second pitch and my gift card."

Sophia nodded. "You got it."

"I'm going on a smoke break early." The woman smiled like a thought just occurred to her. "Maybe I'll take two. Who will notice?"

"Not us," Sophia sang, filing through to the main area and leaving the woman behind.

She knew they were in an airport hangar, but it didn't really hit her until she halted in front of a large plane, sitting squarely in the middle. It was like a dragon, not as awesome, but still great for mortal technology.

A guy with a bandana wrapped around his head rolled out from under a helicopter next to the plane. "Who you?"

Sophia held up her clipboard. "We're with Best Designs, an inventory organization business. We're all about providing solutions for expanding businesses that are constantly losing track of their supplies because they are growing at an alarming rate and can't keep things too—"

"Don't care," the guy said, rolling back under the helicopter.

He was another mortal, which was good for them. Cyborgs might have magitech to sniff them out, but so far, it appeared Trin Currante had left behind the real bare bones of Medford Research.

Sophia nodded to the upstairs area, where they were told not to go. That was where she was going to scout. She pointed for Mahkah to search out a ton of equipment at the back of the warehouse. They were supposed to be assessing inventory needs, so he'd need to catalog that, or at least pretend to.

Looking over her shoulder, Sophia snuck up to the offices on the second floor. Thankfully, she found the area empty.

Unthankfully, she found the main offices locked. Luckily, she had a few pieces of her own magitech she was employing for this mission. The first was an unlocking device she'd gotten from Liv. She slipped the universal key into the lock and waited for it to do its job. A moment later, the door clicked and opened slightly.

Sophia sucked in a breath as she pushed back the door to find a dark office. Her eyes adjusted immediately, and she slipped into the space, closing the door behind her.

She knew she had to have found the boss's office based on the size of the desk chair. The boss always had the biggest chair even if they maintained a small workspace.

Not wasting any time, Sophia slipped another piece of magitech Liv had given her into the computer. It made a zinging sound and lit up as it went to work, copying the files of the computer. They sprung up on the screen at once, scanning through various screens as they were copied onto the drive.

Sophia's eyes soaked in as much as she could, trying to make sense of it all. They would probably have to sort through the information when they returned to the Castle, but she was curious about what Medford Research did.

The drive flashed red when it was done copying files. It might give them enough information on what Trin Currante's company did and what she did with the eggs, but it might not. Sophia hadn't deluded herself into thinking the dragon eggs were simply lying with the inventory downstairs. She continued her search of the area. They still had a few more minutes until she had to give a bogus presentation to Tammy and then give her a legitimate Amazon gift card.

Sophia snuck through to the neighboring offices, finding them all empty. She was just about to copy files on other workstations when the artwork covering the walls caught her attention. They were all maps, but not ordinary maps. They were maps that showed the topography of the land. Over the top of the maps was a certificate signed by the President of the United States. It read, "To Medford Research for their dedicated efforts, detecting and cleaning up UXO worldwide."

Sophia's eyes squinted at the sign, trying to make sense of it when a door opened at her back. She dropped to the ground, hearing two strange voices as the lights flipped on. Sophia crawled for the other door on the far side, hurrying before she was spotted.

Thankfully the two chatting strangers seemed so engrossed in their conversation, they didn't hear her moving to the other side of the room. She flicked her hand at the area by the opposite door, where she remembered seeing mail cubicles. The papers all flew out, falling to the ground and stealing the attention of the strangers.

"What the hell?" one of them yelled.

Sophia didn't wait to hear how they responded as she slipped the other door open and snuck out. There was no one waiting, which was good because she was certain she would throw a lousy kick in the pencil skirt she was wearing.

Hurrying, Sophia trotted down the stairs and slid up next to

Mahkah just as two paranoid faces ducked out of the office door up the stairs. Their angry eyes connected with Sophia briefly before skirting around, looking for what could have caused the disturbance.

"I got the files," Sophia said, showing him the flash drive.

He nodded. "I think I've figured out what they do and why we can't destroy them."

Sophia expected him to point to a piece of the strange equipment sitting on a shelf. Instead, he leaned forward and indicated a man behind them sweeping the floor. "He told me."

"Oh?" Sophia questioned. "I thought I told you not to talk to anyone."

"He's the custodian, and they see everything," Mahkah told her. "It felt natural to talk to him, and it's not like I know what I'm looking at here." He indicated all the strange equipment she didn't recognize either. "I used my observation skills and discerned he felt underappreciated and wanted the opportunity to feel important, so I had him tell me what they do here as though he did it himself instead of cleaning the toilets."

Sophia had to give it to him. Mahkah, as shy and reserved as he was, could be a very good people person. "What did you learn?"

"They clean up old bombs and shrapnel from wars and military sites," Mahkah explained.

"UXOs," Sophia said, putting it all together.

"Yeah, they save thousands of lives yearly with what they do," Mahkah continued. "Even more importantly, their work saves Mother Earth."

Sophia let out a heavy sigh. "Okay, so we can't destroy this place finding our dragon eggs."

Mahkah nodded, conviction in his brown eyes. "We will still figure out how to get our dragon eggs back. As adjudicators, we are in the perfect position to find solutions, preserve peace, and make this work for everyone."

"I still get to rough up some cyborgs who trespassed on our home, right?" Sophia asked, her face quite serious.

A smile broke across Mahkah's face. "But of course."

CHAPTER FIFTY

Hiker read over the report Sophia had put together several times in silence before bringing his gaze up to meet hers. "I'm not sure I understand most of this."

"They use lasers to detect the presence of UXOs in the ground, which roughly means unexploded ordnances," Sophia explained.

"I get that much," Hiker stated. "But these cyborg pirates figured out how to break into the Gullington. How? They were created by the Saverus, who play into this how? They're actually good guys who clean up the Earth, but we have to stop them because they have our dragon eggs."

Sophia nodded. That all was accurate and to the best of her knowledge after reviewing the data. "I don't know, sir. Maybe Medford Research is a front for something else, or it's a bad business Trin Currante pretends is noble so she can do bad things, like steal dragon eggs. I think we need more information. I'm all up for breaking noses to get our dragon eggs back, but I just think we need to be careful not to wipe out Medford Research in the process since it appears, at least on the surface, the organization might be good."

What Sophia couldn't say was that her source, the Brownies, had confirmed Medford Research was good.

"Okay, so we're supposed to formulate a plan where you all storm in there and find the eggs, rough them up, but not kill them and not level the company, but also achieve our goals? Is that right?" Hiker asked.

"Correct, sir," Sophia chirped.

He sighed. "Your review of the data didn't find anything pointing to where the dragon eggs could be?"

She shook her head. "Honestly, sir, I couldn't understand much of the information. It was riddled with industry terms I'd need three engineering degrees to decipher. I know they use a technology called LIDAR to detect things in the ground coupled with aviation. That's about it. With your permission, I'll forward it over to my magitech source in Los Angeles, but it might take a while for her to review it."

He nodded. "Go ahead, but I'm getting antsy to make progress. Each day we let Trin Currante hold onto our eggs is another day they get farther out of our reach. I mean, who knows what she could have done with them already. They might be tested on or used for experiments."

Sophia shuddered at the thought, although it had already occurred to her.

Hiker blew out a breath. "I need to consider our options, but at this point, the best one might be to copy their approach."

"You mean, storm them with as much ammo as possible when they aren't expecting it and use force?" she asked.

Solemnly he nodded. "I don't like it, but we need to make progress here. If we can capture them, then we can get answers."

"Remember we need Trin Currante," she reminded him. "Otherwise, she has the kill switches she can use to disable the other cyborgs like she did with the prisoners we captured."

Hiker seemed to have considered this. "Yeah, I know. It's just that—"

Both Hiker and Sophia froze at the same time. They had different voices in their head, but they were saying similar things. Sophia was certain Bell wasn't voicing things quite like Lunis. His words rang clear in her head.

Some more heathen dragons are breaking free of their prisons! Get over here, Sophia!

CHAPTER FIFTY-ONE

Unsurprisingly, it was raining on the Expanse as Sophia crossed to the Nest. She'd seen rain before and it came down in little droplets, covering the Earth. This felt more like someone was taking buckets, hundreds of them, and tossing them out from overhead, drenching the land.

Sophia covered her head with her hood, knowing who was throwing buckets of water all over the Expanse. Just like why Quiet was waking her up in the middle of the night, she didn't know his reasoning and suspected she'd have to work her way through the mystery since he wasn't talking. If he was, she couldn't hear it.

By the time she made the long trek to the caves where the Nest was located, Sophia was soaked through. She'd slogged through thick mud for the last bit, and now her boots were covered in gunk.

Lunis was sitting nobly by the entrance to the cave under an overhang, staying dry and out of the rain.

"Thanks for the lift," Sophia grumbled, trying to kick mud from her boots since it was making her steps lopsided.

What do you think I'm an Uber? he joked, winking at her. Even though he was teasing her, she caught him looking her over, checking she was okay.

She was fine, although chilled to the bone and shivering.

Come here, he encouraged, holding out a wing for her.

She folded herself into his body before he wrapped his wing all the way around her, holding her in close, but leaving a space for her head. The heat of his body instantly took the chill away. Sophia could feel his insides like a coal-burning heater, drying her clothes and making her teeth stop chattering.

"Thank you," she said when she felt more normal.

Well, it's the least I can do since you have to walk using legs and don't have wings, Mortal.

Sophia laughed. "Yes, I'm such a simpleton with my two legs and no fire breathing ability."

You're quite short too and can be easily crushed. He pretended to threaten her and squeezed in extra tight before releasing her.

"More eggs are hatching?" she asked, looking toward the Nest entrance where she could only see the glow of the torches coming from around a bend. "How do we know they are devilish?"

You'll have to see for yourself, he said ominously.

Sophia nodded. "Oh, look at you selling the suspense."

The pair entered the Nest to find Hiker and Mama Jamba were already there. The Viking was drenched, as Sophia had been. Even with his increased speed, he wasn't able to escape the rain entirely. Mama Jamba appeared as pristine as ever, not a single hair out of place and her makeup not at all smudged. She must be able to portal around the Gullington, unlike the rest of them. It made sense, though, since she was in charge of...well, everything.

Hiker shook his head as she strode up next to him, displacing water droplets onto her like a wet dog shaking off.

"Hey, I just dried off," Sophia said, shielding herself.

"Well, use another drying spell," he commented, looking her over.

Sophia smirked at him. "I didn't use a drying spell." She pointed to the dragon behind her. "Lunis dried me off."

Hiker gave her an annoyed expression. "You two are very strange. We ride dragons, not hug them."

"You don't hug them," Sophia fired back. "In all your time with Bell, you haven't given her a big bear hug?"

He rolled his eyes. "I'm going to pretend this conversation never happened if it's all the same to you. Your strange behavior with your dragon might be the reason your crop acts so strangely."

Sophia followed his gaze to three newly hatched dragons that were battling. They were small, about the size of terrier dogs, and thankfully they didn't have fire. They were representing the primary colors in red, blue, and yellow. What was startling about them was they were nipping at each other, whipping each other with their horned tails and taking turns wrestling.

"Since you don't have any experience with dragons hatching since this is a first for us, how do you know this behavior is strange?" Sophia asked, although she had to admit there was something very off-putting about how the newly hatched dragons were acting. There was undeniable aggression in their movements like they were fighting for resources in the new world they'd come to.

"I don't have experience being around young dragons," Hiker answered. "And the collective consciousness of the dragons, according to Bell, doesn't offer much help on the matter since the first batch of eggs wasn't congregated like this."

Sophia nodded, remembering this bit from the *Complete History of Dragonriders*. The first one thousand eggs were scattered all over the Earth and hatched seemingly randomly over centuries. Sophia's batch was all together, setting another new precedent.

"Maybe the issue is the eggs are all together and they should be separated," she offered.

Hiker glanced in Mama Jamba's direction. She was squatted, regarding the three fighting dragons with a placid expression. "I know who can answer that for us."

"She isn't talking, is she?" Mama Jamba answered with a snicker, rising from her low position.

"No. Why offer your Dragon Elite any inside information on this subject," he remarked, a rare bit of sarcasm in his tone.

"I've given you everything you need to find out the information," she said, drawing out the words with her Southern accent. "It's all here for those who wish to look." Mother Nature made a broad motion, indicating to the world around them.

Hiker nodded, annoyance heavy in the movement. He turned his attention back to Sophia. "Have you had any luck finding information in the *Complete History of Dragonriders*?"

"Honestly, I haven't had much time," she admitted.

"With all the tasks you have burdened her with, I'm not sure when you expect her to figure this out," Mama Jamba stated, standing back as the three dragons started to take over the space fighting.

"Yes, there are many mysteries to solve right now," Hiker said with a sigh. "The Elite Globe, the newly hatched dragons, Trin Currante and of course, Wilder. I only wish we had a resource that would talk." He cut his eyes at Mama Jamba, but she didn't seem to notice or care.

A thought suddenly occurred to Sophia that she wasn't sure why she hadn't had before. "Oh, I know someone who might be able to help. I'll be back."

Hiker grunted. "Just be back before the mission starts tomorrow."

"I think what my dear son meant to say, Sophia, was thank you," Mama Jamba told him with a wink.

She nodded, running for the exit of the Nest, Lunis following her onto the Expanse, knowing exactly what her next move would be.

CHAPTER FIFTY-TWO

Thankfully, Liv knew where to find the person Sophia was looking for. She texted over the coordinates and Lunis and Sophia took off, *The Complete History of Dragonriders* in tow.

For as long as Sophia had lived in California, which was pretty much the whole of her life, she'd never been to this place—one of the rare wonders of the world.

"They are simply incredible," Sophia said, gazing up at the Redwood trees towering over her in this particular grove of the National Sequoia forest.

Eh, Lunis replied, not impressed. *Just look like trees to me.*

Sophia gave him an annoyed expression over her shoulder. "They are the largest trees in the whole wide world."

So I shouldn't rub up against one to scratch my back then? he asked. *Because I have an awful itch that really needs to be scratched.*

"No!" Sophia exclaimed, much louder than she intended. "You'll break the old trees with your spikes and strength."

Then you'll have to scratch this for me. He indicated with his snout. *It's right over there, to the left.*

Sophia patted her sword on her hip. "I'll scratch it with Inexorabilis."

And in return, I'll scratch any of your itches with my teeth.

Sophia flashed him an amused expression. She really wouldn't have him any other way. Without the banter, Lunis would be like all the other dragons, which in her opinion, were too dry.

Taking off in the direction of the coordinates indicated, Sophia kept her eyes out for the expert she was searching for. After only a few paces, it was clear Lunis wouldn't fit through the narrow paths that snaked between the trees. He could use a compartment spell, consolidating to fit, but Sophia sensed he'd rather do other things.

"Go on then," she encouraged, waving him away. "Go kill some innocent creatures."

He lowered his head and gave her a repugnant stare. *Did you want the dragon to become a vegan as to not harm any animals?*

"Yes," Sophia teased. "You can sustain yourself on hummus and carrots or figs and berries."

I'm considering eating you, Lunis warned.

"You wouldn't," she protested, pretending to be offended. "My life is connected to you, so if you kill me, you won't last long."

Actually, he said, looking off as he recalled a distant memory. *There's no account of a dragon eating their rider. Maybe like when your twin dies, it actually makes me stronger. I would inherit all of the power, and then world domination would be mine.*

Sophia giggled. "You sort of scare me, weirdo."

Same, he retorted. *Don't worry, I won't eat you because I'm certain your bad jokes would give me indigestion.*

"Good reason," she replied.

Lunis started forward, pulling up before meeting the majestic grove of trees that towered in front of them. The blue dragon contrasted magnificently against the canopy overhead before he disappeared into the blue sky.

CHAPTER FIFTY-THREE

For a girl who grew up in a magical house and was used to seeing bizarre things, she was in awe of the majestic Redwoods. They stood like skyscrapers, towering over her with quiet elegance. Sophia felt like she was in the presence of wise mages who held the secrets of the world.

It shouldn't have surprised her then that the person she was searching for was standing beside one of the larger trees, making it somehow appear small.

The three-hundred-foot-tall tree put Bermuda Lauren's height into perspective. She was large by mortal standards, but the giantess was considered big to her own magical race.

Her back tensed as Sophia took a step forward, a twig breaking underfoot. With a typical annoyed Bermuda glare, she turned and put her hands on her hips.

"And just like that, you ruined it," Bermuda snapped, disapproval covering her face.

"Good to see you, as well."

Bermuda shook her head. She was wearing a safari hat with a net around it and a camouflage outfit. "I've been tracking the knock-

knock bird for days and was just about to close in on it when you scared it away."

"Sorry," Sophia said guiltily.

"Don't make a joke about how I should ask who is there or try ringing the doorbell instead to find it," Bermuda warned.

"I wasn't going to."

This seemed to surprise the giantess. "Oh, well, that would have been your sister's reply."

Sophia held in her giggle. She could just see Liv saying something like that and earning a contemptuous glare from Bermuda.

Seeming to resign some of her frustration, the giantess took a seat on a fallen tree, making it sag a bit from her weight. "Well, let's have it then. Why did you come here and ruin my expedition?"

"I really didn't mean to mess things up for you," Sophia said, striding over, *The Complete History of Dragonriders* tucked under one arm.

"Is that...?" Bermuda asked, her eyes widening with alarm.

Sophia nodded. "Yes, and I was hoping you could help me locate some information in it unless you already know the answer."

"May I?" Bermuda held out her hands, her tone completely changed to one of awe.

"Sure." Sophia handed over the book. Before, she would have been reluctant to have a non-dragonrider take the book. It was the only copy in the world. However, Trinity, the librarian, had read it. Bermuda Laurens was also one of the most respected experts on magical creatures. Sophia reasoned she could be trusted.

With a great fondness, Bermuda ran her large hand down the front cover of the thick book. "Now, what's your question? Then we will tackle how to find it."

"Well, the dragon eggs are starting to hatch," Sophia began.

"How many so far?"

"Four," Sophia answered. "This is new territory for us since there's never been an incidence of so many eggs collected in one spot. The ones that have hatched so far, they appear to be..."

"Be what?" Bermuda snapped, impatience flaring on her face again.

Sophia gulped, disbelieving what she was about to say. "Evil. Maybe bad-tempered is a better word and evil is overdoing it bit, but that was my first inclination."

"Your first inclination is usually correct," Bermuda stated. "Learn to trust it. You'll be better off the rest of your life if you tune into that gut instinct. It's never wrong."

Rory, Bermuda's son, had said something similar to her once. Sophia nodded. "Anyway, I know the answer has to be in this book, but it's so vast, and I was hoping..."

"You're not asking me to teach you how to read, are you?" Bermuda asked, her face stone serious.

"No, I just thought that as an author and an expert on magical creatures..." Sophia instantly doubted her decision. Time was important. It always was, really. At the end of the day, time was all anyone ever really had. It was the currency of the world.

She slumped with defeat, thinking she should be back at the Gullington, resting up for the mission the next day, or working to find out how to help Wilder. She needed to research the twin factor and the Elite Globe. Sophia was just about to call Lunis to her and return when Bermuda randomly opened the book in her hands.

Her hazel eyes ran down the page before she pointed, a victorious glare on her face. "There you go."

"Wait. You found something on why the dragons are being born evil?" Sophia asked.

"Not just something, but the exact reason," Bermuda answered mildly.

"How did you do that?" Sophia questioned shock on her face. "You just randomly opened the *Complete History of Dragonriders*."

"I didn't." Bermuda sounded offended. "Nothing in life is random, child. As soon as you understand that, then you'll see the signs and cosmic force in your life, leading the way."

Sophia scrunched up her brow. "I don't understand."

Bermuda nodded as though Sophia's confusion was just a part of her DNA and couldn't be helped. "Everything in life is driven by intention. When we enter a space with a certain intention, then we change that space. When you're about to be presented with options to choose from and desire a particular one, you are time traveling to a certain extent, coloring that which will be offered to you. When an ailment befalls us and we make plans for a funeral or for a wellness party, again, we are creating the future. Intentions make this world go round. Does that make sense?"

Sophia thought for a moment. "So, before you opened the book, you thought about what you were looking for, didn't you? You set your mind on that, and then when you opened the book, you found what you were looking for because your intentions paved the path."

Bermuda twitched her mouth to the side. "The Beaufonts, for as many criticisms as I give your lot for being wasteful with smiles and careless with sarcasm, are actually very intuitive and intelligent."

"Thank you," Sophia stated.

"Learn not to thank people when they state the obvious, would you?"

Sophia shook her head. "I think I'll do as I please. Besides, my gratitude is more for me than for you."

An almost appreciative expression crossed the giantess's face before she whisked it away and pointed to the book. "Yes, I found what you were looking for using intention. It should always lead the way. Too often I see people focusing on what they don't want and wondering why they get it. You see people confused, overwhelmed even, thinking they will never find that which they seek. How can they be surprised when they don't? I just had the confidence to know I'd find what you seek, and I must say after you explained what's happening with the dragons hatching, I was curious too."

The forest around them was so quiet it made it easier to think. "The dragons are being born evil. Is this batch bad? Is it me?"

Bermuda pushed the book over so Sophia could read it. "I think you better read this passage."

Sophia focused her eyes on the words on the page, reading:

"Dragons are predisposed to a certain affiliation. Unlike humans, they aren't dictated by nature versus nurture. In creating the balance of the world

through these magical creatures, great reason was put into the set number of dragons that would reign the Earth one day. As previously discussed, the Archangel Michael's blood infiltrated the Earth, soaking into the dragon eggs, according to the legend.

"However, in order to ensure things remained balanced, other blood was spilled at the same time by the demon Nergal. Half the eggs on Earth absorbed the angel's blood and the other half, the blood of the demon. Although it was always the intention that dragons and their riders would serve as the world adjudicators, promoting justice and peace, to ensure yin and yang laws were observed, it was necessary that half the population also promote the opposite. For every dragon in a batch that's born good, there will always be one born evil."

Sophia's head jerked up after finishing the passage. "So they are supposed to be like this? They are evil?"

Bermuda nodded. "I'm as surprised as you to learn this, but it makes sense when you think about it. If a thousand dragon eggs had hatched originally and they were all good, then maintaining peace would never have been an issue. But we don't evolve in the times of peace and goodness. It's through adversary and overcoming the struggles of war that mankind has always made the most progress. Mother Nature and the angels set it out that there would be guardians of this world—you and the Dragon Elite—but you'd have a natural enemy, and it's one of your own."

Sophia shook her head, wondering why things could never be easy.

"You see, Sophia," Bermuda continued, seeing the frustration building on her face. "We are as in danger of being overrun by goodness as by evil. Those who run this show know it's in maintaining a balance between the two that the world continues to go round. I've learned as much in my travels and explorations of this great planet."

"But it says dragons are born one way, either good or bad," Sophia reasoned. "Then it said humans aren't. An evil dragon magnetizes to a rider with the same affiliation…"

Sophia paused, thinking. She recalled Thad Reinhart and what she knew about twins. They were also born either good or evil. Neither was both. If Jamison, her twin, had survived, he would have supposedly been a dragonrider and evil, according to Hiker. That was why the leader of the Dragon Elite had asked Mama Jamba to stop allowing twins to be chosen as dragonriders.

"Maybe some of us are predisposed to being one way or another," Sophia continued, trying to work things out in her head.

Bermuda shrugged her large shoulders. "Maybe. I think your situation is a bit more complicated than most."

It was like the giantess knew what Sophia was thinking about with the twin factor. "What if…" Sophia began slowly. "What if a rider changes? What if they turn good or evil? Does that change their magnetism to a dragon?"

Bermuda held out her hand, sighing softly, obviously irritated by this question. She randomly flipped through the book and pointed to a passage. "There you go."

Sophia leaned over, reading the words:

"Riders don't magnetize to dragons until their personalities are set, which usually happens around middle age. It's then that it's unlikely they will shift even when faced with great circumstances."

Overwhelmed by this, Sophia shook her head. "This is nuts."

"It's actually very extraordinary you magnetized to Lunis so early on in life," Bermuda lectured. "You are an anomaly, and I don't think we will see this situation repeated again. You were born good, and there was no changing that. And my son, for all his eccentricities, had the forethought to spot you as having dragonrider qualities."

"But, like the dragons, I was predisposed," Sophia said, her heart suddenly racing. "I was meant to be good, just as Hiker was. And Thad Reinhart was meant to be evil."

"I'm afraid it's not that simple," Bermuda disagreed, giving her a sympathetic expression.

"What? How do you know what I'm even talking about?" Sophia questioned.

"Because I see where your intention has led you," Bermuda stated, pointing at the book.

Without realizing it, Sophia had opened it randomly, and her finger was resting on a chapter related to the twin factor.

A chill ran down Sophia's arms as she read over the first few sentences:

"Intentions choose the affiliation of a twin which is sealed when the first act of magic is performed. That act, whether good or evil, sets in stone what the person will become and is countered by their twin. They are much like the dragons they will magnetize to, sharing the act of balancing the world. The issues for those who have the twin factor is in balancing their powers, especially when they absorb the other's strength."

"May I suggest," Bermuda interrupted, pulling Sophia's gaze away from the book, "that since you have learned what you came here for, you return to this section later. I dare say it can wait now that you know how to use the book with your intention. What can't wait's you preparing for a time-sensitive mission."

Sophia's mouth dropped open with surprise. "How did you know I'm about to leave on a time-sensitive mission?"

The giantess had a twinkle in her eyes when she said, "I would point my finger at something intangible like intention, but alas, it was that."

She pointed, and Sophia looked up to find her dragon standing in the distance. He was sitting on his hind legs, tapping on his wrist with a single claw to indicate time was of the essence.

CHAPTER FIFTY-FOUR

Before they had geared up for this mission, Sophia had a brief moment to explain to Hiker what she'd learned in *The Complete History of Dragonriders* with Bermuda Lauren's help. She'd handed him the book, explaining how he could look into the twin factor for himself and find the information she hadn't had the time to research. However, once the book was in his hand, it disappeared and then reappeared in her room.

For whatever reason, Quiet didn't want the Viking to have the book. He wanted Sophia to find the information, or he had some other strange reason for his actions. It was hard to understand why things were playing out the way they were.

Hiker didn't seem as disappointed as Sophia would have expected. "I'm busy enough I don't need the extra work, researching that which I've assigned to you to figure out."

She nodded bitterly, not wanting to remind him he'd pretty much placed the bulk of the projects on her shoulders. When she drilled down into it, she thought if she did complain, he might think twice about entrusting such big projects to her. He might conclude she wasn't strong enough. If she was really honest with herself, she might be overwhelmed, but she selfishly wanted all the major projects.

"Half the dragons being born evil though," Hiker began, gripping his beard, "actually makes sense based on my experience."

He paced in his office in thought for a long moment. "If my experience with the Dragon Elite has taught me anything, it's that not every dragonrider who comes to us is suited for what we do. I'd say, exactly half the time, a rider and their dragon hasn't worked out. You remember Gordon Burgess?"

Sophia nodded, having thought specifically of that man when this came to light.

"Well, he's just one of many examples," Hiker stated. "Of course, we went through a dark spell when mortals weren't able to see magic, and few came to us. Even then or before then, it was always a roll of a dice whether the rider who showed up on the steps of the Castle would make a good addition to the Dragon Elite, and it was always clear from the beginning. Either they were like Wilder or Mahkah or...well, I guess you."

"You are so kind, sir," she said dryly.

"Don't mention it," he replied dismissively. "Or the rider was the opposite, full of their own selfish desires and not willing to sacrifice or risk anything for the betterment of the world."

"The dragons and their riders are divided," Sophia commented. "They are either good or evil."

"I don't think I have to elaborate to you that this makes our mission more complicated," Hiker lectured.

She nodded, having thought about that. "We don't have a thousand eggs…"

He shook his head, frustration taking over his features. "No, we have half that. Now we have to figure out what to do with the other five hundred that hatch and how to minimize the threat they could cause."

"Sir need I remind you the text says they create balance in the world," Sophia urged, realizing the Viking thought an easy solution would be to just destroy the bad eggs. "We don't even know which ones are which. Many babies are born with colic or something and appear bad-tempered, but simply have an upset stomach."

Hiker actually laughed at this. "You'll have me believe those three angry dragons that just hatched are just having an upset tummy?"

"You said 'tummy,'" she joked, trying to make light and sensing Hiker was close to a new edge. She didn't want him to do something rash, which was exactly where she thought he might be headed with this new information.

The power had made it harder for him to think rationally. Now he knew the three dragons that just hatched, and probably Blackey could be evil. She didn't want him to do anything that might doom them to a worse fate than before. Yes, they had a thousand eggs and had just learned half of them were evil, but they still had more than they did previously. They simply had to figure out how to manage things.

First, they had to get back the thirteen eggs that had been stolen. Then they could turn their attention to fixing things.

CHAPTER FIFTY-FIVE

It was decided Hiker would stay behind while they charged Medford Research. He thought retaliation might be inevitable when Trin Currante and the other cyborgs got ambushed. Although the Barrier was back in place, no one wanted to chance the steampunk pirates ransacking the Gullington again. Sophia still didn't know how they managed to figure out how to trespass, and that was the main reason they needed to be so careful.

Hiker and Bell would stay behind to guard things. Wilder would stay behind because Hiker didn't trust him around Sophia. He thought being in her presence would only make Cupid's spell stronger, making him "illogical with feelings of love."

"At some point, son" Mama Jamba began, putting a coat of nail polish on her toes as she sat on the front steps of the Castle, "we're going to have to discuss your corrupt view on love and reconcile your memories with what your reality should be."

Hiker gave her his usual irritated expression. "Does this happen before or after you start sharing pertinent information with me that would make my job as the Dragon Elite leader easier?"

"Way before, since that other thing is never happening," Mama Jamba stated, her attention mostly on her nails.

"Insufferable woman," Hiker complained, turning around to face his riders, all of them suited up and sitting high atop their dragons.

"What was that, son?" Mama Jamba asked in a sing-song voice.

"Nothing, Mama," he said at once, a bit of fear creeping into his voice.

Hiker cleared his throat, facing the three riders, his chest held high. "It has come to this. We have dragon eggs that have been stolen from us, and I believe the best way to recapture them is to act fast and swiftly. Those steampunk pirates started this, and we're going to end it. I want you all to go in there, use force and find out where our dragon eggs are. Steal them back, the way they did to us. Show no compassion. No mercy, just as they did to us when they ransacked our border, devastated our lands, and took what didn't belong to them. Stay vigilant. Remember who you are. And return as quickly as you can, with that which we seek—that which belongs to us. All who agree!"

Mahkah and Evan yelled their agreement.

Sophia opened her mouth, but nothing came out, and no one noticed.

She, of course, didn't agree. Using brute force had never been her way. She would have preferred to research these enemies more, find out their motivation, and use that to get back what they wanted. But Hiker was determined they act and swiftly, and she couldn't argue that time wasn't of importance. She only hoped that while at Medford Research, a strategy occurred to her, because currently, she was coming up blank.

CHAPTER FIFTY-SIX

Although Sophia hadn't been able to decipher much from the records she'd copied from the computer in Medford Research, she'd been able to find security codes. That was going to make their jobs that much easier. She liked this part of the plan because it felt organized. What she didn't like was the storming part and the hoping against hope part.

That was the opposite of the way she operated. Sophia was banking on faith at this point. She felt certain if she held onto that, in a moment of inspiration, she could see the strategy and everything would fall into place.

You might be deluding yourself with hope, Lunis cautioned as they landed on the hillside where she and Mahkah had first watched over Medford Research before their reconnaissance mission.

The door to the airplane hangar was open, and there was much more activity happening around the building than the last time they were there. The crew appeared to be unloading equipment, maybe from their last mission.

Sophia narrowed her eyes, telescoping to see better. She was able to spot many cyborgs working, hanging around, or chatting. There were at least a dozen, but they weren't any match for three riders and dragons, she believed.

Starting to seriously dislike Hiker's plan, Sophia considered abandoning the whole thing and going back to the Gullington. It wasn't worth endangering themselves to search a facility they'd already been roughly through. Then she watched as none other than Trin Currante disembarked off the plane that had gone on the most recent mission. The cyborg appeared similar to the other two times Sophia had seen her, her wiry black hair moving around her head like snakes on Medusa's head. She wore black goggles, and her billowy pants caught the wind as she stepped off the plane. Her appearance wasn't what stole Sophia's attention and spiked her motivation. It was what she was holding in her hands.

The bag she used to steal the dragon eggs, Lunis remarked in her head.

Sophia nodded, recognizing the magic sack that had allowed Trin Currante to carry many large objects at once. She and Evan had used something similar when they stole back a few of the first batch of dragon eggs from Thad Reinhart.

Sophia watched as Trin wadded up the burlap sack and threw it at one of the men, slouched against a wall. "Put this somewhere I can find it when I need to."

He grabbed the bag as it connected with his midsection and nodded. "Yeah, boss."

Sophia turned up her enhanced hearing, hoping to learn more from the exchange.

"Hey boss," another of the many lackey of Trin Currante's asked, stepping forward. He was dressed similarly to the others with belts strapped diagonally around his midsection and around his waist. Over his shoulders, he wore a long black coat, and on his head, he had a top hat that had seen better days. These steampunk pirates seemed confused like they weren't sure if they were going to a fancy dinner party or straight into a war.

"What, Clive?" Trin asked, narrowing her eyes at the guy before her gaze darted to the side, seeming to spy something out of the airplane hangar.

"Now that we've hidden the—"

"Shut your face and don't talk so plainly," Trin Currante scolded.

He cleared his throat. "I was just going to say, can we get a break soon? We've been working nonstop since the escape."

"And we will until we're really free," she stated boldly, her mechanical eye scanning the grounds outside of the airplane hangar.

"Yeah, and I want that as much as the men," Clive declared. "It's just that we were hoping for a leave. Just a day or two now that we've got to wait for the...well, you know...to do what they do."

Trin Currante brought both her eyes to center on Clive as she shook her head of wires. "No, this isn't the time to relax. We will continue with our work for Medford Research. When the time comes, then hopefully what we've recovered will save us."

Sophia looked beside her at Mahkah and Evan, knowing they'd heard what she had.

"Save us," she mouthed confusion in her gaze.

They both mirrored her gaze.

"For now," Trin Currante continued, pointing out to the hills where the three dragonriders were camouflaged, "you all need to go after the dragons stalking us from the perimeter."

CHAPTER FIFTY-SEVEN

"Dare I say, I think we've lost our element of surprise," Evan called, sitting high atop Coral, his purple dragon.

Sophia let out a heavy breath. Apparently, Trin Currante could see through the glamour of their dragons with her strange cyborg vision. There were many surprises about this woman, but now she knew Trin Currante had done something with the dragon eggs, maybe on the mission they'd just returned from since she was carrying the sack down from the plane. The cyborgs needed the dragon eggs for an important reason—to save them.

"Yeah, I say we go," Sophia said, finding her voice strangely authoritative. "Evan, you want to go straight through the front door?"

"I like the way you think," he agreed, saluting at her.

"Mahkah, do your thing on the runway outside of the hangar," Sophia ordered and received a curt nod.

"I'll go in the back." Sophia didn't even wait to finish her sentence before taking off on Lunis, veering down as cyborg soldiers ran out of the hangar carrying guns and missile launchers, many of them attached to them like extra body parts. Trin Currante had disappeared inside, but Sophia had every intention of catching the ringleader. She was the one who would lead them to the dragon eggs. As far as she was concerned, the rest of the army of cyborgs were ones Trin Currante would terminate if they endangered her mission—whatever it was.

CHAPTER FIFTY-EIGHT

E van knew exactly how to plan the right attack on these jerk faces. After what they had done to his home, he was going to enjoy it.

He pointed Coral at a cyborg wearing a getup that would have looked better on a clock. The guy was mostly gears and gadgets, and his face was covered in a respiratory mask. He held a pistol in his hands, pointed at the dragon flying in his direction.

"Hahaha," Evan called to Coral, who never appreciated his humor, but that only encouraged him. "Gotta love a man who thinks his dumb gun will do any good against a fire-breathing dragon."

The man fired, and what shot out of the tiny pistol wasn't what Evan expected.

"What the hell, dude," Evan bellowed, twisting Coral to the right to avoid a collision with a blast ten times the size of the gun the man held. The dragon and Evan spiraled and crashed into a helicopter taking off.

"That wasn't how the plan was supposed to go," Evan stated, finding himself discombobulated as he tried to yank Coral back up into the air. She wasn't injured, and thankfully he wasn't either. On the list of good news, they'd decommissioned a helicopter.

"Dragon Elite, one," Evan cheered. "Stupid Cyborg Pirates, zero."

He realized almost immediately he might have counted the score too soon as three more helicopters took off, spinning around in his direction, all of them appeared to be locked and loaded with artillery.

CHAPTER FIFTY-NINE

It felt natural for Mahkah to take orders from Sophia. He didn't think she knew it yet, but she was a born leader. That wasn't something most in the Dragon Elite were destined for. In order to be a dragonrider, two parts of a whole had to work together.

A leader stuck out in this clan because the rider had to be slightly more confident than their dragon. Yes, they relied on them. That was inevitable. However, they had to have a certain knowing that made it so they could lead men or women, who were much more irrational than dragons. They had doubts and emotions and so many things that made it difficult to motivate them when fear set in.

Mahkah had witnessed something so pure and right in Sophia Beaufont when she stepped up and directed them, not glancing at her dragon once for affirmation. She simply knew and that was beautiful.

It was especially impressive to Mahkah because Sophia Beaufont was so young and inexperienced, but proved to him those things mattered very little in this world. He took orders without question from the young dragonrider not just because he trusted her implicitly, or because, unlike Hiker Wallace, he had no desire to lead or give orders.

It was because when she spoke, there was a fire in her eyes that was full of conviction. He didn't think anyone who witnessed it in the young magician would ignore it. If they did, they'd pay the price.

Mahkah knew without a doubt what Sophia intended for him and Tala to do. He barreled down on the strange assortment of men gathering on the tarmac. He'd seen these men before when they stormed the Gullington. They were covered in strange armor, with weapons attached to their body in weird places. They were half-man, half something else.

What Mahkah felt at that moment wasn't a vengeful desire to crush his enemy. He felt sorry for them that they were so far from what they'd been. He hoped to make their ends as swift and painless as possible. Unfortunately, they'd have to be ended, if the Dragon Elite were to survive. That was the cost of battle. The cost between good and not as good, the way Mahkah saw it. He hardly ever saw evil in the world.

As his dragon flew past attacks on the ground, weaving through the various shots, they—dragon and rider—used their collective power to open up the Earth. This was Tala's element, and he knew it better than any. The ground under the cyborgs began to quake. It split and they fell, sliding into a chasm that would swallow many of them, ending their attacks and making their deaths hopefully quick.

CHAPTER SIXTY

This wasn't how Sophia had planned for this battle to start. They were supposed to have the element of surprise, but regrets were about as useful as a bunch of pennies for a wishing well, so she let it go.

She was going to do what she did best and find out the strategy behind winning this whole thing. First, she needed to blast a bunch of pirate steampunk cyborgs, and by she, Sophia meant Lunis.

Several men cloaked in armor and wires and weapons faced her and Lunis as they neared the back of the warehouse, the dragon opened his mouth and unleashed fire unlike she'd ever seen him use before.

Sophia felt the rush of heat under her as it streamed through the blue dragon's body and flew out of his mouth, catching the men and making many of them combust at once. They had to be fueled by something flammable she realized, watching as fiery men ran in different directions. She didn't like what they were doing to them, but it was necessary.

That was part of war and conflict. More importantly, it was why the Dragon Elite did what they did. They presided over matters to make justice and peace happen to avoid further conflict. That was the hope anyway.

Many of the men on the ground darted away from the attack, but Sophia was proud to watch as her dragon swiveled his head around, sending fire at them. They either were hit or scattered toward the hills. As long as they kept as many away from the airplane hangar as possible, that was good news.

As Lunis neared the tarmac, Sophia dropped from her dragon when he was still twelve feet off the ground. He knew what she'd do, and she knew he'd serve as cover for her. Without saying a word, without a telepathic message, they knew what each other was doing.

That was the beauty of soul mates.

CHAPTER SIXTY-ONE

Evan wished he was Wilder. Not because he had great hair or dimples, although he would never say that to the dragonrider. It was because his dragon controlled the element of wind, which could have demolished the helicopters speeding toward him and Coral.

If the last one-hundred years had taught Evan anything, it was how to adapt. When the three aircraft raced in his direction, his dragon made a water main burst followed by a tank beside the airplane hangar to also explode.

This threw all three pilots off and gave Evan the advantage. Stealthily, he slipped up high in the air above the helicopters. Their guns were all pointed straight ahead. When the pilots brought their chins up, they realized what the moment of distraction had cost them.

Coral sent fire raining down on the helicopter to the right as Evan sent magical attacks to the other two. Like a baseball pitcher throwing for a batter, he threw one after another, assaulting the crafts and beating them closer to the ground with each assault. It was exhausting work neither dragon nor rider could keep up for long, but from the corner of Evan's vision, he saw Sophia slip into the back of the airplane hangar. If they bought her time to find the dragon eggs, it was worth it.

CHAPTER SIXTY-TWO

Mahkah had nearly emptied the tarmac of all the enemies at the front of the airplane hangar. From a quick glance, he noticed Evan had a pretty good handle on the aircraft where they were trying to make the most of him but thankfully failing.

They appeared to be making quick work of Trin Currante's crew, which was surprising since they hadn't gotten the element of surprise they had been hoping for.

Several centuries of experience had taught Mahkah Tomahawk one thing—when you think you have the advantage, you're dead wrong.

Just as there were no more enemies for him and Tala to bury into the earth, he saw Trin Currante inside the airplane hangar closing the door, just as Sophia slipped in through the back.

That wouldn't have been enough to make him worry, except he noticed lasers streaking through the space. Lasers he had heard the janitor talk about when he'd questioned him during the reconnaissance mission. He'd said, "We have a security system here you don't want to mess with. When put into action, it will fry you in place. No magic can defy it. That's why it makes Medford Research great, well, besides we save nations from destruction."

CHAPTER SIXTY-THREE

S ophia wasn't sure why, but she giggled when she found the door at the back of the airplane hangar unlocked. She felt like she was winning.

She entered the airplane hangar and froze, hearing the door shut behind her.

"It's locked now," Trin Currante said, standing in front of her, feet shoulder-width apart and a strange crooked smile on her face.

A dozen feet divided them. And lasers. Many, many lasers.

Trin stood next to a plane whose engines were roaring like it was going to take off, but that seemed unlikely since the airplane hangar's door was shut, closing the large bird inside the building.

If Sophia moved too much, she was sure she'd hit one of the lasers. Even from this distance, she guessed they wouldn't simply trip an alarm. They were way past tripping alarms at this point. The villains knew they were there. These lasers were hot, and Sophia guessed they would burn her flesh off.

She stayed frozen, darting her eyes around to check out her options.

"What's locked?" she dared to ask, knowing in this kind of position, the best thing to do was to get the enemy to talk to buy time. She needed that.

Trin Currante laughed, her mechanical eyes lighting up. She was such a strange thing to look at up close. Her hair was hers and yet not. It meshed with wires that moved as if controlled by an electrical current, and her face moved like a human's with facial expressions, but there was a strange mechanical aspect to it. Trin Currante brilliantly pulled off acting human while also seeming robotic.

"The door you just came from," Trin Currante said, stepping up on the stairs that disembarked from the airplane next to her, unfolded by an unseen pilot on the other side of the plane.

Sophia didn't understand. Why were the plane's motors going? Were they going to open the doors to the airplane hangar? She hoped the guys were there with their dragons ready to shoot fire at them. Then she realized she'd be at the epicenter of that attack.

Maybe not.

"So," Sophia fired. "I don't need to go anywhere."

She knew Lunis could hear her and he was panicking, as he should be. Sophia couldn't go through the door at her back. If she even flexed her hand, she ran the risk of hitting a fire-hot laser. She was stuck and facing a madwoman.

Please Lunis. Find an option, Sophia urged, realizing she had to do her part and stall.

"So, Trin Currante," she began. "Why don't you tell me about your childhood?"

CHAPTER SIXTY-FOUR

There was only one thing clear for Lunis: He had to get Sophia back.

He'd destroy this place, Medford Research, even if they did altruistic work. He'd demolish everything around. He'd ruin their chances of finding the dragon eggs.

All that mattered—all that ever mattered was Sophia.

She had to know that.

Whether their lives were connected or not, Lunis was in love with his rider. As it should be, but it actually wasn't.

Tala and Mahkah were bonded. Coral and Evan were partners. Wilder and Simi had a deep relationship built on trust and love. And Hiker and Bell were one of the same in many ways.

But Lunis…he unabashedly loved his rider Sophia.

He broke all restraints and bore not just into the minds of the dragons around him, but into their riders, coordinating an effort he hoped would free the girl locked inside the airplane hangar, imprisoned by lasers.

CHAPTER SIXTY-FIVE

Stall, Sophia thought, looking around for options.

Trin Currante laughed. "Like I'd tell you anything. I have no plans to tell you what I have in store. But I'll thank you, Sophia Beaufont, for giving me everything I needed to get there."

"Me," Sophia asked. "Don't you mean the Dragon Elite?"

She shook her head of wires. "No, I mean you, my little rider. Without you, I wouldn't be here, about to take my prize and get what I've worked so hard for."

How could Sophia be responsible for this, she wondered, racking her brain. She was also hitting herself upside the head, wondering how she'd been led in to this, potentially ruining so much for the Dragon Elite.

"I'm sure I haven't helped," Sophia said. "I'm sort of a dimwit. Haven't you heard I'm a new dragonrider? So green, I hardly know how to do anything of any use. Just ask Hiker Wallace!"

Trin Currante laughed. "You made it to the Great Library in record time and found it faster than most."

"Yeah, but—"

A shock hit the warehouse, making Sophia nearly topple to the side into a set of red lasers.

Was that you? Sophia asked Lunis.

Well, Evan, but yes, he answered.

Nearly sawed off my arm, she protested. *But thanks.*

Sorry, he replied.

"Well, that seems like my alert to go," Trin Currante remarked, boarding the stairs for the plane, which was still facing a closed hangar door. She waved, and half of her fingers were metal attachments. "See you later, Sophia. Thanks for helping me unbury that which will save me."

CHAPTER SIXTY-SIX

Lunis had no idea how to save his rider. He could blow up the airplane hangar, but that would also blow Sophia up. He was panicking, but he'd done what he set out to do, and the others were recalculating, directing their efforts to save Sophia.

He watched as Mahkah and Tala changed directions, heading for the back of the airplane hangar.

Soon, Evan was heading for them too, no longer having to battle with aircraft.

The two riders slid off their dragons and ran for the door Sophia had entered. Never before had Lunis felt such love for the dread headed Evan when he pulled out a pocket knife.

"I nicked this off Sophia, and was looking to use it," he said proudly.

To Lunis' surprise, the pocket knife was the one Subner had given her, the one with the glass slipper engraved on it.

Lunis normally would have scorched Evan for such a thing, but right then, he was so grateful the little heathen had been a conniving thief. At the end of the day, Evan was good through and through. Lunis knew by how he worked fast to try and undo the lock imprisoning Sophia. No one wanted her to die in that building. Anyone who knew Sophia Beaufont, really knew her, knew she was worth saving.

CHAPTER SIXTY-SEVEN

"Oh, just so you know," Trin Currante commented after ducking into the jet like she was checking on something and then retreating back out. "This whole place is set to blow when my plane leaves. So even if you don't touch the lasers, it's still…BOOM. You'll die and your friends trying to save you on the other side of that door probably will too. I had to use enough explosives to ensure none of my secrets got out there."

She pointed to the door at Sophia's back, where she'd heard tinkering.

"Thanks," Sophia said dryly. "Do I get one more question?"

Trin Currante tilted her head to the side, like trying to consider. Finally she shrugged, her movements robotic. "Why not."

"Why are you doing this?" Sophia asked, cutting past all the bullshit.

The woman who was mostly not human gave her an expression that was purely human. "Because all I want is to be like you. Is that so wrong?"

There was unmistakable sadness in her face and so much more. Something that spoke to Sophia's spirit, unlike any villain she'd encountered.

Sophia felt so much grief for Trin Currante and so much emotion for the predicament that seemed to have befallen her at the hand of Saverus Corporation. She also felt respect for the Medford Research organization. It was short-lived as Trin Currante cued a smile and grabbed the rails to the stairs of the plane.

"Anyway, I better be off," Trin Currante stated. "I'm sorry for blowing you up and taking all your secrets and your dragon eggs, but a girl has to do what a girl has to do to become a girl once again. I'm sure you'll understand in another life."

As she boarded the plane and the stairs folded up behind her, the roof of the giant airplane hangar pulled back to show the clear Oregon sky. Sophia didn't think much of it at first, knowing planes needed runways to take off.

Then, as if propelled by defying her thoughts, the plane Trin Currante was on rose up into the air like a helicopter, hovering just above the hangar before it zoomed off and raced away from Sophia and the building armed with bombs.

CHAPTER SIXTY-EIGHT

"Don't worry, guys," Evan said, squinting as he turned the pocket knife in the lock, listening for the tell-tale sign it worked. "I've honed my lock picking skills hunting around the Castle. Quiet thinks I can't pick his locks, but he's wrong. I've found manual entries into places like the showers and the dungeon."

Evan halted and turned to look at the three dragons and one rider regarding him with intense stares. "Oh…" He shook his head. "I've got no lock picking skills, do I?"

He backed away from the door, realizing he was going to be the reason Sophia Beaufont, probably the best thing to happen to the Dragon Elite since him, was going to die.

To Evan's shock, Mahkah, the most reserved of the dragonriders, stepped forward, urging Evan back behind him. Evan got more than the impression he should back up. He followed the lead of the dragons and took several large steps away.

All but Lunis moved back as Mahkah held up his hand and directed it at the door with a focus Evan had never seen him wear in one hundred years.

CHAPTER SIXTY-NINE

Sophia never thought she'd die alone. She'd been hoping not to die in this century, but it looked like fate had a change of plans for her.

She gave up hope about the time the picking in the lock ceased.

All she could think about were the strange things Trin Currante had told her. Too many of her messages had hit a nerve in Sophia. How did Trin know about how long it took her to find the Great Library? That was as strange as her knowing how to take down Quiet so she could bring the Barrier down and ransack the Gullington.

Then there were the dragon eggs. Why would she want those? She'd mentioned to her men she wanted them to save them, but from what? There had been a strange sadness in her that made Sophia want to relate to her. The worst part of it all was when she said all she wanted was to be like Sophia again. But what could that possibly mean? Sophia was just a girl who was about to be killed, buried by a huge explosion.

Buried....

That struck a nerve as Sophia prepared herself to die.

Buried....

She was so stressed she couldn't even form a connection to Lunis.

He had to be busy trying to save her. She was sad his efforts would be for nothing.

More than that, Sophia was sad she'd figured it all out and couldn't tell anyone how Trin Currante had done it and where the dragon eggs were located. Sophia was sad she'd never figure out why the steampunk pirate cyborg was doing this all since Sophia sensed it was for a very good reason.

CHAPTER SEVENTY

Mahkah had never been good with mechanics or spells related to it, but he also knew there was no better way to enhance skills than to employ motivation. He needed to save Sophia Beaufont.

That was the most important. As he held his hand up, trying to disengage the lock that was binding the dragonrider behind the door, he knew he didn't have what it took.

There was no way he alone could unhinge the lock. It was reinforced ten different ways, and breaking through the wards was beyond him. The dragons could fly through the opening of the roof where the plane had taken off, but according to Lunis, there were lasers all around Sophia, so that wouldn't help.

It appeared they were out of options. Then Evan stepped up next to him, his hand out at the ready and fierce expression on his face. He flexed his hand, a meaningful expression in his eyes.

"Come on, brother," Evan encouraged. "Together, we can do this."

There was his motivation. Evan was offering his powers to help.

If that wasn't enough, and Mahkah wasn't sure it was, the three dragons by their sides, stepped up and channeled their energy to the two dragonriders, loaning them their strength so they could use it to undo the locking mechanism dividing them from the most important dragonrider they'd had in centuries.

The three dragons and the two riders concentrated like they'd never done before, using all their power to unlock the door and free Sophia Beaufont in time.

CHAPTER SEVENTY-ONE

Dying alone wasn't so bad, Sophia told herself as she looked out at the empty airplane hangar, surrounded by the red lasers.

She'd tried to portal, with zero luck.

She'd tried to call Lunis, also with no luck.

She'd considered sprinting through the lasers but was pretty sure she'd be turned to ash. So she stood frozen, wondering how she could communicate what she knew so it didn't die with her.

She heard a churning at her back. It sounded like a chainsaw cutting down a tree, but there were no trees around.

She spun around until she saw where the sound was coming from.

The lock on the exit.

It was glowing.

A moment later, before doubt or wonder could set in any further, the door to the airplane hangar burst off, flying far off into the distance and leaving a cloud of dust and bright light that streamed into the dark hangar.

Sophia covered her head, shielding her eyes until she saw figures approaching. Figures she recognized. Ones she loved.

With a rush of emotion, Sophia jumped up and sprinted out of the hangar, throwing her arms around the blue dragon's neck and hugging him with a fierce love that expressed how happy she was to see him again in this life.

CHAPTER SEVENTY-TWO

The reunion had to be short-lived. Sophia yanked away from Lunis, darting back in the direction of the airplane hangar, and ducking through the door she'd just escaped from.

"Are you mad?" Evan yelled. "We just got you out of there! What, did you drop your purse?"

"Shut your face and come and help me!" she exclaimed, reaching to grab equipment from the shelves lining the walls. "We don't have much time."

The lasers snaked around the entrance to the hangar, making an arch around the shelves lined with strange gadgets and devices. Sophia didn't know what it all was, but she knew without a doubt she needed it for what would come next. The lasers cut into the shelves at about the halfway mark, so they couldn't get to all the equipment, but this had to be enough.

The first thing Sophia tried to grab was too heavy, nearly falling on her toe as she tried to lift it.

"Damn, girl," Evan said, catching the large object before it hit the ground. "You're nicking her stuff? Is that the way you're getting retribution for her taking the dragon eggs?"

"Less talking and more moving," Sophia demanded. "This place is set to blow any moment."

Evan's eyes widened. "Seriously? Why aren't we running?"

"We are going to, but we need this stuff," Sophia urged.

Mahkah didn't argue, simply went to work, hauling things off the shelf and delivering it back to the outside where the dragons were.

After two loads, they had as much as they could get to. They had loaded it precariously on the dragons, and for a short flight, it would hold. They didn't bother tying it down before lifting off and flying as fast as the dragon's wings would carry them away from Medford Research—the place where Trin Currante thought she'd left her secrets, but Sophia had figured them out.

CHAPTER SEVENTY-THREE

Thankfully there had been a delay on the timer for the bomb.

Yay for timing, Sophia thought as they landed just as the facility blew, sending a wave of heat and fire in their direction.

No one spoke until they landed outside the Gullington. Lunis didn't even communicate with Sophia, although they were sharing thoughts again and he now knew what she did. If anything happened to her, he'd know what to do. But nothing was happening to her, not now that her team had risked everything to save her.

Sophia slid off Lunis' back before his claws even touched down on the grassy lawn. She ran as fast as she could for the Gullington, screaming over her back as she crossed the Barrier. "Drag that equipment in here. I'm going to the Castle."

"Please," Evan yelled. "I think you meant to add a please in there."

Sophia was breathless by the time she barged into Hiker's office. He jerked his head up at the sight of her, his eyes scanning her for injuries. Mama Jamba was stretched across his sofa, doing a crossword puzzle.

"You're back!" he said, jumping to his feet.

"And she's got answers," Mama Jamba agreed in a sing-song voice.

"Did you find the dragon eggs?" Hiker asked, continuing to look her over like she might have the thirteen eggs stashed somewhere on her person.

Sophia shook her head. "No, but Mama Jamba is right. I know where the eggs are and how to get to them. More importantly, or probably just as importantly, I know how Trin Currante discovered how to take down the Gullington."

CHAPTER SEVENTY-FOUR

As Sophia had expected, the portal door to the Great Library was closed.

"There's no way in there then?" Hiker asked. "It's locked from the other side?"

Sophia nodded. "It doesn't matter. She's not there anymore."

Mama Jamba smiled at Sophia from behind Hiker, a twinkle in her eyes. "Good on you, figuring it out, my dear."

Sophia held in the prideful look, returning her attention to Hiker. "That's how she knew so much about the Dragon Elite. I dare say, she now knows more than we do. That was how she knew who Quiet was and that he needed to be poisoned to bring down the Barrier. She knew if he was sick the Gullington's defenses would go down."

Hiker chewed on his lip, his eyes darting to the book which had magically appeared in Sophia's hands when they'd halted outside the portal to the Great Library.

"She's read *The Complete History of Dragonriders*," Hiker stated bitterly.

Sophia nodded. "I'm sorry. I didn't know it was her."

"How were you supposed to know, dear?" Mama Jamba questioned. "Trinity has been the keeper of the Great Library for centuries.

It appears he's been gone for a while and was replaced by a cyborg who can glamour herself to look like him."

Hiker was really going to town on his lip as he studied the door to the portal. "You gave him the book, but it was Trin Currante, and that's how she knew all of our secrets?"

"She must have done something to Trinity long ago," Sophia guessed. "She wanted to get her hands on that book so she could find out about the Dragon Elite. She's been planning this for a while."

"But why?" Hiker questioned. "So she could steal dragon eggs? How would she know we'd get a new batch?"

"Maybe she didn't," Sophia mused. "Maybe she just wanted to know more about the Dragon Elite or thought we had some eggs. I mean, we did have a few before the new crop that went bad. She was definitely taking a risk by impersonating Trinity. This has been a long game."

"Taking up residence in the Great Library would benefit her even if Trin Currante didn't have you waltz in there," Mama Jamba explained, strangely offering up information. "I'm sure she thought she'd hit the jackpot when you did, but it's also inevitable for a new Dragon Elite to visit the Great Library. Remember, it's a rite of passage for you to complete training and get your wings."

Sophia nodded, remembering having to enlist King Rudolf to help her find the Fierce, which led her to the Great Library.

"Even still," Mama Jamba went on, "if a new Dragon Elite didn't enter that library and give her the hope of finding the *Complete History of Dragonriders*, the Great Library is quite possibly one of the most powerful places on my Earth."

Sophia's eyes widened with comprehension. "Because besides this book," she held up the volume in her hands, "it has every book ever written in the history of mankind."

"That's right, my dear," Mama Jamba stated proudly. "And knowledge is power."

"Trin Currante obviously wants to do something of great significance," Sophia warned, telling Hiker about what she'd overheard the cyborg say to her men.

"She needs the dragon eggs to save them," Hiker speculated, his brow creasing. "She wants to be like you. Does she think that by having the dragon eggs, she'll become a dragonrider?"

"I don't know," Sophia replied, not having worked out that part. That would come later. She smiled victoriously. "I've figured out roughly where the dragon eggs are and how to get to them."

CHAPTER SEVENTY-FIVE

"What exactly am I looking at?" Hiker Wallace said, peering down at all the strange equipment they'd recovered from Medford Research. The guys had dragged it inside the Barrier and now it lay just outside the Castle in the brisk morning sunshine. For once, it wasn't raining inside the Gullington, but Sophia didn't trust that, so they'd move it all into the Castle soon.

She shook her head. "I have absolutely no idea."

Hiker's eyes fluttered with annoyance. "Then why did you take it from Medford Research?"

"Yeah," Evan complained. "You made me risk my life to nick that stuff. Are you planning on selling it on Tbay?"

"Ebay," Sophia corrected, realizing she'd have to help him with his modern cultural references. "I don't know exactly what it's or how it works, but I know people who will. I recognized this equipment from reviewing those files on Trin Currante's computer. This," she waved her hand at all the strange equipment, "is part of some of the devices Medford Research uses to see into the ground to recover UXOs."

"What did you call it?" Hiker asked. "LiDAR?"

Sophia nodded. "Yeah, it stands for light detection and ranging. It's a system that uses the idea of radar but with light. Anyway, they use this at Medford Research to look deep into the ground to recover unidentified ordnances and other explosives that could go off, harming innocent people."

"That's all very fascinating you've figured out what Trin Currante's company did after she blew it up, but why do we care?" Evan asked, toeing one of the larger pieces of equipment.

"Because Trin Currante let a few things slip when she was holding me," Sophia stated. "She'd just returned from a mission when we got to Medford Research. I think Trin Currante was using what she knows about LiDAR to her advantage, namely, she didn't take things out of the Earth, but instead put them back in."

Hiker's blue eyes shone when they widened with surprise. "You think she buried the dragon eggs?"

Sophia nodded triumphantly. "Yeah. She let something slip about burying stuff. It was just a hunch. I pieced it together with what I'd recently learned in *The Complete History of Dragonriders* about how the original eggs were all buried in the ground where Archangel Michael and the demon Negal's blood seeped into the dirt, making the eggs either good or evil. That wasn't enough, so I asked Lunis, and he confirmed my suspicions."

Hiker's mouth popped open, a smile actually lighting up his face. "Dragon eggs buried in the ground will hatch faster, won't they?"

Sophia nodded. "So now we know Trin Currante wants the dragon eggs to hatch."

"Because she wants to be a dragonrider," Hiker guessed.

"I don't know, but it makes sense," Sophia agreed. "We now know she used her company resources to bury the dragon eggs somewhere."

"But where?" Hiker asked, looking out at the ground, an overwhelmed expression on his face.

"Well, I have another guess based on something I saw when doing reconnaissance at Medford Research," Sophia explained. "There was this topography map that was pretty prominent in Trin Currante's workspace. It was of a military base in Colorado. I don't know that it's the site, but it's worth checking out."

"And the files you recovered?" Hiker asked.

"They will probably confirm or deny parts of this," Sophia guessed.

Hiker nodded. "And this equipment?"

"It's going to help us find the dragon eggs," Sophia declared proudly.

"But we don't know how to use it," Hiker argued, eyeing the equipment with slight disdain.

"No, but my scientist friend in Los Angeles can help," Sophia replied. "We have what we need, we just have to figure it out, and I'm certain we can."

Hiker was silent for a long moment, thinking all of this over. Finally he nodded, giving Sophia a sturdy expression. "I have every confidence we can, and that's mostly because I know you're not going to rest until we do. Good work on this, Sophia."

CHAPTER SEVENTY-SIX

Springtime in the Gullington was like a dream out of a movie. The Expanse was a gorgeous shade of green that almost hurt Sophia's eyes, it was so bright. It contrasted perfectly with the blue skies. All of the constant rain had done something for the grounds and now it was the picture of fertility with the thistle blooming everywhere and new life springing up all over the place.

Sophia couldn't think of a better place to celebrate Easter. Yes, she missed being with her family, but the Dragon Elite was her family now.

To make the celebration even more magical, all of the dragon eggs had been moved out of the Nest. Quiet had done that overnight, so when everyone came out to the Expanse that morning, it looked like a magical field with Easter eggs everywhere, waiting to be hunted.

Although no one knew why the groundskeeper had moved the eggs out of the Nest, Lunis had some ideas on the subject.

The bad eggs have less of a chance of fighting if they are spread out, he explained to Sophia as they stood on the Expanse, looking out at the green grounds speckled with large dragon eggs of every color.

"Bad eggs," Sophia said with a laugh.

Well, that's what they are, Lunis muttered. *Those heathens who have hatched so far are making me want to move out of the Cave. They steal my food and fight incessantly, and Blackey snores something awful.*

Sophia continued to laugh. "I'd offer to have you move in with me inside the Castle, but I think you've outgrown those days."

Lunis leaned in close to her. *Don't tell, but I'm moving my things to the Nest since it's no longer occupied.*

"Things?" she asked. "Like your clothes and books and other worldly possessions?"

As well as my stamp collection and keyboard, he replied.

She nodded. "That makes sense."

I think he began speculatively. *That Quiet also moved the dragon eggs out of the Nest for a couple of other reasons. Following the logic we learned from Trin Currante, dragon eggs that are underground or in caves, have a higher chance of hatching.*

"Because they are being properly incubated," Sophia guessed.

Lunis nodded. *Correct. One theory is that to stall hatching, they should be out in the open. We don't feel as welcomed to the world if we're in the cold open air.*

Sophia remembered how Lunis, when still in the shell, had asked for Rory to make him a warm oasis in his yard. He was very happy, half in rich soil and surrounded by lava.

"So Quiet is trying to stall the dragon eggs from hatching?" Sophia asked.

Maybe just a bit until you figure out more about things, Lunis agreed. *You've just learned half a crop is born good and the others evil. There will be much more to learn if we are going to manage things. Currently, we have four eggs that have hatched, and they are all evil. What we do with them, I don't know, especially if they want to leave and magnetize to a rider.*

The thought was overwhelming to Sophia. "Yeah, then on top of recovering the dragon eggs from Trin Currante, fixing the world's problems, discovering how to solve our own problems here at the Gullington, we'd have evil dragons and riders to deal with."

Exactly, Lunis affirmed. *I think not having a bunch of dragons hatching right away would be best for everyone. We need to gear up for what's to come, but not before we figure out how to deal with what's already happened.*

Sophia nodded. "Yeah, and now we know what Trin Currante knows and how she knows it, the Gullington can remain safe again, so there's no risk of the dragon eggs being on the Expanse."

I don't think she's coming back to the Gullington anyway, Lunis said, beginning to meander through the dragon eggs, Sophia strolling next to him.

"Yeah, I think Trin Currante has what she wanted," she remarked, making their way to the men and Ainsley in the distance. The house-keeper had decided to serve breakfast on the grounds, laying out a picnic of pastries, fruits, meats, and an assortment of other foods on a blanket.

Now we just have to figure out why she wants the dragon eggs, Lunis added.

"And get them back," Sophia declared.

We will, Lunis promised with confidence. *I'm going to leave you to it. Don't tell anyone about my new hiding place, or the other dragons will probably try and move in with me. Bell is livid that one of the evil babies keeps biting her tail when she sleeps.*

Sophia winked at her dragon. "Don't worry, your secret is safe with me."

A glint of affection sparkled in his eyes before he looked at the sky and took off for the Pond in the distance.

"Get over here and get something to eat before Evan finishes it all off," Ainsley encouraged, waving Sophia over.

The Easter brunch spread was incredible. Ainsley had really outdone herself, making everything look pristine. Her cooking skills had come a long way in the absence of Quiet's help.

The elf pointed proudly to one of the dishes. "In honor of our newly hatched eggs, I've made deviled eggs."

"Haha," Hiker said, not appearing amused.

"And then, we have Every Bunny's Favorite Cake." Ainsley indicated a three-layer chocolate cake.

"Oh, for the love of the angels," Evan groaned. "Those jokes are as bad as Sophia's puns."

"Hey now," Sophia scolded.

"I happen to like Sophia's jokes," Wilder disagreed, batting his eyes at her from the other side of Hiker.

The leader of the Dragon Elite held out an arm and blocked the other rider. "Remember to keep your distance from her or you're going back in the Castle. I won't have this Cupid spell getting any worse and making you further lose your wits."

"Yes, sir," Wilder agreed and blew a kiss to Sophia.

She couldn't help but smile in return, her cheeks blushing.

"Where are the pancakes?" Mama Jamba asked, looking around at the spread.

"Well, I didn't make any, but I did make you some hot cross buns," she answered, indicating rolls lying on a platter.

"Right…" Mama Jamba started, not at all looking pleased.

"Well," Hiker began as Ainsley passed champagne flutes around, "you all eat up because after this celebration, we have many important things demanding our attention."

"Oh, there's always something to be done," Mama Jamba said, taking a sip of her champagne and smiling. "There's always a world to save and mystery to solve. But none of those are worth it if you don't take the time to enjoy the spring air and love the ones around you. Remember what I taught you, son."

Hiker looked strange with his bulky hand holding a dainty champagne flute. "That you know everything and will tell me nothing?"

Mama Jamba giggled into her flute. "No, that we celebrate every win." She held up her glass. "You know much more than you did. You know where the dragon eggs are roughly and how to recover them. It will take a lot of work to get there, but this is progress. This is worth celebrating."

"Here, here," Wilder stated, holding up his glass to join Mother Nature's.

Everyone else looked at Hiker, watching for his reaction. Finally he sighed. "Yes, that's something to celebrate." Holding up his own glass, he said, "To a new spring full of possibilities. To new life." He glanced around at the dragon eggs littering the Expanse. "And to the

Dragon Elite. May we overcome the challenges presented to us in order to make this planet a better place."

Everyone held up their glasses, smiling and clinking each other's flutes. "Cheers."

Sophia took a sip of her champagne, enjoying the bubbles as they danced in her mouth. The world was changing all the time, but never before like it was now with so many possibilities sprinkled around them. Her eyes swept over the dragon eggs on the Expanse. She realized something beautiful then.

The world was full of so much good and so much evil, but the Dragon Elite was ready to help maintain the balance between both.

CHAPTER SEVENTY-SEVEN

L asers.

They streaked back and forth in the narrow hallway, a security measure to keep trespassers out of the highly restricted area at Langer Technologies.

Sophia was so tired of stupid lasers. They were a constant theme of her current life. After being imprisoned and nearly burned to death by lasers at Medford Research, she confessed she would be happy to never see a laser again.

Unlike at Medford Research, these lasers were not static. They were moving back and forth, ready to catch any thieves who dared to go further. Thankfully, these were just security measures and wouldn't turn her to ash like the ones at Medford Research.

She would prefer not to bring out a bunch of security guards who she would have to put in headlocks and tie up.

"So how about you do some fancy moves to get past these things," Evan suggested as he stood next to her, facing the long corridor and eyeing the solid reinforced door at the end. "That's where we need to get through, after passing the lasers."

"I don't think so," Sophia said, thinking as she scanned the tech devices installed on the wall.

"Oh, come on," Evan stated. "You can do some fancy flips and then a slow-motion backbend like that one movie you made me watch. What was it called? Pattern?"

"*Matrix*," Sophia corrected. "How come you can name all of the Jonas Brothers, but you refuse to remember names of anything else from modern culture?"

"Have you heard the Jonas Brothers?" Evan asked, gawking at her. "They're great."

"They're a boy band," she argued, continuing to study the area in front of them, inches from where the lasers were located.

"And I'm a boy," he agreed. "That's what I'm supposed to listen to, right?"

"Yeah, flawless reasoning," Sophia told him sarcastically. "You're a boy."

"Man," he corrected, knocking his fist into his chest.

"There has got to be an easy solution to this." Sophia chewed on the inside of her cheek.

Evan rolled his eyes. "Sometimes you just have to suck it up and do what's got to be done. Let me show you how a man does it."

He stepped forward, ducking as one of the lasers flew overhead. Then he jumped as another ran across the ground. The dragonrider looked like he was doing a dance as he progressed across the long corridor, bending and stretching to avoid the lasers. To Sophia's surprise, he was avoiding them.

Making a strange limbo move, Evan nearly lost his balance and fell backward onto a laser as it streaked by. He sucked in a terrified breath and Sophia bit her lip, ready to fight whoever came through the door at their back when Evan triggered the alarms. He caught himself in time and rushed forward, avoiding the rest of the lasers and arriving at the door on the far side.

Sophia let out a relieved breath. He was in a safe zone.

"And that's how it's done, Pink Princess," Evan said, clapping his hands and brushing off his shoulders. "Your turn. Show me a cartwheel, and if you add a spin and a leap, you get six extra points."

Sophia nodded and narrowed her eyes at a small black box. She lifted her hand and pointed, making it burst. Smoke and sparks sprayed down from the device, but a moment later, the lasers all faded away, making her path clear.

"How much do I get for doing that?" she asked.

Evan shook his head. "Sure, take the easy way out. Anyone could bring down the security system so they could waltz through the high-security area."

"But real men break a sweat to get the job done, is that right?" she teased, turning to face the last door dividing them from what they were after.

The equipment they had stolen from Medford Research wasn't complete for what they needed to recover the dragon eggs from underground, where Sophia suspected Trin Currante had buried them.

The LiDAR equipment was missing some important components according to Alicia, the magitech scientist she had enlisted to help them with this project. She had shown Sophia what to look for and even given her the idea to steal it from Langer Technologies, a place where she used to work.

Alicia had outfitted Sophia with the security badges she needed to get inside after hours. She had explained they would have to get by the rest of the security measures on their own.

It was actually pretty genius, Sophia thought. What better place to steal the LiDAR technology from than one of the competing firms to Medford Research. Getting it from Langer ensured they would be able to find what they needed.

First, they had to get through the last major obstacle, a thick metal reinforced door.

"Why don't you try that handy dandy spell you just used to fry that electronic box?" Evan suggested.

"That was an exploding spell," Sophia explained. "I don't think you want me throwing that at a solid metal door with us standing so close."

Evan gawked at her. "You used an exploding spell on something just over my head?" He pointed to the burned-out part of the wall, only a few feet away.

"Oh, what are you worried about?" she joked. "You could have employed some of those sweet moves you did to get around the lasers to avoid the explosion."

"What are you telling me, I can dodge bullets?" Evan asked, repeating a line from the *Matrix*. That had not really stopped since Sophia showed him the movie. She was seriously considering never showing him anything ever again.

She shook her head, centering her attention on opening the security door.

"No," he said with disappointment. "You were supposed to reply with, 'No, Neo. What I'm telling you is when you're ready, you'll not have to.'"

"I'm not calling you Neo," she declared. Alicia had given her a universal key, but ironically it wouldn't work on this. For as helpful as the key was, it didn't work on a lot of locks.

The door could only be opened with three keys and a password, all of which Sophia didn't have. She had maybe been a bit naïve to think she would figure this part out once she got to Langer Technology.

"How are we going to open this door?" Sophia muttered.

"Have you considered there's no door?" Evan speculated.

"Have you considered how you'll look when I break your nose?" she asked.

"I'm trying to free your mind," Evan said, doing his best impression of Morpheus, which was pretty awful. "I can only show you the door. You're the one who has to walk through it."

"That's it," Sophia said. "You're brilliant. You figured it out."

He nodded smugly. "About time you see that. What did I figure out exactly?"

"I kept trying to figure out how to open the door," Sophia explained. "But we're magicians. We don't need to open doors when we can walk through them."

"You're my kind of woman, Blondie," Evan said, looking

impressed. "You're already drunk, and it's morning our time in Scotland."

Sophia sighed. "I'm not drunk. Remember that spell I was trying to master the other day?"

He yawned. "I know you think that like Wilder, I pay attention to every bloody thing you do, but I really don't."

"Fine," Sophia stated. "It was a reverse object permeance spell."

He nodded, seeming to be following her. "Totally. I just need you to explain what that is."

"Well, object permeance is the idea that something tangible continues to exist even when it can't be seen," Sophia began to explain. "And—"

"Wait, I'm going to need you to explain this to me like I'm five years old," Evan said, making a reference to *The Office*. After he finished the *Matrix* and highjacked Sophia's account, he had started marathoning episodes of the show. She was certain she would hear Michael Scott lines for the rest of her very long life.

"Okay, remember when you were a kid and would close your eyes and think it meant you were hidden?" Sophia asked.

He shrugged. "When I was a kid. Last week. Sure."

"Object permeance states the thing continues to exist even if you can't see it," Sophia explained.

"Can we call it something else like Thing Still There theory?"

"Well," she said, drawing out the word and ignoring him, "the spell my brother Clark was trying to teach me is the reverse. If you close your eyes, using the spell, then the object doesn't exist and therefore…"

"We can blow it up," Evan said proudly, triumph on his face.

Sophia slumped with defeat. "No, I thought we could walk through the door.

"Oh," he said, looking equally defeated. "I guess, but that doesn't seem as cool."

"Walking through walls doesn't seem cool to you?" she asked skeptically.

He shrugged. "At what point do you offer me the red or blue pill and give me the decision to jump down a rabbit hole?"

"At what point do you stop being a pain in my butt?" Sophia queried, mock seriousness in her voice.

Evan laughed. "Hah-ha! That's what she said."

"Okay, let's do this before I murder you." Sophia turned to face the door, calling the spell to her mind. "You'll need to close your eyes and hold my hand."

"At last, you get to have your way with me," he said, holding out his hand.

Sophia had to refrain from laughing. "If that was true, then you would be gagged."

"Ew...Kinky."

"Shush it and close your eyes," she ordered and took his hand. It was sweaty in hers. "I'll tell you when to walk through."

"If you make me hit a wall, I'm going to be mad."

"Noted." Sophia closed her own eyes and hoped this spell worked. She had been working on it since Clark shared it with her but hadn't gotten it to work entirely yet. It was her hope she could get into places in the Castle Quiet had on lockdown, but either she was bad at the spell, or Quiet had outmaneuvered her. She expected the pressure of the moment would make it so she was successful with the spell where she had failed in the past.

She repeated the ancient words that evoked the spell in her mind, forcing all of her energy around them and honing her attention on a single idea. Sophia knew there wouldn't be any signs it would work based on what Clark had told her. She would just have to have blind faith.

She nearly giggled at the pun, but refrained, keeping her power focused.

When she felt there wasn't anything else she could do, Sophia stepped forward, expecting her boots to meet a solid surface. She didn't and continued forward, walking through something that felt like cobwebs. Like the silk of the webs, it registered but didn't hold one back.

"Oh, that tastes weird," Evan remarked.

"Dude, stop being a mouth breather," Sophia whispered, walking blindly. It was hard to know when they had gotten through since the door was much thicker than most. She didn't want to stop part of the way through and have Evan stuck in a metal door....or maybe she did, on second thought.

Sophia took a few extra steps for good measure, and when she sensed she was nearing something, she halted and opened her eyes.

They were in a brand-new room lined with shelves full of strange and awesome technology. Evan's hand was still in hers. To her relief, they'd made it through the metal door.

"Open your eyes," she whispered in the darkened room.

"Oh, baby," Evan said, smoothly. "Now things are heating up."

"I'm about to roundhouse-kick you in the head," Sophia threatened.

His eyes popped open and he flashed her a smile. "I know kung fu," Evan remarked, doing his impression of Neo when he would download lessons.

Sophia shook his head. "No, no, you don't."

CHAPTER SEVENTY-EIGHT

L unis was disguised with glamour as a U-Haul truck when he and Sophia pulled up outside of John's Electronic Repair shop in West Hollywood with all the parts she and Evan had snagged from Langer Technologies.

She disembarked from his back and unloaded the equipment he had carried through the portals.

"Need help with that, young lady?" a guy asked from the other side of the street.

"No thanks," she said, looking over her shoulder. The last thing she needed was some mortal getting too close and figuring out her moving truck was actually a giant blue dragon.

The man didn't listen to her and came across the road with a dignified swagger in his movements.

Sophia rolled her eyes, taking the first load to the front of the shop and leaving it on the step.

"Oh, come on, sweetheart," the man with a black beard and a white tip said, smiling at her. "I'll work for pizza."

"I'm broke, which is why I hired a U-Haul instead of movers," she stated, giving Lunis a commiserate expression as she pulled another load from the saddlebags attached to his back.

"Oh, well, maybe tacos are more your style," the man insisted. "We could share some."

"No," Sophia said more forcefully.

"If you're not into tacos, then you're nacho my type," the guy said.

Sophia froze with her back to the man. Holding a heavy load, she turned. "Plato, is that you?"

The lynx transformed immediately, shrinking down into his usual unassuming form as a black and white American shorthaired cat. "Guilty, as charged."

Sophia sighed and set the box of equipment down. "Do you seriously have nothing better to do than annoy me when I'm trying to save the world?"

He seemed to think for a moment, his whiskers twitching. "Yeah, I find it brings meaning to my life to stall your noble missions with tomfoolery."

"You would." She headed back for her dragon to pick up the last load. "I didn't know you could transform into a human. I've never seen you do your voodoo in front of anyone."

"Well," he said, drawing out the word. "You're not just anyone. And I can transform into many things. It doesn't rob me of life to transform in front of a rider or dragon, little known fact."

"Always full of surprises, aren't you?" Sophia pulled the last of the LiDAR equipment off Lunis' back and gave him a grateful smile. "You can buzz off if you like. I'll be back to the Gullington after I figure out LiDAR technology and charter a plane."

Fine, he said with a wink. *I'll just buzz on home like a good little bee.*

"Charter a plane, huh?" Plato asked casually, licking his paw. "Why ever would you do that when you have dragons who are so much more emission friendly?"

Sophia took the last of the equipment and set it down shaking out her hands from the heavy load. "Because apparently the technology can mess with their cosmic forces or something. That was Hiker's concern anyway. Medford Research and all the other firms use aviation coupled with LiDAR, so that's what he wants to do."

"But," Plato countered, tilting his head back and forth, "It goes to reason the dragon's magic could also enhance the LiDAR, making it more efficient. Then you don't have to charter a plane and get to save your dollars. Next time you can hire movers and buy friendly old men pizza."

Sophia thought about this. She wasn't even sure it would work, using the LiDAR equipment on the dragons, but Plato had a point that the dragons could turn it into magitech. "Technology doesn't seem to bother Lunis," she reasoned, looking at her dragon for confirmation.

It makes my life better, he declared. *However, I'm the new generation. The other dragons are against it, subscribing to Hiker's mindset that it detracts from their powers.*

"He isn't completely wrong," Plato explained. "Anytime technology enters into an equation, it takes something away."

Sophia leaned back on her dragon, crossing her arms casually. "Settle in, Lun. We're about to get schooled by the wise Plato. Take notes because all lessons will involve a riddle and a test later."

Plato gave her a cross look. "Ten points from Ravenclaw for that remark."

Her mouth popped open. "Ravenclaw? I'm so Gryffindor."

He dipped his chin and gave her a challenging expression. "Are you sure about that, because I hear the parties are more fun in Ravenclaw house."

"Are we even having this conversation on the heels of trying to decide whether to attach LiDAR to ancient dragons?" Sophia asked, amused by the strange lynx.

"You know, Soph," he began snootily. "Making references to Harry Potter is always appropriate, especially when discussing things such as these. When I was at Hogwarts—"

"Not a real place," Sophia interrupted, rolling her eyes.

Plato sighed. "It's thinking like that which limits you into thinking dragons wouldn't be the preferred transportation when using light radar technology. I'm guessing you're one of those people who think hobbits aren't real, and Alice never found Wonderland."

"Well…" she said, trailing away.

"Keep in mind for many centuries many factual history books fell out of that section in the Great Library and got classified under the fiction genre," Plato explained. "This has never been sorted out, and now most of the population reads works of fiction, never knowing they detail real events from our past."

"That isn't a real thing," Sophia disagreed skeptically, wondering if the lynx was messing with her. They were known to be very mischievous creatures.

"It is. I assure you," he argued. "It was known as The Great Reorganization Error of the Great Library."

"I think we could have come up with a better title," Sophia said dryly, glancing up at Lunis. "Are you buying this?"

It's common knowledge among the dragons, Lunis replied to her surprise. *Why do you think I'm obsessed with the Princess Bride movie?*

"Because you're a strange dragon with extraordinary tastes in books and movies," she stated.

Because it tells a very important and forgotten part of history, the dragon corrected.

"Anyway," Plato said, regaining their attention. "The GREGL, as it's often abbreviated—"

"By whom?" Sophia interrupted.

"By the dragons and me," Plato stated. "We're pretty much the only ones who know about this. Well, and now you. I told Liv once, but she was asleep and she never remembers what I tell her when she is asleep, which is why she is still struggling to discover the meaning of life, although it has been explained to her many times."

Forty-two, Lunis said with a snicker.

Plato gave him an appreciative expression. "Another great nonfiction book, placed in the wrong section."

"So, some librarian error caused all this?" Sophia asked, starting to buy in, although she had not ruled out the notion that both her dragon and Liv's sidekick were pulling her leg for fun. It seemed like something they would do—working in cahoots with one another.

"Yes," Plato answered. "The Great Library's classification system is the master for the world. Wherever Trinity puts a book is where it's classified worldwide."

"Why didn't he just move those nonfiction books back to the right sections, then?" Sophia questioned.

Plato gave her a very sage-like expression. "Oh, well, then the secret would have gotten out and he would have lost his job, so naturally he covered the whole thing up, and now few know about the whole debacle."

"Well, what is going to happen now there's no librarian for the Great Library?" Sophia asked.

"I'm glad you asked. I was asked to do the job."

"You said no, right?" Sophia asked. "I mean, that's got to be a full-time job."

He nodded. "Of course. I declined."

Who even makes those assignments? Lunis asked.

"Mama Jamba and Papa Creola, naturally," Plato replied. "When Sophia informed Mama Jamba that Trin Currante had impersonated Trinity, the librarian, they went to work to find a replacement for the librarian. The place is currently on lockdown until they find the right person. Security measures are also being updated so Trin Currante can't do what she did again. Finding the Great Library will get even harder."

Sophia sighed. "Because risking your life to follow a tiny flying bug around Zanzibar for what could be weeks isn't hard enough."

"You have a portal you can use, now don't you?" Plato offered. "I mean, once I elect a librarian and they unlock it."

"You're making the assignment?" Sophia asked, impressed.

"Yes, since I turned down the position, they then stuck the responsibility on me," Plato explained. "I'm interviewing mild-mannered women with severely straight hair and shy demeanors."

"Isn't that a little stereotypical?" Sophia challenged. "Not all librarians are the mousy type or wallflowers."

"That's true, but they do make the very best, in my experience," Plato imparted. "Actually, there's one person I'm considering for the position who doesn't meet that description in the slightest, but she has to be able to live outside the Gullington, and currently that isn't possible."

Both Sophia's and Lunis' mouths dropped open. Before she could say something, her dragon said, *But Sophia is horrid at filing stuff. She would make an awful librarian.*

Sophia playfully slapped her dragon. "He is referring to Ainsley, you dweeb."

"Good one," Plato said. "Calling your dragon a nerdy name. That seems about right for a Beaufont. And yes, I mean Ainsley. She has the right skill set, and I think after her imprisonment in the Gullington, she will enjoy the freedom of living at the Great Library."

"What do you mean?" Sophia argued. "Why would she want to go from being trapped in one place to being imprisoned in another?"

Plato clicked his tongue and shook his head. "Oh, dear. You have been in a library before, right?"

She rolled her eyes. "I pretty much mastered getting around the library in the House of Fourteen, which is a maze and will trick you if you're not careful. The books run the show there."

Plato nodded. "Yes, that's a very impressive library, indeed. Your time in libraries should remind you that a person surrounded by so many books has endless possibilities. They can go anywhere and experience anything. They're able to live a thousand lives. You know how the quote goes."

"Well, it's null and void because Ainsley can't leave the Gullington," Sophia stated.

"She can't yet," Plato said, a hint of foreboding in his voice. "I'm sure someone will find a way to change that." He gave her a very sharp expression.

"Yeah, maybe when I don't have to find dragon eggs, help Hiker not destroy everything in the Castle with his mammoth powers, fix Wilder and do everything else on my list," she told him.

Don't forget I need a bath, Lunis reminded her. *I haven't had one since I hatched.*

Sophia peeled away from him and grimaced. "Gross. Why not?"

Because you're supposed to do it and you neglect me, he answered, a pout on his face.

"No, I'm not." Sophia pointed to a carwash down the road. "I order you to go wash yourself."

He huffed, appearing offended. *As if. They don't use organic, vegan soap at that place.*

"Oh, for the love of the angels." Sophia shook her head.

"As I was saying earlier, Hiker isn't completely wrong about the dragons and technology," Plato began. "Anytime technology enters into an equation, it takes something away."

"Oh, wow, we really derailed the conversation since that topic," Sophia remarked, trying to remember what they were talking about with the LiDAR and dragon discussion.

Plato nodded. "It's a gift of mine. Anyway, when technology is involved, something has to be sacrificed. It's the natural law of things."

"Of course it is," Sophia said sarcastically, rolling her eyes at Lunis.

He stiffened, stepping slightly to the side like he didn't want to be associated with the class clown. *I'm listening, Plato. Please continue.*

The lynx gave Sophia a cross expression before clearing his throat like a college professor. "Thank you, Lunis," he stated regally. "As I was saying, the price of technology is a sacrifice. So you can have your phones, but you lose privacy. Fly your planes, but the clouds will smell of gasoline, and the birds will lose their wonder. Have television but endeavor to exercise less. You get the idea."

"What is the price we would pay if we outfitted the dragons with LiDAR for this upcoming mission?" Sophia asked.

Plato lifted an eyebrow and grinned. "It's cute you think I would tell you the answer."

CHAPTER SEVENTY-NINE

Sophia was still annoyed at the lynx when she approached John's Electronic Repair shop a few moments later, leaving Lunis parked on the curb. Plato, in his normal fashion, had disappeared right after not telling them what using the dragons instead of planes would cost them. However, Sophia was still playing with the idea.

She thought there was merit in using her dragon for the mission instead of chartering a plane. It wasn't that technology involved a price. It was a tradeoff, the way she saw it. Phones kept them connected all over the world and provided so many benefits. To her mind, it was worth the fact that as a society, they had become somewhat addicted to the devices. Tradeoffs. That's all.

John's terrier, Pickles, barked at Sophia when she entered the repair shop.

"Oh, would you hush it," John Carraway encouraged, reaching down and stroking the dog's head with a laugh. "It's only Little Sophia."

John would always see the dragonrider as a little girl even if she was wearing armor, had her elfin made sword on her hip, and her dragon parked in front of his shop. It was actually nice to just be a normal person to someone instead of him seeing her as this warrior who did impossible things and was expected to continue to risk her life for the good of the world at large.

The terrier was actually an ancient chimera meant to protect the Mortal Seven for the House, transformed and took up a large portion of the front shop area. He waved his tail, which was in the form of a goat, and the snake on his back hissed as his lion head growled.

Alicia, who was working on something behind a workstation, flipped her goggles up onto her head and pointed to the window where Pickles' attention was centered.

"I think the dragon glamoured as a U-Haul truck is what has got him all worked up," the scientist said.

John squinted out the display window and scratched his head. "Well I'll be, I had no idea."

Alicia smiled, indicating to the goggles on her head. "I have a no glamour lens on these since much of the magitech I work on is disguised in one way or another."

"Just a regular Tuesday in this place, isn't it?" Sophia joked, petting the large chimera and settling him back down. Pickles instantly purred from the affection, bumping his head into her, and nearly knocking her to the ground. He was the size of a medium-sized refrigerator when he shifted forms.

"We like to keep things interesting around here," John agreed, spotting the equipment outside. "Oh, I better pull that stuff in for you, Soph."

"I'll help you with it," she said, opening the door.

He waved her off. "Don't be ridiculous. I don't want you getting your hands dirty."

Sophia was going to argue she had carried all the stuff to the door and she was a dragonrider who spent more of her time dirty than clean, but she decided not to. Again, John saw her as the little girl he knew who wore lacy dresses and curtsied to all she met. She was still that girl, it was just impractical to wear dresses when riding dragons.

"Thank you, John," Sophia said over her shoulder and went over to the workstation where Alicia was. "Thanks for reviewing those files from Medford Research."

"Quite the firm there," Alicia said, pulling the goggles all the way off her head and shaking out her long, silky brown hair. "I mean, as you know, I did contract work for a similar organization at one point, Langer Technology. They were more about using LiDAR for financial profit. From what I've been able to discern, Medford Research takes only government contracts that benefit making the planet a safer place."

Sophia slumped slightly, blowing out a breath. "Yeah, that's in line with what I've learned about them."

"Why the sad face?" the Italian scientist asked, her accent making her words sound like music.

"It's just hard to wrap my head around taking down a villain who does good things," Sophia related.

Alicia nodded in understanding. "I don't think most people are good or bad, they fall somewhere in the middle. We're an assortment of grays, rather than blacks and whites."

"Yeah," Sophia agreed, thinking of the dragons and their riders and how they tended to align to one end of the spectrum or the other. There were not any grays when it came to the adjudicators of the world, and that was probably for the best, Sophia reasoned.

"Maybe there's more to learn about your villain," Alicia offered thoughtfully. "I'm sorry I can't give you much insight into her other than what I already have, but it seems to me it would be unwise to destroy someone whose intentions you don't understand fully."

Sophia nodded, having thought the same thing. She was definitely getting her dragon eggs back. Those belonged to the Dragon Elite. Once she did, she wasn't certain what she was doing with Trin Currante.

Usually an enemy would be imprisoned, punished, or taken down, like Thad Reinhart. It wasn't smart for the Dragon Elite to leave potential adversaries out there who could come back and seek retribution. But what if they were not inherently evil? It went back to the whole philosophical question, does a man who steals bread to feed his starving family deserve to be punished?

Some would contend the man should be let off since he wasn't hurting anyone and only trying to save the ones he loved. Others think that stealing regardless of the circumstances was wrong. As an adjudicator presiding over the world's affairs, Sophia didn't actually know. She thought it depended on specific factors. It was a case by case basis for her.

"I think I have everything you asked for," Sophia said, holding out her hand in a presenting fashion as John brought in the equipment. "Thanks for helping with this."

"It's my pleasure," Alicia told her, coming around the workstation to check out the devices Evan and Sophia had recovered. "Yes, this should give me what I need to get your LiDAR up and running."

"How long do you expect it to take?" Sophia asked.

Alicia considered the question, pushing out her lips. "Not long. I suppose you're anxious to get this mission going, though."

Sophia nodded. "Another question. What would you say if I said I was considering using the LiDAR on Lunis rather than in a plane, as most firms do?"

The smile that lit up Alicia's brown eyes made her more beautiful. "I think that would enhance the technology quite a bit."

"That was Plato's thought too," Sophia commented. "Could there be any drawbacks?"

Alicia thought for a moment. "Most certainly. However, that's outside of my experience since I've never even met a dragon, let alone used LiDAR equipment around one."

Sophia nodded, and then something occurred to her. "Well, I think it's overdue. Would you like to meet a dragon?"

Alicia's face turned red with excitement. "You mean the U-Haul truck out there?"

"Yes, I've got to send him through a carwash after this, but before that, I bet he would enjoy the opportunity to meet you," Sophia explained.

Alicia brushed her hands off on her slacks and made for the door.

When there, she paused, pointing to the back of the shop. "Oh, and Sophia…"

She paused too, picking up on the excitement in the scientist's tone. "Yes?"

"Your 3D printer is almost ready," Alicia said, pride in her voice.

CHAPTER EIGHTY

The smell wafting out of the kitchen of the Castle was so horrible Sophia considered skipping dinner altogether, but she needed to give Hiker an update on the LiDAR mission and the best way to catch him was at the dinner table.

Mama Jamba and Evan were already dutifully seated with expectant expressions.

Sophia gave them both a tentative look. "Anyone know what that weird smell is?"

"I thought it was you," Evan remarked, sticking his tongue out at her.

"It's something special Ainsley is making," Mama Jamba affirmed proudly. "Not something I'll eat, but she has promised to make me pancakes for dinner, since well, I'm the boss."

Sophia smiled at Mother Nature. "It's good you don't let the power go to your head."

"I just ask for pancakes at every meal," Mama Jamba said, moving the salt shaker slightly so it was more in line with the pepper.

"If I were you, I would demand a lot more stuff," Evan said, puffing his chest out. "No one would be able to argue with me. I would have anything I wanted instantly. And anyone who irritated me would be imprisoned."

"Absolute rule gets pretty boring pretty fast, my dear," Mama Jamba explained. "I tired of it early on."

"I would probably make it mandatory that women had to wear bikinis," Evan said, not hearing a word Mama Jamba stated.

"I think you misunderstand me if you think I created this planet to rule it," Mama Jamba said placidly. "A mother doesn't have children to run their lives and rule over them. If she does, she quickly realizes only suffering will be a result of such choices."

"Why do mothers have children, then?" Sophia asked, her chin on her fist resting on the table.

"For the same reason a writer tells a story, I believe, sweet child," Mama Jamba explained. "Because deep down, she feels there's a part of her that needs to breathe on its own. When we bring children into this world, we do so with the understanding they came through us, but they're not us."

"That's beautiful," Sophia said, enchanted by Mother Nature's world.

"So purdy." Evan kept glancing at the door to the kitchen. "If this food isn't any good, Pink Princess, will you order me food from that phone app of yours?"

"I'll if you learn to ask politely," Sophia replied.

Evan rolled his eyes. "Never mind. I'll starve."

"Your call," Sophia fired back as the rest of the men entered the dining hall, all of their faces registering the strange smell in the air with different degrees of speculation.

Wilder appeared completely put off. Mahkah simply batted his eyes briefly, and Hiker Wallace scrunched up his nose and shook his head.

"What is that woman up to this time?" Hiker asked, thundering across the dining room and taking his seat.

"No good," Evan answered. "I'm certain of it, sir. You should fire her."

"It doesn't matter if I do," Hiker replied. "She refuses to leave."

Sophia flashed him a punishing expression. "Maybe she would if she could. If she had not sacrificed herself for—"

"Have you figured out how to fix Wilder?" Hiker interrupted her, knowing what she was about to say. "Since he was hit with Cupid's arrow while with you and is now hardly much use to me."

"I'm fine, sir," Wilder argued.

"You're not thinking clearly since becoming infatuated with Sophia," Hiker countered. "I asked you to do research for me, and what happened?"

Wilder's eyes cut to the side. "I was distracted, sir."

"Funny thing." Sophia tried to take the heat off Wilder. "When I met with Cupid, he had something interesting to say about you, sir. And Ains—"

"Dinner is served," the housekeeper chirped, backing into the dining hall carrying a large platter of fish.

When she set it down, everyone but Quiet, who Sophia had not seen enter the room and take a seat, backed away from the table.

"What is that?" Hiker asked, narrowing his eyes at the dish.

"Surströmming," Ainsley answered. "It's a fermented fish that—"

"I know damn well what it is," Hiker cut in. "Why are you serving that when you know no one will eat it?"

"His name is Quiet," Ainsley corrected. "Not 'No One.' Gosh, you would think after all this time you would learn my name isn't 'Would You' and the groundskeeper isn't 'No One.'"

To everyone's surprise, Quiet was digging into the herring, loading it onto his plate.

"Hey, Quiet," Evan said in a sugary, sweet voice. "If you want, little guy, you can have my serving."

The gnome mumbled something and took a bite.

A sharp cackle fell out of Ainsley's mouth as she made for the kitchen. "You feel the same way about Evan, Quiet, as I feel about you."

"Wait, what?" Evan asked, looking between the housekeeper and groundskeeper. "I'm trying to be nice to him. Why doesn't he like it?"

Sophia shook her head at him. "Because being nice to get something is wrong. You should be nice because that's the right thing to do. Better yet, because that's what is in your heart."

Evan pretended to gag. "I think you made it here by accident, Sister Sophia. The convent is down the street and much better suited for your holy ways."

"I hope you're going back to the kitchen to fetch real food we can eat," Hiker called over his shoulder.

"Ainsley is still mad at Quiet for keeping being the Gullington thing a secret, I see," Wilder said in a whisper in Sophia's direction.

She was about to respond when Hiker leaned forward, a challenging expression on his face. "Don't talk to her. It makes you act weird."

"Weirder," Evan corrected.

Wilder shook his head. "It doesn't, sir. I'm totally fine, I tell you."

"Okay, then answer these questions for me," Hiker demanded, folding his hands on the table. "What is your name?"

"Wilder Thomson," he proclaimed at once.

"Who are you?" Hiker continued.

"A rider for the Dragon Elite."

"Are you in love with Sophia?" Hiker asked.

"One-thousand percent," Wilder said, brandishing a wide grin.

Hiker pounded his fist on the table, making the plates jump. "See, you're not well. Cupid has corrupted you and I'll not stand for it."

Ainsley returned, a sneaky grin on her face as she laid down another tray. This time everyone but Quiet jumped up from the table as if the housekeeper had served a severed head. It was a mound of custard looking rice, but the smell was what repelled them.

"Is that..." Mahkah asked, looking sideways at the dish.

"A mistake I made, my dears," Mama Jamba apologized. "I'm sorry. Durian was supposed to...well, not smell quite so horrible. The taste isn't bad if you can get over that it smells—"

"Dead?" Evan supplied.

Mama Jamba nodded. "Yes. All my creations haven't been fantastic. Sometimes I lucked out and created something like the cocoa bean, and then sometimes..." She gave the durian dish a long look of regret.

"Sometimes you didn't," Hiker stated, shaking his head before glancing at Ainsley. "Tell me you made something edible for tonight's dinner."

"I did," Ainsley said, sticking her hands on her hips. "There you go." She threw her chin in the direction of the surströmming and durian.

"Ainsley!" Hiker bellowed.

She smiled sweetly. "Yes, sir?"

"You're fired!"

She nodded obediently. "Well, if there isn't anything else you all need, I'm going to take my dinner in the kitchen. My chicken pot pie is just fresh out of the oven."

"Wait!" Hiker called as she retreated. "We want chicken pot pie!"

"Oh, too bad," Ainsley said over her shoulder. "I only made enough for me."

"Why are you eating that instead of this?" Wilder asked.

Ainsley laughed. "Because that stuff is gross."

Hiker growled when the housekeeper went into the kitchen. He gave Sophia a pointed expression. She nodded at once and pulled out her phone. "Fine, do you want Chinese or Mexican?"

"Pancakes," Mama Jamba stated.

Sophia was about to order something from Uber Eats when she noticed she had a message from her fairy godmother, Mae Ling. Her eyes widened. "Actually, I've got to run right now, but I'll order you all something on the way out."

"Where are you going?" Hiker asked as she ran for the exit.

She turned, her eyes briefly meeting Wilder's. "To see someone. They think they know how to fix him." She pointed at the guy who always regarded her with such affection.

At the conclusion of her words, he shook his head, disappointment on his face. Hiker didn't notice.

Instead, the Leader of the Dragon Elite urged Sophia to leave. "Yes, get on that. And order me something with lots of meat from Really Eats."

"Uber Eats," Sophia corrected, trying to catch the look on Wilder's face before she rushed away.

CHAPTER EIGHTY-ONE

S ophia was never so happy she had to eat a macaroon to open the portal to Happily Ever After College than right then. She was hungry after not eating at the Castle, although she had ordered food for the others before leaving. Ainsley was acting out and Sophia could not blame her.

The housekeeper was hurt Quiet had kept his secrets from her. She was confused that she could not leave the Castle without getting sick. There was no doubt a lot more confusion over why she didn't have any memories from early on. Then there was Hiker Wallace, who took her for granted, but Sophia suspected he was keeping her at a distance for a very good reason.

After stepping through the portal to the fairy godmother college, Sophia expected to find herself on the lawn outside the front door. She should not have had such expectations. The young dragonrider should always expect when things were supposed to follow a pattern, they would be turned upside down.

When Sophia stepped through, she found herself in a garden nursery she had only ever spied traces of at the back of the college when headed to Mae Ling's office. On that trek, she had seen through the window to the large greenhouse that seemed to have many strange and mysterious plants.

Now Sophia was standing in front of one that was more akin to a monster than a plant. It reminded her instantly of Audrey 2 from Little Shop of Horrors. The carnivorous plant was the size of a bear and arched over its huge pot, towering over her.

She looked up into the giant mouth of the beast with teeth full of bits of flesh and its bad breath wafting over her face. The Venus fly trap-like plant appeared ready to eat Sophia, but for whatever reason, she didn't pull out her sword. She just looked up at the gaping mouth that was ready to snap shut on her at any moment.

There were a long few seconds where Sophia didn't breathe and her pulse stopped beating. She prepared for these to be her last moments on Earth.

Then the plant let out a high-pitched wail and shrank back, twisting round and round as it grew smaller until it sat in its pot of fresh soil as a tiny, unassuming seedling.

Sophia hardly had a moment to digest what had happened before applause broke out all around her. It wasn't until then that Sophia realized she was surrounded by a class of students from Happily Ever After College.

The girls, all wearing their school uniforms and pleased expressions, continued to applaud her as Mae Ling stepped forward. "And that's exactly how one faces off with an Audrey, my lovies. Sophia Beaufont, dragonrider for the Dragon Elite, showed you the perfect strategy. Good work, my Cinderella."

"Thank you," Sophia said, her eyes shifting from side to side as she tried to figure out what was happening.

"One must never try to fight an Audrey," Mae Ling continued, lecturing the class as she strode along with the crowd of girls. "If you do, then you'll only anger them and make the situation worse. They simply want a stare-off in a way, although I get they don't have eyes. Be the last to react, and they will become bored and go back into hibernation."

"Miss Ling," a student asked, holding up her hand. "When would we encounter an Audrey?"

Mae Ling nodded, having expected the question. "It isn't common, but many of your travels to aid Cinderellas will be hampered by evil witches, bad queens, and other villains who want nothing more than for you to fail, preventing more love from entering this world. You must overcome these obstacles, help your charge, all while looking fabulous and spreading glamour." Mae Ling spun around, looking very theatrical in a way Sophia had never seen her. "How does that sound, students?"

"Wonderful!"

"Fantastic!"

"Awesome!"

The group of women cheered.

"Very well, my lovies. Now off to lunch," Mae Ling said, clapping her hands and ushering them toward the exit. "Get your refreshments and be punctual for your math lessons this afternoon."

This was met with reluctant groans. "Do we have to?" a girl with braids complained.

"Yes, you have to," Mae Ling told her. "We're changing the curriculum, and you're all going to embrace it. Most of you are messing up your crochet patterns and baking recipes because you can't do simple math. We were wrong to keep it out of our studies, so you're going to like it, or you know where the door is. Others would love to have your positions here."

"Okay, Miss Ling," many of the girls agreed with dutiful nods.

The fairy godmother nodded proudly and waved them toward the door.

When they all had exited, Mae Ling swung around to face Sophia with a smile. "Just as I planned, you performed perfectly!"

CHAPTER EIGHTY-TWO

"Wait," Sophia nearly stuttered. "You planned for that? I was supposed to show up and nearly get eaten by a plant?"

Mae Ling nodded. "Yes."

"But what if I had tried to fight it, and it attacked and killed me?" Sophia asked in a rush.

"Then I would have had a free lunch period," Mae Ling observed matter-of-factly, heading for the door of the nursery.

Sophia took the hint and followed her fairy godmother out of the nursery, although she would have enjoyed some time to explore the greenhouse. There were so many strange plants surrounding her, and the sweet smells of the flowers were intoxicating. Not to mention the sunlight streaming through the glass warmed her up just enough, making her the perfect temperature, like an incubating plant, waiting to bloom.

They passed several chatting students on their way down the now-familiar trek to Mae Ling's office. Once inside the private area, Sophia's fairy godmother took a seat behind her desk by throwing herself down in her overly large pink chair quite dramatically, as though she was exhausted from the events of the day.

Sophia stayed standing in the entryway and watched the strange woman roll her head back and forth, her eyes closed. Finally Mae Ling rose, her eyes open and disapproval on her face.

"Well, don't just stand there," she scolded. "Take a seat and eat your meal before it melts."

"My food…" Sophia wondered. Her eyes found the hot chocolate fudge sundae that had just appeared on the other side of the desk, next to the empty oversized pink chair opposite Mae Lings. "Oh, that's for me?"

"Of course, silly girl," Mae Ling said, a chocolate sundae appearing in front of her too, along with a long whimsical spoon. "You didn't have dinner, and I dare say if you had gotten food from Uber Eats, you probably would have ordered some vegetables or chicken something."

"I've been trying to eat fewer fruits and vegetables," Sophia admitted, taking a seat.

"Good girl," Mae Ling said. "I'm sorry for my outburst. I'm just so tired having to deal with the girls adjusting to the new curriculum, but it really is for the best."

"I understand." Sophia took a bite of the sundae. The vanilla ice cream was perfectly balanced with just enough vanilla bean, and the fudge was just cold enough it cracked from her spoon but instantly melted in her mouth. There was just a smidge of whipped cream and no banana or cherries or other fruit to ruin the sundae. Fruit always messed up seemingly perfect desserts.

"So you intended for me to face off with a man-eating plant for a demonstration for your class?" she asked Mae Ling.

The fairy godmother nodded. "Yes."

"You seemed to know I wouldn't fight the plant," Sophia guessed.

"It's your nature," Mae Ling explained. "You never fight when there are other options. It isn't your instinct. A man would have pulled his sword at the sight of Audrey. And he would be dead. Which is why men make awful fairy godmothers. Well, and also for the fact they're men."

Sophia found herself giggling uncontrollably, probably from the rush of sugar. "I got your message." She tried to regain her composure. "I hadn't told you about Wilder being hit by Cupid's arrow. How did you know it was a problem to be solved?"

Mae Ling gave her a look that seemed to say, "How do you think, child?" Instead, Mae Ling explained, "My message to you said I know how to help with Wilder, but you have a very different way of putting things. Why is it you think he is a problem to be solved? Maybe you're the one with the problem?"

Sophia considered this. "Well, it's just Hiker keeps saying he needs to be fixed."

"That's a very Hiker Wallace thing to say." Mae Ling dug into her hot fudge sundae.

"What can I do for Wilder?" Sophia asked. "He really isn't right since getting hit by Cupid's arrow, and he is getting himself in trouble with Hiker. He isn't thinking clearly. He is easily distracted and acting a fool at times."

Mae Ling looked off with a dreamy thought. "Oh, love. It does the most wonderful things to people."

"I don't think you understand," Sophia said, pushing her sundae away. "Wilder is a dragonrider, and this is a serious time for us. If he doesn't get it together then—"

"Oh, I'm perfectly aware of what will happen to Wilder, and I know you're always facing something or another," Mae Ling told her. "What you have to understand is that love isn't what you find when the day's battles have been fought and won. Love is *why* you fight the battles. But you're not quite ready for that lesson yet, so I'm going to help you with a different one."

"I don't know what you're talking about just so you know." Sophia felt slightly grumpy from her lack of sleep and now the rush of sugar.

"Yes, and you need rest, which is why you're irritable, but that gnome will not let you." Mae Ling shrugged. "I can't help you much there. I can tell you who to look for that can help with Wilder."

"Thank you," Sophia said. "That would be great."

"He will not be easy to find, though," Mae Ling cautioned.

"I sort of expect that now," Sophia moaned.

Mae Ling held out her small hand and a pink envelope appeared in it. "The last time I met Saint Valentine, he was gushing about these shops in London. If there are any clues about how to find him, they will be found there. I'm afraid that's all I can offer you."

"Did you say, 'Saint Valentine?'" Sophia questioned. "That's who I need to find to help me with Wilder?"

Mae Ling held up a finger, pausing Sophia. "I don't know that Saint Valentine can help you or you can even find him. But it's worth a shot. He is an expert in love, after all."

"Saint Valentine..." Sophia took the small pink envelope. "He is still around?"

Mae Ling toggled her head back and forth. "In a way."

"And this won't tell me where to go to look for clues of where to find him?" Sophia questioned.

Mae Ling nodded. "I'm sorry, he didn't leave a forwarding address with me, but I have every hope with skills like yours, if Saint Valentine can be found then you'll do it."

Sophia pressed the note to her chest, feeling a strange bit of hope, although it sounded like she would have to go on a series of convoluted adventures to get where she needed to be.

"Thank you," she said, standing from her chair and looked down at the sundae quickly turning into a puddle of sauces.

"Don't thank me just yet," Mae Ling said, her face turning serious. "I'm giving you what you want, a way to 'fix' Wilder. But at the end of all this, you have to ask yourself, do you really want to fix him?"

"I don't know," Sophia said honestly. "I don't want Hiker to be upset or toss us out. And I want Wilder...well, if he is going to love me, I want it to be because he does and not because of a spell."

Mae Ling smiled and nodded, approving of this answer. "Then go and find Saint Valentine. I think that's the only way to find closure in all of this. As a bonus, I believe he might be able to offer you some insight into another case you want to be solved."

"Another case?" Sophia asked, her mind coming up blank about what her fairy godmother was referring to.

"The one regarding Ainsley Carter, of course," Mae Ling answered. "If anyone knows how to help the shapeshifting elf, it's Saint Valentine."

CHAPTER EIGHTY-THREE

Kensington High Street was definitely one of the more refined places Sophia had an opportunity to visit. The buildings that lined the busy street blocked out some of the London wind she realized when she came to an intersection and got blasted in the face by a gust that sent her hair in a flurry around her face.

Not only was she momentarily confused by the traffic since the cars drove on the opposite side of the road from what she was used to, but the street signs were also all foreign to her. She followed the pedestrians around her, crossing the roads when they did and hurrying before the aggressive drivers nearly clipped her heels.

She had to admit she was distracted by the homes, all of them nestled right next to each other. Each had five steps that led to the front doors where she expected a dignified lady of the home would answer with a polite smile. Her name would maybe be Hyacinth or Elizabeth or Dorothy, and she would have a little dog named Gregory who sat dutifully beside her, not barking at the visitor calling at the odd hour.

Sophia wasn't going to knock on any of the doors and interrupt tea time for the lovely people who lived on the High Street. The little pink envelope Mae Ling had given her had a specific address of a pub which was down the road a bit.

At the next intersection, Sophia checked her phone for directions, careful to stay out of the way of the heavy traffic that streaked by her on the crowded sidewalk. Sirens blared in the air as ambulances sped by.

After spending the majority of her time in the quiet of the Gullington, it was sensory overload to be in the center of busy London where the noises, smells, and sights all competed for Sophia's attention.

Following the directions to the pub, she turned down a cobbled road that looked out of place next to modern architecture. Hanging plants hung from the side of the buildings, flowers draping down and offering a welcoming sight.

Soon the crowds died away, and when Sophia turned the next corner, she could not hear the traffic of the busy High Street anymore. It was replaced by birds tweeting and branches making gentle music from the breeze that wafted through the area.

Sophia glanced over her shoulder, wondering if she had accidentally stepped through a portal to another place. In the distance, she could just spy details of the bustling part of Kensington she had come from. On the small cobbled street adjacent to a community garden, she felt a million miles away from busy London.

She found herself meandering down the road where there were no other people, her hands in her cloak and her chin lifted to the blue sky like she didn't have a worry in the world. It was the opposite of her present reality, but in this idyllic oasis she had stumbled upon, it felt like she had been given some respite from her cares.

Sophia would have walked right by her destination, lost in her blissful thoughts, but the pub could not be ignored. It belonged on the enchanted street with a low wrought-iron fence enclosing the patio and umbrellas covered in green moss from the winter rains. Dozens of hanging plants decorated the front, and topiaries stood around on the second-story balcony.

Even if this wasn't the place Mae Ling had sent Sophia to, she expected the charming exterior would have drawn her into the Scarsdale Tavern. Sophia smiled at a few patrons who sat at mismatched tables and chairs when she entered the pub and restaurant. Most were older men, soaking up the sunlight that streamed through the stained-glass windows while enjoying an ale.

The barman glanced up from behind the counter where he was polishing a glass. His expression shifted from a welcoming smile to a tentative look at the sight of Sophia.

"Oh, you can't see him like that," the man said, his British accent strong.

Sophia peered down at her attire, confused. She was wearing her usual getup, a blue and silver armored top, leather pants, a traveling cloak, and Inexorabilis on her hip.

"Wait, you know why I'm here?" she asked, wondering why he didn't think she could be a patron about to order fish and chips and sit by the fire.

"Of course I do," the man said. "I've been expecting you." He eyed his watch and smirked a little. "Actually, I expected you more like next month. It looks like the timeline got pushed up a bit."

Sophia shook her head, uncertainty making her doubt everything around her. Maybe the pub wasn't real and she had stepped through a portal. She could still be asleep and this was all a dream.

"You knew I would come to you and ask to see—"

"Don't say his name," the man interrupted, cutting his eyes to the side to ensure the customers eating nearby didn't overhear them.

Sophia leaned forward. "Then how do I know we're talking about the same person?"

The guy nodded, seeming to understand. "You have got an issue that involves the heart. Is that right?"

Sophia twisted her mouth to the side, agreeing with a curt nod.

"And you're seeking an expert, is that correct?" the man asked.

Another nod.

"Then I know who you're looking for and I can help," the man said with a toothy grin.

"How did you know to expect me?" Sophia asked, grateful the guy was going to help, but also skeptical.

He held up a pad of paper. "I keep his appointments. They were made centuries ago, and most get canceled for one reason or another, but it looks like you made yours and are a bit early, which is much better than late. I can't tell you how many show up for their appointments late, having put off matters of the heart. They let taxes and work and fears of rejection and commitment get in the way. Then they show up and learn it's too late."

Sophia scratched her head, thoroughly bewildered. She figured at this stage of her career she should be used to unexplained situations such as this, but she never got used to it.

"Who made the appointment?" Sophia asked. "Was it Mae Ling?"

The man eyed the pad of paper, squinting at his messy writing. "No, no. I haven't heard of a Mae Ling. Appointments are always made directly by the person."

Sophia's confusion deepened. She pointed at her chest. "You're saying I made this appointment with...You-Know-Who?" She hoped You-Know-Who was the same person she wanted to see—Saint Valentine.

"Of course you did," the guy stated. "Who else would?"

"When did I do this?" Sophia asked, wondering if she was sleep-walking at night, or in this case, sleep scheduling.

The barman flipped through the pad of paper, furrowing his brow. "I'm not certain. Doesn't say. But time is relative with these things. Appointments are made well in advance and ironically after their occurrence."

"Wait, are you saying I could have made this appointment in the future?" Sophia queried, wondering how in the world things could have gotten any stranger.

"Sure. I get this is confusing. Events are rarely linear. As a great man once said, 'It's a big ball of wibbly-wobbly timey-wimey stuff,'" the guy affirmed, picking back up his rag and continuing to polish glasses. "The important thing is you have an appointment because without one, you could not see...well, you know."

"Okay, but you said I can't see...you know...like I am," Sophia related. "What is wrong with my dress?"

The guy chuckled. "He will hate it for one. When you meet...you know who, you have to look like someone he would fall in love with. That's the only way he ever helps anyone. Appearances are important."

Sophia sighed and lifted her hand, ready to transform her appearance. "Fine, what does he want? A dress? My hair up? Makeup? I can do that."

The guy shook his head. "I'm afraid it will not be that easy."

"Figures," Sophia said darkly.

"You would have gotten these instructions for dress code when you booked the appointment," the guy continued, glancing at the pad. He shrugged. "You probably made this appointment in the future, then."

"Well, what *is* the dress code?" Sophia asked. "I'm pretty good with wardrobe changes and really need to get going."

The man shook his head. "You can't rush things." He leaned forward with a serious expression. "Don't you know that by now? Love can't be rushed. Matters of the heart take time."

Sophia nodded. "So, what do I need to do to get ready for this appointment? You say I have a month?"

The guy peeled back, relaxing a bit. "Yeah, but hopefully it will not take you too long. It looks like you just gave yourself some wiggle room in case the seamstress took a while or was delayed working on other orders."

"Seamstress?" Sophia asked.

"Yeah, I can imagine your puzzlement since your future self got these instructions and your present self is hearing them for the first time," the guy continued. "You-Know-Who only will take appointments with those elegantly and expertly dressed. He has a favorite seamstress he prefers. It's in your best interest to go and see this person. Once they make you a dress, then come back to me, and I'll give you the key to the meeting chamber for your appointment."

Sophia nodded slowly, doubt heavy in her mind. Something told her this wasn't going to be as easy as just getting a dress and a key. She gulped, preparing herself for a many-headed monster and deranged murderer she would probably have to face to actually meet this Saint Valentine.

The man didn't seem to notice her doubt. Instead, he held out his hand and a small pink envelope appeared in it, identical to the one Mae Ling had given her with the address for the Scarsdale Tavern.

"That's the address of the seamstress," the man said, handing her the envelope. "Good luck. When you get your dress, come back and see me."

Sophia took the note and backed away, wondering if she forgot to ask the barman something. "Should I make the appointment now?"

He shook his head. "No, it doesn't work that way. I assure you, when it's time, you'll know. Then give me a call. My name is Gregory."

CHAPTER EIGHTY-FOUR

In contrast to where Sophia had been, she was sent to the other side of the world and to a place that could not be any more different than the area of Kensington in London.

Whitefish, Montana was the exact opposite of the bustling feel of the High Street. The shops that lined the mountain town of Whitefish were quaint and squatty compared to the buildings in Kensington.

She eyed the note from the pink envelope and wondered if she was missing something. Glancing up, she matched the address on the card to the one in front of her. It was an antique store, not a seamstress shop.

Sophia strode across the main road, which had no traffic, and decided she would check it out. She had not expected Saint Valentine's receptionist would be a British guy in a pub, so she needed to keep an open mind.

Laughing to herself, Sophia could hardly believe with everything going on, she was going to have a dress made. It seemed like the wrong thing to be spending her time on with everything else on her plate.

She reasoned there wasn't anything she could do to find the dragon eggs until Alicia fixed up the LiDAR equipment, and meeting with Saint Valentine would help Wilder and Ainsley. That seemed sufficiently worthy of Sophia's time. She did like the idea of having a fancy dress made that would make her worthy of a meeting with Saint Valentine.

The antique shop smelled of lavender and chocolate when Sophia entered. The store was cluttered with tons of shelves overflowing with trinkets, lamps, and old books. In the center of the small shop was a round pink sofa. In the center was a round back, and Sophia highly doubted the thing would be comfortable to sit on.

She eyed a few objects, pretending to be a shopper, and searching for a store clerk. There didn't appear to be anyone attending to the shop.

To add to the irony of meeting a barman who scheduled Saint Valentine's appointments and was named Gregory, a small dog trotted into the area around the round sofa and jumped up onto it. He focused on Sophia with a pointed glare.

Sophia returned the expression and said, "Where is Hyacinth?"

The dog yelped.

"Did someone call me?" a woman's deep voice said from behind a set of shelves.

Sophia peered in that direction but didn't see the source. "Hello?" she called.

From around the short set of shelves toddled a female gnome who had a thick cap pulled down over her gray hair and was wearing a dress similar to the brown burlap ones Ainsley always adorned.

"Hi, I'm looking for a—"

"A seamstress shop," the woman interrupted, snapping her fingers at the dog. "Get down from there. We have a customer, Dorothy."

Sophia narrowed her eyes at the dog. "The dog's name is Dorothy?"

"Yes, and as you know, my name is Hyacinth," the gnome said, pulling a pincushion from the pocket of her dress. "Weird, Gregory doesn't usually give customers my name. Just the address." She shrugged dismissively. "He must have let it slip."

"Your name really is Hyacinth?" Sophia asked, not believing the irony. "Don't tell me there's an Elizabeth here too?"

The gnome pointed to the back. "She is taking a lunch break. Elizabeth is my apprentice."

Sophia felt a chill run down her arms. What a strange thing her imagination had done in Kensington.

"Now, you need a dress to see Saint Valentine," the gnome said, standing back and closing one eye at her, as though trying to see her from a different point of view. "Oh, yes, this will be fun. You have a nice figure and good boo—"

"You're the seamstress?" Sophia interrupted, confused why the dressmaker worked out of an antique shop.

"Yes, and welcome to my workshop," the gnome said, casting a short arm around. "Oh, it still looks like an antique store to you, doesn't it?" She waved her hand in the air, and before Sophia's eyes, the entire store transformed, all of the little trinkets and old furniture disappearing. They were replaced with row after row of beautiful fabrics. There were patterns of all sorts in a wide array of colors.

Drawn to the nearest one, Sophia reached out to touch a paisley red silk fabric, craving the soft feel on her fingertips.

"Oh, lovely choice," the gnome said, arriving at Sophia's side and looking up at the bolt of fabric.

Sophia's hand paused before touching the silk. "May I?"

The gnome's bulbous nose wrinkled when she smiled. "Of course. Its magical properties will not work on you until I've fashioned it into a dress."

"Magical properties?" Sophia asked.

The gnome nodded, chuckling. "Well, of course. You didn't think I ran a normal seamstress business I disguised as an antique shop, did you?"

"I'm not sure what to think anymore."

Hyacinth pointed to a bolt of fabric next to the red one. "This one will make the wearer skinnier if made into a dress or outfit." She ran her eyes over Sophia, the spectacles on her nose sliding down a bit.

"Not something you need, magician. Oh, in my next life I get to be like you, eating whatever I like and not having it stick to my bones."

"Wow," Sophia said, amazed by what she was learning. "This fabric will make people skinnier?"

She shook her head in reply. "No, it makes them appear skinnier. Nothing but good nutrition, exercise, and genetics can make anyone skinny. Not even magic. Well, not for long. There are certain things that can't be done with magic. You can't make someone fall in love with you, can't make yourself skinnier, and you can't bring back the dead. There are of course exceptions, as with everything, but let's not get off task."

Sophia knew the gnome was correct. For the most part, magic could not be used for major things, as she said. However, King Rudolf Sweetwater had proven he could defy the laws by bringing back his wife Serena from the dead using magic Father Time had forbidden. Of course, he was an exception, and that was probably one of the only cases in the entire history of the world where magic brought back the dead.

"What are some other magical properties these fabrics hold?" Sophia asked, turning around to study the shop filled with rows of material. The round pink sofa, she realized now, was a seamstress stand, with measuring tapes and pins and scissors. Beside it was a standing mirror Sophia remembered seeing when the workshop had been glamoured to look like an antique store.

"Well," Hyacinth began, pointing around the room, "this could take a while so I can't run you through them all. But for instance, that one there will make others think the wearer is rich." She indicated a shiny metallic fabric and then pointed to a black one beside it. "That one makes others believe you're famous. The spring line over here."

Sophia turned to spy the row of fabrics in pastels.

"These do everything from increase fertility to protect against sun damage," Hyacinth explained before laying her hand on the red fabric that had pulled at Sophia's attention from the start. "But the one you chose, well, it's very special indeed and perfect for a dress worn for a meeting with Saint Valentine."

"What does it do?" Sophia asked.

The gnome's face lit up when she smiled. "It will make you flawless."

CHAPTER EIGHTY-FIVE

Holding the red silk up, Sophia peered at herself in the full-length mirror. "So, when you fashion me a dress with this, it will make me appear flawless?"

The seamstress was on her hand and knees, busy taking measurements. "That's right. It enhances all of your features. Your hair will appear healthier, shiner. Your skin will glow even more. Your eyes will sparkle. You get the idea."

"Wow, that's really incredible," Sophia mused, already liking the way the red fabric looked on her, although its magical properties were not working yet. On its own, the silk was beautiful.

"It was a good choice on your part," Hyacinth advised, measuring Sophia's legs. "Saint Valentine only likes to look at beautiful people. That's why he requires I make their attire prior to meetings. I usually pick out something that will make the wearer even more attractive, but you found the perfect fabric right away. I would have chosen it for you."

"I can't wait to see this dress," Sophia related, trying to remain still so Hyacinth could do her work.

"Unfortunately, you'll have to wait a bit," the seamstress told her. "I have a few orders in front of yours." She glanced up suddenly, worry in her eyes. "When is your appointment with Saint Valentine?"

Sophia shook her head, trying to dispel the concern. "Not for another month, apparently."

Hyacinth blew out a relieved breath. "Oh, good. I'll have it done by then. Hopefully well before then. Being early is always good for these appointments."

"That's what Gregory said," Sophia remarked.

"Okay, so tell me about your reason for making this appointment," Hyacinth asked. "That will help me to craft the right design."

"Well, I need Saint Valentine to help my friend," Sophia began but then found her mouth dry. Calling Wilder a friend felt weird.

The gnome must have picked up on the tension. "No one has ever gone to see Saint Valentine about a friend. Try again."

Sophia gulped, trying to make her throat not close up again. "There's a guy…"

"That's better," Hyacinth said with a laugh. "Keep going."

"He got hit by cupid's arrow," Sophia said in a rush.

With wide eyes, the gnome looked up at her. "Oh."

Sophia nodded. "Now he is in love with me and well…it isn't that I don't want him to be, but we're not really allowed to be together. If he did love me, I would prefer for him to do it because…"

"Because that's how he truly felt and not because he was forced," Hyacinth said, finishing Sophia's sentence.

She nodded, her chest tightening.

"That's a good reason to see Saint Valentine." Hyacinth stood from the floor, her height not changing much. "He will be able to fix your friend." There was a sly expression in her eyes when she said the last part.

"Thanks. That's a relief. I do have another friend I would like him to look at too," Sophia said, thinking of Ainsley. It suddenly occurred to her Saint Valentine would have to come to the Gullington, since Sophia doubted she could get Wilder and Ainsley to him. The shapeshifter could leave, but not for long. She made a mental note to make a special request with Quiet to let the saint into the Gullington.

Hopefully he could make an exception. It might be a way to start making amends with the housekeeper by allowing the one person who could help her have access to a place usually restricted to outsiders.

Hyacinth took the red silk from Sophia and gave her a pleasant expression. "I'll be in touch with you once the dress is ready."

"Will I need to come back for fittings?" Sophia asked, knowing she didn't need to clarify how the gnome would be in touch. Those in the magical world had ways of sending messages.

She shook her head. "Not only am I the only seamstress in the world who works with magical fabric and makes dresses people literally have died for, but I never make a mistake and defy the old cliché. I measure once and cut twice. Your dress will fit better than anything you have ever worn. I promise you that."

CHAPTER EIGHTY-SIX

A craft shop that appeared too whimsical to not be spelled with magic caught Sophia's attention when she left Hyacinth's store. She realized it was filled with magic when the ceramic in the front window came alive. It was a frog, and it hopped over to Sophia and croaked before saying, "Get in here and make something special for your mom."

"My mom's dead," Sophia said, offended.

It croaked. "Then make something to put on her tombstone."

"Why don't you shut your mouth, you stupid, insensitive talking frog," Sophia refuted, considering marching into the shop and telling the store owner off.

"That's fine," the frog said, appearing suddenly bored. "I bet whatever you made would be awful and not even worthy of hanging on a refrigerator."

"What? How dare you?"

The ceramic frog painted in many different shades of blue licked his lips. "You don't seem like the crafty type. I bet you don't even know how to hold a paintbrush."

"That isn't true," Sophia argued. "I'm totally crafty, and if you're not careful, I'm going to come in there and smash you to pieces."

"Do it!" he encouraged. "Come show me a thing or two. While you're in here, you can sign up for a craft class. We have some for beginners. You won't mind the rest of the class is preschoolers, do you?"

Sophia tipped forward about to take off into the craft store. Someone caught her shoulder and held her back.

She turned, surprised to find the person standing at her back had a warning expression on their face.

CHAPTER EIGHTY-SEVEN

Only Liv would have been able to sneak up on Sophia like she had. For a moment, the dragonrider thought she was dreaming. How could her sister be there right then? When Liv threw her arms around Sophia and hugged her tightly, she knew it was anything but a dream.

"What are you doing here?" Sophia asked when Liv released her.

"Looks like I'm saving you from beating up a defenseless ceramic frog," Liv remarked. She pointed at the jerk frog who was sticking his tongue out at the both of them.

"He had it coming," she argued. "He was taunting me."

Liv nodded understandingly. "I get it. Then you would have waltzed into that shop, fallen under the 'buy everything' spells the shop owner is using to take customer's money, and I would be bailing you out of the local jail when you figured it out and torched the place." She held up her hands. "I'm here to save the day."

Sophia shook her head. "Seriously, why are you here? How did you find me?"

Her sister smiled. "With a bit of cosmic fate, I believe." She pointed to the boardwalk that lined the sidewalk in front of the shops. "Shall we walk? There's a fantastic ice cream store just down the way."

"Sure," Sophia said, realizing the only thing she had had to eat recently was ice cream. "Maybe we can stop off at a restaurant and grab some real food, but whatever you do, don't tell my fairy godmother if I have a salad."

"Gosh, you and I really live in a strange reverse-y world, don't we?" Liv winked at her. "Your secret is safe with me."

The pair started down the path, petting dogs tied up outside of shops while their owners browsed and waving at the locals as they passed. After a moment, Liv said, "So like I said, cosmic fate seemed to have brought us together. I had a mission to go and reinforce magical law with that craft store you found. As you can see, they're breaking tons of laws spelling their ceramics to taunt potential buyers to come into the shop. Once in there, mortals and even magical creatures fall under a dozen other spells that rip them off, leaving them penniless and with a bunch of crafts that will clutter up their homes. I'm all for art, but let the consumer choose to purchase a gigantic ceramic dragon on their own."

Sophia whipped back in the direction of the craft store. "They have a large ceramic dragon. I want it."

Liv encouraged her to turn around. "No, you don't. I'll deal with that shop after we have had a chance to visit."

"That's so weird your mission brought you here and I was here as well," Sophia mused.

The Warrior nodded. "That's often how the universe works. It's wonderful and mysterious. For instance, how many times have you been thinking about someone and they call or message you?"

"Tons of times," Sophia answered.

"We're all connected, and when we think about each other, it's like little beacons that shine on us, ringing a phone."

Sophia smiled, loving this concept.

"I was thinking about you," Liv continued. "As I often do, but not just because I was missing you. I knew I needed to relay some information, so I checked your coordinates and found you were here. It worked out perfectly!"

"You checked my coordinates?" Sophia asked.

Liv chuckled, steering her into a restaurant with a buffalo on the sign. "This work?"

Sophia nodded, thinking she could eat just about anything. "Coordinates. Do tell."

"You haven't figured out I have one of those location sharing apps installed on your phone?" Liv gave her an incredulous expression.

Sophia whipped out her phone. "Are you serious? Why didn't you tell me?"

Liv gave her an embarrassed grin. "Because when you left for the Dragon Elite, I knew you needed to prove you could do things on your own. And I believed in you. Clark was worried as hell, though, because he's Clark. Anyway, to make him feel better and because I'm your big sister, I installed a location-sharing app on your phone covertly. It works in the magical world for all the strange places you go that wouldn't register otherwise. You've been to other planets, which is very cool." Her sister looked impressed.

Sophia laughed, remembering going to Oriceran. "Yeah, my travels take me to as many interesting places as I'm sure yours do."

"True that," Liv said, waving at the hostess as they entered the restaurant. She led them to a corner booth tucked away from the rest of the busy place.

"Are you mad?" Liv asked as they slid into the booth.

Sophia shook her head right away. "No, why would I be? You're just looking out for me. I left home to join a secret society of dragonriders stuck in the seventeenth century. I think I would be offended if you hadn't installed a location-sharing app on my phone."

Liv nodded. She hadn't even glanced at the menu when the waitress came to their table. "I'll have nachos with extra cheese. No sour cream. If there's sour cream on it, I'll send it back. While you're at it, substitute the guacamole for more cheese."

The waitress gave her an uncertain expression. "You want nachos with extra cheese and then more extra cheese?"

"That's right," Liv affirmed.

"Okay," the woman said, drawing out the word and turned her attention on Sophia. "And for you?"

"Make that two orders of nachos with triple cheese," Sophia stated.

"The nachos are actually pretty big," the waitress told them. "Do you two want to share?"

Liv and Sophia both laughed.

"Yeah, right. I would cut this one if we had to share," Liv laughed.

"Um…all right," the very confused waitress muttered as she walked away, probably rolling her eyes.

Liv looked across the table and smiled proudly at her little sister. "I taught you well, didn't I, ordering nachos and making mortals rethink if we should be allowed loose in public."

Sophia nodded. "Now, you said you needed to talk to me about something, and that's why you tracked me down with your secret location-sharing app. What is it?"

The light expression on her sister's face dropped. "Yeah, about that. I have some bad news."

CHAPTER EIGHTY-EIGHT

"Is it Clark?" Sophia asked in a rush but immediately dismissed the idea. There was no way Liv would be laughing and ordering nachos if something had happened to one of the three last remaining Beaufonts.

"He is fine," Liv assured her. "Well, he's Clark, so he isn't really fine. He is neurotic and annoying me to death. Even for as big as my place is, he seems to always be in my space, reorganizing the pantry or complaining I don't use a coaster. Can he come and live with you at the Gullington? You all have a few extra bedrooms, right?"

"A few," Sophia agreed, knowing dozens of dragonriders used to call the Castle home. "I'm afraid the one time you all were able to come to the Gullington might be the last. Outsiders really aren't allowed inside the Barrier, which is why I've got to figure out how to get the gnome to allow Saint Valentine into the Castle."

"I have so many questions related to that string of words, but we will get to them later," Liv said as the waitress slid two huge mounds of nachos in front of the two women.

"Should I bring a to-go container?" the waitress asked with a snobbish glare.

"If you like wasting time," Liv replied. "Come back in a few. I might need to order some more food."

Sophia stared at her food, not as hungry as she had been while she waited for the bad news. Liv didn't wait to dig into her pile of nachos, looking as ungraceful as ever as she crammed chips into her mouth. She paused when she realized her sister wasn't eating and pushed back from the table.

"Oh, sorry," Liv apologized. "You want to know about the bad news."

"You think?" Sophia fired.

"Well, it isn't horrible news," Liv corrected. "It's a challenge and I have solutions, but I fear those might sound like more bad news to you."

Sophia pushed her food away. "You're really making me feel better," she said, sarcasm dripping in her tone. "Usually people say things like, I have good and bad news. You could try that approach next time."

Liv nodded and wiped her mouth. "Great idea. I have some bad news and some good news. Followed by some more bad news. What would you like first?"

"Bad news," Sophia remarked.

"Well, the first set of bad news is that Alicia needs money to fix up the LiDAR equipment," Liv explained. "She didn't know how to tell you and didn't want to disappoint you."

Sophia lightened. "Oh, is that all? We need money. That makes sense. I mean, I know she had gotten the equipment but—"

"She needs a lot more," Liv told Sophia. "She can get it on her own, but she will need the funds to do it."

Sophia, feeling much better, dug into her nachos. "The Dragon Elite have money. This is a non-issue."

The look on Liv's face told her it was still a major issue. "I don't think the Dragon Elite will have nearly enough."

"Okay," Sophia said. "Well, the House of Fourteen has pretty deep pockets. Maybe they can loan it to us. I don't know, give it to us for having to hide in the Gullington for many centuries thanks to one of their own making it so mortals could not see magic."

Liv laughed. "I like the way you think. Retribution for what the Sinclairs did to the magical world. Don't give the gnomes any ideas or they will sue us, too. However, I don't think the House of Fourteen can loan the money."

"Oh, really." Sophia was disappointed. "Why?"

"Because they don't have it," Liv informed her. "Well, honestly, they don't have this much."

"How much does Alicia need?" Sophia asked, bracing herself.

All humor left Liv's face. "Twenty million dollars."

CHAPTER EIGHTY-NINE

"What?" Sophia exclaimed, earning the attention of the other patrons in the restaurant.

She pushed away her nachos, having lost her appetite. "How can she need that much? I gave her most of everything she needs."

"I don't know entirely," Liv professed. "It's complicated tech stuff to do with magitech software and nuts and bolts. She explained it to me, but honestly, I tuned her out after a minute or two. She is just so pretty to look at it distracts me."

"Twenty million dollars," Sophia said, looking off. "Yeah, the Dragon Elite doesn't have that. The House of Fourteen probably doesn't either, and if they did, they wouldn't loan it to us. I'm not sure where to get it, but we need to get that LiDAR. We need it to recover the dragon eggs."

"But that's all based on a hunch," Liv argued. "Are you sure they're buried in the ground?"

Sophia didn't answer, only gave her sister an angry stare.

Liv held up her hands in surrender. "I believe you. I trust my hunches all the time. I just had to check before I gave you the good news."

"Now you're talking." Sophia rubbed her hands together. "Tell me something good."

"I know someone who will give you the money," Liv declared triumphantly and took a bite dripping with cheese.

"That's great news! Who is it?"

The smile faded from Liv's face. "Remember I said I had bad news, good news, and more bad news."

"Oh, right." Sophia deflated a bit. "Okay, I'm ready."

"The person who I believe will give you the money is…King Rudolf Sweetwater."

CHAPTER NINETY

Having to ask King Rudolf for twenty million dollars wasn't bad news. It was horrible news. After Liv had told her, Sophia then lectured her on the use of proper adjectives.

Liv listened dutifully, realizing her sister was freaking out. When Sophia had vented sufficiently, the Warrior for the House of Fourteen cautioned her on several things.

"Any and all agreements with a fae are binding," Liv explained, having finished off her entire platter of nachos, much to the waitress's surprise. She then asked for a dessert menu. The waitress seemed insulted by the gluttonous behavior. "I don't guess she would like to hear I can't really gain weight since I'm a magician and my fat fuels my powers," she had related when the waitress stomped away.

"So, I just have him give me the money and don't agree to anything," Sophia asked, not having done as good a job with her own pile of nachos.

Liv shook her head. "No, he will say something like, you can pay me back later, or I'll do you this favor. You have to shut that shit down. Otherwise, later will come and that sneaky fae will demand a hundred years of servitude."

Sophia gawked. "He can't do that. I work for the Dragon Elite."

"Their agreements supersede all else. Believe me, I have been down this road with that airhead fae before. Remember, I risked my life to save his equally dumb wife. Why do you think I did that?"

"Because you unknowingly agreed to something, and later he held you to fine print you didn't know was there," Sophia guessed.

Liv fired a finger gun at her. "Bingo. Again, I've taught you well."

"So, what do I do?" Sophia questioned as the waitress brought the dessert menu.

Liv pushed it away, not looking at it. "We will take one of everything."

The waitress, not appearing impressed, pivoted sharply and marched back toward the kitchen. "Should I also tell the mortal I age slower than her and will live much, much longer?"

"Why are you such a pain in her ass?" Sophia wasn't used to seeing her sister being rude to anyone who didn't deserve it.

"I'm working," she answered. "As well as overindulging with my little sister." She leaned forward. "You see, the waitress is married to the guy who runs the shady craft store."

"Wait, he's married to a mortal?" Sophia asked.

"Yes, and he uses her to test the spells he puts on the shop," Liv explained. "I'm getting the range of her emotions so I can figure out how he does it and shut the operation down."

"She is his barometer for the spells." Sophia put it all together.

"Exactly," Liv affirmed. "If I can push her to an edge, I can figure out a way to break his spells. Then I shut him down, cart him away, and fine the hell out of his wife."

"If they're scamming so many people, why does she have to wait tables?" Sophia asked.

"You're about to find out," Liv told her as the waitress returned, carrying several plates. She laid a large slab of chocolate cake down in front of Liv, followed by a slice of apple crumble, a thick piece of cheesecake, and a bowl of chocolate mousse.

"Thanks," Liv said, looking at the waitress. "Hey, we're not from around here."

"No kidding," the waitress remarked.

"Yeah, I know, shocking." Liv stuck her finger in the mousse and licked it off. "Any suggestions on things to do?"

"Yeah, there's a craft store down the road a bit." The waitress's demeanor changed entirely. "You should stroll down that way and check it out."

Liv nodded and smiled at her sister. "Thanks. I'll definitely stop by there."

When the waitress left, Sophia gave her sister an impressed look. "So that's why she works here. She sends unknowing tourists down to her husband's shop. She also has a crush on the cook, but I just know that because I've got mad investigation skills."

"People are so complicated and convoluted," Sophia related.

"Except for King Rudolf," Liv stated. "Let me tell you how you're going to deal with that clown."

CHAPTER NINETY-ONE

The lights and energy of Las Vegas were again a stark contrast to Sophia's last location. She already missed the quiet and quaintness of Whitefish, Montana.

Las Vegas had never been appealing to Sophia. It was one reason she enjoyed the Gullington so much. In the quiet of the Expanse, she could hear her thoughts and feel at peace with Mother Nature, both literally and figuratively.

If she wanted the funds, they desperately needed to move the LiDAR project along, then she would have to stomach Las Vegas since it was where the fae palace was located. She brought her chin up to look at the Cosmopolitan that stretched up to the sky before her. It was the location of King Rudolf's throne. Although Sophia had told Liv she had run into him on Roya Lane and didn't think he was currently home, her sister assured her he was back, having to attend to fae affairs. She then advised Sophia on how to go about getting the money so she didn't get stuck in some crazy binding agreement where she owed part of her life to Rudolf.

The smoke hit Sophia in the face when she entered the casino and made her way to the entrance to the King's chambers.

"Do you have identification?" a fae guard asked when she tried to speed by him.

She patted her sword and smiled.

"That isn't going to work," the guard said. "We stopped using weapons as identification when there was a series of accidents from us sitting on our swords. King Rudolf says we're not allowed to carry them anymore, so I'm going to need an actual ID."

Sophia rolled her eyes. The sword as an ID had been a joke, but she was reminded never to underestimate the stupidity of the fae. "Actually, King Rudolf is a friend of mine. I'm Sophia Beaufont, a rider for the Dragon Elite."

The guard was incredibly attractive but apparently had cotton balls for brains grinned. "Cool. I'm a driver for Uber in my spare time. Maybe I can give you a lift some time."

"No, riders..." Sophia shook her head. "Can you just tell the king I'm here? I need to speak with him right away."

He nodded, walking down the hallway and poking his head in through a doorway. "There's a girl here who says she is with the Monster Elite or something, I don't remember entirely. She has a sword and blood on her shirt. Should I let her in?"

Sophia jerked her head down to look at her top. She was in fact wearing salsa from the nachos.

"Sounds good to me," she heard Rudolf call. "What could be the harm."

The guard turned, waving Sophia over. "He said yes."

"I heard," Sophia replied with a grateful smile, although she wanted to slap the guy in the head for being so dumb. She worried about anyone who rode in his Uber. He should not be allowed to cross the street by himself, let alone drive a motor vehicle.

"Oh, it's Sophia!" Rudolf cheered when she entered. The king of the fae was sitting on a blanket on the floor, the three Captains all wiggling around him, apparently enjoying some tummy time.

The room where they were hanging out had probably been a grand chamber for kings and queens of the fae to preside over courtly matters at one time. It was lined with large columns, and huge chandeliers hung overhead. There was a stunning view of the Bellagio fountains and the Las Vegas strip from the top of the Cosmopolitan. Under its current king, the large chamber was full of baby accessories and toys, making it look more like a nursery than a king's quarters.

"May I suggest that in the future," Sophia began, "when the guard informs you there's someone with a sword and blood on their clothing coming to see you, you maybe not welcome them in while your children are lying on the floor."

Rudolf shrugged. "Where is the fun in that? I figured it was probably Liv, but I like you nearly as much, although you're shorter and have that weird dog always following you around."

"That's my dragon, Lunis," she corrected.

He tilted his head to the side. "Are you sure?"

"Positive," she affirmed.

"Oh, well, you're just in time," Rudolf stated. "The Captains and I are playing hide and seek. It's my turn to be it."

"Oh no," Sophia sang, drawing out the two words.

"Yeah, it's fun, but they're not very good at it," he informed her. "But practice makes perfect." Rudolf covered his eyes and began to count to ten, which should have been fairly easy, but he reversed several numbers and skipped eight. When he got to ten, he yanked his hands off his eyes. "Ready or not, here I come."

His excited expression dropped when he realized the wiggling babies hadn't moved. Captain Morgan had actually fallen asleep. Captain Silver was gnawing on her fist. And Captain Kirk had scooted a few inches.

Rudolf shook his head. "Seriously, children. Do you need me to count longer?"

"Yes, keep counting until they're like five years old," Sophia suggested.

He shook his head. "I can't count that high."

"This is so shocking that when I recount it to my friends, they will hardly believe me," Sophia said, preparing herself for what she was about to do. "I didn't come here to watch you play with the Captains. I actually need your help."

Rudolf popped up to a standing position, a wide grin on his face. "And I'll of course help you. As your godfather, I promised I would always be there for you, my goddaughter."

Sophia shook her head. "Nope. You're not my godfather."

He patted her shoulder. "I know that since we don't look that much alike, it's hard to believe. Anyway, I remember when you were born and—"

"Again, no," Sophia interrupted. "You were not there."

He cradled his arms, looking fondly down into them as though he was holding a baby. "You were the ugliest little thing, but I promised myself if you should ever need my help, I would be there for you."

Sophia sighed. "I appreciate the sentiment, but honestly, I plan to give you something in return."

He nodded. "Obviously, I already planned you would name your firstborn after me."

"Nope," she said quickly on the heels of his statement.

"Just think about it," he encouraged.

Sophia shook her head. "Thought about it. Not happening."

"Maybe we should drink," he said, looking around as if expecting cocktails to arrive magically. "I think I have some milk and some... what is that clear stuff that tastes horrible?"

"Water?" Sophia offered.

He nodded. "I think I can get us something more adult."

"We're in Las Vegas," she said dryly.

"What does that have to do with anything?" he asked as he went over to a bar at the back of the room.

"Oh, for the love of the angels." Sophia followed him and wondered if she really needed the money that badly. She decided she probably did and swallowed her pride while bolstering her patience.

Rudolf glanced at the babies on the floor as he made them two cocktails at the bar. The children seemed fine, wiggling around, drooling, or sleeping.

"Where is Serena?" Sophia asked.

"Oh, she is sleeping," he answered.

Sophia narrowed her eyes. "It's the middle of the day."

"Yeah, but she was up working really hard for our family."

"Well, that's something at least," Sophia said, taking the drink he had made her only because she watched everything he had put in it. She did wait until he took a sip first before taking her own.

"She is exhausted after gambling all night and really heartbroken about losing a ton of money," Rudolf stated proudly.

Sophia tilted her chin to the side. "How is that working for the family?"

"Well, I own this casino." He held an arm up. "She is helping to keep my business thriving."

"By spending your own money at your casino?" Sophia questioned.

He nodded, not getting the point at all.

She knocked back the drink and set the empty glass on the bar. "Anyway, I've come here because I need money. I can't pay it back but—"

"Say no more," he interrupted, holding out his hand. A checkbook appeared. "How much do you need?"

Sophia held up her hand. "No, I want to do something in return for the money."

He pressed out his lips. "Yeah, okay. But first, tell me how much you need."

"Twenty million," she answered. "Seriously, first I want to do something for the money."

Rudolf waved her off. "We will figure something out. How about you just write me an IOU."

She adamantly shook her head, remembering what Liv had told her. She had to pay the debt first so Rudolf could not come back later with a binding agreement, making her do something she didn't want to do. "No, I can't take the money unless I earn it."

He frowned. "Really? But it's only twenty million. It isn't like I'll even notice that chunk of change missing."

King Rudolf was such an extraordinarily strange individual. Sophia pushed her glass forward. "I'll take another."

"I mean, twenty-million isn't even close to Serena's monthly gambling budget," Rudolf continued, mixing up another round of drinks.

"Doesn't matter," Sophia argued. "I want to do something for you first. Call it a code of the Dragon Elite."

He seemed to think for a moment, although Sophia sort of doubted much was going on in his very small brain. "Can you teach the Captains how to play hide and seek?"

Sophia glanced at the infants. "In a few years, but I need something I can do now. Something I can actually do that completes things. That way, we're even."

There was the word Liv stressed — even. He had to agree they were even before he gave her the money. Then after, she wouldn't owe him anything.

"Let's see, something you can do for me." Rudolf handed her a drink. "Well, I need something to test a theory I have about how sewer water can be recycled back into drinking water."

"Nope," she disagreed at once. "Next idea."

"Hm...Oh, well, I need someone to break up Liv and Stefan so she can spend more of her free time with me."

Sophia shook her head. "No, I refuse to do that."

"She always says she wants to hang out with her boyfriend instead of helping me take care of the Captains," he argued.

Sophia took a sip and found this drink stronger than the last. "Deal with it."

"Well, there's this guy I really don't like, and I want him offed," Rudolf offered.

"Is his name Stefan?" Sophia asked.

Surprise registered on his face. "How did you know?"

"I'm not committing any crimes for you or murdering anyone," she imparted. "There has got to be something you want that I can do for you."

"Technically you could break Liv and Stefan up, but you just will not do it. She is my best friend, and I'm lonely up here by myself with my fae all hanging around, asking for things."

Sophia felt sorry for the king of the fae. "Have you thought about asking your wife to spend time with you? Or, I don't know, help you raise the babies?"

He slumped, draining his drink. "She is depressed. She says she knows that since I'm fae and she is mortal she is going to grow old and look all wrinkly. I tell her that even when that happens in a few years, I'll still love her, even if I'll not look at her directly or touch her, but that doesn't seem to help."

"Shocking," Sophia said, rolling her eyes.

He nodded. "Yeah, and I get it. I've got another few hundred years of looking fantastic and living my best life. She has only got maybe another fifty years and will quickly degrade. She won't even live long enough to see the Captains enter their first stage of life since that doesn't happen for the fae until our one-hundredth birthday. So, she doesn't want to bond with them and is afraid of getting close to them and then dying."

Sophia shockingly found herself feeling sorry for the mortal. Sure, Serena was really dumb and selfish, but it must be difficult to love a man who was so different from her. As a mortal, she did have a severely shorter life than a fae, and although her babies were halflings, they would still have an extraordinarily long life. It was unclear how long, though, since as half-mortal and half-fae, they were an anomaly.

"I wish you had not said that part about not doing anything illegal," Rudolf said, blowing out a defeated breath. "Because then I would ask you to break one tiny little law that could bring my family together."

Sophia drew her chin down. "I'm probably going to regret this, but what is it?"

His blue eyes drifted fondly to his babies before returning to her. "There's a herb found in India. I've heard a rumor that if I find it, and if it's prepared a very special way and given to a mortal it will slow down a mortal's aging."

"Rumor?" Sophia questioned.

"Yeah, well, I tried to find it already, and Papa Creola shut me down."

She nodded. Anything that messed with time, such as aging, was considered against the law protected by Father Time. "When you say Papa Creola shut you down, what exactly do you mean?"

"His little minion told me that if I went after the herb, she was going to shave my head."

Sophia sighed. "Do you mean my sister Liv? Your supposed best friend?"

"Yes, I do!" he exclaimed, making the babies who had all fallen asleep wiggle, but they remained in dreamland. "I'm surprised you pieced that together."

"She works directly for Father Time," Sophia said dryly. "As in, she is the only delegate he has."

He shrugged. "Yeah, when you put it that way, I see how you figured it out."

"You want me to go after a herb my sister told you not to get, is that right?"

"Yes, but she likes you a lot," Rudolf answered. "I mean, it's like you two are blood, whereas—"

"We're blood," Sophia interrupted.

He waved her off. "Anyway, I'm sure she will not even notice if you pinch a bit of that herb. Then you just have to find bakers who are experienced with working with magical ingredients. They have to make it into something that will increase its potency. I give it to Serena and then she ages slower, hopefully rejoining our family and making me happy, which will save me from enslaving my people with demoralizing laws and overly taxing them."

"Well," Sophia said, drawing out the word. "When you put it that way..."

He prayed his hands together. "Please, Sophia. Please, please, please. If you do this for me, then I'll give you the twenty million dollars, and we will be completely even."

She considered her options. Ironically, she knew two bakers who were experts working with magical ingredients, Cat and Lee at the Crying Cat Bakery. It might be easier and more forgivable if she hired Lee to murder Stefan. She dismissed the idea. She really liked Stefan Ludwig, and Liv did too. But going behind her sister's back wasn't something she could do. That meant she had to pull her sister card and enlist Liv's help.

Finally Sophia let out a tired breath, feeling the alcohol hit her. "Fine, I'll do it."

Rudolf ran around the bar and threw his arms around her shoulders. "You're the best, Sophia. Thank you. I promise you'll not regret this."

She pulled herself out of his tight grasp and shook her head at him, but still smiled. Sophia was doing this for the twenty million dollars, but she would probably have done it anyway, just to help the king of the fae. Rudolf was a lot of things, and one of them was a very good person.

Her eyes drifted to the Captains asleep on the floor. He was an exceptionally attentive father and deserved for his wife to be there by his side. If she could bring their family together, well, she would do that for free.

CHAPTER NINETY-TWO

"Now I know you have lost your damn mind," Liv said, shaking her head at Sophia.

She had returned to Montana to find her sister on a stakeout outside the craft shop.

"I knew you were going to say that," she argued, having told her what she needed to do for Rudolf in order to get the money. "But think about it. Serena needs this. The king of the fae needs this. Those halfling children do."

Liv's eyes fluttered with annoyance. "Don't bring my godchildren into this. Keep in mind I brought that woman back to life, defying all sorts of laws. That dumb bimbo should just be happy she isn't dead anymore. Now she wants us to slow down her aging."

"Well, think about it from her perspective," Sophia countered. "She only has so long left, and her husband and children will live for centuries without her. Of course, she is spending her days in the smoky casinos. She is probably inviting a quicker end at this point."

Liv crossed her arms over her chest and gave Sophia a very rude stare. "Don't try to appeal to my softer side. I don't have one."

Sophia bumped her hip into Liv's, batting her eyes at her. "Yes, you do. You care about the world and you love Rudolf. He is like your best friend."

Liv shot her a fiery glare. "You're my best friend. Stefan is. Clark is when he is asleep and not pestering me. Rory would be if he would wise up and realize my jokes are hilarious. But Rudolf, well, he is a lavish fae who needs to go to college."

"Liv…" Sophia pleaded. "I know that, but you also know I'm right. Rudolf is worth helping. Saving Serena will save the fae kingdom; otherwise, that man is going to fall further into depression and his people will suffer. His children will, too."

"Soph, you don't know what you're asking me to do. I'll have to go against Papa Creola. Do you know what that man does when he gets angry?"

"No," Sophia said quite seriously. "What?"

"He does this whole silent angry thing," she insisted. "It's really annoying because I know he is mad at me, but when I ask, he is all like, 'Nothing. It isn't anything.'"

"Really? That's it?"

"Well, he can hold a grudge forever," Liv said with a laugh. "Literally forever."

"But he loves you, and you have special privileges," Sophia argued. "If anyone could get away with doing this, it would be you. We have so many reasons. It helps the fae. It helps the first halflings in who knows how long. It helps the Dragon Elite. Need I go on?"

Liv considered this. "I don't know, Soph. This is a lot."

She shrugged. "Okay, then the only option is you spend all your free time with Rudolf so he isn't lonely."

"Fine!" Liv threw up her hands. "I'll do it."

Sophia smiled. "Thank you! You'll not regret this."

"I'm certain I will, but I would do just about anything for you."

"What are you going to tell Papa Creola?" Sophia asked her sister.

She shook her head. "I'm not telling him anything. We're going with the whole ask for forgiveness, not permission strategy on this one."

CHAPTER NINETY-THREE

L unis wasn't taking the news well at all, and Sophia didn't know what to say to make him feel better.

The silence that stretched on between them hurt her heart. She knew it hurt him too because she could feel it.

Sophia had returned to the Gullington to rest up, change, and grab supplies. When she woke at ridiculous o'clock, or as everyone else called it 'sleep time,' she made her way out to the Expanse where her dragon met her.

The Gullington was unsurprisingly dark at three something in the morning. But the glow of the stars and the half-moon in the sky made the grounds glisten.

In the distance, she noticed a short figure. Quiet was standing on the Expanse, doing whatever he did.

Lunis flew down from the Nest when she took a seat, pulling her attention away from Quiet. Business with him would have to wait. Sophia knew Lunis had made quite the bachelor pad for himself at the Nest. Then they had argued until they both went silent.

Finally, Sophia tried to change the subject. "Don't the other dragons ask you where you're sleeping at night?"

Yes, he answered sullenly. *I tell them in their mom's bed.*

Sophia laughed, the sound echoing in the quiet night air. "That's funny because you all don't have mothers."

That's always their reply, but it's all very clinical, he said, clearing his throat and shaking his head, preparing to do a Bell impression. *'As dragons, we know no parents. Therefore, you can't sleep in my mother's bed.*

Sophia continued to laugh. No one but Lunis made her really laugh like this. "Did she push you on where you're hanging out when not in the Cave?"

Lunis shook his head. *Just once, telling me she wasn't buying I was sleeping in her mother's bed. And I replied by saying, 'Your mom goes to college.'*

Sophia shook her head. "I'm guessing she didn't get the Napoleon Dynamite reference."

You think? he asked, giving her an annoyed expression.

Sighing, she said, "I know you don't like this…"

You're supposed to go on missions with me, he said, cutting her off.

"And I do," she argued. "Once I secure the funding, you're going to lead the LiDAR mission."

Really? he asked, hope springing to his eyes.

Sophia nodded. "Yes, I decided we will take our chances. We will put the LiDAR equipment on you and have the other dragons fly behind you for backup, in case something goes wrong."

He seemed to like this. *I want to be your plane.*

"But this time," she said each word carefully, taking great care picking them, "I need to go alone."

He slumped. *But you just went on several missions alone. You went to London without me—*

"Because they don't take kindly to dragons strolling down High Street," Sophia cut in.

Then, he continued, *you went to Montana without me.*

"Because I had to get fitted for a dress," she argued.

I like to go shopping with you.

"I can't wait to show you the dress," she told him.

Then you went to Las Vegas.

She shook her head. "And I lost half my brain cells to do it."

The young dragon shook his head. *Now you're going off on a really cool mission to fight aliens in India and I have to stay behind.*

Sophia giggled. "It's a scorpion goddess."

Same thing, he cut in.

Liv had informed Sophia about the mission. The herb Rudolf sought was located in the southern region of India and was known as *kanike,* but to get to it, they had to break into a temple guarded by a scorpion goddess who was literally a huge scorpion with the body of a woman on the top half, and a deadly stinger on the back half. If they got past her, then they could get the herb and take it to the Crying Cat Bakery.

Apparently, the herb had formed through some cosmic Hindu force after worshippers long ago left gifts at the shrine of a goddess known as Chelamma. The best or worst part was that Liv said they could not kill the scorpion goddess. Instead, they had to defend themselves the best they could and use strategy and trickery to get past her. Sophia was fine with the idea of using strategy. But what if Chelamma, as she was still known, used deadly force against them? They were simply supposed to stun her, not causing injury, to get away. That seemed difficult. Sophia remembered her recent adventure battling the giant worm with Wilder, and if she had been told she had had to get past it without killing the monster, she would be dead.

"I want you to go, Lun."

But Dumb Face doesn't, he protested melodramatically.

She sighed. "Liv doesn't think a dragon in India is a good idea. You'll draw attention, and we need to be stealthy."

I can glamour myself, he argued.

"We have to maneuver through tiny temples," she continued.

Are you calling me fat?

Sophia laughed. "You do weigh a few tons."

So you're calling me fat, he said with a wink. *I'm thinking of trying out keto. I mean, I already eat meat almost exclusively.*

"Yeah, if you could just stop eating so much chocolate chip cookie dough," she said, still laughing.

Oh! he exclaimed, obviously excited. *You know those chocolate chip cookie dough protein bars you pretty much live on?*

She nodded. "Yeah, the Quest bars."

The other day, I accidentally breathed fire on one of them, and guess what?

"What?" she replied.

It totally turned into a fresh-baked cookie.

Sophia shook her head. "I'm not surprised."

First it was a protein bar flavored like chocolate chip cookie dough, he said, excitement filling his voice. *And then poof, it was a steaming hot cookie. Really good too. I ate through your entire stash after that.*

She cut her eyes at him, scowling.

Is this when you call me fat again? he challenged.

"I haven't done that once," she protested. "And Lun, I want you with me all the time, and in a way, you always are. But you can't go on every mission with me. The more urban ones, if you were there, it wouldn't be right. You get a lot of attention because you're an amazing and magnificent dragon."

And I don't fit in pubs, he pouted.

She nodded. "That's true. But the most important missions, like recovering the dragon eggs or fighting the biggest baddies, I can't survive those or be successful without you."

You're just trying to make me feel better, he said.

She shook her head. "I would never do that."

Lunis huffed. *I'm just feeling left out and maybe a little lonely.*

"That's understandable." Sophia scooted over and put her arm around her dragon, which was awkward and looking like a flea trying to comfort a human. "Maybe you should think about moving back into the Cave. Being around your own is important."

He shook his head. *No, those new hatchlings are the worst. They have awful tempers, make a mess of everything, and put the other dragons in horrid moods.*

Sophia considered this. "Well, maybe then offer for Simi or someone to join you in the Nest."

He cut his eyes at her. *You think that because you're with Wilder, your dragon should hook up with his?*

"First of all," Sophia trailed away, shaking her head, "I don't even know how to go about addressing that."

He smiled at her. *Go on your mission with your sister, Soph. You never have, and I think it will be good for both of you. She loves you fiercely, and even if she annoys me to no end, simply because she likes getting under my skin, I can't not like anyone who adores you so much.*

"Thank you, Lun," she said, leaning her head against him, enjoying his warmth. He was right that going on a mission with Liv meant a lot to her.

Then go on your mission to "fix" Wilder, he told her. *And when all these side quests are done, I'll be ready to step in and save the day. How does that sound?*

She looked up at him with adoration. "It sounds like you're the best dragon in the whole wide world."

He combed his foot through the air, as though waving her off. *Oh, shucks. You stop it, would you?*

CHAPTER NINETY-FOUR

S ophia made her way carefully out to where Quiet stood on the Expanse, looking to the hills in the distance. She wasn't sure why, but she approached him like he was a flock of birds that might take off if spooked.

When she was only a few feet away, he turned to look at her, like he had been expecting her all along.

"Hey," she said awkwardly, wishing she had picked a better greeting.

He returned his gaze to the hills, studying them. She didn't know what it was like for him—to be the grounds of the Gullington, controlling every aspect. There were so many mysteries about the gnome, and she almost didn't want to solve them because it was more fun not knowing.

"I have a request to make," she began, formulating all the reasons in her head in categorical order so as to present her case as succinctly as possible.

He turned to face her, lifting his chin so she could see his eyes under his cap. "Yes," he said in a quiet yet audible voice.

"Yes?" Sophia questioned, unsure she had heard him or that he even knew what he was saying yes to.

"Yes, to Saint Valentine entering through the Barrier," he expressed.

"Oh, thanks," Sophia said, finding herself speechless. It was what she wanted, so she didn't know what else to say. There was something else bothering her.

"While I have you here," she began, noticing the early signs of sunrise starting over the hills in the distance. "Why are you waking me up early every morning? You let the others sleep in. I dare say, some of them sleep much longer than they should." She laughed but was also secretly jealous. Not that keeping secrets from Quiet worked.

He was still studying the dark hills, which were quickly gaining light from the new day dawning. "This is the quietest time of the day when most are asleep and you can hear things that are usually over-powered by the hum and drum of the day," the gnome said at an audible volume. "If you want to hear the secrets, the ones you have longed to know, or maybe even have hidden away from, at this hour is the time."

The groundskeeper of the Gullington strode off for the hills, leaving Sophia to contemplate his strange words.

CHAPTER NINETY-FIVE

"Wow, that's beautiful," Sophia remarked.

Liv brushed her hair off her shoulder and batted her eyelashes. "Why, thank you. I've switched shampoos."

Sophia giggled at her sister and pointed straight ahead. "I was referring to the ancient Indian temple."

"Oh," Liv said, pretending to be offended.

Before them in the southern region of India was an exquisite temple so intricately carved its thousands of places seemed to call for Sophia's attention at once. It was several stories high with a dozen steps leading to the entrance. Columns surrounded the structure, and behind it, rainstorms were forming.

"Well, I guess we better make haste, or we're going to get soaked," Liv said, hurrying up the stairs.

"Are you serious?" Sophia asked, hurrying beside her sister. "You're rushing to meet the scorpion goddess to avoid getting sprinkled by a gentle rainstorm?"

Liv halted, turning to face her sister. "This is your first time in India, then?"

Sophia nodded.

Liv laughed. "I would take the scorpion goddess over the torrential downpour, to be honest."

"Well, before the crazed Chelamma or the crazy storm, do you want to tell me what the plan is?"

Liv nodded. "Absolutely. We're going to walk in there and get the *kanike*. Then you're buying me enough drinks to get me delightfully buzzed. After that, I'll go and tell Papa Creola I broke his rule, as his sole and only trusted delegate. He will be angry and probably sulk for a bit, but he will not fire me because I'm the only one willing to put up with his bad attitude and horrible management practices. Also, I think in the end, he will agree this needed to be done. Then you'll toddle off to that bakery and get the cupcake or whatever they make and ensure Serena continues to be a total pain in my ass for upwards of a century. Any questions?"

"Yeah, just one," Sophia said, trying not to laugh. "You sort of glossed over the whole, getting past a giant scorpion goddess without killing her. You want to elaborate?"

"Right," Liv said, drawing out the word, seeming distracted by the dark clouds brewing overhead. "You've got fire magic, right?"

Sophia nodded. "Yeah, it came via the chi of the dragon thing I inherited."

"Lucky," Liv said, doing her best Napoleon Dynamite impression. "I had to battle tons of hot-headed gnomes to get that skill."

"You know," Sophia said with a sideways smile. "I think you and Lunis are more alike than either of you care to admit."

Liv seemed surprised by the sudden mention of her dragon. "Why would you say that? I don't have bad breath and sharp skin, do I?"

Sophia shook her head, laughing. "No, but he always makes Napoleon Dynamite references, as well as bad jokes."

Liv regarded her under hooded eyes. "I'm going to take offense to that last part. My jokes are awesome."

"They're so bad they're good," Sophia countered. "I think he is jealous of you, and if I'm honest with you..." She paused, assessing her sister's reaction. "I think you're jealous of him."

Liv pretended to study the storm clouds like she was a meteorologist about to give a report. She pursed her lips and said, "It's hard not to be jealous of him sometimes." She turned to face her sister directly. "He is your dragon, and that's amazing. You're amazing. You're the first female dragonrider in history. You have created a new batch of the last dragon eggs this planet will ever see. You're a legend in the making and have already changed so many things for the better in the time you have been on this Earth. Why wouldn't everyone want to be the closest one to you? That just happens to be Lunis and that's how it should be, but yes, at times it's tough because after you magnetized to him, you grew up rapidly, literally maturing overnight and left for the Gullington. It isn't his fault. It's no one's, just life, but sometimes it's hard to accept."

Sophia put her arm around her sister, hugging her tightly. "There's always room in my life for you. I need you both."

Liv pulled her in and hugged her back. "I know. I get it. I think we both just love you so much. That isn't a bad thing."

Sophia smiled, feeling the tender love of so many amazing people in her life.

CHAPTER NINETY-SIX

"Where do you think the light switch is?" Liv asked when they entered the ancient temple. Being Father Time's delegate came with loads of advantages. One of them being that Liv was able to open a secret entrance no one had come through in many centuries. The temple had been sealed long ago when Chelamma went into hibernation. Now only those who were thought to be after the *kanike* would dare to trespass. That would be Liv and Sophia.

Once the scorpion goddess realized there were thieves in her temple, she would wake up as an angry creature from her slumber and try to sting the hell out of them.

Sophia had Inexorabilis in her hands and her eyes darted to the side at the sound of every noise, which so far was only the emergence of tiny little scorpions. Never in Sophia's life did she think she'd be relieved to see small scorpions scampering under her boots. Her thoughts were literally, "Oh good, the queen of the scorpions has not arrived yet." She would delightedly put up with Chelamma's little babies until the moment their momma arrived.

Liv, beside her, had out her sword known as Bellator. It had been made by none other than the novel-writing giant, Rory.

There was something special about being on a mission with her sister that made Sophia proud. Being the youngest of five, she had always looked up to her older siblings but none more than Liv. Ian was always so serious. Reese was especially eccentric, and Clark was uptight. They were all wonderful in their own ways, but Liv was well balanced with a practical side and a sense of humor. As Sophia grew up, she had always wanted to be more like Liv than any of the rest, and here she was, back to back with her idol about to gently take down a giant scorpion without killing her and steal the treasure. Sophia could not think of a better bonding trip for the two sisters.

CHAPTER NINETY-SEVEN

The pair had illumination orbs hovering beside them, providing the light they needed to see as they progressed through the temple. Liv had been right. Light switches would be ideal. Sophia was reluctant to touch anything, though, since most surfaces were covered in cobwebs and dust.

"Come on, Chelamma," Liv complained as they entered a different room of the ancient temple. "Would it kill you to clean a little?"

"She is hibernating," Sophia corrected.

Liv rolled her eyes. "I've used that line before. It means I'm curled up on the couch and watching Netflix. The goddess could still sweep on occasion."

Sophia shook her head, but then froze when she heard a scampering louder than the small scorpions they'd encountered. "Do you think that's her?" she asked her sister.

"Or it's the cable guy, fixing the Netflix," Liv said in a horrified whisper.

"Ha-ha," Sophia replied dryly. "You don't need a cable guy to get Netflix."

"You don't," Liv agreed. "But Clark is awful at that stuff. He needs all sorts of help. He was trying to run our Netflix through the Wii."

"What is he from 2010?" Sophia laughed.

"One would think."

The scampering grew louder. Sophia was relabeling it scuttling. It sounded like a thousand little legs headed in their direction rather than eight.

Sophia braced herself for the mother of all scorpions and a strategy that would involve not killing her, while also incapacitating her and getting to her treasure.

The temple went from brown to black as hundreds of tiny scorpions sped into the room, covering the walls, the ceiling, and the floor.

CHAPTER NINETY-EIGHT

"Question," Sophia said, suddenly breathless. "When you said we could not kill Chelamma..."

"That didn't apply to her little babies," Liv fired, pivoting to face the arachnids directly.

The little jerks might seem small, but with their large pincers and arching tail tipped with a menacing stinger, they were anything but unintimidating. Facing a few hundred at once made Sophia want to run for the exit. As rain thundered ever louder over the temple, she realized she had to literally choose her battles.

Liv said the rainstorms in India could create flash flooding within minutes, making for instant danger. As Sophia faced off with a few hundred beady-eyed scorpions, she considered which was worse, drowning or death by scorpions. She decided to take her chances with the latter.

"So the plan?" Sophia asked from the corner of her mouth.

"I say we compete to see who can take out the most," Liv replied with a laugh.

Sophia shook her head. "Really, we're going to have a competition right now?"

"It's always a good time for healthy competition, Soph," Liv told her and turned to her side of the room, which had stopped filling with the scuttling legs of scorpions. They all flexed their tails, like soldiers trying to decide when to charge.

Sophia pivoted to face the army she had to battle. A hundred scorpions with pincers at the ready seemed ready to run up her body and sting her all over.

"Ready for this?" Liv asked.

"As ready as I'll ever be," Sophia said as thunder cracked overhead and the scorpions took off in all directions.

CHAPTER NINETY-NINE

*Y*ou're having all the fun without me, Lunis sulked in Sophia's head.

You're not seriously doing this right now, she replied, powering up her attack in the final seconds she had before the little jerks reached her.

Well...

Sophia could feel his unease. If he were there, he could open his mouth and scorch all these heathens back to hell. But he wasn't, and he wouldn't have fit through the temple entrance anyway.

If you want to have a part in things, then tell me what spell to use, Sophia asked her dragon.

She felt him smile. *Now you're asking the right questions. Do the one where you scorch them with fire from your mouth.*

Sophia nearly laughed, realizing he had read her thoughts. *Try again. How about something I can actually do, like a combat spell?*

Let me think about it, he related. *Give me a bit and I'll get back to you.*

The scuttling feet of the scorpions pounded the ground, walls, and ceiling of the temple like a drumbeat as they formed groups.

Um...cool, but I'll be scorpion dinner by then, Sophia informed him.

Lunis sighed. *Okay, fine. Why don't you try the knock-knock joke you tried on me the other day? It made me want to die.*

Sophia, facing total peril, tried not to laugh. Leave it to Lunis to make jokes in the face of death.

Lunis, I was hoping for something a bit faster acting than bad humor, she said a bit tersely, gripping her sword, although she didn't think it would do much good against a bunch of tiny scorpions.

Fine, fine, he said, sounding bored. *Then you'll have to rely on a cedar oil spell.*

Are you freaking serious, Sophia questioned, tensing as she feared the scorpions were going to attack at any moment. It was like they were stalling to see which one of the Beaufont sisters would wet their pants first.

I'm totally serious, he answered. *Cedar oil has long been known to not only repel arthropods but also kill them. Now, you'll have to ramp up its effects to make it fast-acting, but I have faith you'll come through. Or you'll die there, alone without me after leaving me to go on a mission with your sister.*

Do you feel better now, Sophia asked her dragon.

Sort of, he answered.

Now this cedar oil spell, Sophia urged. *How do I do it?*

I'm uploading the protocol, he said matter of factly.

Seriously, Lun.

It's all there, he told her. *Just pull it up from our shared drive.*

If you don't stop being so modern I'm going to..., she trailed away, realizing she knew the spell. He might have been joking, but Lunis had given her the perfect way to deal with the little jerks facing her.

And not a moment too soon as they took off in her direction.

CHAPTER ONE HUNDRED

As the little beasts charged at Sophia, she sent the essential cedar oil spell in their direction, holding up one hand while the other held her sword. The spell, which she had never practiced, seemed to flow naturally from her hand and hit the hundreds of scorpions, covering them with a light coating. It slowed them at first before making them lock up completely. Then one by one, they popped over on their backs dead.

The spell worked, she rejoiced to Lunis, watching as the league of enemies died off. Sophia continued to spray the little jerks with the spell, shooting her hand around the room.

Naturally, Lunis said, sounding smug. *Just call on me whenever you're about to lose your butt.*

Thanks, Lun, Sophia said as she fired off shot after shot at little scorpions that had gotten through and were making their way to her.

I'll never let you down, Soph, he said, before going quiet in her head.

Behind her, Sophia knew Liv was battling her own army of scorpions. By the good bit of cursing, it sounded like it was going mostly well. It was when the language got really colorful that things were not going to plan.

Sophia turned when she had stamped out the last of her scorpions to find Liv had too. She had used a different chemical spell.

"What was that?" she asked her sister.

"An acid spell," Liv answered. "I figured if it melts off your face, it should melt a scorpion. But caution, don't walk over there." She pointed to the area of the temple she had been defending. "I think the floor might cave in since I used...well, acid."

"It was effective," Sophia said, smiling at her sister and finally breathing again, although she realized that was a bad idea since the air was filled with chemicals in the enclosed area.

"Thanks," Liv said, sizing up Sophia's area. "You did mighty fine too. What was that spell you used?"

"Cedar oil," Sophia answered. "Lunis gave it to me."

Liv nodded proudly. "You used the 'Call a friend' option. I approve."

Sophia could not help but smile. She was on a mission with her sister, with her dragon helping telepathically. In the end, a family would benefit, and they would get the funding they needed to save the dragon eggs. It felt like everything was working out right finally.

Something that wasn't thunder shook the temple hard and Sophia realized she had spoken too soon. The devil was on her way. She was wearing eight shoes on her long legs and had a stinger ready to take out whoever had awoken her from her long slumber.

CHAPTER ONE HUNDRED ONE

"Is it too late to tell you I don't want to do this sibling mission with you?" Liv asked, pressing her back against Sophia's and holding up her sword, Bellator.

"Yeah, I think so," Sophia said, finding herself trembling as she clutched Inexorabilis.

"I mean, in hindsight," Liv remarked, her voice vibrating, "I should probably not be here right now. It's really a conflict of interest for me."

"I think you're in over your head at this point," Sophia observed as the noise from the other chamber got louder.

"Remember when you asked about having a plan earlier?" Liv asked.

"Yeah," Sophia replied.

"And remember when I said we should not kill her?" Liv continued the odd questions at the worst possible moment.

"Yep," Sophia answered.

The beast thundered into the temple room. Chelamma was at least ten feet tall and was almost not able to make it through the doorway. She appeared similar to a centaur in that she had the body of a scorpion but the top half was of a naked woman. Her genetics were all messed up in multiple ways because her face wasn't that great to look at either if you could get over the fact she had a huge stinger arching over her back. Her eyes were too small and her chin too pointy, and her teeth were very prominent. Her clawed hands were reaching forward even as she stalled in the archway of the entrance and looked at the two sisters. On top of all of the physical problems preventing Chelamma from getting a date was the fact she was super rude.

Instead of greeting the first guests she had had in a few hundred centuries, she opened her mouth and screamed, making a sound that made the temple vibrate and dust rain down from the ceiling.

"Yeah, as I was saying," Liv continued. "All protective acts are over. I'll suffer the repercussions. Let's take this horrid creature down. It's kill or be killed time!"

CHAPTER ONE HUNDRED TWO

Being able to kill the scorpion goddess was a huge relief to Sophia because she didn't know how they were going to incapacitate Chelamma without harming her. Now it was a no holds barred situation, which meant no limits.

Sophia unleashed a series of fireballs at the exact same moment her sister did. The good news was many of them hit the scorpion goddess. The bad news was many didn't, and they ricocheted off the walls of the temple and flew back at the sisters, making them both have to dive and duck to avoid getting scorched by their own attacks.

This gave Chelamma the chance to pounce, and her heavy pincers sliced in both Sophia and Liv's direction. The Hindu goddess remained stable on eight legs as her torture devices went to work, snapping at them.

Sophia rolled, bringing her sword up to counterattack the claw headed for her face. The pincer and her blade met in a battle of steel against claw. The harder Sophia tried to press against the pincer, the harder Chelamma pushed. It was like an arm-wrestling contest, except the prize was life and the punishment was death.

"Not today, Satan," Sophia said through gritted teeth, mustering extra strength and pressing the claw down. When she forced past it, she brought her sword up and around slicing through the pincer, severing it completely.

A scream like nothing Sophia had ever heard before reverberated through the chamber and made both sisters cringe. It gave Liv a momentary advantage, and instead of lopping off the pincer she had been battling, she swung Bellator around in a flash of green light in an attack powered up by magic. With a series of movements, Sophia's sister took her breath away, chopping off the scorpion goddess's head and sending it rolling to the side of the dusty temple as her large body fell to the opposite side, crashing as her many legs gave way.

Liv somersaulted in the air away from the awesome attack and landed in a crouched position, Bellator to the side of her and her blonde hair partially obstructing her face as she breathed hard.

Sophia was breathless for many reasons, but the biggest was that she had just witnessed the coolest act of heroism of her entire life.

There was no one like Liv Beaufont in all the world.

CHAPTER ONE HUNDRED THREE

"Chelly is even scary when dead," Sophia remarked, peering down at the decapitated head.

"Ugly too. I definitely wasn't asking her for fashion or makeup tips," Liv joked.

Sophia looked her sister over, ensuring she was okay and realized that was what Liv was doing as well.

"Did you even break a sweat?" Liv asked her.

She patted her forehead lightly. "Just a tad. Should I powder my brow? Am I shiny?"

"Not at all," Liv said. "You're picture-perfect. But I fear your hair is going to get wet when we leave." She pointed to the ceiling of the temple where the rain continued to pound overhead.

Sophia shrugged. "I'm cool with it. I like rain now."

Liv actually laughed at this. "A Los Angeles girl saying they like rain is a first. Usually when it rains in La La Land everyone stays home, afraid they will melt."

"Well, their hair and eyelash extensions probably would," Sophia remarked.

"Yeah, or when they do actually go out but only wreck their cars,"

Liv added, stepping over the massive body of Chelamma. "Let's go get that *kanike*. Being in here gives me the creeps."

"Really?" Sophia questioned. "Is it the hundreds of dead scorpion carcasses or the giant one that gets to you?"

Liv glanced around as though seeing all the arachnid bodies for the first time. "Oh, those. I rather like them. They give this place a bit of flair and personality. But the dust is awful for my allergies and I can't stand not having windows. Really, would it kill the Hindus to install a window in their temples?"

She was about to stride into the next dark room when a figure appeared, blocking the path. For a woman who had not appeared the least bit fearful facing a giant scorpion goddess, Liv jumped backward and screamed like she saw a ghost.

Sophia pulled out her sword at the same time her sister did, both of them taking fighting stances.

The figure stepped forward into the light cast by the orbs. It was a man in a long yellow robe with a white beard and mustache. His hair was fashioned into a bun on the top of his head and he was barefoot as he shuffled forward, his hands held together in prayer.

Sophia eased a little, realizing this must be a monk of some sort who watched over the temple. As if he didn't notice the two sisters standing ready to strike, he strolled around them and eyed the dead body of Chelamma.

"Um...hey dude," Liv said, cutting her eyes at Sophia.

She knew what her sister was thinking. Finding Chelamma in the temple was expected. But a man was strange since the place had been sealed up for a long time.

Without responding to Liv's casual opening, the man turned to face them with an unreadable expression on his face.

Liv indicated Chelamma. "She started it. We just had to finish things."

"Whenever you point your finger at someone, three of your own are pointing back to you," the man said, reciting a famous Hindu proverb.

"Right," Liv said, nodding to the doorway. "We're just going to pop into the next room and grab a little something." She backed for the dark archway before pausing. "The shrine for Chelamma is this way, right? I would prefer to take the most direct route."

Sophia shook her head, disbelieving Liv was having this conversation with the strange monk.

"There are hundreds of paths up the mountain, all leading to the same place," the man began, his voice sounding like he was chanting. "It doesn't matter which path you take. The only person wasting time is the one who runs around the mountain, telling everyone his or her path is wrong."

"So, not this way?" Liv dared to ask, pointing at the doorway where Chelamma had come through.

Sophia indicated the opposite side of the room, where there was another door. "Maybe that way?"

"We could try splitting up," Liv offered.

"Help your brother's boat across," the monk began, reciting another famous Hindu proverb. "And your own will reach the shore."

Liv shook her head. "No, she is my sister. My brother isn't nearly as attractive, but don't tell him that. Not that I picture the two of you meeting. He never gets out and definitely doesn't frequent old haunted Hindu temples."

Sophia could not help but laugh now. "Okay, let's just go on this way. It makes sense Chelamma was guarding her shrine where the *kanike* is located."

"The three great mysteries: air to the bird, water to a fish, and mankind to himself."

Liv shook her head as she walked past the monk. "Yeah, okay, Frank. We're going to catch you later. Thanks for the words of wisdom."

"Frank?" Sophia asked when her sister strode up next to her.

"Well, he didn't introduce himself, so he got named," Liv explained.

"We didn't introduce ourselves either," Sophia said, giggling.

"I said, 'Hey, dude,'" Liv argued. "He didn't even say hi back. He just started pushing his holy agenda on us."

Sophia cringed slightly as they entered the other room, their light orbs following them. "Do you think it's possibly bad form to tease the monk in his own temple?"

"What do you mean?" Liv questioned, looking around the large room and trying to make out the details. "You think it's sacrilegious? Then I've got a whole bunch of people I need to apologize to. If Frank has a problem with it, he can take it up with my boss. Usually people let it go when they find out I work for Father Time."

"Who, by the way, is going to kill you for murdering Chelamma."

Liv nodded. "Don't I know it. The irony isn't lost on me. But don't worry, I'll deal with him. First, though, we need that herb, but this place is huge."

"Shut out the physical world," the monk chanted, following them into the large temple room. "Control the mind. Then you become free."

"Oh good, Frank is here," Liv said.

Sophia laughed, taking in the space. It was much larger than any of the rooms they had come through. Most of the area was empty, save for artwork and sculptures on the wall. The ceiling was domed and Sophia could make out more carvings on it, like on the outside of the temple. At the far side, she spied something that looked like it could resemble a shrine.

"Hey, over here," she called to Liv.

Her sister looked away from a mural on the wall she seemed to be trying to decipher, Frank at her back, calmly watching her like a museum docent ensuring she didn't touch the artwork. He didn't seem to mind they'd slaughtered Chelamma, but get too close to the murals and they were getting booted, Sophia thought, laughing to herself.

"What did you find?" Liv asked, hurrying over and Frank shuffling behind her. She glanced over her shoulder. "Yeah, you can come too, Frank."

"Certain things catch your eye, but pursue only those that capture the heart," he said as if in response to a conversation they were having.

"Dude, this guy is like how Subner was before you fixed Cupid's bow," Liv complained. "Constantly spouting hippie phrases."

"I think he is trying to help," Sophia told her, eyeing the man at Liv's back.

Her sister turned around and stuck her hands on her hips. "Here is something that would help. Where is the herb we seek? Our prize for slaughtering Chelamma."

Frank bowed his head slightly, his hands still in prayer. "When you were born, you cried and the world rejoiced. Live your life so that when you die, the world cries and you rejoice."

Liv sighed, turning back around. "That's why he isn't getting invited to dinner. Thoroughly unhelpful." She leaned forward and whispered, "He is a bit preachy and I bet silently judge-y."

Amused, Sophia spun to face the large structure on the back wall. It was a shrine for sure. The large statue of Chelamma made her shiver, the memory still fresh of facing her and all her babies. Around the shrine were many tiny statues and Sanskrit writing on the floor. There were no bowls of herbs or other offerings, as Sophia had expected.

"Hm... maybe it's in another room," she mused, striding with her light orb and taking in the space fully to ensure she wasn't missing something.

"Maybe," Liv said, her tone speculative as she knelt and ran her hands over the Sanskrit. "But something tells me it's here and we have to figure something out."

"Like a riddle," Sophia said with a sigh. "There always has to be a riddle, doesn't there?"

"Yes, because defeating a bunch of scorpions and their goddess is never enough," Liv joked.

"There's nothing noble about being superior to some other man," Frank stated, not having moved from his spot. "The true nobility is in being superior to your previous self."

"You know what, Frank," Liv said, glancing up from the writing she was eyeing. "Be a part of the solution, not the problem. Have you heard that one?"

That seemed to shut the monk up momentarily. Liv continued to study the Sanskrit as Sophia explored the artwork on the wall, looking for clues.

"As a Dragon Elite," Liv began, ruminating on an idea, "don't you speak all languages automatically since you're world adjudicators?"

Sophia nodded. "Yes, but I can't read it if that's what you're wondering."

"That was exactly what I was thinking," Liv replied, disappointment in her tone.

"Yeah, the translation happens automatically," Sophia explained. "Kind of like how the Doctor's Tardis does the translation for him and his companion."

Liv glanced up, a glint of pride in her eyes. "You're like the Doctor. I love it."

"I bet *he* can read it." Sophia pointed at Frank.

Liv shook her head. "We haven't spent much time together, and I already have little faith that he's a team player."

"What does a monkey know about the taste of ginger?" Frank replied, not looking offended.

"Look who is calling me a monkey," Liv retorted, appearing offended. "I'm not the one who lives in an ancient temple surrounded by a forest full of monkeys, now am I?"

"When an elephant is in trouble, even a frog will kick him," Frank imparted.

"Enough with the animal clichés," Liv groaned.

As if delighting in doing the opposite of what Liv asked, Frank said, "Love is a crocodile in the river of desire."

She rolled her eyes. "Dude, you really know how to push my buttons. Is your last name Sweetwater? Could you possibly be related to a fae I know?"

Sophia didn't think so since he didn't have that drop-dead gorgeous factor all the fae shared. She pulled her attention away from the random, weird thoughts. They had a mystery to solve and a herb to secure for the king of the fae.

"Do you have one of those translation apps on your phone?" Sophia suggested, pulling out her own device to check.

Liv did the same, and they shared frustrated expressions. "Absolutely no service." She flashed her phone at her sister.

Sophia nodded. "Magitech is a fickle thing. I've had cell reception on a different planet, but inside a Hindu temple, not."

"The power of God is with you at all times," Frank chanted. "Through the activities of mind, sense, breathing, and emotions, and is constantly doing all the work using you as a mere instrument."

Liv rose and gave the monk an annoyed expression. "I would like to use you as an instrument." She tapped her finger on her lips. "What are we missing? Besides a thorough knowledge of Sanskrit and a restraining order on Frank?"

Sophia laughed, pausing beside her sister and staring at the writing. "I get you two don't get along," she said, looking back at Frank, "but I think he is trying to help. We just have to decode his proverbs."

"Yeah, I think you're right," Liv agreed. "We have got to ask the right questions." She pointed down at the Sanskrit and pointed. "What does this say? Preferably in your words and not the Bhagavad Gita."

"A book is a good friend, which reveals the mistakes of the past," Frank replied.

Liv nodded. "Yep, that seems about par for the course. Thanks for nothing, Frank."

"No, but I think there's a connection here," Sophia said, her eyes drifting back and forth as she thought. "You mentioned the Bhagavad Gita and he replied with a proverb. I think he is limited in the ways he can communicate."

"You think?" Liv asked sarcastically.

"But," Sophia continued as she worked things out in her head. "If we, like you said, ask the right questions, he can offer us insights via proverbs."

Liv glanced up to the ceiling, a pleading expression in her gaze. "Seriously, you can't just ever give me something after I defeat the baddie. No, I have to make friends and decode a bunch of riddles."

Sophia pressed her hand onto Liv's arm, encouraging her sister to shush it. She looked directly at Frank. "How do we get the *kanike*?"

"They who give have all things; they who withhold have nothing," he replied.

"I've got something I can give you," Liv joked.

"That's it," Sophia said, putting it all together.

"What is it?" Liv asked. "I'm supposed to give Frank a knuckle sandwich?"

Sophia shook her head. "No, we have got to give something to the shrine."

"But we killed Chelly," Liv argued.

"Yeah, but the *kanike* is formed by the offerings and gifts given to the scorpion goddess," Sophia said, watching Frank's reaction for any clues as she spoke. "So even though we slew her, we have to give something to get something. I bet that's what the Sanskrit says."

"Well, Frankie?" Liv asked, looking to the monk for confirmation.

"Great minds discuss ideas," he began. "Medium minds discuss events. And little minds discuss people."

"A yes would have sufficed," Liv said, rolling her eyes.

"I think that was his way of saying yes," Sophia stated, feeling around her person for something to offer. She had her sword, her clothes, her phone, and pretty much nothing else. "I'm not sure what to offer, though. Does it need to be something valuable or does it not matter?"

As if in reply, Frank said, "Rivers don't drink their own water. Trees don't eat their own fruit. Clouds don't swallow their own rain. What great ones have is always for the benefit of others."

"I think he is saying it doesn't matter," Sophia imparted. "It just has to be something from us."

"Yeah, my boss talks in the same riddle-like way." Liv patted her cloak. "I have a bag of gummy frogs and a two-minute timer." She pulled the candy and a small hourglass from her pockets.

"What is with the timer?" Sophia asked.

"Don't ask," she answered. "A bad joke on my bosses' part."

"You two are cute." Sophia double-checked her pockets. Usually she carried a chocolate bar or something to refill her reserves, but she was all out.

"Here, I'll leave the timer." Liv handed Sophia the gummy frogs. "You can eat those and pretend they're that jerk frog from the craft store."

"Gladly," Sophia said, taking the candy but offering one to Frank first.

He held up his hand, as if declining and said, "Eating while seated makes one of large size; eating while standing makes one strong."

"A simple no would have worked, Frank." Liv put the timer in front of the shrine.

Nothing happened.

Thinking, Sophia popped a gummy frog into her mouth. "I wonder if we both need to give something."

Both sisters looked to Frank for confirmation.

He said, "He who does kind deeds becomes rich."

"Well, there you go," Liv exclaimed. "What do you have?"

Sophia frowned. "Only important stuff like my sword and phone."

The monk pressed his hands back together. "Kill a cow to donate shoes."

"I don't know what that means," Liv began, "but I think you have to give up something no matter what."

Sophia sighed and removed her cloak. She had just replaced it, but that was fine. There wasn't anything else on her person she wanted to let go of. Folding up the garment, she placed it next to Liv's hourglass and stood back.

For a moment, nothing happened, and it irritated Sophia. Then a moment later, the two offerings disappeared with a whirl of sparkles, like fairies were suddenly there. Seconds later, they were replaced with a pouch tied with gold rope.

Excitement filled Sophia's chest as she grabbed the sack. She opened it with shaking fingers and peered down.

"Well, is it..." Liv asked, her question trailing away.

Sophia had no way of knowing if it was the *kanike*, but she reasoned it had to be. Sitting in the bag were dried herbs that smelled bitter and sweet at the same time. "Yeah, I think so."

"Fantastic!" Liv turned to face Frank. "Well, just when you were starting to grow on me, we have to take our leave, Frank. Thanks for all the sage wisdom. Anything else you want to leave us with?"

He bowed slightly, a peaceful expression on his wrinkle lined face. "The most beautiful things in the universe are the starry heavens above us and the feeling of duty within us."

"Well put," Liv said, winking at the monk. "We're off to fulfill said duty. Take care and try to get out every now and again. Oh and sorry about leaving the mess in the other room. Just shut that part of the temple off until the smell of the rotting scorpion carcasses goes away."

Sophia waved to the monk as they made their way to the exit. When they were almost there, she heard Frank say, "Farewell, Beaufont sisters."

CHAPTER ONE HUNDRED FOUR

"I can't believe that funky monk could talk freely the entire time but instead communicated in riddles," Liv grumbled once they portaled to Roya Lane.

Sophia laughed. "Well, maybe he couldn't. Maybe he could only speak freely when saying goodbye."

"Yeah, because they don't have a Hindu proverb for that, huh?"

"I don't know," Sophia replied.

"They probably do," Liv remarked. "And it goes something like, real friends never say goodbye."

Sophia giggled "I'm just glad we got the herb. Thanks again for taking the heat on this from Papa Creola. I hope you're not in too much trouble. Well, actually, I hope you're not in trouble at all."

Liv dismissed her with a wave. "Don't worry about it. But if you hear thunder, then you'll know Papa Creola has struck me down with a bolt of lightning."

"Let's hope that doesn't happen," Sophia said with a laugh. "Okay, I'm going to go see about getting the *kanike* turned into a baked good for Serena. If you need me to come to your defense, just holler."

"Yeah, if you don't hear from me, please come and question that hippie elf known as Papa Creola," Liv joked. Her face then turned serious. "Seriously, it isn't a big deal, and more than anything, I'm grateful we got to go on a mission together. I like working with you, not that I'm surprised. However, I usually don't like others playing in my sandbox. I'm sort of the lone warrior type."

Sophia knew that about her sister and was glad to hear her say she had enjoyed their mission together too. "I think we work really well together, and if nothing else, you keep me laughing."

"The key to saving the world, I've found, is while risking your life, to do it while telling a joke."

Sophia giggled as she walked down the alleyway the opposite of her sister, leaving her in the middle of Roya Lane. "That's true. As a wise man once said, 'Laughter and tears are both responses to frustration and exhaustion. I myself prefer to laugh since there's less cleaning up to do afterward.'"

Liv flashed her a confused expression. "I don't remember Frank saying that."

"He didn't," Sophia informed her sister. "It was Kurt Vonnegut."

CHAPTER ONE HUNDRED FIVE

Sophia probably should not have been surprised to find Lee sharpening a long blade when she entered the Crying Cat Bakery. What did surprise her was Cat sitting in a chair in the corner with one leg elevated and an icepack on her knee. Wrapped around the baker, pinning her arms down was a bunch of bubble wrap.

"Is she okay?" Sophia asked Lee because Cat had her head back and appeared to be talking to an unseen entity on the ceiling.

"She is fine," Lee said, continuing to sharpen the blade. "Cat took another fall down the stairs in the back, so I fixed her up, gave her something strong for the pain, and wrapped her in bubble wrap so she can't hurt herself again. She is very accident-prone."

Sophia gave the wanna-be assassin a skeptical expression. "You get it's difficult for me to accept that she 'fell' on her own when you're constantly threatening her life? Also, you kill people in your side business."

Lee straightened, fear on her face. "Where did you get the idea I was an assassin? Who told you that?"

Sophia pointed to the blade in her hand. "You're sharpening a knife right now."

"It's for cutting cakes," Lee argued.

"Really thick cakes that have bones and need to be chopped into smaller pieces?" Sophia asked with a laugh.

"How did you know?" Lee replied.

Sophia pointed behind the counter. "There's a sniper gun on the table back there."

"That isn't mine," Lee said in a rush.

Nodding, Sophia pursed her lips. "Oh, and then there's this." She held up a poster she found pinned on the wall outside the Crying Cat Bakery.

It read:

"Is there someone who has pissed you off? Do you want them gone? Banished from this Earth, never to annoy you again? Inquire in the Crying Cat Bakery. We're running a special two for one. Take out both your in-laws. Get your ex and his bimbo girlfriend. Or use one and save the other for when someone new pisses you off. It's bound to happen. This is an investment in your future."

"Oh, that..." Lee's eyes darted to the side. "It says nothing about assassination."

Sophia stuck it on the counter. "I believe it's implied."

"Reason is implied in most situations and yet few use it," Lee retorted.

"Anyway, I'm here because—"

"Where is that man of yours?" Lee asked, interrupting her. "The one whose heart you broke?"

"He fell in love with me, so now he's no longer allowed to be around me," Sophia remarked.

"Oh, is that how it works?" A smile broke across Lee's face as she looked over at her wife, who was still incoherently muttering at the ceiling where fairies danced. "I'm so very in love with you, dear."

"See, it's things like that which make me think you pushed your wife down the stairs."

Lee gave her an offended expression. "I would never. She seriously has clearance issues. She walks from point A to point B and hits ten different things on the way. Believe me, if I wanted her dead, then she would be."

"You're not making me feel much better."

"Well, it's really all about you and how you feel, isn't it?" Lee spat. "Now tell me why you're here. I have to see a man about a thing in a bit."

"A man about a hit?" Sophia asked.

"No, he doesn't want his neighbors making so much noise."

"So, you're going to kill them?"

Lee shrugged, holding up both her hands. "I'm going to cut a hole in the floor next to the man's bed. If he falls through it to the basement below after stepping out of bed, so be it. If he breaks his neck after slipping on the marbles I lay on the basement floor, well am I really to blame?"

"That's your assassination attempt?" Sophia questioned. "There are like a hundred things that could go wrong. What if he hears you sawing through his floor? Or he gets out of bed on the other side? What if the fall from one story doesn't kill him? And slipping on marbles, is this a cartoon? Do you have an anvil you're going to drop on him too?"

Lee seemed to think. "An anvil is a good idea."

Sophia shook her head. "I'm just saying, I think there are more direct methods if you really want to take someone out, although murder is wrong, and as a member of the Dragon Elite, I encourage you not to kill."

"But you're not saying I can't, right?" Lee asked, her chin tilted to the side and a tentative expression on her face.

Sophia laughed. "Bad neighbors are the worst. I guess I can turn a blind eye this time but try to be a bit more discreet in the future. No more flyers posted on Roya Lane."

"That's fine," Lee agreed, laying down the knife and picking up a cake box. "We have got new shipping materials for our baked goods." She handed it to Sophia.

On the front of the box it read:

Crying Cat Bakery, where the baked goods are to die for. Literally. Get a hit on your least favorite person with each cake.

Sophia handed it back to Lee. "I'm going to pretend I didn't see that."

"You're being awfully easy-going about this," Lee said slyly. "What gives? This guy being in love with you have you down?"

Sophia shook her head. "No, I'm getting a dress made, and then I'll fix him."

"Usually a dress makes a guy fall harder," Lee offered.

"It's complicated," Sophia muttered, realizing how much more she had to do when she was done completing all these side quests for King Rudolf Sweetwater and the others.

"Complicated like his ex-girlfriend is stalking you and you need someone to take her out?" There was a spark of hope in Lee's eyes.

Sophia shook her head. "No, I don't think he has any exes. If he did have one who was stalking me, well, you wouldn't have to take her out." She patted her sword. "I would cut that skunk-smelling-two-bit-loser myself."

Lee nodded smugly. "I see why he fell for you."

"It wasn't anything I did," Sophia corrected. "It involved a crazed maniac and a bow and arrow."

Lee's mouth dropped open. "That's how Cat and I fell in love too! What are the odds?"

A laugh burst out of Sophia. "Anyway, the reason I'm here is I need your help." She held up the bag of *kanike* and offered it to Lee. "That's—"

"*Kanike*," Lee said with astonishment before even opening the pouch. "I thought I smelled the infamous herb. This stuff will extend a mortal's life."

"Oh, good, you're familiar with it."

Lee nodded. "You had to go through some pretty crazy stuff to get this."

"Yeah, if I see a scorpion or a monk this century, it will be too soon."

Lee took a closer whiff of the herbs. "You need me to put this into a baked good, right?"

"Yes. Can you do it?"

Lee seemed to consider, her eyes going to her wife, who was now peacefully asleep in the corner and snoring loudly. "I think I can sneak away from Mrs. Lee-You-Need to-Trim-the-Hedges-Walk-the-Dog-and-Rub-my-Tummy for a little bit."

"Wow, that's a long surname," Sophia said with a chuckle. "I'm guessing you didn't take her last name when you got married?"

"No, I kept mine."

Sophia looked around. "I didn't know you two had a dog."

"We don't anymore," Lee answered darkly. "It fell down the stairs."

CHAPTER ONE HUNDRED SIX

"What do you mean, you're okay with what I did?" Liv exclaimed when Sophia entered the Fantastical Armory. She had an hour to kill before Lee would have the baked goods ready and decided to stop by to ensure Liv wasn't getting murdered for helping her get the *kanike*. It appeared she wasn't.

The elf known as Father Time was smoking what appeared to be a peace pipe and regarding Liv placidly. He gave Sophia no notice as she came into the shop and halted next to her sister.

The hippie elf was wearing a T-shirt that said, If you're not barefoot, then you're overdressed. He blew out a plume of smoke. "I'm Father Time—"

"Yes, we have met," Liv said, her fists by her side. "You gave me that stupid two-minute timer because I'm always two minutes late and you thought it would be cute, but as an elf, you're just annoying. You were cute as a gnome."

"I also liked myself better when I didn't make friendship bracelets and smoke peyote, but alas, this is the form I've reincarnated into," Papa Creola relayed, laying the pipe down on the countertop. "I, of course, knew from seeing glimpses of future events that Sophia would ask you to help her get the herb to delay Serena Sweetwater's aging. I knew that since you'll do anything your family asks you to, you would help her, thereby ignoring my law about messing with aging, death, and time."

"But you're okay with it!" Liv roared, strangely upset she wasn't in trouble.

Papa Creola nodded. "Who do you think let it slip to King Rudolf Sweetwater there was such a herb in India that could extend his wife's life?"

Liv's eyes widened. "It was you? I've been keeping him from it for weeks! You could have clued me in and saved me a ton of time and trouble."

"As was your job to keep others from things that mess with the flow of time and aging. You were not supposed to allow him to get to the herb. The timing had to be just right. It had to be in exchange for the twenty million dollars Sophia needed." Papa Creola picked up the pipe and offered it to Liv.

She pushed it away. "Get that away from me, you dirty hippie."

Not at all offended, he took a pull on the pipe, shrugging like it was her loss.

"So you coordinated this whole thing, even though it defies your own laws?" Liv asked, still livid. "I don't get it. Explain."

"Liv, there's a time to uphold and defend the laws, and then there's a time when I must know when to flex them." He pointed to Sophia. "As your dragonrider sister so thoughtfully explained to you when convincing you to break my laws, this is for a good cause. The king of the fae will be happier, and a happy king makes for prosperous people. His halfling children will have a better future, which is important since they have an important destiny. And the Dragon Elite really needs to get those eggs back and further things with Trin Currante in order to keep the timeline on track."

"I don't suppose you're going to elaborate on that last bit, by chance?" Sophia asked, deciding to cut in.

He lowered his chin and regarded her from under hooded eyes. "What do you think?"

"It was worth a shot." Sophia took a step backward.

"It's just not fair." Liv stomped. "Even when I defy you, it's part of your plan. You knew I was going to do this, and it was all part of some scheme."

"Would you rather be in trouble?" he asked her.

She thought for a moment. "Maybe. I did kill the scorpion goddess. Doesn't that make you angry?"

He shrugged. "That was really the only way. It was a necessary part of the equation, and she will not really be missed. Who likes scorpions, anyway?"

"No one," Sophia said, shivering from just the thought of the gross things.

"I'm not in trouble and I did everything as you had intended, even though I broke your laws?" Liv asked.

Papa Creola nodded. "Yes, but if you break another of my laws in the future, there will be repercussions."

"Will I get fired or lowered into the pit of doom or die?" Liv asked.

"There's no pit of doom," Papa Creola told her. "I got rid of it ages ago when lemmings kept falling into it."

"Just so I know, if by chance I somehow slip up and break one of your laws, what is the repercussion?" Liv asked.

He pulled at his T-shirt. "I'm going to require you to wear this every single day."

Liv shuddered. "Fine. Okay. I won't break your laws. Just don't be so harsh."

CHAPTER ONE HUNDRED SEVEN

Relieved Liv wasn't in trouble with Papa Creola, she decided to stop by to see Mortimer at the Official Brownie Headquarters before going back by the Crying Cat Bakery to get the cupcakes.

Mortimer had agreed to look into a few things for Sophia. She was grateful to have the brownie's help, and he seemed happy to do anything she needed.

For Sophia, there was something not adding up about Trin Currante and her band of steampunk cyborg pirates. She asked if he'd had his Brownies research Saverus Corporation to find out what the company was up to. All she knew at this point was this company had been where Trin Currante escaped from, according to the hostages she had questioned after they raided the Gullington.

Apparently, Trin had gone back to Saverus Corporation and rescued the men, turning them into her allies and ensuring they did whatever she asked, like when they sacrificed themselves to invade the Gullington. After that, all the leads on the Saverus Corporation had dried up. Mahkah had not been able to dig up anything more. In order to discover what Trin Currante wanted with the dragon eggs, Sophia felt finding out what the organization had done was crucial.

Mortimer agreed to get right to work, finding information for her.

With that in motion, Sophia returned to the bakery to find Lee had made two oversized cupcakes. They were individually wrapped up in paper boxes with the Crying Cat Bakery's new, very long slogan plastered across the box, advertising its assassination side business.

"I figured if one of the cupcakes didn't work or you knew another mortal you wanted to live longer, then you could give it to them," Lee explained when she handed them over.

Sophia pointed at the boxes and magically covered up the assassination advertising by covering them in white. "Thanks. I had not really thought about it. I don't really know many mortals."

John Carraway, Liv's old boss at the electronic repair shop, and Alicia's partner, was mortal, but because he was one of the Mortal Seven at the House of Fourteen, he was already slated to live longer. His chimera, Pickles, protected his lifespan and kept him young. Still, it made Sophia feel more confident knowing she had two cupcakes, instead of one.

Something occurred to her, and she jerked up her chin suddenly. "You're sure the cupcakes will work, right?"

Lee nodded. "Oh, yeah. I'm not as good a baker as my drunk wife, but I can manage." She indicated the side workstation where Cat was lying on it like it was a bed. Her head was resting on a bag of flour. "I gave her another dose of painkiller since her knee was bothering her still after her fall."

"By painkillers," Sophia began, a question in her tone, "do you simply mean hard liquor?"

"Lick her?" Lee asked with a laugh. "I only lick her softly."

Sophia shook her head. "Please stop."

"Okay, well, you get those cupcakes to the mortal you risked so much to help," Lee encouraged. "I've got to go see a guy about a thing."

"You're not still going with the cut out the floor strategy, are you?" Sophia asked.

Lee shook her head. "Nope. I'm going with the anvil idea. Precariously hanging it over a partially open door."

Sophia sighed. "Yeah, I still think you could go with something a bit more direct."

"Like removing the reinforcement from his third-story balcony? Then I leave a loop of rope out on this balcony floor and I call him and wait until he walks out and steps into the loop, then I yank the rope and draw him off the side of the balcony and kill him with the fall?" Lee asked, her face quite serious.

Sophia scrunched up her brow. "You seriously are the worst assassin in the world. Why don't you just try using a sniper gun?"

Lee glanced back at it. "Oh, I don't like guns. I don't use that for the rifle. I just have it for the scope, but I do keep the safety off the gun because I like to live dangerously."

"Seems about right," Sophia said and wondered how she managed to make the strangest friends in the world.

Lee pointed to the cupcake box and squinted. "So you owe me something for that."

Sophia blushed, feeling bad for not offering something initially. "Yes, of course. How much?" She felt around in her pockets.

The baker slash assassin shook her head. "No, your money is no good here, dragonrider. Instead, I want you to do something for me..."

Dipping her chin, Sophia regarded her with hooded eyes. "Of course you do. That's always the way it is. Why don't the people I work with ever just want money in compensation?"

"Because that's boring," Lee explained. "We'd much rather put your talents to use. I've got money, but what I haven't got is a katana sword that has ten different magical properties and is revered for its healing abilities by the person who holds it."

"Wait, what?" Sophia pretended to ask. "You don't have that sword? I'm surprised. I thought everyone did."

Lee shook her head. "No, I dropped my katana sword in some suburban neighborhood on Halloween, as one does."

Sophia nodded. "As one does."

"That one I got at Walmart though and it didn't have any magical properties," Lee stated and then added, "Well, besides that it was dirt cheap."

"You can buy a katana sword at Walmart?" Sophia asked, realizing that really shouldn't be the take away from this all.

Lee shrugged. "I went in to buy milk and eggs and came out with a katana sword and a lawn mower."

Sophia laughed. "Yeah, neither of those are usually spontaneous purchases."

"You're telling me," Lee replied. "I don't even have a lawn so you can guess that Cat is pretty pissed about it taking up space in our living room."

"Why did you buy a lawn mower?" Sophia had to ask. "And why keep it in your living room?"

"Well, it was in the bedroom because I thought it made for a nice art piece, but Cat just kept draping clothes on it like it was a treadmill." Lee shook her head, disapproval on her face. "And both the katana sword and the lawn mower were on sale, so I couldn't really pass up the deal."

"But you don't have a lawn," Sophia argued.

Lee scowled. "I don't have a boat and you think that stopped me from personalized sails? And I don't have a car, but do you think that stopped me from buying custom rims?"

"I'm guessing no," Sophia said dryly.

The baker shrugged. "When I see a good deal, I get it. Of course..." She leaned forward, looking over her shoulder toward the back where Cat was probably sleeping. "My wife is really peeved about all these purchases."

"Because it's a waste of money?" Sophia asked.

Lee shook her head. "No, because they all end up in the bedroom, taking up space."

Sophia couldn't help but laugh. "It sounds like you'll need to get a bigger place with all that money you like to throw away."

She scoffed, like this was a bad idea on Sophia's part. "That would be a total waste of money. Real estate is a horrible investment. Everyone knows that."

"And what's a smart investment, according to you?"

"Toilet paper," Lee whispered. "I have a feeling that it will one day be quite the expensive commodity."

"Yeah, maybe..." Sophia gave her a doubtful look.

"Hey, when you're down to your last roll, you stop by here and I'll sell you some at an outrageous price," Lee offered.

"Thanks," Sophia replied. "But let's settle up for these cupcakes you made. You want me to go get this katana sword for you?"

"Yes," Lee stated. "But first you'll need to track down an expert in weapons."

A smile broke across Sophia's face as she thought about Wilder. "I don't think that will be too hard."

"You'll also need something that can project fire," Lee said, a disparaging expression on her face.

Sophia's grin widened. "Again, I think I can figure this out."

"Oh, good," Lee stated. "Then the last part will be easy. You just need a magic compass, Zack Efron and a pack of magic chewing gum."

"Is that all?" Sophia asked with a laugh.

"Well..." Lee toggled her head back and forth, thinking. "You could also use the ashes of a thousand warrior horses, preferably all black ones, but we could settle for only eighty percent of them being mono-chromatic."

"Ummm...I don't think I can get that."

Lee stuck her hands on her hips and scowled. "Not with that mind set you won't. Really, it's thinking like that which keeps you stuck in the dark ages."

"I'm the youngest dragonrider in history and the only one who has a knowledge or appreciation of modern culture," Sophia argued dryly.

Lee waved her off. "Forget the ashes of warrior horses. You can manage without it, so long as you have Zack Efron."

"Why him?" Sophia asked, thinking of the movie star who played one of her favorite roles in the Greatest Showman.

"He can tap dance," Lee answered at once.

"Well, I think there's a lot of people who can tap dance," Sophia argued. "Can you settle for someone who isn't famous and possibly difficult to locate and convince them to do whatever it's you have planned to get this katana sword?"

Lee rolled her eyes. "You're one of those people who puts nonfat milk in her coffee when ice cream is an option, aren't you? If I teach you anything, it will be not to settle. I want the best tap dancer there's and that's Zack Efron. Also, he has a winning smile and a great voice. I think that will be important."

"Okay," Sophia said, drawing out the word. "I need a weapons expert, a dragon, Zack Efron, a magical compass and magical chewing gum. Anything else?"

"No, but you might have to secure some strange treasure in compensation for the compass and the chewing gum."

"And how do I get those?" Sophia asked.

Lee shook her head. "I can't do everything for you. The compass has to be elven made and the chewing gum has to put the person who chews it into a fantastic mood no matter what the situation."

Sophia glanced around at the bakery. "You make magical treats here. Can't you help with that one?"

"No," Lee said at once. "We make baked goods. We're not a candy store. For that, you'll have to find the one somewhere on Roya Lane here. It's run by elves, so I apologize in advance for the hippie nonsense they will inundate you with."

Trying to remember where such a place was, Sophia's brow scrunched. Roya Lane was full of strange shops and government offices and it was impossible to know where everything was since it always changed around. However, she was certain she'd never seen a magic candy store on the street. "Do you know the name of this place?"

Lee nodded. "It's called Midnight Lunar Eclipse."

"Oh, I definitely haven't been there before," Sophia remarked.

"No, it hasn't been opened in a while," Lee explained. "It's only open during a tiny window."

Sophia huffed. "Let me guess. It's only open at midnight during a lunar eclipse?"

Lee's face broke into a smile. "And here I thought I'd have to spell it out for you."

"So I have to wait until then to get this magical chewing gum?" Sophia asked. "Is that all right?" She didn't want her debt to go unpaid.

Lee nodded. "It's what it is. I've waited this long for my katana sword. And you've got to get that cupcake to the mortal who is going to eat it."

Sophia glanced at the small white boxes, thinking of Rudolf and the money and all the other things she needed to accomplish. She wasn't excited about adding another mission to the list, but she was going to make good on things with Lee for baking the cupcake.

"Okay, well when is the next lunar eclipse?" Sophia asked.

"In a year," Lee replied. "So if you can secure some time traveling device that takes you to that spot, that would be ideal."

Sophia had already defied Father Time once. She wasn't sure that she could do it again. But also, he probably already knew about it and was going to assist her or have Liv stop her.

"Okay, time travel to the future," Sophia began. "Go to Midnight Lunar Eclipse and buy magical chewing gum. Recruit Zack Efron. Find a magical compass and then what? Where is this katana sword?"

Lee shrugged. "Beats me. But I've got a lead on it. So you go and feed a mortal that cupcake and get back to your day job. The next time that I see you, I'll have the location. Then you can go about getting the rest of the things you need for this mission."

Holding up the boxes, Sophia offered a smile. "Well, thanks for doing this. And I'm happy to make good on the deal once you have the location for the sword."

A wicked chuckle fell from the baker's mouth. "Don't be so willing to repay. If my suspicions are correct, you might be paying with your life or at least a limb or two. This won't be an easy mission, recovering the katana sword."

Sophia nodded, darkly. "It never is."

CHAPTER ONE HUNDRED EIGHT

Not happy to be back in Las Vegas, but thoroughly grateful to have fulfilled her end of the bargain for King Rudolf, Sophia strolled into the Cosmopolitan hotel and casino carrying the two small white boxes with the magical cupcakes.

She didn't really know what she would do with the extra one. According to Lee, it had to be consumed in the next twenty-four hours to work. Sophia could not really think of any mortals to give it to. She had considered giving both to Serena for good measure, but the assassin baker had warned that could be dangerous. Less was more in this case.

Sophia reasoned she would figure it out after she had completed this part of her mission.

Rushing through the lobby, she paused by a pillar and noticed a horde of crazed mortals glaring all around. Sensing there might be a security issue involving the king of the fae, Sophia listened in and tried to discern what was happening.

"He went that way," one of them said in a terse whisper.

"No, he went that way to Jesse Rae's," another argued.

"I'm telling you, Michael is here, hiding somewhere in the lobby.

We have to find him and tell him about all the ideas for books we have that we want written."

One of the others shook their head. "No, there's no way he could do that. He would have to live for like another hundred or two hundred years."

"But we need those books," one of them demanded. "I need more Bethany Anne. We all have characters we want more of."

"Well, then we'll just have to divide up," someone suggested. "If we spread out, then we will be able to find him."

A short woman with an adamant glare in her eyes stepped forward. "I don't want to get all *Misery* about this, but if he isn't willing to do what we want, I say we take action into our hands."

The others looked to one another, searching for someone to disagree with this dangerous mindset. When no one voiced a concern, they all nodded.

"Okay, let's divide up and find the Yoda."

Sophia peeled out from the pillar and watched the crazy mortals scatter. She didn't know who this Michael was, but he sounded like he was in trouble—in maybe a good way. He had crazed fans who were very demanding. That wasn't such a bad thing.

Shrugging it off, she made her way to the private elevators that led up to King Rudolf's chambers. She boarded the elevator, careful to keep the cupcakes level so they didn't get messed up in the small white boxes.

The doors to the elevator were just about to shut when a guy rushed through just before the doors slammed shut.

"Whew," he said, throwing his back up against the wall of the elevator and closing his eyes. He was taking deep breaths like he hadn't breathed properly in a while. He wore glasses, and his black hair had a cowlick in the front. He appeared young with his boyish facial features, but he had a maturity about him.

Sophia realized she was staring when he opened his eyes and looked at her like she was a crazy stalker.

"Sorry," she said, tearing her gaze away. "You just seem stressed."

He nodded. "I am. I have some pretty demanding followers stalking me. I think I just got away from them."

Sophia thought it was none of her business.

"Oh, we're not going anywhere," the guy noticed, looking at the panel of buttons on the elevator.

"Sorry," Sophia admitted. "I had my hands full and forgot to hit a button."

"No, problem," the guy said. "What floor do you need?"

"The very top," she stated.

He pressed the button and the one under it. "There we go." He smiled good-naturedly at her. "How are you today?"

She wasn't used to being asked that question, and for a moment she didn't know how to answer it. Finally she said, "I guess everything is okay. I've got to deliver these cupcakes, then deliver a payment to a hard-working scientist. And then I have to get a dress from a seamstress and keep an appointment I don't remember making."

He shook his head. "Although I appreciate all the information, I was asking, how are you? Not how is everything going that's demanding your time and attention."

Sophia was shocked by the phrasing. He was right. That was a different question. He had asked how she was, not what she was doing.

"Oh," she said, assessing how she felt. "I guess I'm overwhelmed and a little tired. But all in all, I'm really good. I feel happy I get to help the ones I love. That's a good thing."

He grinned, nodding. "That's a great thing."

"How are you?" she asked, returning the question, watching the slow progress of the elevator.

"Well, a bunch of fans are chasing me because they want me to write all these different stories, and I want to do it, but I just don't know how I'll find the time."

"Michael!" she exclaimed.

His face registered his shock. "How did you know who I am? Are you a fan?"

She shook her head. "I mean, maybe I should be, but I hardly have

384

time to read. There's one book I need to read before any other, in its entirety." Sophia thought about *The Complete History of Dragonriders* sitting on her desk in her room in the Castle at the Gullington. "I heard your readers strategizing about how to track you down. Don't worry, they went in the opposite direction."

He let out a breath. "Well, I'll catch up with them. I don't like disappointing them. I just don't know what to tell them when they unload all of their great ideas. How do I say there isn't enough time left in the day for that many stories?"

Sophia grinned, grateful to the universe for once again providing a solution. She took one of the cupcakes and offered it to Michael. "I know we don't know each other, but I'm a rider for the Dragon Elite."

"The Dragon Elite?" he asked in astonishment, having heard of the organization.

She nodded to the sword on her hip. It was her universal identification. "Yes, and I hope you trust me when I tell you this cupcake here will extend your life and make it so you live longer than any normal mortal. Maybe if you do, then you'll be able to craft all the stories they demand."

The guy peered at the cupcake tentatively and then smiled. "Seriously?"

She nodded. "I know it seems like a strange thing for someone to offer you, but I have an extra one and you...well, you seem like someone who needs to stick around for a long time."

Michael grinned at her as the doors to the elevator bounced open. "I don't know what to say."

"You don't have to say anything," Sophia explained as he backed out of the elevator. "Just enjoy your life and make it worth it."

He nodded and held up the small white box. "Thank you."

CHAPTER ONE HUNDRED NINE

Still amazed she had randomly run into the guy the crazed mortals were looking for, Sophia walked into King Rudolf's chamber in a daze. She almost strode by the baby sitting in a bouncy seat outside of the main room.

"Captain Morgan!" Sophia exclaimed, wondering why the child was sitting by herself in the hallway. She pulled her out of the seat and cradled her to her chest. Sophia checked her over and ensured she was okay. She appeared fine and wasn't fussing at all.

"What are you doing out here?" Sophia asked the child.

Since she was an infant, she didn't answer, and Sophia was forced to go into the main chamber to find out more. She was certain it would kill most of her brain cells. Juggling holding the baby and the magical cupcake, she entered the large room to find more confusion.

Rudolf was kneeling over Captain Kirk, also perched in a baby seat. "I don't know how they taught you at school since we didn't use common core, but I'm certain you carry the one."

"What is going on?" Sophia asked from the doorway and saw Captain Silver was sitting in a car seat with a steering wheel attached to the front.

"Well," he said proudly, popping up to his feet. "I realized parenting

386

full-time was detracting from my job as king. Since I have heard so many say one should make all businesses family businesses, I put the Captains on the payroll."

"No," Sophia said, shaking her head and not needing the explanation he was no doubt going to give to her.

King Rudolf Sweetwater nodded proudly. "Oh, yes." He pointed to the baby in her arms. "Captain Morgan is my new bodyguard. Looks like she let you in." He reached forward and tickled the baby's chin. "Good work, little love."

He ran over and presented Captain Silver, who was sitting with paper, crayons, a calculator, and an abacus in front of her. "I present to you my new accountant."

"Angels above," Sophia whispered.

"But it gets better!" Rudolf exclaimed, holding up a single finger victoriously.

"I don't see how."

He rushed over to where Captain Kirk was drooling on a plastic ring of keys. "Here we have my chauffeur."

Sophia shook her head. "I admire your problem-solving and that you want to have a family business, but you get why this won't work, right?"

His smile dropped. "There are some sort of tax complications, aren't there?" He spun around. "Captain Silver, look into this! I'm sure it will involve filing a Form 899 or whatever. Drop everything and do it."

The baby threw her hands in the air like she was fed up with the job. Sophia didn't blame her.

"Rudolf," Sophia began, carefully putting Captain Morgan on a blanket, "I can appreciate that as a king of a busy empire you're overwhelmed, and I love that you want to make things involve your family. But your babies are just that. They're babies and not ready for such jobs."

"So, I need to wait a year or so?" he asked, looking between the three babies.

Sophia shook her head. "Try like eighteen or more years. They have to grow and learn first. Then you can incorporate them into the business. I think I have something that could help." She held up the white box containing the magical cupcake and presented it to the king of the fae.

His mouth fell open. "Is that it?"

She nodded, hardly able to contain her excitement. After all the complications, it had actually worked out. She was going to get her twenty million dollars, and everything would work out for everyone.

"My half-birthday cake!" he exclaimed, rushing forward. "You remembered!"

Sophia yanked it away before he grabbed it. "No, King Rudolf. This is the cupcake containing the special herbs from India you asked me to get for Serena."

"You actually did it?" He sounded surprised.

"Of course, I did," she told him. "This is the solution to your problems. If you help Serena, then she will pitch in with the babies, and you won't feel so stretched between your role as king, father, and husband. Remember?"

He seemed to have difficulty recalling the conversation but finally nodded. "Yeah, that's probably a better solution than me employing the Captains or killing Stefan or ordering all my people to off themselves so I don't have to rule over them."

"None of those are solutions," Sophia agreed with a sigh, handing him the cupcake. "Now, Serena has to eat this right away. I want to see her do it."

"Not a problem," Rudolf announced. Turning to a couch covered in blankets, which Sophia hadn't realized had a person strewn across it. She was draped in covers, her hands and feet sticking out in various places. "My love. I've got a treat for you."

"What?" Serena exclaimed, twisting over and putting her back to Rudolf. "I don't want it."

"Oh, but you do," he sang. "It's going to make you age slower so you live longer and can raise our children."

"No," she said, half-asleep. "I just need to sleep for another day or so, and then I'll eat it."

Rudolf looked back at Sophia for support.

"She needs to eat it soon," Sophia encouraged.

Rudolf nodded and turned back to his wife. "Just take a tiny little bite. Then you can return to your two-day naps. I promise."

The mortal threw the covers over her head. "NO! I'm not hungry."

Rudolf gave Sophia a defeated expression. "What can I do? I guess I'll just slip further into depression and fall further into the role of a horrid dictator. Thanks for trying. How much do I owe you?"

Sophia was pissed. No, she was beyond pissed. She had gone through too much for this. Father Time had broken his own laws for this mortal. King Rudolf Sweetwater had shouldered too much of the responsibility. Everyone, including Liv, had sacrificed. The least Serena Sweetwater was going to do was choke down a carrot cake muffin. And she was going to like it.

She stomped over to the sofa, glad the Captains were not old enough to remember what she was about to do.

Grabbing the blankets, she yanked them off Serena Sweetwater and exposed the mortal cuddled on the couch in pajamas, even though it was the middle of the day.

She shielded her eyes immediately. "Ack, it burns."

"Deal with it," Sophia said, grabbing the mortal by her shoulders and hauling her up to a sitting position. She was surprised by how weak the woman was, although she didn't hurt her as she made her cooperate.

"Why are you doing this horrible stuff to me?" Serena asked, crying.

"Making you wake up?" Sophia demanded, eyeing the time. "At three o'clock in the afternoon?"

"Is it that early?" Serena wailed.

Sophia glanced up at Rudolf. "Seriously, I'll drop everything right now and find you a new wife. Someone who will be a good mother to the Captains."

Adamantly he shook his head. "No, she is the love of my life. I went to the valley of death and back for her, and I would again."

"Fine." Sophia let out a tired sigh. She grabbed the white box from

Rudolf and shoved it into Serena's hands. "You're going to take this cupcake laced with magical ingredients, and you're going to eat it. You're going to eat all of it, and afterward, you're going to get up, shower, and take care of your children, because you're going to live a very long life after ingesting it. You'll see your children grow up and be able to be productive members of the fae empire."

Serena considered this, opening the box and peering at the expertly made cupcake covered in cream cheese frosting and little bunnies. "And if I don't?"

Sophia shook her head and wished it hadn't come to this. She withdrew her sword from its sheath and brought it close to Serena's face, only inches away from her eyes. They widened. "Then I'll ignore King Rudolf's pleas and practice something I saw Liv do earlier and learn what it's like to decapitate someone."

Serena shoved the cupcake into her face so fast, Sophia was certain she swallowed without chewing. She didn't like having to bully the mortal into cooperating. She knew Serena felt hopeless, and sometimes when people feel that way, they need to be pushed. Once she got the dose of the magical herb, she would feel better. She would be better, and there was hope she would act better.

CHAPTER ONE HUNDRED TEN

After Sophia had affirmed Serena had eaten all of the cupcake, King Rudolf Sweetwater gave her a check for twenty million dollars. She gratefully accepted and ensured he said the magic phrase, "We're even."

She called Alicia and told her she had gotten the funds to finish the LiDAR project, then opened a portal to Montana. The timing of everything was working out perfectly. On the heels of finishing this mission, her dress was ready according to the message she got from the gnome at the seamstress shop.

Sophia stepped out of the portal, right in front of Hyacinth's shop. Her eyes went to the other end of the boardwalk, where the craft store was located. She saw a warrior in a long black cloak, with a giant-made sword entering the store and felt only marginally sorry for the guy who was about to get his ass handed to him by her sister, Liv Beaufont.

Then she remembered her newly assigned, random mission from Lee at the Crying Cat Bakery and decided this might be a good opportunity to start putting things into motion.

Cupping her hand to her mouth and using a whispering spelling, Sophia said, "Hey, over here."

The words she said were inaudible to anyone between her and her sister. However, when Liv halted and turned around, Sophia knew that her sister had heard her. Her gaze found Sophia standing across the street. She waved her forward only feeling marginally bad for interrupting her mission again although she knew that Liv wouldn't mind so much. The craft store swindler was going to get his reckoning one way or another. None escaped Liv's wrath.

"You just can't get enough of me lately, can you?" Liv flashed her a smile as she approached.

"You know it," Sophia replied. "Sorry to interrupt you yet again, but I figured since I saw you that I could ask for something…" The guilty expression on her face might have given her away.

'Well, do you need me to defy my boss because I haven't done that in a while," Liv joked.

Sophia felt her face flush hot. "Actually."

Liv dropped her chin, giving Sophia an annoyed expression. "You can't be serious?"

"I wish I wasn't, but to repay the baker, I need to get a katana sword that has ten different magical properties and heals the bearer—"

"Whoa," Liv interrupted. "This thing sounds awesome. Where do I get one of these?"

"Not at Walmart," Sophia said dryly.

"Who would get a katana sword at Walmart?"

"You'd be surprised," Sophia stated. "Anyway, you can't have the sword because it's for the assassin baker."

"Makes sense," Liv said, not missing a beat.

"And to get this sword—"

"Which is located where? Inside an Egyptian tomb where you have to battle a god of fire or something?"

Sophia chuckled. "Probably on the moon or in the center of the Earth, knowing my luck."

"We share similar luck," Liv related.

"I actually don't know the location of the katana sword yet,"

Sophia explained. "But there are a few items and a person I have to secure first."

Liv laughed, nodding. "We live parallel lives. Let me guess, all the items are ridiculously hard to obtain and just getting them before said mission will be nearly impossible, right?"

"We do live similar lives."

"And," Liv drew out the word. "Let me also guess that you need something that makes you time travel, is that right?"

Sophia gave her sister an apologetic look. "There's this candy store on Roya Lane that's only open during a very specific time."

"Midnight Lunar Eclipse!" Liv exclaimed. "Yeah, it's not open until next year. I've had my calendar marked. This girl needs some gummy frogs that jump around and chocolate kisses that you blow on and they swirl across the air and smack someone on the kisser."

"Oh, are the chocolates for Stefan?" Sophia asked.

Liv gave her a surprised expression. "Gosh no. We're not sappy like that. I want to blow them at Clark and thoroughly gross him out. Then I'm putting the frogs in his bed because he told me that eating desserts in bed was disgusting."

"That's great that you've wanted to visit this magical candy shop." Sophia did her best to lace persuasion into her voice.

"Soph..." Liv's tone had a warning. "Papa Creola probably already knows about this act of defiance."

"Then this time, ask for permission," Sophia encouraged.

Liv shook her head. "No, because of course he orchestrated a mission that would help the king of the fae. I don't think he's going to do it for an assassin baker who wants a weapon that sounds like it should be kept out of her reach."

"Yeah, but if you think about it, this is part of the Rudolf and Serena mission," Sophia reasoned. "Lee made the cupcake that I needed for Serena. So it makes sense that Papa Creola knows that we'll need this time device. And all we need to do is travel to the next lunar eclipse. We visit this candy shop and then we're done. Easy, peasy."

"No, you then need to do what?" Liv questioned. "It's never easy. You must realize that by now."

Sophia agreed with a nod. "Okay, so I need to buy magical chewing gum that makes the chewer happy, no matter the circumstances."

"Why?" Liv asked.

With a shrug, Sophia said, "I don't know exactly. I was just told to get a few things first and then Lee would tell me where to go for the katana sword."

"And what are these other things?" Liv asked.

Sophia started listing them off on her fingers. "I need a weapons expert, a dragon—"

"This is sounding too easy," Liv cut in.

A rebellious smile flicked to Sophia's mouth. "I need a magic compass that's elfin made."

"There we go," Liv said, having expected this curve ball.

"I also need Zack Efron."

"Who doesn't," Liv said with a laugh. "I'd like to rewrite the stars so that he could be mine."

Sophia gave her an annoyed look. "Your boyfriend is a badass demon hunter who is part demon, but only with all the good parts like enhanced powers and longer life. Oh and he's so flipping cute."

Liv nodded with a shrug. "Yeah, but Zack Efron is a fantastic singer and tap dancer."

Surprised, Sophia laughed. "How is it that's what Zack Efron is most known for?"

"Have you tried tap dancing?" Liv asked. "It isn't easy."

"Yeah, I'm sort of busy with other projects and don't have time for tap dancing lessons."

"We all need hobbies, Soph."

She grinned. "Anyway, can you please help me with the time device? You can go to the candy shop with me. We will load up."

Liv seemed to consider this. "I have good and bad news."

"Oh, so you're getting the hang of this good and bad news delivery style. I approve."

Her sister rolled her eyes at her. "So the good news is that I can help you. I'll ask Papa Creola permission and we'll figure something out. You're right that it's a part of the overall mission which he orchestrated. The bad news is I can't do it right now. I really need to deal with that craft store guy who is swindling mortals money. Then I have a few other cases that I've got to handle before evil villains accomplish world domination."

Sophia nodded. "That's perfectly understandable."

"Oh, but I have more good news," Liv said, triumphantly.

"Oh, tell me!"

"Well, I happen to have a magical compass that was given to me by the elfin king," Liv related.

"Shut up!" Sophia exclaimed.

"Fat chance of that ever happening," Liv fired back.

"And of course you have a magical compass."

Liv held her hands up. "You know how I do."

"Okay, well, that gets me one step closer to fulfilling this mission," Sophia said, trying hard not to be overwhelmed. "In the meantime, I just have to figure out how to recruit Zack Efron for this mysterious journey."

Waving her off, Liv said, "I'd save that for last. We can do that together after we go to the magic candy shop."

Sophia smiled. "I'm looking forward to going on another mission with you."

Liv returned the expression, proudly. "I'm looking forward to going on a bazillion missions with you. This will just be one of many."

"That's right," Sophia said, remembering the Beaufont family motto. "*Familia Est Sempiternum.*"

Liv gave her a fond expression. "*Familia Est Sempiternum.*"

Sophia then watched as her sister crossed the road, headed for the craft store. She waited until she disappeared, turning her attention to Hyacinth's shop where her magical dress awaited her.

CHAPTER ONE HUNDRED ELEVEN

W hen Sophia entered the seamstress shop this time, it looked like one instead of being glamoured to look like an antique store.

The gnome seamstress was smiling at Sophia, her hands behind her back. "Your dress is ready in the dressing room over there. Put it on and we will just check it over, although I know it will fit perfectly. I just want to ensure all the magical properties are right and I don't need to make any tweaks."

Sophia nodded obediently and made for the rooms at the back Hyacinth indicated.

The audible gasp that fell out of her mouth made the shop owner giggle.

"Oh, then you like it, huh?" she called through the curtain at the back.

"Like it?" Sophia questioned. The red dress of subtle paisley designs was extraordinary. The sleeves hung off the shoulder, and the plunging neckline left little to the imagination. The dress would fit Sophia snugly around her waist and then flare out at the bottom, like something Marilyn Monroe wore back in the day. It was one of the most perfect garments she had ever laid eyes on. "I love it," she exclaimed.

"Well, put it on, and I'll get you buttoned up in the back," Hyacinth remarked from the front room. "You'll need to go directly from here to your meeting with Saint Valentine, so I hope you don't have anything else scheduled."

Sophia was grateful she had made arrangements with Quiet when at the Gullington last. She had a ton to do, but none of it was ready for her yet. The meeting with Saint Valentine was going to fit in perfectly.

Finding it tough to walk with the tight dress and long train, she nearly toppled over when she exited the dressing room. When she caught sight of herself in the mirror, she almost fainted with disbelief.

She. Was. Absolutely. Breathtaking.

Sophia had never seen herself appear more like an angel than at that moment. The dress by itself was striking, fitting her perfectly, and the magical qualities were definitely at work, enhancing all of her features, making her totally flawless.

Her hair, which had been a wild mess from all of her adventures, was fashioned up high into a lovely bun, a few stray curls falling down beside her face or down her bare back. Her makeup was both striking and understated, and her skin seemed to glow like she had just been in the sun, although she could not remember the last time she had had the luxury of such things. The dress made by the exceptional seamstress was flawless.

"Oh, I do great work!" Hyacinth cheered, clapping her small hands at the sight of Sophia. "Now stand here and I'll button you up." She indicated the stage where she did all her measurements.

Sophia agreed with a nod, moving forward and nearly falling on her face. The tight bodice part of the dress didn't allow for a lot of mobility. When she pulled up the long train, she realized she was wearing nude heels.

Hyacinth grinned when Sophia gave her a questioning expression. "They go with the dress. You really can't wear combat boots with this exquisite number, now can you?"

Sophia shrugged. "I guess not, but movement is tough."

The gnome nodded. "I can adjust that after I get you buttoned up."

She came around behind Sophia and went to work, fastening the many buttons in the back. When she finished the last one, she waved a squatty finger in the air and brandished it at Sophia. Instantly the dress seemed to release her and give the freedom to move without restriction. It was more comfortable than her combat clothing or her pajamas, and the shoes that had been pinching her feet suddenly felt like she was wearing Ugg boots.

Sophia pulled up the dress to make sure she was still wearing the pointy heels. She was.

"Wow, this is amazing," Sophia said with amazement.

"It's magic," Hyacinth explained. "I'm glad to see it works, and everything fits perfectly. You really do look flawless."

Sophia turned around, admiring her appearance in the mirror. "Thank you. I really don't know what to say."

"Well, when you see that guy of yours, you should be wearing this dress and say, 'I only got this dress so you could take it off.'"

"I'm not saying that," Sophia disagreed, shaking her head at the gnome.

"You wanted him to fall in love with you for you," Hyacinth argued. "Men love a good flirt."

"Well, like you said, I wanted him to fall for me, and I'm not the kind to throw myself at guys. He either likes me for me or not at all."

The seamstress smiled, nodding proudly. "I have no doubt he will. But right now, you have a date with a saint."

CHAPTER ONE HUNDRED TWELVE

Feeling overdressed for the Scarsdale Tavern, Sophia kept her head down and avoided eye contact from the patrons who gave her curious stares as she strode up to the bar.

Gregory seemed quite pleased with her when he glanced up from the bar. "Very nice, indeed. You're ready for your appointment."

"Yes, is the timing okay?" she asked, looking away from several individuals who regarded her like she was a looney who had escaped a mental house.

"Oh, yes," Gregory answered. "As I've said many a time, it's—"

"Better to be early than late," Sophia said, finishing his sentence.

"Exactly," he chirped, waving her around the bar. "Now, just follow me to the back, and I'll take you to the next room for your appointment.

He paused outside a rickety old door in the back. Holding onto the handle, he turned to Sophia, giving her an apologetic expression. "Now, this isn't my favorite part of the job, but necessary it is."

She lowered her chin. "What?"

"Well, you look simply marvelous, which is key to seeing...well, you know." He lowered his voice.

"What else must I do to see this, person?" she asked. "Is there another hoop you would like me to jump through?"

He laughed. "Oh, no. It isn't anything like that. I'm going to lead you into the next room, and that's a waiting area for you."

"How long do I have to wait?" she asked, sensing a trick.

He held up a single finger. "That's up to you. You see, to pass into the area where…you know who is located, you have to find your way out of the waiting room."

"Oh, angels," she muttered, really wanting to swear properly. "What is this going to involve?"

He turned the handle, opening the door. "Nothing complicated. All you have to do is find the key to where Saint Valentine is."

Sophia peered into the waiting room, dread filling her. "Oh. Dear. God!"

CHAPTER ONE HUNDRED THIRTEEN

Thousands of shiny keys winked at Sophia when she looked into the waiting room. She glanced back at Gregory.

"You have got to be kidding me," she said with a gasp.

He shook his head, an apologetic expression on his face. "I'm afraid I'm not."

"But there are so many keys," she argued, looking through the room to the other side where a large, regal door stood importantly.

"To open that door," he pointed across the room, "you only need to find the right key."

"Only?" Sophia questioned. "That could take forever."

Gregory nodded. "Some have perished while attempting the task, but I hope that doesn't happen to you. Just remember to stay organized in your approach, and hopefully you'll shave some time off your attempt."

"Like a few years?" she questioned, looking over the room. Tables and shelves were piled with thousands of keys. There was a huge chest sitting under a desk, and she assumed it was filled to the brim with keys. The desk too. Then she noticed cigar boxes, jewelry boxes, and other totes that had to also contain keys. "Isn't there another way?" she asked Gregory.

He sighed. "I'm sorry, but the rules are very clear, and you agreed to them when you took this appointment. You even heard the clue for how to bypass this room quicker."

Sophia lowered her chin, giving him a murderous expression. "I haven't made the appointment yet according to your timey-wimey thing, remember?"

His face flushed red with embarrassment. "Right. Then you don't know."

"And you're not telling me?" she questioned.

"I'm sorry, but I can't," he apologized. "I already gave you a tip on the dress code, but I'm really not allowed to tell the waiting room information except to the person who makes the appointment."

"Which was me!" she argued.

He nodded. "I realize that. I'm certain it will not take you long... ish. Just stay organized."

Before she could argue or object, he pulled the door shut, leaving Sophia alone in the waiting room full of keys.

CHAPTER ONE HUNDRED
FOURTEEN

Glancing down at her gorgeous dress, Sophia laughed. She wasn't dressed for this task. She wasn't dressed for anything she had done recently. She was going to have to adapt.

Sophia felt naked without her sword, but Hyacinth had refused to allow her to wear it. She had had to send her sword and other personal effects to the Castle. Now she wished she had the sword so she could tear up the room of keys. It would make her feel marginally better, although not solve the actual problem.

Sophia tried to summon her phone or her sword with no luck. There was a magical ward in the waiting room that prevented summoning spells, but the one thing that could help her seemed to still be working.

Hey, Lunis said in her head, taking in the view she saw through her eyes.

"Well, you wanted to help, and now you can," she said, sounding defeated. "I need to find the right key in all this mess for that door." She pointed her vision at the arched door in front of her.

Hm. Her dragon ruminated on everything he had been shown. *I think the key is to keep an open mind.*

"Now your jokes are making me want to kill myself."

All is fair, he teased. *This is quite the conundrum.*

"Yeah, it could take me forever," Sophia complained. "And I don't have forever. I feel more like Cinderella than ever. This dress might evaporate if I don't hurry."

It's a nice dress, Lunis told her, having seen her reflection through her eyes in one of the pictures on the wall.

"What am I going to do? I guess I could try every key in this room, but am I wrong to think that's the dumbest approach ever?"

It's what a loser would do, Lunis agreed. *You're better than that.*

She slumped as she looked at the table piled high. "Am I? Gregory told me to keep things organized, so apparently he thinks I'll use the 'try every key approach.'"

Forget Gregory, Lunis declared. *We're going to figure this out.*

Sophia smiled as she realized her dragon needed this. She was glad she invited him to the challenge.

Go take a closer look at the door lock, Lunis urged. *I think the key... sorry, the solution to this lies in figuring out what we're looking for. Then we can rule out anything that doesn't fit.*

Sophia did as she was told, and went over to the door. She peered at the lock so both her and Lunis could see it properly.

Oh, well there you go, he declared matter-of-factly.

"What do you mean, there I go?"

You're looking for a key that fits in that hole.

"That isn't as helpful as you think," she related with a sigh.

If you notice, the key isn't a modern one, he explained. *It's one of those old-timey ones.*

"It's cute when a dragon describes something as old-timey," she said with a laugh.

Clear out all the modern keys, he told her with conviction.

She had not heard him be so bold or order her about, so Sophia paid attention. "Okay, but what do I do with those keys?"

Stay organized, like Gregory told you, he insisted. *Create a bin. I'm sure the room will allow for it.*

"It will not allow for summoning, but we will see." She attempted to create a large receptacle in the corner by the door where she came through. It was the only empty area in the room, and since she figured she wasn't going back through that door, she might as well make use of the space.

Nothing showed up when she tried to create a bin.

Just dump the huge chest, Lunis suggested.

Sophia did as she was told, turning her hand over and making all the keys in it spill magically onto the floor. Then she pushed the chest into the corner.

All right, Lunis began. *Send all modern keys into that area.*

Sophia thought hard about the spell for this. She began muttering and watched as keys flew like little birds trying to find their nest. The number of keys became so great that Sophia had to drop to the floor to avoid being assaulted by all the flying objects. When she lifted back up, the large chest was overflowing with shiny keys that all looked like they had been cut by a modern machine.

"Okay, well, that eliminated a lot," she said, turning to the room and finding her heart sinking. There were still many more keys lying all over the space.

Well, I've got to go, Lunis said. *My microwave dinner is calling my attention.*

"Lunis," she said in irritation.

Fine, I'll let my bean burrito get cold for this, but you owe me, he said, amusement in his voice. *We got rid of the modern keys. Now we just need to eliminate others. Go take another look at the lock again.*

Sophia did as she was told, peering through the keyhole.

It needs a key with two prongs, like a skeleton key, Lunis crowed, sounding excited.

"Okay, so more elimination," she stated.

Yeah, that should narrow it down some more.

"Where am I going to put them?" she asked, looking around the room and trying to figure out how to stay organized.

Just pile them in the corner with the modern keys, he suggested.

Sophia nodded and tried another spell. This time she had to drop to the floor to avoid getting pummeled by little metal objects flying at her. She worried her dress had gotten messed up, but when she rose, it seemed in fine condition. She shrugged it off and noticed the exit out of the room was now fully obstructed by keys.

"Let's hope I don't have to go out that door again," she said to Lunis before turning around. Lying on the desk in front of her were only two keys. The entire room was empty, to her surprise. She could not believe it. There were only two skeleton keys left.

"This will be easy," Sophia stated, about to reach for one of the keys.

Wait, Lunis urged.

Sophia halted. "What is it?"

Well, I don't know this for a fact, but it seems to me that if you have two options and you choose the wrong one, there could be repercussions.

She shook her head. "I don't like the sound of that."

Me either, he agreed. *I think you have to carefully consider your options. You can't choose blindly. You have to think this through and pick the right key the first time.*

Sophia ran her eyes over the two keys. "But how do I know which one is the right one?" she asked her dragon.

That I can't answer for you, Soph. Honestly, I'm sorry to say this, but at this stage of the game, I think you're on your own.

"Why?" she said, feeling close to tears, which would ruin her perfect makeup.

Sophia, you're there because you want to help a guy who is in love with you. As much as I'm a part of you, I can't fully relate. I think you have to look at those keys and pick the one which will unlock the answer to your problems. You're the only one who can do that.

She rubbed her lips together, considering her dragon's words. They made sense, and yet, she didn't even know how to go about fixing this puzzle.

I'm here, Sophia, Lunis said, offering a last bit of encouragement before going quiet in her head.

"Thanks," Sophia said to her dragon, looking at both of the keys.

She trusted Lunis. If he was right, she had to pick the key that unlocked the solution to her problems. This made her consider what she faced—her actual problem.

Wilder had been hit with Cupid's arrow, and now he was crazy in love with her. Hiker was pissed and there was tension in the Castle. But to Sophia, none of that was what she wanted to fix.

Sophia had to pick the key that made everything right with Wilder. Not make it so he didn't love her, but rather so he loved her for the right reasons. She didn't care if Hiker accepted them. She wanted to get to the point where she didn't care what he thought. Then there was Ainsley. Sophia knew giving the housekeeper her memory and her health back would ultimately lead to her leaving the Gullington, but if it was what made Ainsley happy, that was what she wanted for her friend.

She closed her eyes, meditating on these thoughts and realizing that she was actually there to see Saint Valentine for many different reasons than what originally drew her.

When Sophia opened her eyes, to her amazement, one of the two keys was glowing on the desk. She could hardly believe it, but that was how life worked when she trusted it.

With an excited hand, she reached out and took the glowing key, almost expecting it to burn her fingers. It didn't.

When she stuck it into the lock, she expected everything to be reset in the room and all the keys to fly back into place, creating another puzzle for her to continue to solve until she grew old trying.

However, the key turned in the lock with a gentle click, opening the door to Saint Valentine.

CHAPTER ONE HUNDRED FIFTEEN

I t wasn't that Sophia expected to be greeted by a glowing room filled with roses and orchestral music when she pulled back the door dressed as a princess. It would have been nice. What she found was exactly the opposite of what she had expected.

When she pulled back the magical door, she was faced with a dark staircase that led down into a chasm of the unknown. Wafting up from the cold darkness were strange smells and eerie harp music.

Sophia considered shutting the door and retreating back into the pub for an ale or three. Then she resigned her frustration, hiked up her dress, and made the trek down the rickety staircase to an unknown location.

Once she was about a dozen stairs down, the light from the room above disappeared and she had to rely on magic to light the way. Immediately she wished she had stayed in the dark because climbing on the walls all around her were dozens of spiders. Their webs covered the wall so thickly it was hard to see the surface. The spiders were huge, about the size of Sophia's palm.

She would have shrunk back, but that would only send her into another set of webs. She considered ignorance was bliss. At least when she was in the dark, she didn't know there were creepy crawly things all around her.

Sophia didn't know why she had had to dress up in her finest attire to descend into a dark basement with huge spiders, but she hoped Saint Valentine had some champagne and had brushed his teeth because the first thing she was going to do was take a drink and punch that guy right in the kisser.

She was about to laugh at her own joke when a low cooing sound made her catch her breath. Sophia halted. Squinting into the darkness.

Then the noise came again. It wasn't cooing like that of a dove, she realized. It was an "oohing" sound. Like ghosts make.

CHAPTER ONE HUNDRED SIXTEEN

T he low howling almost sounded melodic though it certainly carried an ominous tone to it. Sophia froze, rotating to find the source of the noise, although she was starting to embrace the whole ignorance is bliss thing.

That had never been her style before—quite the opposite, but if she hadn't lit up the stairs, then she wouldn't know Franklin and Abraham were hanging out on the walls next to her in their giant webs. That was what she had named the spiders, going with a Founding Father-slash-presidential theme. They probably should have been Romeo and Casanova because they took up residency in Saint Valentine's home, which was where she realized she was heading.

Sophia could not believe she had deluded herself into thinking her meeting with Saint Valentine would be in some classy room with crystal goblets and fine linens covering a dining table. She reasoned that since she had to have a magical dress made, she might have expected a fancy meeting environment. By the smell in the dusty stairwell, it seemed more like they would be meeting in a morgue.

The light orb didn't show her what the source of the ghostly

topped all her recent adventures. She didn't know what would happen if Simon caught her, but by the way he had his arms stretched out as he chased after her, she didn't think he wanted to give her a hug.

This would have been the perfect time to social distance, but Sophia didn't think the plague-carrying mummy was going to heed her warning if she asked for some space. She continued to run as fast as her heels would carry her. The light orb stayed by her side as she jumped down stair after stair, leading farther down.

When she checked over her shoulder, not only did she see Simon gaining on her, but racing behind him as if joining the party were Abraham and Franklin.

They probably think he is going to make the kill for them, she thought morbidly. Then they can all sit down and enjoy a Sophia dinner.

Simon reached out as he ran, desperation in his glowing yellow eyes. His sharp fingertips scraped her back like bits of broken glass. Sophia screamed and picked up her speed, using magic to fuel her. It didn't matter because as she sped up, so did the mummy.

Its hands reached out for her again and clawed at her arms. Sophia ripped herself away and pointed over her shoulder, attempting a spell in the closed space that would either save her life or end it rather fast.

Desperate times called for desperate measures. She employed the explosive spell, knowing it might be the death of her if it backfired.

CHAPTER ONE HUNDRED EIGHTEEN

The explosion was immediate. The blast was bright, like lightning striking. It sent her flying down the stairs, tumbling head over feet down until she hit a wall. She thought it was a wall, but in the chaos of the aftermath of her spell, she could not really tell.

For a moment, Sophia felt like she was buried in an avalanche and didn't know which was up or down. She felt something under her that must be the floor—a cold stone that seemed to hum with a strange beat like it was alive.

The light orb had been extinguished during her fall, so all Sophia could see was blackness. All she could hear was the ragged breathing of an unknown thing.

She pressed up to a sitting position, her back against the wall behind her. At least she thought it was a wall. In the total blackness, it was hard to know up from down.

The breathing grew closer, and Sophia knew she was about to find out where Simon was. She was trapped at the bottom of the stairwell, at a dead end, and there was definitely something in the dark with her. She clenched her eyes shut, as she created another light orb, hoping the ragged breathing was Saint Valentine.

CHAPTER ONE HUNDRED NINETEEN

I t wasn't Saint Valentine.

Sophia's heart nearly jumped into her throat at what came into view.

The spell had worked to get the mummy off Sophia's back because it had taken off its legs. Now crawling down the stairs and moving like a strange beached fish was Simon.

He was dragging himself on his hands, his legs severed by the blast. His mouth was open, but there was no sound emanating from the black opening framed by his penetrating yellow eyes. The only sound was his ragged breathing, which sounded a lot like Sophia's fearful sips of air.

Flanking Simon were Abraham and Franklin, scuttling down on the wall, unhurt by the explosive spell.

Sophia rose to her feet, trembling as she pressed back into the wall. She turned and pounded on the stone dead end, wondering how it had all come to this.

"Hello! Help!" she screamed, beating on the wall, desperate for rescue.

In a sad bit of irony, Saint Valentine appeared to have stood her up.

She whipped around, trying to decide what spell to use on the mummy and man-eating spiders. Her reserves were low from the use of magic to get to this point. She didn't have anything to restore her energy, and as she combed her hair out of her face with a shaking hand, she realized exactly why her magic was so severely depleted.

There was a large gash in her head.

CHAPTER ONE HUNDRED TWENTY

Sophia loathed when people said stuff like, "Well, things can't get any worse."

Things could always get worse, she had found, and this was proof of it.

She was facing a crazed monster advancing in her direction. It wasn't hurried like before. Simon must have realized there was nowhere for her to go. Even if she had a good bit of magic to take the monster out, there would still be Franklin and Abraham remaining. The icing on the rotten cake was she had split her head open on the fall down the stairs. Blood trickled down her face on both sides, seeping onto her shoulders and staining her dress.

At least it's red, Sophia thought morbidly.

The mummy wiggled down each step, one hand at a time clawing its way on the stairs. Behind him was a trail of bandages dragging and leaving behind black blood. As he progressed, the bandages tore, revealing more of the disgusting creature. It was like he had wrapped himself in toilet paper, which in a time of shortage would have made him a real jerk for hoarding the precious tissue.

Sophia wondered if Lunis was witnessing what she saw through her eyes right then. Her connection to him was severed due to her injury. Usually, she was a very positive person, but right then, she wasn't sugar-coating it for herself. Her head wound was bad. As her vision started to go black and dizziness took over, she realized she was close to fainting.

Maybe that was for the best, so she wasn't conscious when the mummy ripped out her heart and ate it. Sophia swayed as Simon neared, only five feet away. Franklin and Abraham were hot on his tail, their red eyes intent on the mummy rather than Sophia.

She found this strange, but everything was relative when being pursued by a blood-hungry mummy and huge spiders.

A yelp actually escaped Sophia's mouth when Simon was less than two feet away. She pressed herself as close to the cold wall as she could, but it was no use. There was nowhere to go. She was stuck. Her fate was that she had to die at the hands of a possessed mummy.

CHAPTER ONE HUNDRED TWENTY-ONE

The two spiders rose up on their back legs as the mummy reached for her with unmistakable hunger in his eyes. Just when Sophia assumed they were going to attack her, Abraham and Franklin fired silk from their spinnerets. The streams of thick webbing shot straight at the mummy and wrapped around him.

It happened so quickly, it was like a movie in fast forward. Sophia watched the threads of silk wind tightly around the mummy. It continued to stream from the spiders, who seemed to be working together.

To Sophia's amazement, they were saving her. They had saved her, she realized as Simon attempted to reach for her one last time before freezing up and dropping to the floor at her feet. He was completely wrapped up by the cobwebs. She didn't know how they had done it or why, but in a strange turn of events, Abraham and Franklin had come to her rescue.

She sucked in a breath, finding her chest on fire and her lungs straining to pull in oxygen. "Thank you," she said to the spiders, still worried they might have stopped the mummy so they could have her all to themselves.

As her vision dimmed and her head lolled back, she realized it didn't really matter. She was too injured to get back up the stairs, back the way she had come. She was stuck at the dead end.

Sophia's eyes fluttered as she realized she was losing her grasp on consciousness. She swayed, sure she was about to faint as a bright light shone at her back and a cool draft hit her.

CHAPTER ONE HUNDRED
TWENTY-TWO

The wall at her back wasn't a wall at all, Sophia realized, only partly conscious.

It was a door.

Someone had opened it.

Just as her legs gave out and she tumbled to the floor, warm hands reached out and caught her and cradled her close. The person carried her into the light of a place very different from where she had been.

The space was warm and full of sunshine and felt like hope.

Sophia smiled, wishing she could enjoy her new location or thank the savior whose arms continued to hold her, but the waking world wasn't open to her anymore.

She closed her eyes, losing her hold on consciousness.

CHAPTER ONE HUNDRED TWENTY-THREE

T he smell of chocolate and roses was strong in the air when Sophia regained consciousness. She opened her eyes, hearing soft harp music but only saw blurry images.

"Oh, good, you're awake," a deep voice said that was instantly alluring.

She blinked to try to clear her vision, but it did little good. "Where am I?" she asked, finding her voice strangely alert, although her head throbbed with a blinding force. Sophia would give anything for a painkiller right then.

"You're safe," the man's voice said, moving closer to her.

"My head," Sophia groaned, pressing her hand to her temple, expecting to feel the searing wound. There wasn't anything there. Her fingers continued to explore, and she could not find the blood she expected or the severe gash.

"Yes, you took quite the fall, didn't you? Not really, but it was real enough for you, I'm sure," the man said.

Sophia blinked, trying to make sense of what the voice said. "I didn't really fall? I'm not really hurt?"

A warm chuckle filled the air. "The mind does strange things to those who keep their appointments with me. You were a victim of your mind's fears."

Just like that, Sophia's vision cleared, and everything around her came into crisp view. She was lying on a beautiful settee, her red dress perfectly arranged around her and her hands gently clasped over her midsection.

Pushing up, she took in the man perched in an armchair beside her, regarding her with a thoughtful stare. He appeared ready to rush forward and catch her if she might faint again.

Saint Valentine was handsome enough that he might give Cupid a run for his money. He had salt and pepper hair and was clean-shaven. His turquoise eyes lit up as he sat back and relaxed, no longer fearing she would topple over.

He wore a silver suit and a red tie and had a very Sean Connery elegance about him.

"Saint Valentine?" Sophia asked, thinking she smelled his cologne from that distance, although she also picked up the unmistakable aroma of chocolate and roses in the air. She knew immediately why as her gaze slid to a table where a large bouquet of flowers sat, a box of chocolates beside it. They were in a room that was much more handsome than the creepy hallways she had come from.

It was covered in rich fabrics and beautiful paintings and statues. The light was provided by candles, which were literally everywhere, reminding Sophia of the most romantic scene from any movie she had ever seen.

"The one and only," Saint Valentine said, holding out his hand to her. When she took it, he kissed the back, much the same way Cupid had. However, she instantly trusted the man in front of her. He was love incarnate. He was like a religion, powerful, alluring, and supportive in the time of stress. He was faith and poetry. Saint Valentine was the stuff of legends.

CHAPTER ONE HUNDRED TWENTY-FOUR

Sophia's head didn't hurt anymore, but she continued to rub it, expecting to find the missing wound. "I fell. I hurt myself."

Saint Valentine offered a sympathetic smile. "You dreamed you fell. You dreamed quite a bit, didn't you?"

"That was all a dream?" she asked, continuing to study the room. On the far side was a doorway that looked much like the one in the pub. The one she had to find the right key to.

"Indeed it was," Saint Valentine answered. "Most fall asleep on their way through the door." He pointed to the one she regarded curiously. "It's like space travel or going through the channel or breaking through the atmosphere at light speed. Your consciousness simply can't handle it and retreats."

"So, the mummy and spiders were not real?" Sophia asked.

He nodded. "They were real enough to you, but they were a product of your mind. You have many reservations about visiting me, it seems." Saint Valentine indicated her chest. "Your heart is conflicted."

She glanced down at her chest, remembering she was wearing the beautiful dress made by Hyacinth. "It was a dream…" Sophia didn't like that. It felt like she had been cheated. It was a cheap way to give her an adrenaline rush. She never liked it when dreams were used as plot devices, especially in her own life.

Saint Valentine reached out and grabbed the box of chocolates, offering her one. "It was real enough that your reserves were depleted. Try eating something."

She took one and smiled in gratitude.

"You see, the dream is how you got to me," Saint Valentine said. "It might not seem real to you now, but at the time, you were desperate to survive. You did whatever it took to battle your demons...or mummy in this case. That tells me quite a lot. Many have nightmares when they come to see me, and they force themselves to wake up so they don't have to face their fears. But you, well, you didn't just face your fears, you blew them up and enlisted the help of would-be villains to come to your aid." Saint Valentine chuckled, the gesture lighting up his eyes. "I do believe that dress makes you appear like a princess, but it's deceiving because you, Sophia Beaufont, are a true and tested warrior."

She took a bite of the chocolate, enjoying the richness that coated her mouth. Now having a dream to get here didn't feel so bad. It appeared it was the only way to Saint Valentine. Of course, she would have liked a bit of a heads up. She guessed Gregory had explained the procedures and what she should expect when she made the appointment to see the man before her.

"Now, you came to me for two reasons," Saint Valentine began cordially. "Shall we start with the first one?"

"My friend has been shot by Cupid's arrow," she explained, wishing she had something to wash the chocolate down. At the conclusion of her thought, a flute of champagne appeared. She grinned at Saint Valentine. "Thank you."

"I aim to please," he said, giving her an incredibly handsome look. "Cupid." He didn't sound pleased. "I'm glad you were able to fix his bow. He has been creating all sorts of problems for me and everyone else. I can help you with your friend. What else?"

"Well, I have another friend." Sophia drained her glass and felt a hiccup coming. "I've heard you might be able to help her. There was an accident, and she lost her memories and can't leave the Gullington, or she will grow weak and die."

"And you want her to be able to leave?" he asked.

"I want her to have the choice to live her life the way she desires," Sophia stated.

"But her memories," Saint Valentine began. "Sometimes we're better off without them. Are you certain their absence isn't what is keeping her alive?"

Sophia thought for a moment. "Honestly, I don't know. If I didn't have my memories, it would be awful. I wouldn't understand why I behaved the way I did or have something to point to in order to know why I was the way I was."

Saint Valentine gave her a thoughtful expression. "That's a very good point. We're a product of our memories. They shape us. I dare say, at our darkest times, they keep us going. Having memories, the good ones and bad ones, give us hope and tell us how to survive the future."

"You'll help her?" Sophia asked.

He gave her a reluctant look. "I can't guarantee anything, unfortunately. I'll look at your friend. Your other friend, well, I can fix him if that's what you really want."

Sophia nodded. "Yes, it is."

Saint Valentine stood and offered his arm. "Then I say we should take off. Although I would love to have you all to myself, you're not mine to have and must be shared with others."

CHAPTER ONE HUNDRED TWENTY-FIVE

I t felt strange to walk through the Barrier with Saint Valentine, but Quiet had allowed him to enter as he had promised.

"Oh, what a lovely place," Saint Valentine said as they walked up to the Castle. In the distance, Sophia spied her dragon perched at the top of the Cave, regarding her with an affectionate glare.

"Your dragon was worried for you," Saint Valentine observed, pointing at Lunis.

Sophia nodded. "Yes, he is like an overly protective Jewish mother."

Saint Valentine laughed, somehow making his face even more attractive.

It was surreal to march up to the Castle with an old saint who was smartly dressed in a silver suit. What was even more odd was Sophia wearing an elegant gown, holding it up with one hand, the long train dragging behind her.

At the door to the Castle, Saint Valentine paused, taking in the stained-glass window of an angel on it. "Oh, yes, the Dragon Elite, forever protected by the angels." He turned to face her, a glint of flirtation in his eyes. "A girl after my own heart, it seems you are ."

She blushed, pushing one of her loose curls behind her ear.

He reached out and combed a finger over her cheek. "Hyacinth didn't have to do much work on you, I would think."

Sophia was overcome with nervous emotions. Her throat closed up from the affections of this strange man. She didn't know what to say, but it didn't matter because a moment later, the door to the Castle whipped open. Wilder stood on the threshold, an undeniably angry expression on his face. "Well, this is awkward," he spat, looking between Saint Valentine and Sophia.

CHAPTER ONE HUNDRED TWENTY-SIX

"Wilder," Sophia said in a rush, jumping back from the man beside her. "This is Saint Valentine. I brought him here to fix...help you."

The dragonrider looked Saint Valentine over and then drew his gaze to her, taking in her appearance in the red dress. He softened immediately. "You look stunning."

She found herself blushing again, but this one brought butterflies to her stomach. "Thank you."

"You didn't have to do this," Wilder said, his fond expression fading as he glanced back at Saint Valentine.

"Hiker told me to," Sophia explained. "He wants you to have your head clear again."

Wilder chewed on his lip, reservation heavy in his gaze. Finally, he opened the door all the way, welcoming Saint Valentine to the Castle.

"Where is Ainsley?" Sophia asked Wilder.

He nodded to the top of the stairs. "In Hiker's office, dusting the bookcase and going on about how the Castle is making her life hell."

"That seems about right." Sophia picked up her dress and climbed the stairs, the two men following her.

When she entered Hiker's office, his eyes widened at the sight of her. He shook his head as though trying to clear his vision. "What happened to you?"

"She brushed her hair," Mama Jamba remarked from her usual place on the sofa, a book tucked into her lap.

"I would say she did a bit more than that." Ainsley whistled. "Are you wearing lipstick, S. Beaufont?"

Sophia flushed. "I am, but not really. It's the dress. It does my makeup and hair."

"I used to have someone who did my hair and makeup," Ainsley replied, referring to Quiet. She was standing on one of the bookshelves, dusting from a precarious position. "But now he is dead to me."

Mama Jamba gave Sophia an appreciative look. "Hyacinth does good work, and if you're wearing one of her dresses, then I expect..."

On cue, Saint Valentine entered Hiker Wallace's office, followed closely by Wilder.

The leader of the Dragon Elite shot into a standing position, nearly jumping over his desk. "What the hell?"

CHAPTER ONE HUNDRED TWENTY-SEVEN

"Oh, this is going to be good," Mama Jamba cooed, scooting back on the sofa and sticking her book to the side as she got ready to watch the show about to ensue.

Sophia realized that for Hiker, who had never seen an outsider enter the Gullington except when Quiet was sick and the Barrier came down, the presence of a stranger was very alarming.

"Everything is okay," Sophia told him in a rush, trying to reassure Hiker. "Quiet is fine. The Barrier is still up. I asked Quiet for permission to bring him here." She pointed to Saint Valentine, who was smiling warmly even as the Viking regarded him with skepticism.

"And who are you?" Hiker bellowed.

"Saint Valentine, of course." Mama Jamba blushed at the handsome gentleman.

He abandoned his place next to Sophia and went over to Mother Nature, taking her hand and kissing it the way he had with Sophia. To her surprise, the old woman tilted her head to the side and batted her eyes at him.

"An honor to see you, Mother Nature," Saint Valentine said.

She waved him off, smiling. "Oh, the pleasure is all mine."

"What is he doing here?" Hiker asked, sounding angrier than usual.

"You asked me to find a way to fix Wilder," Sophia explained. "My source told me Saint Valentine was the only one who could undo Cupid's arrow."

"Oh, very good," Hiker approved. "Well, get to work."

Saint Valentine thankfully didn't appear offended by the Viking's lack of decorum. He turned his attention to Wilder and ran his eyes over him. "This is the friend you spoke of, Sophia?"

She nodded.

"And the other friend?" Saint Valentine asked, turning his attention away from Wilder and back to her.

Sophia pointed at Ainsley. "She is right there."

His gaze studied Ainsley for a long minute while everyone remained tensely silent. Finally, Saint Valentine graced Sophia with an apologetic smile. "I have some good and bad news for you."

She tensed. "Yes?"

"Well, the good news is I can't fix your friend," Saint Valentine said, indicating Wilder.

"You can't?" Hiker questioned. "Why not? He's never thinking anymore. Always dreamy-eyed and distracted. There has to be something you can do to fix him. That damn Cupid…"

"I can't fix him," Saint Valentine began, his tone speculative, "because there isn't anything wrong with him."

"Of course there is," Hiker argued, pointing. "Didn't you hear me? He is aloof and always has a ridiculous smile on his face."

Saint Valentine nodded. "Yes, that seems right. Those are the symptoms of love."

"Well, there you go," Hiker stated. "Fix him. Undo what Cupid did to him."

Saint Valentine shook his head as he eyed Wilder. "I can't fix him because Cupid didn't do anything to him. He wasn't struck by an arrow."

432

CHAPTER ONE HUNDRED TWENTY-EIGHT

"Say what?" Hiker boomed, his eyes widening.

Sophia's mouth dropped open.

Mama Jamba wiggled, enjoying the show. Ainsley hopped down and took a position next to her on the sofa, wanting a front-row seat to the action.

"This just got good," the housekeeper whispered.

"But I was there," Sophia stated, nearly stuttering. "I saw you get hit."

Wilder gave her a shameful expression. "It nearly hit me. Ripped through my clothes, but it didn't pierce the skin."

"Then why..." Sophia trailed away, confused.

"Then that means..." Hiker also seemed unable to finish his sentence.

"You wouldn't accept my affections any other way," Wilder explained to her, defeated. "Then Hiker caught me confessing my feelings, and it just got out of control."

"You lied about getting struck by the arrow to cover the way you really feel?" Hiker asked, disappointment heavy in his voice.

"Yes, sir," Wilder affirmed.

"You know I'll not tolerate this," Hiker declared with conviction.

"I know, sir, and for what it's worth, Sophia rejected me. She wanted to mind your rules," Wilder told him.

Hiker cut his eyes at her. "About time she started doing what I say."

"I'm sorry for lying," Wilder apologized, his gaze low before he brought his blue eyes up to meet Sophia's. "I'll respect your decision and leave you alone from now on. Just friends."

"Oh, this is hard to watch," Ainsley said in a loud whisper to Mama Jamba.

"Just wait," she replied, patting the housekeeper's knee. "It's going to get worse."

Sophia hoped it didn't. Her heart was breaking for Wilder. She knew why he had done what he did, but having it announced in front of everyone was humiliating, and now Hiker knew, and everything was a mess.

"I'm sorry," Wilder said to her and then bowed to Hiker. "You don't have to worry about this happening again, sir. I'll mind my boundaries."

The dragonrider seemed to have said everything right, leaving Hiker with little to criticize. "See that you do."

Wilder nodded, backing out of the office before taking off, his footsteps getting faster as he ran down the corridor, leaving Sophia to wonder if she had done the right thing by bringing Saint Valentine. She had ruined everything between her and Wilder, and she saw no way to fix it. It occurred to her that maybe he wasn't the one who needed fixing. Maybe it had been her all along.

CHAPTER ONE HUNDRED TWENTY-NINE

Saint Valentine turned his attention on Ainsley, his face grave. "And now for you, my dear."

Ainsley looked over her shoulder like he was talking to someone else. "Me? What about me?"

"Your friend," Saint Valentine indicated Sophia. "She has asked me to help you."

"Help me?" Ainsley questioned. "Why? Because I work for an ungrateful dictator and my best friend is no friend of mine?"

He drew his gaze to Sophia. "She doesn't know."

She shook her head. "Even if she does, she forgets. The Castle has a way of erasing it so as to not hurt her."

"It sounds like you do have a friend, after all," Saint Valentine said, referring to Quiet.

"Sophia, what is this all about?" Hiker questioned.

"I want to help Ainsley," she explained. "I want her to have her life back."

"Help me?" Ainsley's voice was shrill. "With what?"

Hiker dropped his chin. "You have no right to do this, Sophia. This isn't your business."

"It may not be," she fired. "But one could argue Wilder's feelings were none of your business."

"He is my dragonrider and works for me." Hiker's face turned red. "What happens in my Castle is my business, and you would do well to remember that."

"Can someone please explain to me what is going on here?" Ainsley asked, sounding scared.

Hiker shook his head. "No. There are some things we don't need to fix. Some things we just have to let go of."

"I can see why you're taking that position, Hiker," Saint Valentine observed.

"You have done quite enough here," Hiker fired, spit flying from his mouth, his unbridled power building. Once Sophia was done fixing everyone else's problems, she was definitely going to have to help him with that before it got the better of him.

"I don't think I am," Saint Valentine said quite calmly. "Sophia booked an appointment with me, and therefore, she is entitled to my services." Turning to her, he gave her a thoughtful expression. "I'm ready to tell you my assessment of your friend."

"NO!" Hiker yelled. "Sophia, get out. What this man has to say isn't for your ears."

"What is going on here?" Ainsley asked, now standing and trembling.

"I'm not going anywhere," Sophia proclaimed. "You can tell me who I can't love and be with because I work for you, but what you can't do is tell me who I can help. Ainsley is my friend, and if there's a way to fix her, then I'm going to do it."

"You're going too far," he said through clenched teeth.

"What is happening here?" Ainsley sounded on the verge of tears.

Sophia faced her. "Ains, a long time ago, you threw yourself in front of Hiker to save him from an attack by his brother, Thad Reinhart."

At her back, she heard Hiker sigh loudly. She pushed on.

"You survived the attack, but it cost you your memories." Sophia gulped and looked to Mama Jamba for support. She nodded, encouraging her to continue. "You were brought here to the Castle and it healed you. You know how if you leave for long you get ill?"

Ainsley nodded.

"That's because the Castle is keeping you alive," Sophia explained. "For centuries, you have been unable to leave here, and the worst part of it is, even as I tell you this, you'll forget it if the Castle desires it so. It erases the information from your memory so you don't suffer. For as much as Quiet has done you don't like, he wants the best for you. He has kept you alive all this time and tried to make you as comfortable as you can be under the circumstances."

Ainsley's mouth was hanging open as she tried to process this. "What if I don't want to forget this time? What if I want to know there's something wrong with me so I understand the emptiness I wake up with each day."

"Then you simply ask," Mama Jamba answered, pointing to the doorway where Quiet stood, having materialized without anyone knowing.

In a daze, Ainsley walked around Sophia and Saint Valentine, her attention on the gnome. "Quiet, you did this? You kept me alive when I should be dead? You took my memories so I wouldn't suffer? You kept me busy here, so I had a purpose?"

The groundskeeper nodded, his chin low and his hands behind his back.

"Then how can I be angry at you," she said, a tender smile in her voice. "I know you kept secrets, but I realize now, there's a reason to your madness, and I forgive you. I have one request."

The gnome looked up at her, age-old wisdom in his eyes. His expression seemed to beg for her to continue.

"Let me remember this," she told him slowly. "Don't erase this memory from my mind. I wake every morning feeling lost. Now I know why, but if you make me forget again, I'll just live in this perpetual cycle. At least now, when I wake up, I know why my heart hurts. I can't remember who I was before. I can't leave the Gullington.

Knowing that's hard, but not knowing why I feel lost, that's worse. Please, Quiet, don't erase my mind."

He nodded—a simple gesture, but it meant so much. As quietly as he had shown up, the gnome disappeared, leaving everyone in the office in silence.

CHAPTER ONE HUNDRED THIRTY

"I want to know who I was before," Ainsley said, looking at Hiker. "I want you to tell me. You know, don't you?"

He nodded. "Ainsley, this isn't worth it. We did what we could to save you and keep you as comfortable as possible."

"That isn't fair," she argued, her fists by her side. "I want my memories back. S. Beaufont was right to do this for me."

"Ainsley," Hiker began, again using her name, which he never did. "There are some things that are worth forgetting. You're better off this way. I assure you."

The housekeeper whipped around to face Saint Valentine. "You know how to fix me. I want you to do it so I can remember who I am. I want to be able to leave the Gullington. I want to be as far from this man as possible." She pointed at Hiker and he flinched.

Saint Valentine released a pained smile. "I'm sorry, but I can't help you. I cannot cure a broken heart. Only you can do that for yourself."

"Broken heart?" Ainsley asked, her voice full of shock. "I'm suffering from a broken heart? That's the spell Thad Reinhart hit me with?"

"No, but it's the reason you lost your memories," Saint Valentine explained. "And it's what prevents your body from healing yourself

439

completely from the attack. Fix your broken heart and you'll have your memories. You'll be able to leave here for good."

"If I don't have my memories, how do I know how I broke my heart?" Ainsley demanded.

Saint Valentine pressed his lips together, unwilling to answer the question.

"Someone has to tell me what happened." Ainsley looked between the man before her and Mama Jamba, desperate for answers. "Please, I just want to know so I can get my life back. I just want to—"

"It was me," Hiker Wallace said, interrupting her.

All eyes spun to face him.

He cleared his throat, unwilling to look directly at Ainsley. "I broke your heart. You were a delegate advisor to the Dragon Elite from the Elfin Council. We fell in love, but I told you we didn't have a future because I was married to my job as the leader of the Dragon Elite. Then the war came, and Thad attacked, and you sacrificed yourself for me. I'm sorry. That's what happened, and it's history, and there isn't anything I can do to change things. Even if there was, I don't see it playing out any differently. Love isn't a luxury that we, the Dragon Elite, are allowed. We fight wars and resolve disagreements so others can know and have what we cannot."

CHAPTER ONE HUNDRED THIRTY-ONE

The timing of the LiDAR being ready was either going to be a saving grace or make things tenser. Hiker and Ainsley locked up in the Castle together was probably not for the best. The leader of the Dragon Elite didn't think it was a good idea he go on missions until he learned how to fully control his new inherited power.

Sophia figured Ainsley would stay as far from him as possible... maybe for a century or two. It could not have been easy for the house-keeper to learn she had once loved Hiker, and he had loved her. She knew the truth now and she wasn't going to be forgetting it.

To further complicate things, Sophia and Wilder on a mission together wasn't ideal. It was time to recover the dragon eggs. They had what they needed to dig them up, but it would require all of the dragonriders.

Sophia worked to secure the LiDAR equipment onto Lunis with Mahkah's help. He was the right one to be around her right then because he didn't talk unnecessarily and had a calming effect.

I like this new bling look, Lunis said as they secured the last bit of equipment.

She shook her head. "You're not a rapper wearing gold chains. This is very expensive equipment and we need to be very careful."

The other dragons landed close by, all of them giving Lunis strange looks as he got loaded up.

Why don't you take a picture, he spat at them. *It will last longer.*

Bell, like Hiker, would stay behind but it was because she had to babysit the bad dragons. The old dragon was in no way pleased about this.

Sophia stood back, checking Lunis over. "Okay, I think this works. It's a bit bulky, but it should work."

"He will be much slower than normal," Mahkah offered.

That still makes me faster than slowpoke Coral, Lunis said, sticking out his tongue at the purple dragon.

Very mature, she replied, throwing her snout in the air.

I know you are , but what am I? Lunis replied.

Sophia shook her head. "I knew there would be drawbacks to having the LiDAR equipment on him. I suspect he will lose other powers as well."

Mahkah nodded. "He probably will not be able to use fire and have decreased power."

"As a plus," Sophia countered, "the LiDAR should be powerful and work faster, which is good because then we can whip in and out of there."

Yeah, after our ditch diggers get the eggs, Lunis stated, laughing at the dragons.

They had been chosen to dig up the eggs since that would require them to wear less equipment. Their sharp claws would work like shovels, hopefully making fast work of it. The regal dragons were not excited about being turned into magic shovels, but none of them wanted the technology job, so it meant they had to settle for the more manual one.

Evan slapped his hands together as he strode out to the Expanse, which was still littered with colorful dragon eggs. Thankfully no more had hatched. Sophia was hoping they wouldn't until she had a chance to focus on what came out of the eggs. If they had any more evil dragons at the Gullington, things were going to heat up pretty fast.

"All right," Evan said, excitedly. "Who is ready to go on an egg hunt?"

"You are, it seems." Sophia didn't look directly at Wilder as he approached behind Evan. Things were awkward between them after the whole Saint Valentine thing, but time would hopefully ease tension.

She pulled three small screens from the equipment and powered them up, handing one to each of the men. "Once we take the first few readings using the LiDAR, the mapping will show up on these devices. That's how we will locate the dragon eggs."

"Question," Evan asked, studying his device. "How do we know that what registers on these are dragon eggs and not rocks? I don't want to excavate a bunch of junk."

"Alicia tweaked the tech to specifically work on dragon eggs," Sophia explained. "And dragon eggs are naturally hot so they will show up as bright red, indicating a heat source."

"Okay," Evan said, taking off for his dragon. "Let's do this! The last one there's a rotten egg!"

CHAPTER ONE HUNDRED THIRTY-TWO

Much of this LiDAR was based on a hunch, but she had learned that to trust her gut was almost better than relying on solid data.

As the four dragonriders rode through the portal and over the Colorado terrain, worry started to build in her. If she was wrong...

She had spent twenty million dollars on this project. Well, King Rudolf had, but still. Alicia had worked nonstop on getting the LiDAR equipment ready fast, not to mention the guys were all at her back and would witness her failure. The worst part would be the dragon eggs would still be out there, lost.

Believe in yourself, Lunis encouraged. *At the end of the day, the battles we win are because we believe in our abilities. We always have a choice between believing we can or we cannot. That becomes our reality. At this eleventh hour, if you doubt yourself, that's going to influence how things go.*

She smiled, grateful for his sage wisdom. It was ironic to her that her dragon could make silly jokes and then spout great wisdom.

Sophia reminded herself of a Zelda Fitzgerald quote. Since attending the Great Gatsby, roaring twenties party at Cupid's mansion, she had been obsessed with the Fitzgeralds, brushing up on their work in her spare time which there had not been much of, but one always made time for great literature.

The quote was perfect for this momentous occasion, reminding Sophia to believe in herself. Zelda Fitzgerald had said, "She quietly expected great things to happen to her, and no doubt that's one of the reasons why they did."

The words instantly made her feel better as she repeated them in her mind and powered up the LiDAR equipment. It was strange to ride on the back of her dragon while typing on several different workstations, all with monitors and advanced technology, but it was also awesome. She had leaned into this magitech, taking dragon-riding to a whole new twentieth-century level.

The LiDAR went to work, scanning the terrain below. The land-scape was all mountains and prairies—the Colorado spring bringing colors as new life sprouted from the dirt.

Beside them, a flock of birds soared in the opposite direction as a herd of buffalo streaked by on the ground below. This, like Scotland, felt like untouched territory, rustic and untamed. There was some-thing innately perfect about Mama Jamba's planet.

Sophia waited for the first readings to come through as Coral sped by Lunis, doing spirals. From the purple dragon's back, Evan hollered, "Who's the slow dragon now?"

The equipment had slowed Lunis down a lot. That worried Sophia if they were attacked. He didn't have any offensive or defensive measures right now. But like Plato had warned, using technology always came with a tradeoff. Sophia just hoped the benefit of having it on Lunis was worth it.

As the report delayed in loading, the doubt started to build in her mind.

Remember where your faith needs to reside, Lunis told her.

Sophia nodded. "She quietly expected great things to happen to her, and no doubt that's one of the reasons why they did," she repeated to herself.

The screen refreshed. The LiDAR was working. Better yet, it appeared it had picked up thirteen hot objects in the ground below.

Thirteen dragon eggs!

CHAPTER ONE HUNDRED THIRTY-THREE

Sophia and Lunis stayed in the air as the other three dragonriders landed, following the maps on their handheld devices.

Now that Sophia knew where to look, she could see the markings in the soil that indicated it had recently been upturned when the dragon eggs were buried. It still burned her Trin Currante had gone to such lengths—tricking her into giving her *The Complete History of Dragonriders*, reading all their secrets, poisoning Quiet and then stealing the dragon eggs. Even so, she had a hesitation in her loathing for the cyborg.

There was something she didn't know. Something important. She had to figure it out once the dragon eggs were back at the Gullington, safe once more. Even if they were evil dragons that hatched from the shells, they were still hers.

Lunis continued to circle overhead, the LiDAR continuing to operate so as to give the guys more accurate readings on the ground. It wouldn't take long for the dragons to dig up the eggs, but the more specific the location, the faster their jobs would be.

Sophia looked out at the Colorado frontier, taking a moment to enjoy the view. It was never lost on her that she rode on the back of a dragon and got to see everything from the skies, but sometimes the stress of the missions made her miss the beauty of the world.

Sorry to interrupt your respite, Lunis chimed in her head.

She smiled into the wind. "What is it?"

It appears there are alarms on the ground below, he told her.

Sophia pulled her gaze down immediately to see what he meant. That's when she saw it.

On the ground, multiple portals were being opened and steam-punk cyborg pirates were stepping through, looking fierce and ready to fight.

CHAPTER ONE HUNDRED THIRTY-FOUR

L anding wasn't an option for Sophia and Lunis. She needed to monitor the LiDAR equipment, and he needed to stay flying. That left them helpless to watch as the guys were ambushed as dozens of cyborgs ran through the portals, ready to fight.

Sophia had to hand it to Trin Currante. She was alert and ready to respond at a moment's notice. Lunis was right, there had to be some sort of alarm that clued her in when they had landed on this territory where the dragon eggs were.

Having to watch the three dragonriders from the air wasn't what Sophia wanted. She always wanted to be a part of the action. She wanted to fight alongside her friends and to have their backs, but that wasn't her role in this battle. She and Lunis needed to stick to the sky.

They can handle this, Lunis assured her.

She nodded, grateful for his encouragement as she watched three men with face masks and goggles race in Wilder's direction.

From atop his dragon, he pulled out his sword and charged at the men who had guns and flamethrowers. She felt he was ill-prepared to fight such types of warriors.

Have faith, Lunis reminded her. *Guns are fast and easy, but they're not better.*

She was happy to have his wisdom when she needed it most.

As the first of the pirates powered up his flamethrower, Wilder shot in his direction, twirling his sword. The man must have miscalculated either how long it would take for the flamethrower to work or how fast the dragon could run because Simi was on him in seconds. Wilder struck his sword across the man's midsection, sending him to the ground as the dragon's tail whipped around and took out a second man. He fell like a twig being stomped on.

The third man held up a rifle, which was his arm, and pointed it at Wilder. The dragonrider ducked when the first blast was fired. Then as the guy reloaded, the master of weapons held up his hand and closed his fingers. The gun on the man's arm mimicked this movement, closing up on itself, being crushed immediately. The man screamed, turning and running the other way.

See, Lunis insisted. *You don't have to worry. He is a big boy and can take care of himself.*

Sophia knew he was right, but then her gaze drifted to Mahkah and Evan on the ground, and she had similar worries for them.

Mahkah was surrounded.

Evan was off Coral; something had pulled him to the ground and separated him from his dragon.

If things were not exciting enough, another portal opened, but this one was right in front of Lunis and Sophia and the steampunk zeppelin that had attacked the Gullington flew through, Trin Currante easily visible at the front.

CHAPTER ONE HUNDRED THIRTY-FIVE

R emember that positive thinking? Lunis asked.
"Yeah," she said, fear running rampant in her head.

Time to abandon that, he urged. *We're totally screwed.*

She didn't want to admit it, but he was right. They were slow, and he could not use his fire. She had magic, but against the huge zeppelin, she doubted it would do much good.

"I'm going to portal us home," Sophia stated.

No, Lunis said with conviction. *We will lose the mapping, and then they will move the dragon eggs. We stay. We fight.*

Sophia playfully argued with Lunis all the time, but when he was adamant about something, like this, she listened. "Okay, we fight."

She held up her hand, trying to decide what spell would be the best against the zeppelin. She decided to rely on the element that came to magicians best, the one they presided over—wind.

Forcing all of her strength into the spell, she shot it at the zeppelin, deciding it was best to put all her effort into one spell rather than divide it up into several attacks.

The wind spell hit the side of the zeppelin and sent it sideways toward the mountain. It began losing height fast and she almost rejoiced, thinking she had been successful at taking down the huge aircraft. Then it zoomed around and regained height, its panels flapping in the wind like an undeterred bird.

Sophia braced herself on Lunis. She was surrounded by millions of dollars of equipment, but the most important, most valuable thing was under her. Her dragon was irreplaceable.

She was just about to refuse him and open a portal when the first attack came. That stole her attention from creating a portal as Lunis had to move to avoid it, but he was much slower than normal and the missile whizzed dangerously close, brushing his underbelly.

Sophia held her breath as she felt his pain from the attack.

The zeppelin launched three more attacks in succession. Sophia watched them come toward her in slow motion. There was no way they could dodge all those.

They were going down.

CHAPTER ONE HUNDRED THIRTY-SIX

Sophia braced herself for the hits. Lunis naturally wore armor, and she could partially shield him. She might be able to deflect one of the attacks, but three missiles were more than they could safely withstand.

She was just about to knock down the first missile when it dropped from the air and landed on the ground, exploding on top of a band of pirates below.

Stunned, Sophia looked around just in time to see Wilder and Simi cutting across and coming to their rescue. He flashed her a smile as he pushed off the other two attacks, deflecting them at the ground where Mahkah and Evan were making up lost territory, pushing the steam-punk pirates back toward the hills.

With the two missiles racing after the cyborgs, they began opening portals to escape as they realized they were overrun.

Evan was back on Coral and scorching a few men who were slow to react. Coral opened her mouth, sending fire on the men. "Haha!" Evan yelled. "How is that for a flamethrower, you metal pirates!"

Wilder gave Sophia one last reassuring glance over his shoulder as he and Simi raced in the direction of the zeppelin, sending attack after attack at the helium balloon that kept it afloat. The guy looked charged and ready. Sophia almost felt sorry for the zeppelin. It was coming down, she suspected.

CHAPTER ONE HUNDRED THIRTY-SEVEN

From high atop Lunis, Sophia watched as the men battled the cyborgs on the ground and Wilder scared the zeppelin away. It opened a portal, escaping before he could bring it down properly, which she was certain he could do. He appeared very motivated, with a heat in his actions she had never seen.

It was then she recognized he was defending her. Not just her and Lunis while they were mostly defenseless but mostly her. Even after everything, he was protective of her. She wanted to think it was because they were friends and fellow dragonriders, but she knew there was another connection that made him charge after the huge and stocked zeppelin and send it flying for the hills in the distance.

When the last of the pirates had been scared away, the dragons went to work excavating the eggs. It was quick work but still took precision. Digging haphazardly into the ground and crushing an egg would be no good. The LiDAR and its constant reporting were crucial. Lunis and Sophia continued to circle, staying vigilant for the return of any of Trin Currante's crew.

The cyborgs must have known they had won. The Dragon Elite were taking back their dragon eggs. That should have made Sophia proud and happy. She should be celebrating, but for some reason, something felt off about the whole thing. She wanted her dragon eggs back, but she also wanted to know why someone would go to such great lengths to get them.

Trin Currante wasn't someone to underestimate. She was a woman who had somehow overthrown an organization, taken out the librarian of the Great Library, impersonated him, read a book Sophia had yet to even crack, and figured out how to get into the Gullington and steal dragon eggs. Trin Currante was a devilishly smart woman, and strangely Sophia didn't want to fight her.

As the first dragon egg was excavated, Sophia had a strange thought. She wanted Trin Currante on their side.

CHAPTER ONE HUNDRED THIRTY-EIGHT

"You have lost your damn mind," Hiker said, pushing up from his chair and starting to pace.

"I knew you would say that, sir," Sophia argued.

"Good, you're not as dumb as you look right now then."

She rolled her eyes at Mama Jamba, who was crocheting on Hiker's couch. She didn't look like she was going to offer up any help.

"You're obviously still bitter about the Ainsley situation," Sophia stated, returning her attention to Hiker.

"You think?" he queried. "I'm planning on being bitter about that for another few centuries, so be warned. You just had to bring Saint Valentine in here, didn't you? Things were just fine, and then you dragged that guy in here, and he exposed everything I had carefully—"

"Covered up!" Sophia interrupted.

He closed his mouth and regarded her with pure venom. "You'll do well to watch yourself in my presence."

"Is that a threat?" she challenged. "Because I'm not scared of you. I respect you, but I'm not going to be scared of you anymore. Ainsley needed to know the truth. It's her right to know, not yours to cover up."

"Damn it, Sophia," Hiker complained, continuing to stomp around.

"You come to the Gullington with your dresses and makeup and change everything."

"In my defense, my attire has changed nothing around here," she told him. "You don't like that I oppose you and I reveal secrets. Things that need to be revealed. Truths others need to know. I get you see things as black and white. There's the good and the bad. We protect the good and we kill the bad, but sometimes people don't fall into either category, so we have to find a different solution."

He halted and looked at Mama Jamba, then pulled his gaze to Sophia's. "You think Trin Currante is one of these grays, is that right?"

"When I got back," Sophia began, "I got a report from one of my sources."

"The one you'll not share with me, right?" he asked.

She nodded. The report had actually come from Mortimer. His brownies had dug up information on the Saverus organization and found out they had abducted hundreds of people. Mostly men, but there had also been Trin Currante. These were perfectly healthy magicians Saverus had used magitech on to turn them into cyborgs, all in the name of science. Apparently Trin Currante had escaped, but she didn't stop there.

Some might have run as far from their captives as possible, dealing the best they could with all the changes done to her body, enhancing it in some ways, but irreversibly making her inhuman. According to Mortimer, Trin Currante had returned and wiped out the scientists who mutilated her and so many others. Then she rescued and recruited the others, who became her army. Now she was on a whole different mission. One Sophia could not totally argue with.

"Right," she affirmed. "They tell me the reason Trin Currante wanted the dragon eggs is because they're what she needs to fix the cyborgs. They need newly hatched eggs. A good one and an evil one."

He sighed. "If a man steals a loaf of bread to feed his starving family, it's still wrong."

"But it's less wrong than if they did it for selfish gains," Sophia argued. "Sir, she just wants to be normal. That's what she said to me at Medford Research. I misinterpreted it. She said she wanted to be like me, and I thought that meant she wanted to be a dragonrider, but she just wants to be a normal human magician again. Can you blame her? What if you didn't have skin and flesh? What if instead, you were metal and wires?"

He grimaced at the thought. "What are you asking? You defeated them. You got the dragon eggs back. The Gullington is safe. We're done with Trin Currante and her band of cyborgs."

"I'm asking that we help them somehow," Sophia said thoughtfully. "I'm asking that we seek them out and find a way to fix them. That's what they want, and we can help. I'm certain of it."

Hiker pursed his lips, his eyes going to Mama Jamba on the sofa. The old woman shrugged. "You're adjudicators, son. It's your job to settle things."

He huffed. "It isn't my job to help those who have hurt me and mine."

"No," Mama Jamba agreed. "But sometimes when we extend a hand to those who have wronged us, we heal the wounds of the past."

Sophia smiled at Mother Nature, so innocent and sweet curled up on the leather sofa.

Hiker Wallace seemed to think about this before resigning. "Fine. You can seek out Trin Currante and look for ways to help her. But if this gets too complicated, if it costs us, then it's off."

Sophia wanted to hug the big Viking but was certain that would be overstepping boundaries, so instead, she said, "Thank you, sir. I think one day, she will make an excellent ally."

CHAPTER ONE HUNDRED
THIRTY-NINE

Ainsley wasn't even looking at Hiker these days. When she had something to give him, she shoved it into Sophia's arms and said, "Take that to Heartbreaker."

On a bright note, she and Quiet were back to normal. Better.

The housekeeper was lavishing the groundskeeper with attention, making him special food, and giving him extra consideration. Apparently, he was back to getting her ready in the morning. It was a few steps forward and a few back.

Sophia assumed things would get worse with Hiker and Ainsley before they got better. The two had a lot to work through, but Sophia was going to help them, even if neither seemed to want her to. Ainsley wanted her memories before the incident back. Hiker wanted his housekeeper to forget everything. What they actually got was yet to be determined.

On that pristine May Day celebration, those were not the concerns on most minds. The Expanse littered with dragon eggs now had totem poles erected all over. Long colorful ribbons hung from their tops, wafting in the wind.

Evan sidled up next to Sophia and elbowed her in the side. "Do you want me to help you with your problem?"

She cut her eyes at him. "I feel like that's like asking a jackhammer to repair your broken china."

He shrugged. "Hey, just trying to help. You really broke him." Evan nodded in Wilder's direction.

"I didn't," she said, her words stopping short. There seemed to be a lot of heartbreak all over the Gullington lately, but she wasn't taking the blame for the majority of it.

"Don't worry, Soph," Evan said, putting a comforting arm around her shoulder as the ribbons danced in the spring air. Ainsley and Quiet frolicked in the distance, and Hiker pretended not to notice as Mother Nature admired the thirteen returned eggs.

Mahkah and Wilder sat chatting, calm and at ease after a successful mission.

"At the end of the day," Evan went on, "I think you're a good egg. And those, when they hatch, they have something good to offer the world. I'm glad you're here. I just think you also have the extra job of fixing all the bad eggs. And fixing the cracked ones. And then—"

"Your metaphor has failed," she interrupted.

Evan laughed. "Yeah, I know. I just want you to know, for as much trouble as I give you, I'm glad you're here, Sophia Beaufont. It can't be easy to be the only girl dragonrider, but there's a reason it's you. I don't know anyone who could put up with us like you do, and boy, when you make Hiker angry, it's a sight to see."

She found herself smiling affectionately at her friend. "Thanks, Evan. I'm not sure if you knew it, but I needed to hear that."

He winked at her. "I knew it. We're friends, and as such, we look out for each other."

CHAPTER ONE HUNDRED FORTY

"Well, hey there," Sophia said, taking the call from her sister, Liv.

"Hey Trouble," Liv replied. "How's it going?"

Sophia glanced out at the Expanse littered with dragon eggs and all the totem poles with their colorful ribbons dancing in the wind. "Everything is good at the moment."

"Oh, yes," Liv said, a knowingness in her voice. "The quiet before the storm. The moment when everything feels resolved, right before the next big mission hits, surrounded by mystery and uncertainty."

Sophia thought about Ainsley and Hiker. About Trin Currante. About the world outside the Gullington that sorely needed adjudicators. Her eyes scanned the various eggs that could hatch to be good or evil dragons. She thought about all the things she needed to figure out and all the things she knew she didn't know, and worse, all the things she didn't know that she didn't know. She released a tight breath. "It's quiet now. That's all that matters."

"Well, I have some good and bad news, followed by some really great news," Liv said, excitement edging into her voice.

"Tell me!" Sophia exclaimed.

"The first good news is that Papa Creola totally knew you'd need to time travel to the Midnight Lunar Eclipse candy shop to fulfill your end of the bargain with Lee."

"Oh, so he's going to help me?" She asked.

"He doesn't have to," Liv said, a sneaky grin in her voice. "Apparently you already have the means to time travel."

"To the future?" Sophia questioned. "I don't think so."

"No, to the past," Liv explained.

Sophia thought for a long moment before the answer came to her. "The reset token."

"Exactly," Liv stated.

Of course, Sophia thought, remembering the golden coin that she had that took her to the reset point in history. It was the moment in the past that Papa Creola had paused in a way. This was the backup plan if Liv didn't help mortals to see magic again and everything went to hell. Father Time would just send everything back to this time right before the Great War happened and they'd try again.

Sophia had earned this token when she was opening the portals inside the Castle. She'd used it to see the reset point in the House of Fourteen and the Castle inside the Gullington. However, she hadn't considered using it outside of these places, but realized that it must work. She could take the reset token to any place and it would transport her back to the past, to the moment right before the Great War.

"So that must mean…" Sophia began slowly, working it all out in her mind. "That the reset point happened on the night of a lunar eclipse."

"It just so happened," Liv stated proudly. "Don't you love how things work out?"

"I absolutely do," Sophia said. "I'm guessing we have to hang out on Roya Lane until it's midnight to visit the candy store."

"Yeah, Papa Creola said we're allowed to do that," Liv explained. "You can pretty much hang out in the past reset point as long as you like, but it's not advisable. Causes complications if you're there too long, but he authorized it for this."

"Awesome. What are you doing later?" Sophia asked.

There was a long pause. "That's the thing. I can't do it right now."

"Well, by later, I meant tomorrow or in a few days or something."

"Soph, that's the bad news," Liv imparted. "I can't do it for a little bit."

Sophia shrugged, although she realized that her sister couldn't see that reply. "It's fine. Lee hasn't told me where the location of the katana sword is yet. And I have to ask Wilder to help. And there's that whole Zack Efron kidnapping that has to happen."

"I thought you were going to secure his help the old fashioned way."

Sophia laughed. "Chloroform is old fashioned," she joked.

"I meant, by asking him and using your title as a rider for the Dragon Elite," Liv corrected.

"Oh, that way," Sophia said dully. "Yeah, let's go the legal route."

"I'm still curious why you need him for this mission," Liv mused.

"Me too. Anyway, I know you're busy with missions and saving the world and all so don't worry. We can go as soon as you're free."

"Well, remember that I did say that I had really good news," Liv said, her tone now overflowing with excitement.

"That's right. You did. What is it?"

"The reason I'm busy, besides policing the magical world is..." There was another long pause. "Stefan asked me to marry him."

The scream that escaped Sophia's mouth surprised even her. "Are you freaking serious? What did you say?"

"Ha-ha," Liv said, sounding amused. "I said no, obviously."

"Obviously," Sophia stated. "I mean he's only a demon hunter who has incredible powers, a longer than expected lifespan and a cunning sense of humor."

"Don't forget great hair and abs," Liv said, sounding giddy.

"These are the important things when considering a life partner."

"I said yes, of course, you big dork."

"Of course you did," Sophia exclaimed. "I'm so happy for you."

"So there will be a wedding," Liv began. "It will be small—"

"Only Father Time and the king of the fae, right?" Sophia joked.

"Oh dear..." There was sudden dread in Liv's voice. "I have to invite Rudolf..."

"I'm afraid you do," Sophia teased. "And since he made you the best man of his wedding, that means you have to make him the maid of honor."

Liv laughed. "No. Just no. And you know that you're my maid of honor."

Tears sprang to Sophia's eyes. "Really?" She couldn't believe she was asking that question. For sure she'd be Liv's maid of honor. Who else? Well, she had lots of friends, but Sophia was her sister.

"I'm honored, Liv."

"You're the only choice," her sister stated. "But I'm making Clark a bridesmaid."

"And he has to wear a pastel dress, right?"

"Along with Rory and Papa Creola," Liv joked.

"This is going to be the most festive occasion," Sophia said excitedly. "I can't wait."

"Well, you won't have to," Liv explained. "It will be quite soon. We want to be married."

"For tax purposes?"

"Yes, for tax purposes," Liv said dryly. "And because we're in love. And I can't picture my life without him. And I want to put him on my family plan for mobile."

Sophia giggled. "This is the best news ever. I'm so happy for you. And just tell me when the wedding is and I'll be there with bells on."

"Please don't," Liv scolded. "Bells would totally be a distraction. That's something Rudolf would do."

Sophia was smiling so wide it hurt her face. "Okay, I'll wear whatever you tell me to."

"Really, Soph, you're the one who knows fashion. You should tell me what to wear to my own wedding."

Sophia nodded. "I'm on it. I'll put together all the outfits if you want."

Liv sighed. "That's what I love about you. You just know what I need and offer it before I even ask. Well, and I also love that you're funny and courageous and smart."

"Thank you," Sophia said, feeling very loved in that moment.

"Thank you," Liv replied. "You know, I never thought I'd ever get married. Never thought I'd ever find someone I could stand forever or even a few hours. But it just goes to show, we can't underestimate ourselves. I think when I came back into your life, you taught me more than anyone about my capacity to love. It was then that I realized, not only did I want to love the people in my life with all my heart, but I wanted their love like it was oxygen itself. I needed their love to live—to thrive."

Sophia smiled at the poignant remark, realizing the evolution that her sister had taken to get to this point. An evolution of the heart was something that wasn't easy and usually marked by much doubt and confusion. However, she knew from personal experience that it was one hundred percent worth it.

CHAPTER ONE HUNDRED
FORTY-ONE

Sophia's gaze rested nervously on her phone, ruminating on the decision she had been wrestling with since she awoke at the early hour that morning. In the quiet, she had a clear moment of realization. She sent a note to one person, asking him to meet her by the Pond later that morning.

Now she had to go through with the second part related to her realization. If she did, everything would weave together. The question was, did she want it to?

She could go on with the way things were. She could keep her head down, go on missions, and live her life as dictated by Hiker Wallace, serving the Dragon Elite. Or she could have more. Did she want more?

Quiet had been right to wake her up at 3:33 every morning. It was a time when the universe was at its quietest, and in that hour of peace, Sophia was forced to look at the one thing she had hidden from.

The secret the morning breeze had to tell her wasn't a secret at all. Once she came to terms with it, she was going to have to face her fears and that's where the challenge lay.

Sophia pulled up the number for the pub. When Gregory

answered the phone, she almost hung up but instead said in a rush, "Hi, my name is Sophia Beaufont, and I want to make an appointment with Saint Valentine. I need him to fix me."

CHAPTER ONE HUNDRED
FORTY-TWO

After Sophia booked the appointment for a time in the past and got the instructions from Gregory, she hung up the phone. The timing could not have been any better because the person she had asked to meet her was quickly approaching.

Wilder had his hands in his pockets and a reluctant expression on his face as he hiked up to where she stood—the site of their first kiss. It felt so long ago and yet had not been.

She needed to ask him to help her with the mission to recover the katana sword for Lee. However, she'd do that later when that mission was closer. And besides, this meeting wasn't about business. This was absolutely personal.

The look on Wilder's face when he stood in front of her communicated his reservations. All Sophia's note had said was, "We need to talk. Meet me by the Pond in the open part of the Expanse."

This was the general area where they had first kissed, but not hidden from the Castle. From this spot, they could easily be seen from Hiker's office or by anyone.

She knew it probably made a thousand things run through his mind when he got the meeting request, but what she needed to say had to be said in person. He deserved that much.

"Thanks for meeting me here," she began.

"Sophia, can we not make things harder than they have to be?" he asked, interrupting the rehearsed speech she had practiced all morning. "I'm sorry I lied to you. I'm sorry I made things awkward. I respect what you want, and I promise to mind boundaries going forward. I want us to be friends."

"And I want more than that," she said, throwing out the speech and winging it, deciding to talk from the heart.

"W-w-what?" he stuttered. "You do?"

She nodded, a nervous smile breaking across her face.

"What about Hiker?" Wilder asked.

She shook her head. "His rule never should have mattered. I'm sorry I let it. Now I know he has that rule in place for himself rather than for others, but I don't want to live like that. I don't want to look back and realize I missed the opportunity for true happiness because I was afraid and let someone else direct my life. I don't want to realize the only person I've ever been crazy about got away because I wasn't willing to take a chance."

A sideways smile made his dimples surface. "You're crazy about me, huh?"

"I love you..." she began, saying words that had been said a trillion times by so many, but intending to quote Zelda Fitzgerald specifically. Sophia swallowed and smiled tenderly at the man before her, the one she realized she had loved instantly and fully since the beginning. That was the secret of her heart, and now it was out. Catching her breath, she started again from the beginning, the quote etched on her soul. "I love you, even if there isn't me or any love or even any life—I love you."

He rushed to her, desperate to close the distance. Cupping her chin, he bought it up gently so she was looking into his eyes. "I love you too. And the thing is..." He paused to choose his words carefully. The way his mouth formed them was deliberate. "The thing is, I can't pinpoint when I fell in love with you because since we met, I don't know of a moment when I wasn't falling in love with you. Little by little, every second we spend together, I fall harder. I'm not a wise man, but I don't see that ever changing. You're someone people fall for, and I happened to be lucky you fell in love with me."

Wilder was a rare soul. Sophia had never felt so in love with a person. Not her family. Not even her dragon. She had the privilege of knowing the sacred bond between her and a dragon, so she knew there was something more powerful about the love a man and a woman shared.

It made sense since the two crops of the last dragon eggs had been manifested when the first male and female riders came along. It was the balance of life, masculinity and femininity, Mother Nature and Father Time. When the two came together, when the genders worked together, magic was the result.

Sophia welcomed the kiss that graced her lips, soft and full of affection. She no longer worried what Hiker would do to them. This wasn't his life to live. It was theirs. She was certain of one thing: she was going to help her friend Hiker Wallace find the secrets of his own heart. Maybe it wouldn't involve early wake-up calls from the Castle, but whatever it took, Sophia would do because that was what friends did for each other. That was what family did, and the Dragon Elite were her family.

Familia Est Sempiternum.

She pulled gently away from Wilder, staying locked in his arms as the two faced the Castle, unafraid of who would see them. Tomorrow she would take on new missions, one to help Ainsley and Hiker. Missions that hopefully fixed her would-be enemies like Trin Currante and her men. Tomorrow she would help the Dragon Elite bring love to the world. Maybe Cupid was right, and love was the answer. The thing was, it could not be forced.

Love, if nurtured and allowed to be what it was, unbound and organic, could definitely fix the world.

SARAH'S AUTHOR NOTES
APRIL 13, 2020

Thank you so much for reading. Your support of the Liv Beaufont series and this one has been life changing. Thank you! Seriously! Thank you.

It's unavoidable that I discuss what has influenced this book as well as everyone's lives.

Coronavirus.

On March 8th, I went to London for a book conference, but also because my boyfriend lives in Scotland and we wanted to see each other. Honestly, if the conference cancelled, I was probably still going. I think about 30% of people dropped out of the conference at the last minute. Not MA and I though. We had meetings and an awesome fan meet up. And many came out to see us and that was amazing. Thank you!

By the middle of the week, things had shifted dramatically globally. People were getting scared. Many in London changed their flights, leaving earlier. I had to ask myself if I should do that, worried that I wouldn't be able to get home if I didn't leave then. And, of course, I didn't want to get the virus. But my boyfriend, a fellow author, is very logical, as well as optimistic. And together, we reasoned that if I left on Saturday, that I'd still be fine according to Trump's recommendations.

So I stayed. I was the last American to leave. The streets of Kensington were deserted on the few occasions that we left the hotel. Things were starting to change.

I remember walking through the ghost town that was London, wondering if I was insane for staying. But my instincts told me that I wasn't. And in the back of our heads, my boyfriend and I knew that we might not be able to see each other for a long time, although we wouldn't say it. He had to go home to Scotland. I had to go home to Lydia. And the world was about to shut down. So I stayed and soaked in every moment.

And I have zero regrets.

I left London on a Saturday. The US borders closed while I was in the air. I got home and none of my friends wanted to be around me because I'd been in Europe. My pilates place called and asked me not to come in for two weeks. I felt shunned.

That was Sunday.

On Monday, California's governor took immediate and swift action and closed everything that wasn't essential down. Bars, gym, etc. You remember. You lived this. Well, all of a sudden, everyone was in the same boat as me.

Many of my friends remarked, "You're lucky that you work from home already." Here's the thing, people, I work at home so when I'm not home, I love to get out. I'm not at all a home body. I go to the gym every day. I eat at restaurants, more for the ambience, than the food most of the time. I socialize daily. People think that because I'm a writer, I'm an introvert. I'm not. I just need a lot of decompression time after socializing.

My well-meaning friends would also say, "Well, you can just write stories while the rest of us freak out."

Here's the other thing, as a writer, I've very connected to the social consciousness. I couldn't write when I got home. I felt the anxiety of the world and it made it impossible to focus. And for a person who hasn't watched the news in decades, I was hooked to the numbers.

My well-meaning ex-husband kept sending me stuff about the lockdown. Los Angeles was much more aggressive in its approach to the virus than some cities, which at the time was scary. Later, it put us ahead, flattening our curve before many places.

And it was also hard to focus because my heart was still in London, walking the streets of Kensington.

So, like you, I struggled during the pandemic. Homeschooling didn't come natural to me. Common Core is ridiculous. And ironically, I've always said I'd make a horrible homeschooling mom and the universe decided to put me to the test. If allowing Lydia to watch Doctor Who late into the night, sleep in everyday and put off assignments because it's good hiking weather is bad schooling, then stick a label on my head.

With every day that I couldn't write, I felt the pressure. I needed to finish this book and yet, I couldn't concentrate. It wasn't writer block. It was emotional overload. People complained that they couldn't sleep during that time. All I could do was sleep—definitely a sign of depression, something that I'm not at all prone to.

This book was on preorder but Amazon was allowing for push backs on those. And I really considered doing that. Giving myself an extra week or two. But I knew two important things. Firstly, people needed their stories more than ever—a way to escape reality. And secondly, I thrive on deadlines, so if I pushed it back, then I'd just sleep for another week. So I didn't. And it was the hardest push ever. I wrote 45k words in 3 days to complete this book on time. But I did it.

I worried that the push would make the book not as good. You tell me, since I'm obviously not objective on this. However, I love this book. I laughed out loud so many times at Lunis. And Liv came back to do a mission with Sophia and I remembered how easy she is to write. She is me, after all. I became acutely aware of how subtly different she was from Sophia while writing the sisters together. As MA said when we were outlining the Sophia series, the younger sister is more fun—easy going. Liv, well she doesn't put up with anyone's bull shit, whereas, Sophia picks her battle. She sucks it up when she needs to with Hiker and then lays down the law when things have gone too far.

I wrote a majority of this book standing at the kitchen counter or sitting on the front step of my house. I knew that getting vitamin D was important. And even though I was doing video work outs, it wasn't enough exercise. Also, it sort of felt like I was getting out of the house when I sat outside and watched the crows and squirrels play in the trees. And I met lots of friends who happened by. One of them offered me a pizza. I declined, saying that I was keto, but the truth was that I didn't want his corona-pizza.

Later I met him on the street when I was doing a silent disco—see the reference to Rudolf? I was trying to do whatever I could to keep up my spirits and make others laugh.

The guy, my next door neighbor, stopped my dancing to ask me for my number. Since he was my neighbor, I was like, "Sure, seems practical, in case of emergencies." Then he asked me out and I was like, "OH shit!" That was awkward since there was no avoiding him... since he lives next door! AND after that, to make things worse, he would knock at my door multiple times a day, knowing I was home because *we were all* home. I had to give it to the guy, he was finding a way to date during a pandemic. Just go ask your neighbor out!

I told him from the start that I had a boyfriend...in Scotland and he laughed. The next day he brought me a corona-turkey sub. I didn't eat it. Remember, I'm keto.

But also, I realized in that moment, when he was laughing at me for having a boyfriend so far away, obviously thinking it was doomed, that I'd rather be with my Scotsman than with someone conveniently close. Sometimes when you know, you know. More on that later.

My point is that the world was such a weird place during the writing of this book and I know that's reflected in the pages. I had to make a few references to social distancing and TP shortages. And, I had to put in my adventures in London. That pub where Sophia made the appointment to meet Saint Valentine is a real place off High Street that my Scotsman and I stumbled upon on accident.

We were walking down the busy street and all of a sudden turn onto this cobbled road. The sound of traffic was replaced by birds singing and there sitting like it was waiting for us was Scarsdale Tavern. We had drinks while sunshine streamed through the window and he remarked (a Scotsman) that it was unusually sunny in London that week. I told him that I preferred sunshine, unless I'm sad. Incidentally, since I've returned to LA, it's been unusually cloudy and rainy.

The Great Gatsby party in this book was also inspired by a roaring 20's party we went to in London. The Scotsman knows that's my favorite book, hence all the references.

All the pages of the book seem to be heavily inspired by my recent adventures and explorations of the heart. Yes, there's a lot more love in this book than the others. It changes the cadence, but that is what love does to us. I worried that it would detract from the book, but I hope it makes it better.

I don't know where things are going with me and Scotsman. I told you in the last author's notes that you'd have to stay tuned to find out if I dropped the glass slipper for my Prince Charming to pick up. Well, I did. And he did. And now we've entered into something that might make us crazy, living 5k miles apart. However, when I was in the airport, knowing a pandemic was coming, about to get on a plane as the borders of my country shut, and trying to decide if I wanted to be in a relationship with someone so far away, I realized that I hadn't wanted to be in any relationship for a while until right then. No one had stolen my heart like this guy. So regardless of practicality, I had to do what my heart said and embrace uncertainty.

Okay, enough of that.

As some have noticed, I have a thing for Rumi's poetry. Actually, similar to Sophia, I had the morning breeze quote beside my bed for years. I still wake up most mornings between 2 and 4—at the witching hour.

Usually I get on my phone and chat with my UK friends who are all having lunch about that time. However, back in the day, when I had the Rumi quote beside the bed, I would force myself to get out of bed. And that's when I wrote my first series, between 2 and 5 o'clock in the morning. Then I'd go back to sleep for an hour before my infant awoke. Is anyone surprised that my very first novel was entitled Awoken?

Oh, one last thing.

MA and I had a fantastic meeting right before he left London. Funny that we have to fly across the world to meet although we don't live that far apart. Every time I do meet with MA, I always walk away inspired and ready to start a billion projects. We have some really fun stuff in the works. But one of the best parts of that meeting, is that I really think of MA as a friend and we had some nice conversations. I remember sitting across the table from him and saying, "I might be crazy for dating this guy, but I just can't let him go." He said he was happy for me and that meant a lot. And then he said, "Full confession. I thought he was gay...because he's such a good dresser." I laughed. The Scotsman laughed later when I told him. He is a very sharp dresser. Definitely not gay though. He's my Wilder.

Sincerely,
Tiny Ninja

MICHAEL'S AUTHOR NOTES
APRIL 18, 2020

THANK YOU for reading our story!

We have a few of these planned, but we don't know if we should continue writing and publishing without your input.

Options include leaving a review, reaching out on Facebook to let us know and smoke signals.

Frankly, smoke signals might get misconstrued as low hanging clouds so you might want to nix that idea...

Let's just admit I don't know many heterosexual guys who dress fantastic and leave it at that.

I'm very happy for Sarah and her Scotsman (I hear a chorus of swoons when I say 'Scotsman.' I think all of the ladies, and maybe a couple of guys, just put a poster up in the bedroom of their mind.)

Either way, he has a fantastic dress ethic. Where I can't usually be bothered to choose a different color for my shirt than 'figure-slimming black' he is matching his shoes to the ensemble.

I probably should have titled this section 'I'm too lazy to figure out color-coordination.'

I don't dress well.

I used to have long hair when I was in college. It was that 'you aren't in your parents' home, I can have long hair and an earring' time during the 1980's. I shared this rejection of authority by growing my hair long, using hair bands while riding motorcycles.

Yes, I listened to heavy metal and had a Kawasaki EX500... They called it a sport-tourer, I called it fun and thankfully not the death of me.

It was the closest thing to sexy I *ever* had in my notoriously geek life. Except for something recently in the last five years, but that doesn't count.

I'm married. Owning sexy stuff while married takes the sexy out of it. I've lived through the young-family-has-a-van-to-drive days and now I'm in the older-life-kids-out-of-the-house-can-afford-more-expensive-toys days.

Back in the 80's, my hair got long enough that when I rode, I had to use a hair band or rubber band (which HURTS like an SOB trying to get it out of the hair) or spend twenty minutes cussing as I tried to pull a hairbrush through the tangles if I forgot.

I still flinch to this day thinking about pulling the hairbrush through my hair. I am empathetic to any dogs when you have to comb them and they have tangles. I try my best to keep away any pain.

Today I like to wear my hair much shorter because it takes less time to dry.

With the Pandemic, and not haircutting barbershops or anything available, I am trying new ways to style it.

Not very successfully mind you. I'm married, I only have one person to impress and she is usually looking at me strangely. This would be a typical discussion.

Wife: "What is that hairstyle called?"

Me: "Keep it the @#%@# out of my face."

Wife: "...looks nice."

Well, she *SAID* looks nice. Her rolling eyes proclaimed she meant something else.

Mike's Diary: "Sometimes, life just *is*."

So, my company is testing new software to allow us a virtual experience while we work. As of now (4/13/2020), it is performing better than I could have hoped in bringing those who collaborate with LMBPN together, no matter the location or time of day (or night.)

This same software, I hope, will allow us to create virtual meetings with fans, and (I'm trying, but I'm not sure the company behind the software will make it affordable) I want to create a place for fans to get together and create all sorts of fun stuff with LMBPN.

And frankly just have a place to hang a while.

If you would like to know more (and are on Facebook) join us on the Kurtherian Gambit Facebook Group For Fans and Authors

Link: https://www.facebook.com/profile.php?id=127989844503323&ref=br_rs

I hope to have something up to start testing this in the next week or two. We will start with small groups, and possibly move up from there.

Clean is the New Dream

My office isn't messy... exactly. It is lived-in *chic.*

Honestly, a whole *lot* of the lived-in part. (If you add chic to the end of any descriptor, you immediately sound artsy. No, really, try it.

"That's ugly."

"No, that's ugly-*chic.*"

"That man-cave crap has got to go."

"No, that's man-cave *chic.* It stays."

"That's hideous."

"No, that's hideous—"

"If you end that with 'chic,' I will shove my cottony house slippers so far up your ass you will be burping tiny clouds."

"Right. So, what now? I lost my train of thought with that visual."

(You thought 'Hideous *chic,* and that would have worked, #AmIRight?)

I will have to take another set of boxes to the storage room tomorrow after our meetings, and maybe then I'll have a bit of "clean" in my office. Judith cleaned the living room and Kitchen (both places she works from) yesterday, and believe it or not, I am a bit #Jealous of her clean areas.

(Don't worry, I'm having trouble believing it too.)

I'm So Going to Regret This.

So, I have the new 2020 iPad (#SupportApple and #ItsGoodTo-HaveAppleEmployeesWithDiscountsAsFriends along with #Support-FriendsByBuyingApple), but I don't like using it just as it is.

I want either a Smart Keyboard Folio or the new More Magic Keyboard for the iPad, or maybe something clamshell (but won't that effectively make it a Mac?).

Have I mentioned I'm seriously impatient? I work six often seven days a week (#ThankGodILoveWhatIDo), and when it comes to my technology, I splurge on myself. It's the one thing I can point to my wife and say 'it's a write-off' and 'Don't harsh my (writing) buzz, woman.'

(Actually, only one of those responses works on Judith. #Thank-GodAppleDoesn'tRefreshOften and #IReallyDoWait2YearsBetweeni-PhonesNow.)

I swear Apple better not upgrade their keyboard on the larger MacBooks in 2021, or I might have to try therapy to hold-back on an upgrade (yes, I have the 2021 MacBook 16".) If therapy is more expensive than my purchase, doesn't that make it smarter just to purchase the product?

I think it does.

Are you paying attention, Steve? (#StephenCampbellNeedsaNew-Macbook13Pro)

Anyway. My iPad is sitting in its box unopened because I don't have a keyboard for it. I can't get the Magic Keyboard until May at this point, or maybe later. Since I suffer from #ImpatienceIsAThing, I am looking to see if anything cool is out for my iPad that includes a touchpad for mousing around.

You know, if—and this is for the benefit of my fans who might wish to know—I buy a clamshell with touchpad and report that information back here in a future *Author Note*, that's research and something I can write off on taxes, right?

So, I might sacrifice a larger credit card bill on the altar of #Doing-ItForTheFans.

If you happen to write a review for any of our books, maybe drop a line in the review "I Support Mike and his Magic Keyboard!" (Or, if you hate Apple products, feel free to suggest I buy other technology. Especially really expensive hardware that I can point to and show my wife how frugal' I was with the purchases I have already made or might <snicker> make soon.

Ad Aeternitatem,

Michael Anderle

(P.S. – Apple came out early with the Magic Keyboard… Hehehehe.)

ACKNOWLEDGMENTS
SARAH NOFFKE

I feel like I'm on the stage at the Oscars, accepting an award when I write my acknowledgments. I stand there, holding this award, my hands shaking and my words racing around in my mind. I'm not an actress for a reason. I'm a writer and talking to people in "real life" is hard. Not to mention a ton of people all at once.

I picture looking out at the audience and being blinded by spot-lights and forgetting every word of the speech I memorized just in case I won. The speech would go like this and it's meant for all of you, not the guild. For the fans. The supporters. The people who are the reason I would ever stand on any stage, ever.

Okay, here we go. I clear my throat and smile, looking up at the camera, holding the little golden man. And then I begin:

This was never supposed to happen. I was never meant to publish a book and then another one. And then another. I was supposed to write in private and live a life that Henry David Thoreau called a life of "quiet desperation." I would always hope to share my books, but never bring myself to do it. And you would never read my words. But then, in a crazed moment of brashness, I did share my books and you all liked them. And because of that, I've never been the same. And here I am feeling grateful all just because...

That's why I'm here. Because of you. Thank you to my first read-ers. The ones who picked up those books that I didn't even outline and you still liked them. You messaged me and maybe you thought it was no big deal, but when your ego is new to the publishing world, it's a big deal.

I can't thank you readers enough. I've found that reading your reviews helps me to start a chapter when I'm stuck or lazy.

I really need to thank someone who has made this all possible and that's my father. I was going to quit. I can't tell you how many times I quit. But when I wasn't making it, he was the one who told me to not throw in the towel. "Give yourself a timeline," he suggested. If I didn't get to my goal by then, I'd quit. And apparently there was magic in that advice, because I'm still doing this. Dad, you're the pragmatic one, but when you believed in me enough to tell me to not quit, I knew I had to follow your advice.

And I thank all my friends who are constantly supporting me with thoughts of love and encouragement. Most don't read my books. I'm sort of self-deprecating, although I'm working on it and will be the first to tell my friends, "My books probably aren't for you." However, every now and then a friend surprises me and says, "I was up all night reading your books." It's always a total shock. But my point is, that even if they didn't read, I still have the best friends ever. Diane, you're my rock. And I love you, even though you will probably not read this.

Thank you to everyone at LMBPN. Those people are like family to me, although I'm not sure if they'll let me sleep on their couch. Well, who am I kidding? They totally will. Big thanks to Steve, Lynne, Mihaela, Kelly, Jen and the entire team. The JIT members are the best.

Huge thank you to the LMBPN Ladies group on Facebook. Micky, you're the best. And that group keeps me sane.

And a giant thank you to the betas for this series. Juergen you are my first reader and friend. Thanks for all the help. And thanks to Martin and Crystal for being some of the best people I know. What would I do without you? A huge thanks to the ARC team. Seriously, if it weren't for you all I might pass out before release day, wondering if anyone will like the book.

And with all my books, my final thank you goes to my lovely muse, Lydia. Oh sweet darling, I write these books for you, but ironically, I couldn't write them without you. You are my inspiration. My sounding board. And the reason that I want to succeed. I love you.

Thank you all! I'm sorry if I forgot anyone. Blame Michael. For no other reason than just because.

BOOKS BY SARAH NOFFKE

Sarah Noffke writes YA and NA science fiction, fantasy, paranormal and urban fantasy. In addition to being an author, she is a mother, podcaster and professor. Noffke holds a Masters of Management and teaches college business/writing courses. Most of her students have no idea that she toils away her hours crafting fictional characters. www.sarahnoffke.com

Check out other work by Sarah author here.

Ghost Squadron:

Formation #1:
   Kill the bad guys. Save the Galaxy. All in a hard day's work.
   After ten years of wandering the outer rim of the galaxy, Eddie Teach is a man without a purpose. He was one of the toughest pilots in the Federation, but now he's just a regular guy, getting into bar fights and making a difference wherever he can. It's not the same as flying a ship and saving colonies, but it'll have to do.
   That is, until General Lance Reynolds tracks Eddie down and offers him a job. There are bad people out there, plotting terrible

things, killing innocent people, and destroying entire colonies. **Someone has to stop them.**

Eddie, along with the genetically-enhanced combat pilot Julianna Fregin and her trusty E.I. named Pip, must recruit a diverse team of specialists, both human and alien. They'll need to master their new Q-Ship, one of the most powerful strike ships ever constructed. And finally, they'll have to stop a faceless enemy so powerful, it threatens to destroy the entire Federation.

All in a day's work, right?

Experience this exciting military sci-fi saga and the latest addition to the expanded Kurtherian Gambit Universe. If you're a fan of Mass Effect, Firefly, or Star Wars, you'll love this riveting new space opera.

NOTE: If cursing is a problem, then this might not be for you.

Check out the entire series here.

The Precious Galaxy Series:

Corruption #1

A new evil lurks in the darkness.

After an explosion, the crew of a battlecruiser mysteriously disappears.

Bailey and Lewis, complete strangers, find themselves suddenly onboard the damaged ship. Lewis hasn't worked a case in years, not since the final one broke his spirit and his bank account. The last thing Bailey remembers is preparing to take down a fugitive on Onyx Station.

Mysteries are harder to solve when there's no evidence left behind.

Bailey and Lewis don't know how they got onboard *Ricky Bobby* or why. However, they quickly learn that whatever was responsible for the explosion and disappearance of the crew is still on the ship.

Monsters are real and what this one can do changes everything.

The new team bands together to discover what happened and how to fight the monster lurking in the bottom of the battlecruiser.

Will they find the missing crew? Or will the monster end them all?

The Soul Stone Mage Series:

House of Enchanted #1:
The Kingdom of Virgo has lived in peace for thousands of years...until now.

The humans from Terran have always been real assholes to the witches of Virgo. Now a silent war is brewing, and the timing couldn't be worse. Princess Azure will soon be crowned queen of the Kingdom of Virgo.

In the Dark Forest a powerful potion-maker has been murdered.

Charmsgood was the only wizard who could stop a deadly virus plaguing Virgo. He also knew about the devastation the people from Terran had done to the forest.

Azure must protect her people. Mend the Dark Forest. Create alliances with savage beasts. No biggie, right?

But on coronation day everything changes. Princess Azure isn't who she thought she was and that's a big freaking problem.

Welcome to The Revelations of Oriceran. Check out the entire series here.

The Lucidites Series:

Awoken, #1:
Around the world humans are hallucinating after sleepless nights.

In a sterile, underground institute the forecasters keep reporting the same events.

And in the backwoods of Texas, a sixteen-year-old girl is about to be caught up in a fierce, ethereal battle.

Meet Roya Stark. She drowns every night in her dreams, spends her hours reading classic literature to avoid her family's ridicule, and is prone to premonitions—which are becoming more frequent. And now her dreams are filled with strangers offering to reveal what she has always wanted to know: Who is she? That's the question that haunts her, and she's about to find out. But will Roya live to regret learning the truth?

Stunned, #2
Revived, #3

The Reverians Series:

Defects, #1:
In the happy, clean community of Austin Valley, everything appears to be perfect. Seventeen-year-old Em Fuller, however, fears something is askew. Em is one of the new generation of Dream Travelers. For some reason, the gods have not seen fit to gift all of them with their expected special abilities. Em is a Defect—one of the unfortunate Dream Travelers not gifted with a psychic power. Desperate to do whatever it takes to earn her gift, she endures painful daily injections along with commands from her overbearing, loveless father. One of the few bright spots in her life is the return of a friend she had thought dead—but with his return comes the knowledge of a shocking, unforgivable truth. The society Em thought was protecting her has actually been betraying her, but she has no idea how to break away from its authority without hurting everyone she loves.

Rebels, #2
Warriors, #3

Vagabond Circus Series:

Suspended, #1:
When a stranger joins the cast of Vagabond Circus—a circus that is run by Dream Travelers and features real magic—mysterious events start happening. The once orderly grounds of the circus become riddled with hidden threats. And the ringmaster realizes not only are his circus and its magic at risk, but also his very life.

Vagabond Circus caters to the skeptics. Without skeptics, it would close its doors. This is because Vagabond Circus runs for two reasons and only two reasons: first and foremost to provide the lost and lonely Dream Travelers a place to be illustrious. And secondly, to show the nonbelievers that there's still magic in the world. If they believe, then they care, and if they care, then they don't destroy. They stop the small abuse that day-by-day breaks down humanity's spirit. If Vagabond Circus makes one skeptic believe in magic, then they halt the cycle, just a little bit. They allow a little more love into this world. That's Dr. Dave Raydon's mission. And that's why this ringmaster recruits. That's why he directs. That's why he puts on a show that makes people question their beliefs. He wants the world to believe in magic once again.

Paralyzed, #2

Released, #3

Ren Series:

Ren: The Man Behind the Monster, #1:

Born with the power to control minds, hypnotize others, and read thoughts, Ren Lewis, is certain of one thing: God made a mistake. No one should be born with so much power. A monster awoke in him the same year he received his gifts. At ten years old. A prepubescent boy with the ability to control others might merely abuse his powers, but Ren allowed it to corrupt him. And since he can have and do anything he wants, Ren should be happy. However, his journey teaches him that harboring so much power doesn't bring happiness, it steals it. Once this realization sets in, Ren makes up his mind to do the one thing that can bring his tortured soul some peace. He must kill the monster.

Note This book is NA and has strong language, violence and sexual references.

Ren: God's Little Monster, #2

Ren: The Monster Inside the Monster, #3

Ren: The Monster's Adventure, #3.5

Ren: The Monster's Death

Olento Research Series:

Alpha Wolf, #1:
Twelve men went missing.

Six months later they awake from drug-induced stupors to find themselves locked in a lab.

And on the night of a new moon, eleven of those men, possessed by new—and inhuman—powers, break out of their prison and race through the streets of Los Angeles until they disappear one by one into the night.

Olento Research wants its experiments back. Its CEO, Mika Lenna, will tear every city apart until he has his werewolves imprisoned once again. He didn't undertake a huge risk just to lose his would-be assassins.

However, the Lucidite Institute's main mission is to save the world from injustices. Now, it's Adelaide's job to find these mutated men and protect them and society, and fast. Already around the nation, wolflike men are being spotted. Attacks on innocent women are happening. And then, Adelaide realizes what her next step must be: She has to find the alpha wolf first. Only once she's located him can she stop whoever is behind this experiment to create wild beasts out of human beings.

Lone Wolf, #2
Rabid Wolf, #3
Bad Wolf, #4

BOOKS BY MICHAEL ANDERLE

For a complete list of books by Michael Anderle, please visit:

www.lmbpn.com/ma-books/

All LMBPN Audiobooks are Available at Audible.com and iTunes

To see all LMBPN audiobooks, including those written by Michael Anderle
please visit:

www.lmbpn.com/audible

CONNECT WITH THE AUTHORS

Connect with Sarah and sign up for her email list here:

http://www.sarahnoffke.com/connect/

You can catch her podcast, LA Chicks, here:

http://lachicks.libsyn.com/

Connect with Michael Anderle and sign up for his email list here:

Website: http://lmbpn.com

Email List: http://lmbpn.com/email/

Facebook:
www.facebook.com/TheKurtherianGambitBooks

Made in United States
Troutdale, OR
05/10/2025

31258221R00298